TIM SHOEN...

THE SECOND STORM

A HIGH WATER NOVEL

FOCUS
ON
THE FAMILY.

A Focus on the Family resource
published by Tyndale House Publishers

To the Hurricane Ian and Hurricane Dorian survivors.
Your stories have made parts of this book more real. Know that
this book will bring hope, help, and direction to readers.
So, in a real way, realize that your nightmares
will help readers sleep better at night.

Woe to those who go to great depths

to hide their plans from the LORD,

who do their work in darkness and think,

"Who sees us? Who will know?"

ISAIAH 29:15

When the storm has swept by, the wicked are gone,

but the righteous stand firm forever.

PROVERBS 10:25

CHAPTER 1

THE HURRICANE THREAT shouldn't have consumed Parker Buckman's thoughts like it did. The thing would make landfall hundreds of miles away from where he lived. But it wasn't so much *where* the storm was headed that had him on edge. It was *who* was in its path.

The way Parker saw it, tropical storms were nothing short of nature playing the bully. And bullies rarely worked alone. Even storms traveled with six henchmen. Frequent flyers on an unholy voyage. Blinding rain. Shrieking winds. Behemoth waves. Dark clouds thick enough to veil any trace of the sun—or the hope it brings. Confusion is their wingman. And if you're unfortunate enough to be too close when the pack stalks through, you'll surely meet the sixth of the storm's cohorts. The one you never want to face. Sheer terror.

The six of them formed the kind of gang that had the power to change lives—or end them. And right now, they were flexing and elbowing their way toward land—and an old friend.

Parker Buckman stood halfway out on the granite breakwater shielding Rockport Harbor from the Atlantic and scrolled through Wilson Stillwaters's texts from the last couple of days.

> Southern Florida will be hit by Tropical Storm Morgan. Shaping up to be a monster. Winds 50 mph. First exciting thing that's happened here in a long time. Why not come down for a visit, Bucky?

Wilson could sell the cool factor of riding out a storm all he wanted. But there was no way Parker would go back to the Florida Everglades, even for his friend. No, not there. Not ever.

> It's official. Morgan has been upgraded to a Category 1 hurricane. Winds nearly 80 mph. Still heading right for us. Thinking of riding it out on my uncle's airboat. Won't even have to turn on the motor! Yee-ha!

Parker remembered the airboat well. The sound of the engine. The name *Typhoon* painted on the steering fins. He imagined Wilson riding full-throttle into the hurricane winds—and catching too much air under the bow. Would the thing go airborne? It could, right? And if that happened, the flat-bottomed boat would likely flip fast—and hard.

It was probably dumb to let this gnaw at him. Wilson could handle himself in the Glades. Parker had witnessed that firsthand while his own dad had been stationed there as a National Park ranger. Wilson knew the dangers. He was proud of his half-Miccosukee heritage—and he knew how to survive. On the surface, it seemed his whole life was about taking chances. Like every venture into the Everglades was a test of manhood or something.

Actually, manhood had been a topic that Parker's grandpa had talked about with him while in town in August. "What kind of man do you want to grow to be, Parker?" Grandpa's question had replayed in his head a hundred times since then. The bigger question in Parker's mind? Would he have what it took to be that kind of man?

Based on what Parker got from Wilson—and picked up online— authorities had advised residents of Chokoloskee, Everglades City, and the surrounding areas to evacuate. According to Wilson, some locals planned to stay put and ride out the storm. Wilson's dad was among them.

```
Dad says the storm will fizzle, or turn before it gets
here. Not sure he actually believes that. He's finding
plywood to screw over the windows.
```

Parker couldn't shake the feeling that Wilson was in more danger than he realized—or was letting on. And there was something more. A sense that Parker was going to be sucked in if he wasn't careful. Which was ridiculous.

```
My dad laughs at those leaving. Says this will be Dorian
all over again.
```

Hurricane Dorian. September, 2019. Predicted to be devastating to parts of Florida, but it didn't happen. Dorian and the gang camped out in the Bahamas instead, pummeling the island of Abaco almost into oblivion before turning northeast and away from Florida.

```
My dad is never wrong. HA!
But pray for me if you think of it, okay?
This storm is no joke.
Still wearing the gator chomper?
```

The alligator tooth necklace Wilson had given Parker before he left. He'd worn it for months. Not as the lucky charm Wilson claimed it to be. It was as a connection, a way to remember Wilson. But as Parker had become better friends with Ella and then Harley, the necklace found its way to the corner post of his headboard. And sometime after Jelly had moved up here to Rockport, Massachusetts, the gator tooth on the leather lanyard had gone MIA. It had to be in his room somewhere. But he'd avoided answering that part of Wilson's text.

For weeks now, he'd been wearing Kemosabe's spare key around his neck. Once the motorcycle key—and the spare—had no longer been needed for evidence, Officer Greenwood gave them back to Harley. And Harley gave one to Parker.

"God, please protect Wilson." No matter where Parker was, he knew God heard him. But the connection seemed better when he was in a boat on the water—or at least on the breakwater like he was today.

He pictured Chokoloskee and how it must look like a ghost town with every home boarded up. Even now, as he looked over the relative calm of Sandy Bay and the Atlantic beyond, it was hard to imagine how the ocean would be whipping up into a frenzy fifteen hundred miles south.

"Parker!"

Angelica "Jelly" Malnatti strode his way, jumping across the spaces between the giant granite blocks of the jetty without even looking down. "I knew I'd find you here."

Parker smiled. "I'm that predictable?"

She looked skyward and shook her head in a look of total exasperation. "In every way. Where's Harley?"

He pointed to the signal light at the far end of the breakwater. "Thinking."

"About?"

Parker's guess? Harley's foster home. At first, it'd seemed perfect. Right in nearby Gloucester. Close enough to stay at Rockport High and keep his new job at BayView Brew Coffee and Donut Shop in Rockport. But the new foster home with the Gunderson family wasn't going as great as Harley had hoped. "You'd have to ask him."

She shifted her weight to one leg and crossed her arms. "Well, how about giving me a *tiny* hint? Just one word."

Okay. "*Stuff.*"

"Very helpful, Parker," Jelly said.

Time for him to change the subject before she pressed harder. "Looks like you're on a mission. What's up?"

"I see right through your little diversionary tactic, Parker." She waggled her phone. "You following the weather?"

"If I'm *that* predictable, you tell me."

She stuck out her tongue. "Brat. And no, I say you're not paying nearly as much attention as you should."

Had he missed something? He checked the texts from Wilson. Nothing from him in the last couple of hours.

"Morgan *is* going to hit our old hometown. Hard." She nodded. "I really think this is going to be everything they feared Dorian would be. Ella thinks so too."

"Gee . . . have you told that to Wilson? I mean, hey, if he heard *you* two say it will be bad, I'm sure he'd evacuate."

She stood there in her jeans and sweatshirt—with her arms still folded. "Make fun all you like. You'll see. Even Grams has a bad feeling."

Parker loved Grams, but Ella's grandma could get a bad feeling about a plate of Oreos. Besides Wilson, she was the most superstitious person Parker knew. "Well, let's pray you and Ella—and Grams—are wrong."

"And the National Weather Service," Jelly said. "And every other sane person with more than an ounce of brains in their head."

"Wilson thinks—"

"No. He *doesn't* think. The fact that he and his dad aren't evacuating is proof of that. They should've started north hours ago."

"Some guys would rather stay in the ring and fight."

"Yeah, well, Saturday night—which is tomorrow—they're going to get hit in a regular no-holds-barred smackdown."

Actually, her words rang true. A bully was closing in on southern Florida—and he wouldn't arrive alone. He'd bring every one of his henchmen with him. The only one who'd be truly alone was Wilson, the friend Parker had left behind when he and the family moved to Rockport.

"Wilson is in a lot more trouble than he realizes—or will admit," Jelly said.

Parker was pretty sure she was right. Wilson could find himself in a cage fight of sorts. But worse, because once the whupping started, there'd be no ref to stop it. "I feel like I should be doing something to help, you know?" Wasn't that what a real friend would do?

"There you go again." Jelly planted both hands on her hips. "You are soooo predictable. You can't help someone who doesn't want to be helped. They *chose* to stay—remember?"

And it wasn't like he was as close to Wilson as he'd been before. It'd been forever since he'd seen him. "Maybe you're right."

She smiled. "First smart thing you've said today. What could you possibly do to help anyway?"

An idea popped into his mind. The kind of thought a real friend would probably have. But the idea was insane. Absolutely crazy. It was totally beyond the call of duty—and something he'd never actually do. But still . . .

"What?" Jelly locked eyes with him. "What were you just thinking?"

"Nothing. It was stupid." Parker didn't want Jelly digging any deeper. "Do you think Wilson is scared?"

"He should be. Can you imagine anything scarier than being caught in a hurricane?"

That idea he'd had to help Wilson was back. "I really don't want to think about that." And he was dead serious. Because right now—at this moment? It definitely was the one thing that scared Parker more than the hurricane itself.

CHAPTER 2

ANGELICA'S ANTENNA WAS UP, but she didn't want Parker becoming more guarded than he already was. He'd been evasive about Harley, for sure. But it was his thoughts about Wilson—and the Glades—that had her concerned. Her women's intuition said he was holding back—and he was thinking about something extreme. Some way to help. When he got like this, he'd get obsessed with whatever he thought was the right thing to do. Which almost always led to trouble. Angelica just needed to figure out what it was—so she could talk him out of it.

She relied on watching his eyes and body language—the little tells revealing what was *really* going on under his red Wooten's Airboat Tours cap. Something was eating at him—but he was keeping it to himself.

"One to ten." Angelica had learned to watch him without actually looking like she was. It was an art form, and she was getting pretty good at it. "How much danger do you think Wilson is *really* in?"

Parker actually looked to the south. Like he could see all the way to the Glades. "So . . . ten is like walking Gator Hook Trail alone—in high water season—at night—"

"You're stalling. One to ten. I need a number."

"Wilson's dad is convinced—"

"I *know* what he thinks. I asked *your* opinion."

Parker smiled. "Are *you* worried about Wilson?"

"Just as much as you are, I suspect. And don't you dare deny it."

He shrugged in that way he did sometimes when he wasn't ready to admit the obvious. "It doesn't matter what I think. Wilson's dad made a decision. All we can do now is hope it was the right one."

"You think there's a chance he made a good choice?" Angelica lifted Parker's cap off his head. "Anyone in there? C'mon, Parker. They made a bad decision, and you know it."

Parker didn't say a word.

"They decided to stay in the path of a *hurricane*. What kind of chowderheaded thinking was that?" Was she pushing too hard? Maybe. But sometimes that's what it took to get Parker to open up. "Ella. Myself. Anybody with half a brain could make a better decision."

"Soooo . . . you're saying you two only have half a brain?"

She balled her hand into a fist and shook it at him. "Cute. You going to answer my question or not?"

"He'll be okay." Parker nodded like that was all the reassurance she needed. But he avoided her eyes. There was the tell. He'd just given himself away. Parker *was* a whole lot more worried than he acted. And she was pretty sure he didn't even know the worst news yet. "Know what I think, Parker Buckman?"

He gave her a smile like he didn't have a care in the world. "I'm guessing you'll tell me."

Fine. She'd give it to him straight. "This is going to be a disaster."

"Brilliant," he said. "Amazing insight, Jelly—although I'm pretty sure *all* hurricanes are considered disasters."

It was his little game of joking about the very thing that really bothered him. "I'm being serious, Parker. On a scale of one to ten, this is a ten-plus."

His eyes met hers for an instant before darting away. *Bingo.* She was right. This was hitting him a lot harder than he was letting on. Which meant he wasn't going to let this go. Parker wasn't the type to sit back when something bothered him. He'd do something. Probably something stupid. And dangerous.

"Let's join Harley." Parker started toward the signal light at the far end of the breakwater.

Good. It would give her another chance to talk some sense into him. If Wilson wasn't smart enough to evacuate, there was nothing Parker could do.

She kept pace with Parker as he did the long-stepping thing, striding from one massive granite block to the next. She'd promised herself so many times that she'd stop playing the role of Parker's protector. But was it so bad to steer a friend out of harm's way? If Parker got some cockamamie idea in his head, it would be nearly impossible to talk him out of it. She had to stay on the offensive. "Can you think of some way to help Wilson?"

Parker shrugged. "Short of praying for him, nothing that makes any sense."

She liked that answer. Maybe it was time to talk to him about what was really bothering *her*.

"Did you hear about the Everglades Correctional Institution?" Where Clayton Kingman was doing life for trying to kill Parker and Wilson in the Everglades.

Parker shook his head.

What, was Parker living in a cave? "It's smack-dab in the path of the hurricane. Protesters are demanding the prisoners be evacuated to someplace safer."

That got his attention.

"Some say it's inhumane to leave them there—even though the governor insists the walls can withstand anything the hurricane throws at them."

Parker still didn't say a word.

"Kingman shouldn't ever get out of that place."

"You said they might *move* the prisoners," Parker said. "Not set them free."

"Yeah, but don't you think he's planning—right now—how he might use the move as a chance to escape?"

Parker laughed. "Jelly, you watch too many movies. *What if they move him? What if he escapes?* Do you hear yourself? That's a lot of what-ifs. You're overthinking."

"No more than you're underthinking the potential danger."

"So let's say he escapes." Parker smiled. "You think he'd want to pay me a visit?"

That's exactly what she thought. "It's only been a year. What do you imagine he dreams about doing if he got out?"

"Getting a pizza. Going fishing. Running on the beach. Who knows? But definitely not coming after me." Parker stopped at the signal light and looked across the channel to the Headlands. "I didn't put him in prison. He did that to himself. And if he was smart, he'd know God rescued Wilson and me."

Harley sat on a rock closer to the water. Parker jogged ahead to meet him.

Angelica followed but more slowly. Of course God *could* rescue Parker. But why press your luck, right? Honestly, Angelica had tried to step back from her role of being the protector of others. But was it so bad to step it up . . . just a little? She'd ask Ella to help her set some boundaries this time. Parker had a history of doing crazy things to help his friends. Harley wasn't much better. What kind of a friend would she be if she didn't try to figure out what Parker might do—and stop him before he got in over his head?

CHAPTER 3

Chokoloskee, Florida
Friday, October 22, 5:35 p.m.

WILSON HAD BEEN GIVEN the "simple" job of screwing sheets of plywood over every window of the house while his dad made another supply run. The project would've been easy if there'd been no wind. But just getting a piece in position became a wrestling match now. The wind seemed determined to send the plywood flying. Holding the cordless in one hand and driving his shoulder against the wood, he managed to get each sheet screwed into place—although not one of them was straight.

When his dad roared up in the pickup, he tucked the 4×4 in tight to the house. "Stuff to empty out of the back." He glanced at the sky but didn't look concerned. "Let's get the lead out."

Wilson hustled over, dropped the tailgate, and started hauling. Three bags of ice. Two cases of water bottles. Four cases of beer. Bread. A dozen cans of soup. "Think we got enough?"

"I cleaned them out. But we got plenty." Dad walked to the nearest window and tugged a corner of the plywood loose. "We got a shortage of screws or something? I told you to get these up there good."

Wilson knew better than to argue. But for the guy who'd insisted the storm wouldn't dare make landfall anywhere near here, he seemed pretty concerned. The growing knot in Wilson's gut said they were dangerously unprepared.

They'd lose power, for sure. It was just a question of when—and for how long. But Dad had a gas generator out back—with ten gallons of gas. More than enough, according to his dad. Wilson had already charged the mobile phones. Were they forgetting something?

He'd googled "preparing for a hurricane" and didn't come up with anything that they hadn't already taken care of. Except for one little thing: *evacuate*.

Hurricane Morgan was still headed their way—and getting stronger. "Online experts say if winds are expected to hit 130 miles per hour—a Category 4—we've got to get out."

Dad unscrewed the cap of his Bud and took a long pull on it. "You want to run for cover? Say the word and I'll get you out of here. But your dad will come back—and ride this thing out alone. A man has got to protect what's his."

Wilson handed the phone to his dad. "Just check this out." The site posted a video simulating the damage that would occur as the wind intensified—and it was ugly. If the video was at all accurate, their home would never ride it out. "Like, even a well-built wood frame house will be demolished."

Dad looked at him, eyes narrowing. "You *scared*, boy?"

Great question. He shrugged. "Not really." And that was the truth. Mostly. "It's just that everything on the internet—"

"You believe everything you read online?"

Only an idiot would.

"This storm will turn tail and run for Jamaica before it dares come near. Every place a Miccosukee lives is sacred ground, boy. Sacred."

Wilson had grown up hearing how the Everglades was to be protected—and was somehow the protector of its people.

"True Miccosukees don't run." Dad eyed him for a moment, like he was sizing him up. "The wind, the rain—they're your brothers."

Wilson smiled. "And all this time I thought I was an only child."

His dad laughed in a way that made everything seem right. Wilson's fear shrunk small enough for him to hold in his fist.

"You've got some of your mama's blood in you, sure as we're sitting here. That's why you're feeling a little queasy. But you've got more Miccosukee blood in you than most purebloods I know. You'll be all right. You wait and see."

That was the closest thing to a compliment Wilson had gotten from his dad in as long as he could remember. Yes, he was a Miccosukee. He was strong. And the wind and rain *were* his brothers. "I'm staying."

His dad nodded. "When the scaredy-cat neighbors who evacuated come back, won't none of them mess with you. You'll have faced the wind and stood strong. They'll respect that." He jangled the pickup keys. "Last chance. Ride out of here, or ride out the storm?"

"And miss this?" Wilson hoped he sounded more convinced than he felt. His dad was fearless. Had a no-looking-back kind of confidence. Maybe Wilson had more of his mom's blood in him than Dad thought.

The gator-tooth necklace hung around Wilson's neck from a heavy leather thong. He'd strung assorted beads—turquoise, silver, and glass—to either side of the massive chomper to give it a sense of his Miccosukee roots. The necklace was identical to the one he'd given Parker before he left. There was a bond between them. A brotherhood. And both teeth came from the same gator's mouth. Evil twins snatched from the jaws of death. Just wearing it made Wilson feel invincible. Like he possessed a hidden strength. A part of the force of nature.

Wilson's dad stood outside the house, hands on hips. "Tell you what.

I'll throw more screws in the plywood. There's nothing else to do but wait. How about you make sure *Typhoon* is tied up tight. Deal?"

Wilson nodded. He was the only one who'd been using his uncle's airboat for a long time now. Wilson absolutely knew it was secure, but he jumped at the chance to get out of the house. "I'll be back soon."

His dad held the screw gun in one hand, the beer in the other. "Take your time. Ain't gonna be no hurricane here. The weather dudes just need to make their job sound important."

Perfect. Maybe he'd take *Typhoon* for a quick ride into the Glades to check the wildlife. Then he'd find out what was really going to happen. The gators, snakes, birds—all of them had a way of speaking if one knew how to listen. And they were way more reliable than the weather bureau.

Wilson hopped on his bike. Skipped the helmet. Rode like a crazy man for the dock where *Typhoon* was tied, six blocks away. Every house had hurricane shutters or plywood in place. He didn't pass another soul the entire way. Not anywhere. Those few who'd chosen to stay were probably already hunkered inside. He'd always felt he lived at the end of the world. Now he couldn't shake the feeling he was one of the last people on earth too . . . or would be soon.

CHAPTER 4

DAD HAD SOME WEATHER CHANNEL ON THE BIG SCREEN. Mom sat close, her arm around him. Parker stood in the back of the room watching the update on Hurricane Morgan. It did *not* look good.

In the last couple of hours, Morgan had picked up velocity. Size. The thing was shaping up to be every bit the monster the weather people had predicted it would be.

Unless Wilson's dad changed his mind about riding the storm out, they'd catch Morgan's fury sometime tomorrow night.

"Sammy and I talked to our commander," Dad said.

Parker's stomach tightened. He knew exactly where this was going— or rather, where *Dad* was going.

"The rangers down there are going to need help once the hurricane has passed," Dad said. "Water. Food. Fuel. Search and rescue teams. Lots of diehards down there. They just won't evacuate."

Like Wilson and his dad.

Mom shook her head. "Vaughn, it'll be dangerous."

"We know the area. The people. And we won't arrive there until just after the hurricane is over."

They were qualified, for sure. But wasn't Dad making this sound a whole lot more routine than it would really be?

Dad looked at Parker like he'd just noticed he was there. "I know how concerned you must be about Wilson. How'd you like to come with us?"

Not at all what he expected. "Me?"

"Vaughn," Mom said. "Absolutely not. No."

Parker pretty much shared Mom's view. Wilson was his friend, yeah. But not like he'd once been. He hadn't seen him in a year. There was no way Parker was going back into the Glades.

"He's fifteen. Got a good head on his shoulders," Dad said. "And I'm only talking about a couple of days. He's got a friend down there, and he can't sit back at home wondering."

Actually, he'd been telling himself he'd be okay staying home. The idea of going back there . . . to the Glades? It was the very thing he'd been trying to push out of his head since the thought had hit him this morning.

Mom shook her head. "No." But there was a change in her tone. More of a pleading. "That's a man's job." She clapped her hand over her mouth and looked at Parker, wide-eyed.

"Thanks, Mom."

"That came out wrong. I'm so sorry."

But she was right. This was part of being a man, wasn't it? Going someplace he was needed—even though he didn't want to. "I know what you meant."

"It was just a thought," Dad said. "Maybe a crazy one at that."

Parker wanted to be a man. A good one—like his dad. And his grandpa, right? Hadn't he wondered if he'd have the right stuff when the time came? If he stayed at home, he'd never know, would he? Actually, it was worse than that. Saying no . . . now . . . when he had a chance to help a friend—wouldn't that say something about the man he was becoming? And just like that, Parker knew his answer, even if he didn't love it. "When do we leave?"

Dad gave him a quick smile. "Not soon enough. The minute I get the green light from my commander, we're hitting the road. So be ready."

Packing would be quick. But to really be ready to go back to the Glades? That could take a while.

"We drive down with Uncle Sammy. Do whatever we can do to help in Chokoloskee and Everglades City—and find Wilson."

And when they did find him, Wilson would probably ask why they'd worried about him. He'd remind them that he could survive in the Glades for months if he had to.

"Only bring what you can carry—in one hand," Dad said.

Parker flashed an okay sign. "Pack light and tight. Got it."

Dad seemed to be working on his own list already. "We'll bring a tent just in case."

In case there was nothing else standing? That had to be it. But if that was the case, the tent may be worthless. Would they even find dry ground? Likely they'd be sleeping in the bed of the pickup.

"Now," Dad said, "not a word to Jelly. Uncle Sammy hasn't told her anything about us going there, and he wants to break the news to her."

Parker had zero desire to tell her he'd just agreed to be part of a search and rescue effort in the Glades. "Can I tell Harley?" He *had* to talk to somebody.

Dad thought for a second. "As long as he can keep it from Jelly— until Uncle Sammy has talked to her, anyway."

Parker hustled to his room. Gave Harley a quick call. And searched one more time for the gator tooth necklace. Nothing. He switched his focus to packing for the trip. Minutes later, he had the basics lined up in a neat row on his bed.

Gerber survival knife—"Jimbo"—along with calf sheath.

SOG Kukri machete—"Eddie"—with sheath.

600-lumen flashlight with belt case. 2 extra sets of batteries.

Cap with mosquito netting.

Insect repellant.

Parachute cord—100-foot coil.

Snakebite kit.

Rain poncho.

Waterproof "dry" bag.

Cargo pants.

T-shirts—4.

Socks and skivvies—4.

Phone charger.

The cord fit easily at the bottom of the backpack. The poncho was next. He rolled the clothes tight and tucked them inside. He drove the machete deep—with the handle sticking straight up out the top of the pack. An easy grab. Bite kit, flashlight, batteries, and phone charger all fit in zippered pockets. He'd wear the survival knife. Once the pack was on, he'd be hands-free—except for one more thing.

He stood in the center of his room, staring at the gator stick propped in the corner. Six feet long. Inch and a quarter solid oak staff. Dad's vintage Dacor dive knife secured to the business end of the stick with nylon ties and parachute cord. "Amos Moses." The name Grandpa had given the gator stick—a reference to some old song from the 70s. "I never thought I'd be needing you again." But there was no way he'd go back to the Glades without him.

He gripped the gator stick with both hands, pulled the sheath off the dive knife bayonet, and squared off in front of the massive gator skull on his bookshelf. Goliath . . . with its jaws propped open and its menacing teeth bared. Parker jabbed Amos Moses at the skull. "Do your worst, Goliath, and I'll ram Amos Moses down your ugly throat. Again."

Dad popped his head in the door at that moment. "Practicing?"

Parker smiled. Broke off the attack. "Something like that."

"Well, let's hope it doesn't come to that."

Parker's thoughts exactly. "Think your commander will really okay this?" Would Dad see what he was really hoping? Something like *There's still a good chance your commander may not approve this, right?*

Dad sat on the edge of the bed. "I'd be shocked if he didn't. The rangers will need our help—not to mention the locals. I think it's a sure thing. Just a matter of when."

So unless Morgan turned, this was happening. Parker was going back into the Everglades. The place he'd tried so hard to escape just a year ago. And there'd be no backing out. How manly would that be, right? "Okay." Parker nodded at the backpack. "I'm packed." But that definitely didn't mean he was ready to go.

CHAPTER 5

Everglades National Park
Friday, October 22, 7:55 p.m.

WILSON EASED *TYPHOON* BACK TO the pier and cut the motor. He lashed the airboat tight to the dock with every line he could scrounge up.

Wilson didn't have to check updates on his weather app anymore. During his quick trip into the Glades, the wildlife told him all he needed to know. He'd cut the motor far from shore and then paid attention.

There were no gators on the banks or on the mounds of brush anywhere. But he'd seen plenty of them moving against the quiet current of the Everglades. North. Always north. The toughest creatures on earth were evacuating. To deeper water or remote points of the Glades—or both. There was nothing relaxed about their pace, either. Gator after gator passed, each of them creating a silent wake behind itself.

Snakes, birds—all of them seemed to be in a hurry to get to whatever lair or refuge their instincts guided them to. The animal kingdom knew what was coming, and they had enough sense to find cover. If everything

they signaled was true, Hurricane Morgan was coming—and it would
be like nothing Wilson had ever seen. Too bad Wilson's dad didn't pay a
little more attention to what was going on around him. Maybe he would
have evacuated hours ago—like every other sane person had.

Wilson stared at his uncle's airboat. Would there be anything left of
Typhoon after Morgan came to shore? He didn't even want to think of
that. He checked the lines again. Took a selfie beside it—and sent it to
Parker along with a short message.

```
I love this thing, Bucky. Are you sure you don't want to
come down for a ride?
```

He studied the sky before jumping back aboard *Typhoon* and digging out his bug-out bag from where he always kept it stowed below the
driver's seat. He unzipped it and did a quick inventory.

Water bottles.
Beef jerky.
Granola bars.
Waterproof matches.
Dry kindling.
Army surplus rain poncho.
Light-duty sleeping bag.
Single-man tent.
Machete.
Pocketknife with 5-inch blade.
Hatchet.
Sharpening stone.
Spool of parachute cord.
Water-purifying tablets.
Compass.
ACE bandage.
Antibiotic ointment.
1 complete change of clothes in waterproof gear bag.

There was more he'd need, but all that was at home. He shouldered the pack. If the house blew apart the way the simulated video showed, he couldn't bank on making it back to *Typhoon*. A massive thrill shot through him at the thought that he might actually need the pack before this was over.

His phone signaled an incoming text. Bucky himself.

Dad and Uncle Sammy are trying to get permission to come down to help with search and rescue. Jelly is clueless.

Wilson sent a smiley alligator face emoji back.

Be a stowaway. Jelly would croak.

Now it was Parker's turn to send a smiley face.

What did the wildlife tell you about the hurricane?

Wilson snickered and whipped off his reply.

You don't want to know.

CHAPTER 6

ELLA HOUSTON LOVED SHARING HER ROOM WITH JELLY. She couldn't imagine what it would be like when Jelly's dad finished the work at their house and Jelly moved out.

"Are you sure this will be okay with Grams?" Jelly studied the wall—and the quart of red paint in Ella's hand.

"She'll love it. And so will I. Now give me your feet."

Jelly sat on the mattress and rocked onto her back. "This isn't art."

"Says the girl who has never painted anything—not even her toenails." Ella smiled. "Give me your foot."

Jelly wasn't moving.

Ella dipped the foam brush in the paint and slowly moved it toward Jelly's head. "Your face or your feet. You choose." Ella eased to within inches of Jelly's nose. "Final warning."

"Okay—*okay!*" Jelly squealed. "I believe you." She covered her face with her hands and lifted her foot. "You're crazy. You know that, right?"

Ella held Jelly's heel and coated the entire bottom of her foot—and all five toes. "Now, we carefully plant your foot on the wall . . . right about here." Ella guided Jelly's foot to the wall above the headboard of the guest bed. "Do not wiggle one toe." She pressed Jelly's foot flat for a moment, and then she lifted it off the plaster. "A masterpiece. Now give me your other foot."

Ten minutes later, red footprints meandered the section of wall where Jelly so often let her feet wander as they talked. After Jelly was gone, Ella would see those prints and imagine her friend was still there.

"You should have filmed this," Jelly said. "You could have posted it with the title 'How to give your room a new look in ten easy *steps*.'" Jelly rinsed her feet in a bucket of warm water.

Grams stepped into the room and sat on Jelly's bed. She glanced at the footpath on the wall and nodded. "Well, *that's* a nice improvement."

Ella nodded. "See? I told you."

The conversation drifted to the boys. Wilson, too—and what it was like living in southern Florida. Jelly pulled up pictures she'd taken of Everglades sunsets. Massive birds. Close-ups of flowers.

"Looks beautiful," Grams said.

"I used to think that, once upon a time." Jelly explained again how she'd grown to see the area as an enemy. She told stories about how Wilson and Parker had cheated death out in the Glades. Jelly talked about her older sister, Maria, and how Clayton Kingman had been a regular Pied Piper, luring her away from family.

Grams had a way of drawing out whatever was buried deep inside a person. "Your sister trusted a young man who was not trustworthy. What was your heart telling you at the time, Angelica?"

"Of all the dangers in the Glades, none was worse than Clayton Kingman. But Maria thought she understood Clayton like nobody else did. She thought she could 'fix' him. No matter how hard I tried warning her, she wouldn't listen."

"Mmmm-hmmm." Grams nodded. "We girls are good at following

our passions—and deceiving ourselves. We must always test our heart because it can't always be trusted."

"So," Ella said, "you're saying Maria missed something?"

"More like she *discounted* something," Grams said. "Likely she had warning flags pop up, but she explained them away. When we girls get a bad feeling about someone? Trust that, Ella-girl." Grams's voice took on an ominous tone in their dark room. "And don't listen to that civilized, proper voice inside telling you not to be a baby—that you're making something out of nothing. The voice that says you can change a person."

Jelly opened up about Clayton Kingman more than ever before. How he controlled. Manipulated. Could come across as a charmer but had a cruel streak that was horror-movie scary. How the man had tried to kill Parker and Wilson deep in the Everglades . . . and how she feared he'd somehow break free if the prisoners were evacuated.

They talked late into the night. Had they been speaking about some character in a movie, Ella would have loved it. She'd have served popcorn. But Kingman was real. Ella honestly felt she knew Kingman, even though they'd never met. She hoped they never did. But she'd be watching the reports about the prison evacuation with a whole new level of interest now.

"Well, young ladies"—Grams kissed each of them on the forehead and headed for the door—"I'm not sure I'll sleep after all that, but I'm certainly going to try."

"Keep telling yourself that this monster is locked in a cage," Ella said. "He won't bother Parker—or anyone else—ever again."

Grams shook her head. "Then I'd be deceiving myself instead of trusting my heart."

"And what are you feeling—deep in your heart, Grams?" Jelly rolled on her side, propping herself on one elbow. "Give me the first word that comes to your mind."

Grams took Jelly's hand in hers and gave it a pat. "*Uneasy.* Very, very uneasy."

CHAPTER 7

PARKER WOKE FROM A DEAD SLEEP. Someone gripped his arm. He thrashed wildly and kicked off the covers. "Ahhhhhh!"

"Easy . . . whoa, hold on, Parker. It's Dad."

The light of realization dawned on him, even though the room was still dark. "What's going on?"

"Commander called. We're going."

How long had he been sleeping? "The hurricane hit?"

"No. But it will. And it'll be bad. By the time we get there, the storm will be over—or winding down. They'll need help."

Parker was wide awake now. "How long before we leave?"

"Five minutes. Grab your gear." Dad slipped out of the room without another word.

Parker flipped on the light. Pulled on his cargo pants and a T-shirt. Harley's spare key still hung from the leather string around Parker's neck—and he left it there. Honestly, he wished he'd found Wilson's gator tooth necklace, but there was no time to look again. He fired off a text to Harley, telling him he was going—and reminding him not to say a word to Jelly.

Parker shouldered his pack and grabbed Amos Moses. He stopped at the door and scanned his room to be sure he hadn't forgotten anything. He scooped up his phone charger and stuffed it in his pack.

Goliath's massive skull stared at him through empty, shadowed sockets. Mouth propped open, the thing definitely appeared to be smiling at him, like it had him right where he wanted him.

"Yeah, I'm going back," Parker whispered. "And if you have a brother back there that's looking to settle a score, I'll serve him the same thing I fed you." He thumped the butt of his gator stick on the floor.

Goliath's smile seemed to stretch, just a tiny bit. Like the thing was taunting him somehow.

Parker took a deep breath and hiked the pack higher on his shoulder. He hit the light and stood there for just a few seconds, looking into his darkened room. He had to do this, right? Maybe it was some kind of test of manhood. Maybe not. For an instant, he was sure Goliath's eye sockets lit up with that ghastly orange glow he'd seen so many times in the Glades at night. But he'd imagined it, right?

There was only one thing he was absolutely sure of. He was going back to the Everglades for real now . . . and there was nothing he could do to change that.

CHAPTER 8

HARLEY DAVIDSON LOTITTO TORE OUT of the locker room after his shower and ran all the way to the bike rack. He wanted to forget all about this morning's game. He'd stop at Park's house on the way to work and pick up something from his tool chest—to bring to the foster home tonight.

The biggest problem living with the Gundersons? It didn't feel like home. The bunk wasn't his. Neither was the pillow. He wanted something with him that actually *belonged* to him. Something he'd actually had at his real home, once upon a time. Might that help him sleep better at night? He hoped so. The problem was there was almost nothing he had now that he'd had when his dad had been alive—except the tools.

He unlocked his bike and took off on the fly. He never slept great the night before a game. He was too juiced with adrenaline. Itching to hit. To slam into guys wearing a different jersey from his. But last night, it had been the text from Parks that caused him to stare at the ceiling for what seemed like half the night. There was a part of him that wished he'd been asked to go with Parks and the men. But at least Parks trusted him enough to keep a family secret. That said Harley belonged. That he mattered. Hey, he was practically part of the family, right? For a guy living with foster parents, that felt pretty stinkin' terrific. And he'd keep Parker's secret—until his friend broke the news to Jelly himself. Harley was a rock that way. A brick. A vault with no key or combination. He could handle it.

But the thing that had him on edge at the moment? The Massachusetts Correctional Institution "field trip" his foster dad had planned for Harley. Mr. Gunderson said he'd pick Harley up right after he'd finished work at BayView Brew Coffee and Donut Shop this afternoon. He'd rather run wind sprints on a ninety-degree day than see Uncle Ray again—especially in jail. The Gundersons said Harley needed closure, and that the visit wasn't an option.

Mr. and Mrs. Gunderson were okay. Hey, they took him in, right? He'd never had foster parents before—and they were miles better than living with Uncle Ray. They didn't put him on a short leash, which was a plus. But they didn't make him feel like part of the family. Not even a little.

Honestly, the impression he got? They were lifers in the foster care system—and they'd been in it long enough to get the kind of foster kids they wanted. The checks from the state were a needed part of their income—and they didn't want foster kids who gave them any problems.

"Keep your room—and your *nose*—clean," Mr. Gunderson had said. "And we'll get along just peachy." Harley could do that. The room part anyway. Except for the tools stored at Parker's, everything he owned could fit in a backpack. How could he make a mess in his room? The bigger challenge was keeping out of trouble.

The Gundersons didn't go to his game this morning—or give him a ride to school. So he biked it, and that was okay.

Living with them was nothing like when he'd been bunking at Parker's, but at least they lived close enough so he could be with the

Buckmans as much as he wanted. Harley wasn't going to do anything to mess this up, nothing that might make the Gundersons send him packing. What if the next foster home was far away?

Harley pulled up at Parker's home, dropped his bike, and hustled back to the shed. He spun the combination and slipped inside. Big Red, his eight-drawer rolling tool cabinet, stood all the way in the back, covered with a 3-mil plastic sheet. He tossed the cover aside and opened the drawer storing the socket wrenches and accessories. He picked up a hefty ratchet handle and snapped a one-inch socket on the end. He gave the thing a couple of turns. It would do. He dropped it in his pack.

A length of blue masking tape was taped to the inside wall of the drawer. Funny how he'd never noticed it before. Clearly it was taping something in place. Something his dad hadn't wanted to lose. Harley picked off one corner and slowly pulled back the painter's tape. A Harley-Davidson key. "Oh, Dad!"

With shaky hands, he whipped the lanyard from around his neck and compared the cut of the two keys. An absolute match. It was just like his dad to have another spare squirreled away. Now he had *three* keys to the motorcycle he'd worked on with his dad before he'd died. Three keys to a bike that no longer existed. One around Parker's neck. One around his own. And now this one.

He clasped the key in his fist and wrapped his other hand around it. He squeezed tight. Dad had been the last one to touch it. He stood there for a moment, not sure what to do next. He raised his hands to his face in the dim light of the shed. "God . . . I am so . . ." He was so what? Lost? Lonely? Scared? Desperate? "Take Your pick, God. I guess You know what I am . . . but I don't want to be that anymore." He taped the newly discovered treasure back where he'd found it.

He covered the cabinet—and hated the picture that flashed in his mind of paramedics covering his dad with a tarp. He backed out of the shed. *Get a grip, Harley. You've got work to do.*

Harley pedaled hard all the way to town as if he could outrun the shadows chasing him. He locked his bike to a post near the coffee shop.

He was still late for his noon start time. He'd already called Miss Lopez to apologize—and explained that he wouldn't be staying for the full cleanup afterwards. She was great about it. That's just the kind of boss she was.

After the dive shop closed, he'd needed the work. When he wasn't at football practice, he was getting some hours here at the coffee shop. It was one of only two places in town where a fifteen-year-old could get a job that didn't involve pushing a lawnmower. Rockport Yacht Club was the other, but Parker pretty well scooped up all the available hours they had.

Harley rolled his shoulders, hoping to loosen up the bruised and cramping muscles from the game. He pulled open the door to BayView Brew Coffee and Donut Shop. This was a safe place. He drew in the welcoming aromas as if they could heal his battered body.

Right now, he'd need to keep secret the fact that Parker had already left for Florida. *You got this, Harley. Remember, you're a steel safe with no combination.*

Harley hustled toward the counter and stopped dead. Bryce Scorza sat on one of the mushroom-shaped stools, elbows on the counter, leaning toward the shelves of donuts on the back wall. If Harley hadn't been scheduled to work, he'd have done a 180 and gotten out of there.

Ella busied herself wiping the counter, like she was doing her best to avoid any conversation. Scorza obviously wasn't picking up on her body language. Even from this distance, it was clear Scorza was bragging about something. Probably not a word of it was true. But Ella was the only one behind the counter—and there was no way she could leave the front end unstaffed.

She locked eyes with Harley, looking both a little relieved and annoyed. Harley put a finger to his lips, then slipped around the far end of the counter and into the kitchen without being spotted. Maybe Scorza would be gone before Harley got a work apron on. But if today's game was any indicator of how his luck was running, that wasn't going to happen.

Victoria Lopez stood at the back room sink, washing empty donut trays. Sunglasses propped on top of her head—like usual.

"Hey, Miss Lopez." For some reason, he couldn't shorten it to Pez like the girls did—even though she'd invited him to. "Sorry I'm late."

"So is Ella. Is the former Mr. Football Star still dominating her time out there?"

"Yeah," he glanced over his shoulder. "I don't think he even saw me ghost in."

"Tough game today, Harley. You doing okay?"

No, he wasn't. But he wasn't about to admit that. "Fine, I guess." And how did she even know how the game had gone?

She smiled. "You'll get 'em next time."

Not with the way the Vikings had been playing lately. A row of pegs held the official BayView Brew aprons. Most had an employee's name stitched below the logo. Maybe Harley hadn't worked there long enough for his own apron. But he didn't mind wearing the apron with *Trainee* stitched in block letters. He had a job—with people he liked working with. He slipped the apron over his T-shirt and tied it behind his back.

Ella ducked her head into the back room, eyes fiery. "About time you got here. You have to rescue me from his bloviating."

Harley laughed. He had no idea what the word meant, but it sounded like a right fit for Scorza.

"I mean it," she said. "If you don't relieve me in like ten seconds, I'm going to give you a pounding worse than you got this morning." She disappeared out front.

Okay, the game was bad. But she'd been on the schedule here all morning too. Obviously, Scorza hadn't wasted any time giving her the bad news.

Scorza's eyes lit up the moment Harley stepped into view. The guy wore his maroon team jersey—like he was still a player. "Well, look who decided to show his face in public. Not that I blame you for hiding out in the back room. If I'd played like you did, I'd disappear too." He pointed at Harley's apron. "Trainee—oh, that's perfect. You looked like one on the field today too."

"Funny." If Scorza had been quarterbacking, at least Harley would have gotten some decent handoffs—or throws he could catch. But he wasn't about to feed the guy's overweight ego.

"I've got to help Pez in back. This customer is all yours." Ella smiled as she passed.

"Cast is off." He held up his passing arm. Sickly pale—with a thick, long scar running up the forearm like someone had stretched a purple gummy worm and glued it in place. "I start physical therapy next week. A private trainer—comes to the house. He says I'll be throwing rockets next year."

Right now, his arm didn't look strong enough to throw darts. But Harley couldn't say that. He was working for Miss Lopez, and she paid him to be polite to customers. "Can I get you anything before you go?"

"Black Beauty took care of me."

Was the guy deliberately trying to rile him with that name? Of course he was. "So you're all set?"

Scorza slid off the stool. "Actually, I was hoping to find Jelly here."

Harley was kind of surprised she wasn't around. A slight movement caught his eye under a nearby table. *Jelly?* She shook her head frantically and pressed her hands together like she was pleading with him.

Scorza backed away from the counter and shook a paper sack. "I bought her a donut. Wanted to show her my scar."

"You like showing girls your scars? I could give you a couple new ones . . ."

Scorza laughed like he thought Harley was joking.

"When I see her," Harley said, "I'll let her know you're looking for her."

"Don't bother. I'll find her."

Harley wanted to see Jelly's face after that comment. But he resisted the urge to glance her way. "Good luck. Better look high—and *low*."

Seconds later, Scorza was out the door.

"The coast is clear," Harley said, loud enough for Ella to hear in the back too.

Jelly scooted out from under the table just as Ella stepped around the counter. The two of them laughed and hugged and talked over each other like they'd just scored a touchdown. Weird.

"Thanks for not ratting me out." Jelly shook a finger at him. "But telling Scorza to look *low* for me came awful close."

"*Some*body's got an admirer," Harley said.

Jelly shuddered. "That guy creeps me out."

"What?" Harley put on an innocent face. "You don't find it just a teensy bit flattering that he's stalking you?"

"Ew. Ew." She screwed up her face like she'd just sucked on a lemon. "He's just recruiting for his fan club—and I'm not interested." Jelly took a seat on the very same stool Scorza had been sitting on. Then, like she'd realized what she'd done, she popped off the stool, wiped it with a rag, and sat on the next one. "I can handle Scorza. It's Clayton Kingman that has me worried."

Harley knew the name—and his dark history. But Jelly went into it anyway. He'd never heard the story about Kingman staking the retriever by the pond—leaving the trail of dead chickens to lead the gators to it. It was when he heard about Kingman having a video cam set up that he felt the hair on his arms tingle.

"The protestors got their way," Jelly said. "And the prisoners are being moved . . . probably at this very moment."

And at three o'clock, Harley would be leaving to visit a prison himself. He didn't even want to think about it, but Jelly wasn't making that easy. Would Uncle Ray still hate him?

"They're being transported to a handful of places, including Jericho Prison. The place is farther inland—but it's *ancient*." Jelly whipped out her phone and scrolled through with a definite fury. "I saw pictures of the place. There are cracks in the walls big enough to hide a truck. It hasn't been used in over two decades. Are you going to tell me Kingman won't try escaping—along with every other scum-sucking lowlife?"

Ella was quiet—like a dialed-in quiet you get in a huddle when the enemy's score is running up and the clock is running down. What was she thinking—especially with Harley's only relative being in jail too . . . for attempted murder? What if she saw Harley as having bad blood or something?

"And if Clayton Kingman got free, what do you think he'd do?" Jelly looked at Harley like this was a quiz—and Ella already had the answer key.

"He knows the Glades, right? Maybe hide out somewhere."

Jelly shook her head. "Too obvious."

Now both girls were watching him. What was this all about? "If he escaped—which is a big if—he'd probably try to outrun the law. Get out of the state. Run to Mexico."

"You'd figure that, right?" Jelly leaned across the counter. "But he won't do that, either. The guy is smart. And unpredictable that way. But there's one thing I know for sure."

Ella bit her lip like she knew what was coming.

"What?" Harley looked from Ella to Jelly. "What do you think he'll do?"

"It's what I know he'll do."

"Okay . . . what do you *know* he'll do?"

"He'll come here," Jelly whispered. "To find Parker."

Harley rubbed down the goosebumps on his arms. "You should tell ghost stories, Jelly. Miss Lopez could have a little BayView Brew story hour off in the corner. Customers can sit there getting caffeinated and scared to death all at the same time. Nobody will sleep that night—and then they'll be back the next day for caffeine to stay awake at their job."

"If you want great storytelling, have Ella do it. She's got a gift," Jelly said. "All I'm doing is telling you the facts about a very dangerous criminal."

Miss Lopez breezed by, smiling. "Great business plan, Harley. Anytime Ella wants to start a story corner, I'm ready."

That got all four of them laughing, which felt really good. But still, he couldn't shake Jelly's warning about Clayton Kingman escaping. All the more reason to keep Parker's secret from Jelly. If Jelly was this worried that Kingman would escape and somehow travel fifteen hundred miles just to get at Parker? How crazy would she get once she knew Parker was heading Kingman's way?

CHAPTER 9

North of Richmond, Virginia
Saturday, October 23, 1:50 p.m.

PARKER PUMPED GAS WHILE DAD AND Uncle Sammy went inside the mini mart. With two drivers to switch off, there'd be no hotel stops—and no deep sleep. The journey would be broken up by a series of naps. The men had it all figured. How long before the hurricane hit. How long it would likely last. And most importantly, how quickly they'd be on site after it had passed. Parker had just screwed the gas cap back in place when they hustled out, each carrying a handful of snacks.

"About halfway," Dad handed him a chocolate milk. "But we'll be taking that little detour in Georgia." He held up his phone. "Just got confirmation."

They'd be heading to the Okefenokee National Wildlife Refuge. Which was a fancy name for the famous—and downright spooky— swamp that dominated nearly seven hundred square miles. Cypress trees. Spanish moss. Black water. Lots and lots of alligators.

"Fish and Wildlife Service will have an airboat ready for us—and we'll tow it the rest of the way."

Stopping for the airboat was smart. If the hurricane got as bad as the forecasters predicted, there may be a shortage of boats to do search and rescues. A fresh airboat would be solid gold to the NPS in the Everglades City area.

"With a flat-bottomed airboat, we can drive over some of the debris," Uncle Sammy said. "Any boat with an outboard will get hung up or damage its prop."

That made total sense. The only thing that didn't make sense? Parker still hadn't told Jelly that he'd left. Did she wonder why he hadn't stopped at the coffee shop after the game—or did she figure he went straight to work at the yacht club? How was he supposed to explain why he'd waited until they'd driven hundreds of miles before telling her? She'd be soooo bent out of shape, maybe it was good he was so far away. He picked up his phone. Stared at it. He had to tell her. And he would. He'd just give it a few more miles.

CHAPTER 10

ANGELICA STRODE TO THE FRONT WINDOW of BayView Brew Coffee and Donut Shop and flipped the sign from *OPEN* to *SEE YOU IN THE MORNING*. Ella and Pez went to the kitchen to start the cleanup routine. Angelica and Harley took the front end. Something about Harley had changed in the last hour. He seemed more distracted. Checked the clock for about the tenth time.

Maybe he had something planned with Parker. "Somebody looks anxious to get out of work today."

"Just the opposite." Harley busied himself straightening chairs.

Weird. And without offering one ounce of explanation. Chalk that up to one more example of how guys could be absolute mysteries sometimes. Like her dad—and Uncle Vaughn—racing off to the Everglades. On the one hand, she got it. They were part of the National Park Service, and there would be a need for other rangers to help in the rescue and cleanup efforts. But when they'd finally moved away from the Glades,

Angelica had hoped she'd never have to worry about rogue gators again. And after a hurricane? The wildlife could be absolutely unpredictable.

She loved her dad to pieces. But there were some things about him she'd never understand. "What is it with guys, Harley?"

He gave her a suspicious look, like he wasn't sure how to answer that.

"Everybody is supposed to evacuate the area because of the hurricane. People are driving north just as fast as they can. Even the worst criminals are being relocated—because leaving them in this storm is considered inhumane. But *he* has to go the other way—straight to Everglades City and all the danger he'd escaped before. What is it . . . some kind of insecurity? Maybe a need to be the hero of the hour or something?" The truth was her dad was nothing like that.

Harley plopped down on a stool. He actually looked relieved. "I didn't know he'd told you."

"He wimped out." She scrubbed the counter with a clean rag. "He called this morning—while you were probably on your way to the game. He'd been on the road for *hours*."

Harley nodded like he knew—or maybe that he understood her frustration.

"He could have called me when he left. Could have at least said goodbye. But no . . . he said he didn't want to wake me. Which is baloney. He didn't want me talking him out of it. He called when it was too late for me to stop him. That's what I think."

Harley's shoulders drooped a little. "I'm not disagreeing with you. I'm just glad he finally told you."

"He told me he loved me—as if that would make it all better."

Harley stared at her with an absolutely incredulous look on his face. "He said . . . *what?* That does *not* sound like him. I mean . . . I've never heard him say *anything* like that before. Not ever." The guy looked stunned. Like he was off in another world . . . an alien planet.

What was so weird about her dad telling her he loved her? "He said he was s-o-o-o-o sorry, too. But I'm not buying that. If you ask me, he was itching to get down there. To do that hero stuff so many guys are all into. I don't think he was one bit sorry."

"No, really . . . he *was*." Harley seemed to beam back from whatever planet he'd been on. "Trust me, he was really torn up about it. He totally dreaded telling you. You gotta believe him when he said he was sorry. When he talked to me last night—"

"My dad talked to you about the trip—*before* he talked to me?"

Harley's eyes grew wide. "Your dad? You're talking about your *dad?*"

"Of course . . . and who are *you* talking about?"

Harley clamped a hand over his mouth and grabbed the bucket. He turned tail and hustled to wipe down tables at the far end of the room.

"Harley?" But he wouldn't face her. He wrung out a rag and attacked the surface of the table like he was doing mortal combat with a coffee stain. Whatever was inside her stomach swirled. "Harley." But she knew. She *knew.*

A man rapped on the window. He held Harley's bike, and he pointed to the open hatch of his SUV. Harley nodded and waved. "One minute, Mr. Gunderson."

How convenient. But he wasn't leaving until he told her what was going on. Angelica stood in front of the door—just in case—and whipped out her phone. She reread the texts she'd exchanged with Parker earlier. There was nothing to hint that he'd left with the men, but he'd never answered her question about hanging out tonight at Rockport Pizza either. Definitely not like him.

She glared at Harley. "Parker went with them, didn't he?"

His face showed sheer agony. If things were different, she might have felt sorry for him.

"Harley, what have you *done!*" It wasn't a question. It was an accusation, and she said it so loud that Pez and Ella ran up from the back room.

"Parker went with the men—and Harley knew the whole time," Angelica wailed. "Why didn't you stop him?"

"What was I supposed to do?"

"Be a *real* friend—talk him out of doing something incredibly stupid," Angelica said. "Would that have been so hard?"

"He's going to help—and he'll find Wil—"

"Trouble. *That's* what he's going to find." Angelica probably said that a lot harsher than she needed to. But come *on!* "You should know that—even though you haven't been his friend very long."

She'd meant it to hurt—and by the expression on his face, she'd scored a direct hit. He looked as pale as the limp rag dangling from his hand. "Parker is headed right into the jaws of danger—because *you* didn't stop him."

Gunderson knocked on the window again and pointed at his watch. "Now, Harley."

Eyes avoiding hers, he brushed past, still wearing the apron and holding the rag. He slipped out the door without a word . . . and was gone.

CHAPTER 11

ELLA WISHED HARLEY HAD GLANCED her way before disappearing. She would've flashed him a smile, just to make him feel better. "I wonder where his foster dad was taking him."

"No place he wanted to go," Pez said. "It put a pebble in his shoe, for sure. He dreaded going."

And after Jelly's comments, he had been hurting a whole lot more when he left. "I should've thanked him more for rescuing me from Scorza—and for keeping Jelly's hiding spot secret."

Okay, Ella added that last bit hoping it might help Jelly lighten up. Instead, she stormed off.

Pez swung an arm around Ella. "I take pride in the people I select to work here . . . and I am soooo proud of Harley. I do believe shooing Scorza out was the best moment of his day."

Ella got that. "When I see him later, I'll let him know how much that meant to me."

"When you get something in your mind—something good that you just know you ought to do—don't let anything delay you." Pez swung a chair around from the nearest table. "Now you sit yourself down, prop up your pretty cowgirl boots, and send that boy a text. After that awful game this morning and now this, I expect he could use the encouragement."

Jelly seemed to be taking her frustrations out on innocent chairs and tables on the far side of the room. She slid and wrangled them in place, muttering the whole time. "I can't believe that guy."

Harley—or Parker? Ella guessed it was a toss-up.

"Let's give Jelly some space," Pez said. "Text Harley. Then check for news on that prisoner transfer. I need an update on that guy."

Ella stared at her. "Clayton Kingman?"

"Jelly is worried. And when she's anxious, I'm learning that she tends to say stuff she regrets later. If we're going to help her, we need to keep up with what's really on her mind."

Ella watched her boss disappear into the back room. Pez knew how to manage her business well, but her skills went miles beyond that. She understood people—just one more thing Ella loved about her.

The text to Harley came easy—because the words were from her heart. Catching up on the prisoner transfer didn't take long either. But even as she read the article, she found herself tracing the lines of the silver cross hanging from her neck.

Public opinion—from states all over the United States—had been mixed. Some railed that leaving anyone locked in a building smack dab in the hurricane's path was absolutely inhumane. Others argued that the old facility was built strong and perfectly safe for the prisoners. But everybody agreed that the guards shouldn't be forced to stay. They should be evacuating their families, like everyone else. So the move had taken place, and hundreds of convicts had been transported to various prisons around the state, including Jericho.

Stock photos of the retired prison added a definite creep factor. Abandoned guard towers stood watch over the place, and they were showing their age. Named after Harrison P. Jericho—a congressman who later did time there—the prison had been replaced by newer facilities way back in the 1970s. She had to read between the lines a bit, but it didn't sound like the inmates would have regular cells. The prison was a temporary holding spot, and the inmates would be packed in like cattle.

The article was a little sketchy on the details, but honestly, she could see why Jelly was worried. Jericho didn't sound like the most secure solution. Even experts questioned the move. But it was available—and at short notice. Warden Brehman W. Powers seemed to gloss over the iffy condition of the place with the assurance that his guards would make the facility secure, and the prisoners would only be there for a matter of hours. Twenty-four, max.

Ella kept digging. One report claimed close to 120 prisoners had been bused to Jericho. There just wasn't enough room at other facilities. Most of the inmates at Jericho were being held in the open, walled yard. The men selected for transport to Jericho were generally young and fit. Ella could hardly believe what she read. It all sounded a bit barbaric to her. In her gut, she felt that was likely where Clayton Kingman would be sent. What was he, twenty-two? Twenty-four?

Ella gave Pez a quick recap—along with some background Jelly had given her about Kingman.

"She's scared," Pez said. She handed Ella a sheet of paper with tomorrow's specials for the chalkboard. "I love your handwriting, Ella. Post these while I talk with Jelly."

Which was kind of a relief because Ella would hardly know where to start with her friend.

Ella erased the BayView Brew specials board. She used a wet cloth to get a nice, black backdrop, then read the notes from Pez as she let the thing dry. The last line made her smile.

A word from the owner: I choose my employees as carefully as I choose my coffee beans. Treat them nice! ☺

Even now, Pez sat with Jelly at a table across the room, holding both her hands. Tears were coming down her friend's cheeks, and Ella wanted to run to her. But Pez looked like she had everything under control—and she'd already given Ella a job to do.

She picked up the box of chalk and got to work. That last line was going to be in big, bold letters, and not just as a reminder to customers. She hoped Jelly took it to heart too.

CHAPTER 12

Massachusetts Correctional Institution, Concord, Massachusetts
Saturday, October 23, 4:45 p.m.

HARLEY HADN'T SEEN UNCLE RAY SINCE the guy had been locked up back in August. Mr. G said he wanted closure for Harley, but that wasn't the big thing. "Every time I get a new foster kid, I take them to jail—usually in the first couple of weeks. Take a guess why."

What fun. "To show them where they don't want to end up?"

"Exactly."

The tactic might've been good for some—keeping them on the straight and narrow. But it sure didn't make Harley feel like he was part of a family. It reminded him that he was just a kid in the state foster home program—and the prison was just another branch of the same system.

Still, the visit could have an upside. Maybe a couple of months in jail had changed Uncle Ray. Maybe he'd be sorry. Maybe Harley would feel he actually belonged to a family for once—even if that relative was in prison.

Walking inside the correctional facility was enough to make Harley want to keep his nose clean. It made the dingiest locker room look bright and welcoming. They were escorted to a room not much bigger than the washroom at school. Two tables. Four chairs. One door in from the outside. One door leading to who knows what deeper inside the prison.

Harley was instructed to sit, and Mr. G sat at the second table. He pulled out a pocket notepad and pen. The guy was going to take notes?

Uncle Ray smirked when the guard led him into the room. He looked stronger. Leaner. One eye was swollen shut. His forearm mummified in gauze. He sat opposite Harley. "Here to gloat?"

Not a great start. "What happened to you?"

"Nothing I can't handle."

Fights were common in prison, right? Or was this something more? "Was the loan shark behind this?"

Uncle Ray's good eye narrowed. Unreal. He could still do the "Laser Ray" thing—even with only one eye. "I'm not afraid of Lochran—or anybody else."

So he *did* believe this was because of the unpaid loan.

"I'm getting transferred out of this joint. Outta his reach. I'm good." Ray gave him a once-over. "Looks like you landed on your feet too. Maybe you got a little more of your Uncle Ray in you than you think."

Not a comforting thought.

"And you're going to need it. You think life is going to be all good now—with no Uncle Ray?" He laughed and slapped his knee in an exaggerated way. "You're so stupid. You're more alone than ever. You don't have me—or those friends of yours. You got *nobody*. Soon enough, you'll wear out your welcome, and your friends will drop you like you're a moray eel. Trust me."

Trust him? "Parks isn't like that. He—"

"That Buckman kid is only your friend because you're some kind of Christian project to him. That'll get old." Ray gave a slow nod like he'd revealed some great truth. "They're all just putting up with you now, like I did. But you're an outsider. You'll never belong—not to nobody."

Harley sat there, stunned. He couldn't breathe. Couldn't move.

"Why'd you come here? To say you're sorry you didn't sell that stupid motorcycle?"

"Me?" Harley choked the word out. "Sorry?" But this is what Ray did, right? Turned things around so it was Harley who always had to do the apologizing. Harley eased one hand up to his chest like he had an itch. Felt for Kemosabe's keys. Wished it were waiting for him in the shed.

"None of this would've happened if you'd have just listened to your Uncle Ray."

So this was all Harley's fault? That made no s—

"There was a third man in the operation." Uncle Ray smiled and talked so low . . . so quiet that the guard and Mr. G weren't likely to hear a word—or see the need to listen in. "He's the one who ditched your precious motorcycle in the end, and he's the only person who knows exactly where he dumped it. And you ain't never getting it back—because I ain't never giving you the third man's name."

Uncle Ray paused, like he wanted that to sink in.

"Right now, the salt is probably bubbling the paint off the gas tank. Coral is growing on those straight pipes you loved so much. The ocean is claiming it, boy."

Harley slid away from the table. Glanced over his shoulder at Mr. G for some kind of help, but clearly the man hadn't heard what Ray had said. The motorcycle was gone. Harley knew it. Uncle Ray knew it. But the guy couldn't resist the urge to twist the knife.

"Come back when you're ready to admit how wrong you've been," Uncle Ray said. "Do that, and maybe I'll give you the latitude and longitude."

"You don't even know where it is." Harley shook his head. "Only the third man knows. Isn't that what you said?"

"Don't get smart with me, boy. All I got to do is make a phone call."

Right. He'd never give the location—even if he had it. He'd send Harley on dives to anywhere but the spot the cycle had been dumped.

Even now, the bike would have been in the saltwater for nearly three months. Kemosabe was gone. "I got nothing to apologize for."

"You turned on your blood family." Uncle Ray had that laser thing going again. "You betrayed your own kin. Got police involved in family business. Your daddy is probably shaking his head, wondering how he could've raised such a stupid kid."

Harley bolted to his feet. Shaking. "I'm not the one wearing shackles and a jumpsuit, Uncle Ray. I didn't put you here. You did that all by yourself. And there's no way I'll ever be back to visit."

Uncle Ray smiled. "Let's make sure of that." He turned to the guard. "This visit is over. My nephew here is trying to convince me to escape."

Immediately, the guard stepped forward.

"That's not true," Harley said. "He just doesn't want me coming back."

Mr. G grabbed Harley by the arm. "That makes two of us."

By the look on Mr. G's face, Harley was pretty sure the prison field trip wouldn't be part of his "new foster kid" tradition for a long time.

CHAPTER 13

CLAYTON KINGMAN STOOD IN THE outdoor prison yard and surveyed the walls of Jericho. He'd seen dilapidated trailers on the fringes of the Everglades that looked stronger.

The winds blew harder now. Like, amazingly powerful. And the wind was his friend. An invisible ally, promising to bust him out.

Clayton already knew Florida well, and he'd paid attention on the bus ride here. They drove straight north on Highway 27 to the small town of Lake Harbor. Harrison P. Jericho Prison had a uniquely horrible placement. Treacherous Lake Okeechobee straight north. Endless miles of swampy Everglades to the east, west, and south. The place was surrounded by water and swamps. Back in the day, Jericho had been dubbed the Alcatraz of South-Central Florida. The sharks in San Francisco Bay had a way of discouraging would-be escapees from Alcatraz. Instead of sharks, Jericho had hungry gators and deadly snakes. There was only one main road leading in and out of Lake Harbor. Easy to roadblock in case of a prison break—which had never happened. Clayton had always been good with maps, and he'd already drawn one in his head. He knew exactly where he was . . . and where he'd go if the winds of fate blew his way.

He surveyed the yard again. A skeleton crew of guards was posted in the towers, but for how long? Was it even safe that high off the ground with these winds? More than one guard looked mighty uneasy. Warden Powers stalked around like he wasn't at all happy he'd been forced to move the prisoners. Clayton smiled.

The mood in prison could change instantly. And the vibe right now was nothing he'd felt since being locked up. There were no divisions. No gangs. Instead, there was a brotherhood among all who wore orange jumpsuits. They were all on the same team, for once. Only the guards were the outsiders now. Did they feel the eyes on them? Did the guards fear the mob of men in the courtyard, craving the chance to pry the rifle from their hands?

Even from here, Clayton could see the death grip a tower guard had on his weapon. Oh, yeah. They felt the vibe.

A gust of wind blasted the south wall with a fury Clayton had never experienced before. A tower guard's hat blew into the coven of inmates below. Cheers roared as several men pounced on it. An inmate held the hat up and motioned for the guard to come down and get it. The guard stepped back from the rail until his back pressed against the guardhouse.

"Think the walls will hold?" The inmate next to Clayton was older. Hardened. The last two digits on his uniform were twenty-two. He'd never talked to Clayton before, but today, the only walls in this prison were the ones being pounded by the wind.

Twenty-two kept his eyes on the south wall. "Seems to me there's a Sunday school story—or was it a song?—about the walls of Jericho tumbling down."

"Song *and* a story." Clayton liked this guy. "You won't catch me leaning up against any one of these walls." He visualized the walls dropping. Saw it happening. Planned out his first move. Second. Third.

"Too bad the place is surrounded by swamps," Twenty-two said. "We'd have to be part reptile to make it."

Something about that made Clayton snicker. "Maybe we are. You mean nobody has called you a snake before?"

Twenty-two grinned.

Another fist of wind took a swing at the wall. Guards held support beams with one hand, their weapon with the other.

"That wind is promising," Twenty-two said. "But we'll wait and see. It's going to be an interesting night."

"Indeed." But Clayton would do much more than wait to see if the walls held. He'd be busy . . . working on plans for when they fell.

CHAPTER 14

ACCORDING TO THE US WEATHER SERVICE, Hurricane Morgan totally jangled the keys . . . the Florida Keys, that is. Everything from Key West to Key Largo—and they were still getting pummeled. Sustained winds of over 180 miles per hour. A solid Category 5. It would probably rank as a Cat 6 if the rating system went that high.

Flamingo, Chokoloskee, Everglades City. All were getting the tar beaten out of them. And that meant Wilson was too.

Parker sat in the second seat of Dad's pickup. The video clips posted by news crews and stubborn residents who'd stayed behind were absolutely terrifying. How anybody could hold up their phone and get a shot without being blown away was beyond Parker. He stared at the screen, mesmerized. Hurricane Morgan had hammered southern Florida with a rage that seemed unquenchable. Morgan had come in throwing elbows and shouldering its way inland like it was on some unholy vendetta. Any hope that Morgan would give Florida a hall pass was long gone.

Somebody had posted a video of an airboat tumbling up the flooded street like the thing was made of aluminum foil. Parker instinctively looked for a name on the steering fins, praying it wouldn't say *Typhoon*. But between the shaking of the camera and the water on the lens, there was no telling if the airboat had a name or not. The thing sideswiped an abandoned pickup, ripping the cage and half the prop right off the airboat before the video went dead.

Had Wilson found a spot safe enough to ride out the storm?

The face of fear can be different depending on who's wearing it—and how deep the terror strikes. When a guy has to go through someplace scary at night—like down a dark alley or through a graveyard—fear may make him break into a sprint, screaming bloody murder the entire way. It was about getting it over with—and startling any would-be attacker into hesitating just long enough to make escape possible.

Other times, fear made guys go silent. Like, plaster-my-mouth-shut-with-duct-tape quiet. Parker's dad had been quiet for what, maybe a half hour? Maybe fear put Dad's voice box in a full nelson. He glanced at Dad. Whatever he was thinking, he wasn't letting on. Uncle Sammy was asleep. Like he knew shut-eye would be as scarce as an internet signal once they got down there.

Even now, all mobile phone service in the Chokoloskee and Everglades City area was gone—like Hurricane Morgan had already blown down every cell tower. That had to be the reason Parker hadn't heard from Wilson since just before the hurricane hit full force.

He'd gotten five texts. Rapid-fire, like breakers on the shore. One right after another. Too quick to respond between them.

Looks bad, Bucky. Never seen anything like this.

Say a prayer for me. Ask your God to turn this off while you're at it.

It's a for real Everglades Curse—even dad says so. The god of the Glades demanding an offering.

Fresh chills raced up and down Parker's spine like it was a piano keyboard that only played in minor keys. He knew something of the Everglades Curse. At one time, his friends had believed he was the object of the curse—and that it was only a matter of time before he paid the ultimate toll. The thought of Wilson being there now . . . fighting for survival?

"God . . . help him. Please. Help him."

Don't know how much longer I'll be here.

Was Wilson talking about the phone connection—or something more?

The last text had come in seconds later.

Sky dark as the charred gates of hell. Hoping I don't see them for real.

Parker hadn't heard from him since.

The closer they got to Florida, the more okay he was that he'd come along. Not that he felt closer to Wilson—or loved the idea of going to the Glades any more than he had earlier. It was just that he'd hate to be sitting back in Rockport, doing nothing, while men like Dad and Uncle Sammy raced to help.

Too bad Jelly didn't feel the same way. She'd also sent him a series of texts. Each of them a definition—like they'd been cut and pasted right out of the dictionary.

Stupid [adj]: Very dull in mind.

Dense [adj]: Witless. Ignorant.

Brainless [adj]: Birdbrained. Pea-brained. Chowderhead.

She added no further comment. But he got the message. And when he compared them to Wilson's texts? There was no question in Parker's mind that he was doing the right thing.

He'd started typing out a reply to help Jelly understand why he'd gone with Dad and Uncle Sammy. And why he'd left without even telling her. But the more he tried to explain, the more it sounded like he was making excuses. Defending himself. He'd done a lot of thinking on the drive about what it meant to be a man, and not one of his message drafts felt all that manly.

Parker deleted what he'd started and finally settled on something simple.

I didn't want to go—but felt I should. Have you seen YouTube videos? They'll need help. I believe I'm doing the right thing.

He stared out the pickup window for a moment. It didn't take long for a string of responses to stack up from Jelly.

Reckless [adj]: Lacking caution. Hasty.

Risky [adj]: Exposing to possible loss, danger, injury, peril.

Ill-advised [adj]: Not well counseled.

The only things truly ill-advised were her texts. He fired one off to her.

C'mon, Jelly. Talk to me for real, okay?

He waited a full minute for her reply.

Why didn't you have the decency to tell me?

What, so she could talk him out of it? He'd had a hard-enough time convincing himself to go.

You could have manned up and called.

Manned up? Okay, that one stung. He was trying to man up, wasn't he? One reason he couldn't tell Jelly before he left was because her dad wanted to talk to her first. Would a real man have ratted out Uncle Sammy—and just blamed it all on him?

I couldn't do that. It's complicated. Can't explain. Really sorry.

She fired back.

Coward [noun]: One who lacks courage or shows shameful fear.

Okay . . . Jelly could keep the Webster texts going all night. He'd had enough of the vocab lesson—and of her. She was worried about the gators he might meet in the Glades? He couldn't imagine them being any more vicious than what she was being right now.

He sent her one last response before silencing his phone and tossing it on the seat next to him. He regretted it the moment he'd sent it. He was pretty sure she wouldn't need a dictionary to catch his drift, but he'd added the definition anyway.

Adios [interj]: See ya later, alligator.

CHAPTER 15

HOWLING. That was the only word Wilson came up with to describe the sound. Even that wasn't enough. The wind—at a velocity he'd never imagined possible. Even if he stood fifteen feet behind an airboat—going full blast—he'd be talking what? Wind speeds of one hundred miles per hour? The wind tearing at the house was nearly twice that . . . and not letting up. It was relentless.

It was a howling from hell. Like legions of demons had been unleashed—bent on destroying everything in their path.

Half the plywood coverings had been ripped off the windows and sucked away. The windows flexed and bowed like they'd go at any second.

Water from the driving rain was coming in everywhere. Ceiling. Around windows. The seam between the floor and walls. Under the door. At first, he'd used towels, blankets, even sheets to jam into cracks or to sop up water. Now he didn't have a single dry thing to use if they needed it. The oven was the only dry spot left. They stuffed everything they could fit inside. Phones. Chargers. Important papers.

His dad sat next to him, right in the corner, plastering a shoulder against two different walls. Like he was hedging his bets. If one wall blew in, he'd have the other for protection. A half-dozen empty longnecks lay scattered at his feet. They'd been his last-minute storm preparations . . . but that was before the wind speed hit triple digits.

Even in the dim light of the battery-powered lantern, Dad sat close enough for Wilson to see his eyes—all cockiness gone with the wind. Terror cowered there now. Seeing that in his dad was the scariest thing Wilson had seen in his life.

Dad pulled Wilson close. Kept his arm around his shoulders. "Some adventure, huh?" It was his dad's way. Not an apology that anyone would recognize, but Wilson understood exactly what his dad was saying.

"The best." Wilson felt the gator-tooth necklace around his neck. "Miccosukee men don't run."

Dad gave him an extra-tight squeeze. "You know how stupid you look in that bike helmet?"

Wilson had almost forgotten he'd strapped the thing on.

"But you keep it on, hear?"

Something slammed against the house, sending vibrations all the way to where they sat. The demons clawed at the roof, seemingly ripping part of it off as they passed. Wilson stared at the ceiling at the far end of the room. Water dripped and pooled on the floor. "Will the roof hold?"

"Has to."

His dad was right. Because if it didn't, they were goners.

CHAPTER 16

ANGELICA SAT NEXT TO ELLA ON THE TOP STEP of the porch, both of them absorbed with their phones. Ella watched all things Hurricane Morgan— and there were plenty. Angelica scoured the internet for an update on Jericho Prison—which was almost impossible to find.

"Transferring prisoners was stupid," Angelica said.

Ella kept scrolling. "Leaders make dumb decisions when they try pleasing angry mobs, right?"

Hurricane Morgan had altered course just enough to put Jericho Prison in its path. Based on the weather maps, the tired facility was under an all-out assault at this very moment. "They should have never moved them."

"The walls will hold." Ella spoke like it was as much a scientific fact as gravity.

Jericho *had* to hold.

Grams stepped onto the porch with a tray. Three glasses of sweet tea. Three slices of pie.

"You joining us, Grams?" Ella stood and took the tray from her.

"I was rather hoping young Harley might show up."

Just hearing his name sent a flash of anger coursing through Angelica. "We haven't seen him since he left with his foster dad—for who knows where. He was pretty secretive about it. About a lot of things."

"Hmmm." Grams had that way of questioning without saying a word. "That boy shoulders baggage none of us have had to carry. All things considered, he impresses me."

Angelica felt just a twinge of guilt.

"It's not like him to stay away," Grams said.

Angelica had been so focused on the prisoner move—and Parker racing for Florida—she hadn't thought much about Harley. "Where do you think he went this afternoon?"

Ella shook her head. "I've been trying to figure that out." She pulled out her phone and dictated a text to Harley. "Where are you—and what are you doing? How about stopping by? Grams has sweet tea and pie for you."

Angelica watched Ella's screen for his reply.

Sitting on a pier in Gloucester. Thinking. Sorry. Have to get to foster home soon.

"Mmmm-hmmm," Grams said. "Alone on a dock in the dark? Weight of the world."

Okay, now Angelica was really beginning to feel rotten about the way she'd treated him. Was it *really* his fault that Parker had left? And even if Harley *had* told Angelica sooner, would it have made any difference?

"I need to get him talking," Ella said. "Pick him up a bit." Ella's thumbs were flying.

High points of day?

Three replies came fast. She held the phone so Grams and Angelica could read them.

Easy.

1. Your face when I got to work—looks funny when you're
peeved.

2. Keeping Scorza from seeing Jelly.

Ella was smiling now. She texted him again.

Low points?

This time, the answers didn't come back nearly as quickly.

Lots of those.

1. The game.

2. Making Jelly mad.

3. The field trip with Mr. G after work—and don't ask about it.

4. Every minute since getting back from field trip.

5. Totally screwing up when Parks told me he was going to
Glades.

"There," Angelica pointed at the last line. "See? So maybe even
he realizes he should have stopped Parker somehow. Ask him what he
means."

Ella hesitated—and Angelica grabbed her phone and pecked out
her question.

You think you should have talked him out of going—or told
Jelly sooner so she could?

A yes to either one would make Angelica feel a teensy bit better. Like
the frustration she'd poured out on both Parker and Harley was justified
somehow.

It seemed like two minutes before he texted back.

Neither. I should have gone with.

CHAPTER 17

PARKER CHECKED FOR TEXTS FROM WILSON, even though he knew there'd be nothing there. Every internet report he'd found reported that Morgan was still raging as strong as ever.

He tried to imagine his friend riding out a storm like that on the airboat. Had he made it back to his house—or some kind of safe shelter? Was there really any place that could be called safe with winds like that?

Dad was at the wheel. Uncle Sammy stared out the side window. Two of the three most important men in his life. And they were men. Did they feel fear? They had to, right? But they were going anyway.

Dad's backpack sat on the floor behind his seat. The pistol-grip handle of his Ithaca 12-gauge poked out the open top. It had been a regular passenger on the boat when Dad had been a ranger in the Everglades. Parker hadn't seen it since then.

Parker met Dad's eyes in the rearview mirror. "It's going to be bad down there, isn't it?"

"Uh-huh. Still don't want you seeing all that." Dad was quiet for a moment. "But absolutely sure you need to."

Like it was part of being a man.

"There'll be lots for all of us to process—and we'll do that. Together."

Seeing the place he used to live all torn up? Yeah, there could be some things to sort out in his head.

"Seeing a disaster site in person is way different from watching YouTube clips," Uncle Sammy said. "You won't be viewing a game from the stands. You'll be on the field. It'll mess with your head."

Dad looked at him again. "Seeing the power of nature at its worst? It makes you feel something."

Were they thinking Wilson was gone? That he didn't have a chance? "You think we'll see . . . bodies?"

Neither men spoke for a moment. Uncle Sammy looked at Dad— like he knew it wasn't his place to answer that question.

"Likely we will, Son." Dad glanced at him in the mirror again. "It'll change you. But make you into a better man, I think."

Parker didn't feel anywhere near manhood at this moment. And he definitely didn't want to see any bodies. Especially Wilson's.

"When I was your age," Dad said, "I used to wonder when I'd be a man. Wondered if I'd have the right stuff."

It was like Dad was reading his mind. "I'm fifteen, Dad. Got a long way to go, don't you think?"

"Manhood isn't about hitting a magic birthday—like eighteen or twenty-one. And it isn't about driving. Or getting a job. Having a drink. Owning a car."

Uncle Sammy turned to face Parker and grinned. "And it sure as shootin' isn't about having a massively strong body—like your uncle. Otherwise, what chance would most guys have?" He flexed his bicep.

"And manhood definitely isn't about being with a girl," Dad said, "or any number of the other things guys think make them a man."

Parker wanted to know, but he feared whatever it was, he wouldn't have what it took anyway. "So it's about knowing a secret handshake or something?"

Both men laughed—which made Parker feel good. Like he wasn't just a kid but one of them.

"It's about the choices you make," Dad said. "And the person you're becoming. You're closer than you think—and this trip will be another milestone."

"Because of what I'll see down there?"

Dad rocked his head side to side, like Parker still wasn't quite getting it. "That's part of it. But this trip has more to do with seeing beyond yourself."

Parker wasn't sure he got it. But he was pretty sure it had to do with Wilson.

"We'll talk about it more," Dad said. "A lot more."

Dad's phone rang at that moment—and the screen on the dash showed it was the Fish and Wildlife contact near Lake Okefenokee. Both men got involved in the conversation. The talk was about the ETA to pick up the airboat, extra fuel tanks, and other supplies they might need. Even though it was late, it sounded like there was a small crew there getting things ready.

Parker had passed some of the earlier hours watching a movie on his phone. Playing games. He picked up his phone again—and hesitated. Maybe he should get some more sleep. But except for some short naps, how much had Dad and Uncle Sammy slept? They spent their time talking about the mission ahead of them. Preparing for what was to come, in their own way. How much had Parker prepped? Is that what Dad and Uncle Sammy had just been doing? Nudging Parker to get his mind on the target ahead?

If Parker really wanted to be a man, shouldn't he start acting like one—even during something as mindless as riding in the car? Shouldn't he be doing more than running down the battery on his phone?

The voice on the other end of the call gave a quick update as to the status of Morgan—and it didn't sound good. How could Parker think about playing a game when Wilson was likely fighting for his life at this very moment?

Uncle Sammy leaned forward. Thanked whoever was on the phone for the search and rescue airboat they were outfitting. "We'll take good care of her, I promise you that."

The phone call was over, and the men grew quiet. But something was different. There was more energy in the pickup. A vibe of urgency. And Dad drove faster.

Parker set his phone on the seat beside him. Picked up the Rand McNally atlas Dad kept in the second seat. He scanned the road ahead, watching for a road sign to give him a clue where they were. Within minutes, he had their location pinpointed on the map. They were getting really close to Lake Okefenokee.

He studied the map again. Did a rough calculation of how many miles they'd have to go after picking up the airboat—and what time they'd arrive in Everglades City. From what he could tell, they were still on schedule to arrive shortly after Morgan was gone. He could have gotten the ETA a lot quicker by using the app on his phone, but there was something about figuring it out that seemed more satisfying at this moment.

He pictured Wilson. Was he alive? He had to be.

God . . . please. And that one tiny prayer seemed to flip a switch in his attitude. Right now, he just wanted to get there.

"I'm not liking the sound of this, Vaughn," Uncle Sammy said finally.

"Ditto."

Had Parker missed something? "What?"

Dad shook his head. "It sounds worse than we'd feared. Like there'll be nothing left standing."

Parker looked at the darkness outside his window, a sense of hopelessness gripping him. *Nothing left standing?* Dad wasn't just picturing homes and buildings, was he? *Nothing left standing.* No . . . Dad was talking about *people.*

CHAPTER 18

Jericho Prison
Saturday, October 23, 9:25 p.m.

SCORES OF INMATES HAD POSITIONED THEMSELVES along the northern edge of the prison yard—farthest away from the wall taking the worst beating. Clayton didn't stand close to any wall—even though the wind tore at his prison jumpsuit something fierce here in the center of the yard.

Using Jericho Prison had been a gargantuan tactical error. Probably nobody understood that better than Warden Powers right about now.

Clayton shielded his eyes against the rain, watching the south wall guard tower, where the warden was holed up. He'd made it his command post earlier—when the winds were well under one hundred miles per hour. Likely he would've come down long before this, but with the velocity of this wind? Nobody in their right mind would chance that. So the guy was up there in his perch riding out a Cat 5 hurricane—and probably praying he'd make it. Undoubtedly, a whole lot more prayers rose from the yard that he wouldn't make it.

Did the tower sway? By the way other inmates were fixated on it—and cheering—he hadn't imagined it. He ran through a sequence of steps he'd take if fate gave him the nod.

And then it happened. The tower leaned—but didn't right itself this time. Farther. Farther. For an instant, he made out four, maybe five, men in the tower—thrown against the rain-streaked windows by gravity.

"Die! Die! Die! Die!" The inmates' roar competed with the sound of the wind.

All at once, steel beams snapped, and the tower crashed into the east wall with an impact that knocked Clayton off his feet.

The wall crumbled below it, and the tower twisted a full 180° before slamming to the ground.

Moments later, a second tower went down, opening a gap in the south wall big enough to drive a prison bus through.

Chaos. Pure anarchy. Prisoners stormed over hunks of concrete and out the breaches in the wall like rats fleeing a burning dumpster. Clayton stood there, hands cupped around his eyes, watching.

They were fools. They were at the mercy of the winds. It would drive them right into the swamps, where they'd get themselves hopelessly lost—or killed.

Wait, Clayton. You're smarter than any of them.

No guard came out of either tower. Likely they were dead—or pretending to be. They were impossibly outnumbered, and their shotguns wouldn't stop inmates from tearing them apart. There were no other guards in sight. None rushed out of the building.

With the prison yard nearly empty now, Clayton picked his way through the rubble, crouching low to fight the elements. How far would anybody get out in the open with the wind and rain like it was? They weren't thinking.

The guardhouse windows were gone. Clayton worked his way inside. Found the warden dead. From the angle of the man's head, Clayton guessed his neck was broken. "Winds of change, Warden Powers. Winds of change."

Clayton unbuckled the man's belt. Tugged off his pants. Unbuttoned the man's shirt, worked it off his arms—which wasn't easy with only one hand. But he managed—and inspected the clothes. No obvious rips or blood. Amazing. So far, so good.

Even as busted as it was, the guardhouse offered a surprisingly good shelter from the storm now that it was on the ground. Clayton peeled off his jumpsuit and rolled it tight. He'd take this with him for now. Minutes later, he wore the warden's clothes. He checked the pockets, found a set of keys, and smiled. The warden drove a Toyota. And soon, Clayton would too. But he'd wait a little longer—for the eye of the hurricane. That would be his moment.

Clayton passed two unconscious guards on his way out of the tower. He checked the pockets of both and took only cash—no credit cards or ID. He grabbed a pocketknife—and a Glock, too.

A third guard lay close. Eyes wide. Breathing heavily. The guy was bleeding good from a deep slice high on his leg. One arm was pinned under a huge old file cabinet. "Help . . . me."

Clayton eyed him for a moment. Even in the dim light, the terror in the guy's face was obvious. Did he guess that without some help he'd die soon—or fear Clayton was going to speed the process up?

"I'm a new dad." The guy clutched a phone to his chest with his free hand—and turned it so Clayton could see the screen. The kid, maybe a year old, with a smile that could power the screen long after the battery died.

There was no sign of Morgan's eye approaching. Clayton had time, didn't he? And he absolutely knew there was an opportunity for him here. He pulled out the pocketknife and cut one of the pant legs off his prison jumpsuit with jagged, hacking cuts. He pressed the cut end of the pants against the wound and stuffed the rest of the jumpsuit underneath the man's leg to absorb more blood. "I'm going to need your belt to slow your bleeding down."

The guard nodded, and Clayton tugged the man's belt free and cinched it around the injured leg. The bleeding slowed to a trickle. "Okay, you keep this belt on—and you're going to make it. Can you do that?"

The guard nodded.

"Do you know who I am?"

The man hesitated long enough for Clayton to have his answer. He was the only one-armed prisoner in the place. How tough would it be for the guy to tell the police he wasn't buried under the rubble but had escaped?

"You saved my life."

"Don't mention it." And Clayton meant it. "You never saw me."

"I promise."

Clayton eyed the file cabinet. Wondered if the guy would end up with one arm like him. "Tell me you won't try anything stupid."

"I was stupid to let the warden talk me into coming here. I'm done with stupid."

Clayton liked that answer. He pressed his back up to the steel file cabinet and worked his hand underneath to get a grip. He used his legs to push, freeing the guard's hand. "You'll need to keep pressure on that wound."

The guard rotated his wrist, opened and closed his hand. Except for some deep scrapes, the thing looked okay. "I owe you, man."

Clayton dropped on one knee beside him. "And here's how you'll pay me back. You be a good dad. Don't you ever haul off and hit your boy so hard he can't stay on his feet. Don't you ever talk down to him like he's stupid. Or make fun of him because you're bigger."

"I'd *never* do that—I love him."

By the look on his face, Clayton didn't doubt that. "And if your son wants a puppy someday, you get him one, you hear me?"

The guard nodded.

"You name that puppy King. And treat him like one. Then we're even."

"King." The man said it like he was locking it into his memory.

Clayton balled up his bloody jumpsuit and picked his way out of the guardhouse. He'd need to be ready when the eye of the storm passed over.

Nobody stopped him on his way through the wall. Rain stung him like he was being shot with airsoft pellets—at close range. In the distance, men in orange jumpsuits army-crawled their way to the swamps. Clayton fought his way to the parking lot instead.

Economy cars had been flipped on their side. Others upside down.

Most were already in the swamps, up to their windshields in water. Three of the transport buses were still visible, but none stood on its wheels. A handful of heavier cars remained upright in a row—and Clayton fought his way toward them. A Toyota 4Runner sat in the primo spot—the one reserved for the warden.

He didn't use the remote. Didn't want anyone seeing the lights flash on and thinking the car was their ticket to elude capture. If a passenger joined Clayton, he'd double his chances of being caught. He made his way to the far side of the 4Runner—out of the line of vision from the prison and the inmates working their way away from it. Clayton slid the key in the lock. It turned.

At that moment, he knew he'd make it. He pulled himself inside and slammed the door.

He locked the car and slid low in the seat. He'd sit inside and wait for the eye of the hurricane to bring some relief. No windshield wipers could keep up with the rain—and he didn't need to put the car in a ditch. Even now, the winds rocked the 4Runner like it was a toy.

"Sit tight, Kingman. You got this." There was plenty of time to do what he needed to do. And right now, he had to stay smart. He planned out his next step. The key to his survival would be to do the unexpected. To do the things the other inmates *weren't* doing.

The others took flight into the wilds on foot. Totally predictable. Clayton would be taking the highway in the warden's SUV. And he'd be heading south, toward Miami—right into the next wave of the hurricane. But he wouldn't hide out in the city for long. He'd head north—but in his own time . . . and only after he'd gotten everything he needed.

"Clayton Kingman, you are a King!" he shouted. He'd keep doing the unpredictable—practically guaranteeing he'd never get caught. If he played this right—and he would—it wasn't just the police he'd surprise. Young Parker Buckman was going to get the shock of his life.

CHAPTER 19

WILSON WAS THE FIRST TO NOTICE A CHANGE in the winds. His dad's arm was still around him. The howling . . . it had lowered in pitch.

Seconds later, Dad pulled Wilson closer. "The eye. We made it, boy! And we're going to punch through the other side too."

Wilson wanted to believe that.

Dad pulled out his flashlight. Tested it. Wilson rummaged his flashlight out of his bug-out bag. The instant the winds eased enough for them to go outside without being swept away, both of them were out the door.

He peered at the sky. Stars. Millions of them. No clouds at all. Wilson scanned the area and stopped dead. The destruction was incredible. The roof was still on their house, but the shingles were gone. As far as he could see out in the neighborhood, there wasn't another roof or carport fully intact. And there were fewer houses than before. Like some alien tractor beam had lifted them right off their concrete slab.

Wilson's dad did a slow, slack-jawed 360. "It's ruined. All gone."

Cars and boats littered the landscape as if God had shaken them in His hand like dice and thrown them to the ground. Remaining houses were up to their windowsills in water. Wilson's home stood on higher ground, but water surrounded them now. They were an island.

Palms? Gone. Only the mangroves seemed to weather Morgan. Kayaks hung from trees like Christmas ornaments.

Nobody else stood outside. Surely others had chosen not to evacuate. Where were they? Dad had talked about the badge of honor Wilson would earn for riding out the storm. The respect he'd get when neighbors returned. But there was nothing to return to. Who would come back?

"Holy mackerel." Dad stood there . . . stunned. "Hole-ee mackerel." He hustled to the eaves of the house. Inspected them with his light. Swore under his breath.

Half their siding was gone. Gutters. Fascia. Gone. Most areas of the roof were down to the plywood. Even from here, it was obvious that whole sections had loosened. Nail heads gleamed back in the light—like the wind had polished them. And they stood a good quarter inch above the plywood. So . . . the wind had lifted the sheeting enough to raise the nails. "Will it hold?"

"Dunno." Dad checked another corner of the house. "Not looking so good."

"Should I grab a hammer and whack them down?"

Dad shook his head. "The damage is done. Even if you pound them in, they've been loosened. They'll lift quick when the eye has passed. If the roof is going to go, a few extra nails won't do no good." He fished in his pocket for keys. Eyed the water where the road was supposed to be.

His dad was thinking of evacuating? "Can we get out of here?"

Again, Dad scanned with the flashlight. "With the water this high, the three-mile bridge to Everglades City will be under water—and the bay will be an absolute tempest. Even if we got lucky enough to figure out where the causeway is, the chances of staying on it would be slim."

So Everglades City was out. The window for escaping anywhere north had closed tight. But to stay—and face that wind again? Not a chance. "What can we do?"

"I gotta find us a safer place to shelter—right here on Chokoloskee. If the roof goes, we're in trouble."

They were already in trouble—roof or no roof.

"I'm taking the truck. I'll drive to the marina. Then Smallwoods. See if there's a better spot."

It was worth a shot. "I'm coming with."

"What if we already *have* the best spot?" Dad shook his head. "Stay put. Check the neighbors' homes. Grab anything we can use. Bring it back here and wait for me."

"What if the eye passes before you get back?"

"I'll get back. You be here when I do."

It was an order. And like Dad's choice not to evacuate, there would be no changing his mind. Every second Wilson slowed Dad, his chances of making it back went down.

His dad checked the house one more time as if assuring himself of his decision. "I have to take the chance. Nobody can help us now. We gotta help ourselves."

Parker's dad was coming. And Jelly's. That's what Parker's text had said, right? But Dad was right—for now, they were on their own.

Dad was already pulling palm fronds and debris off the pickup. "Give me a hand."

"You think *Typhoon* is okay?" Why Wilson even thought of the airboat at a time like this, he had no idea.

"*Typhoon* can ride it out." Dad flashed a quick smile. "Hey, it survived some crazy driver who sunk it once, remember?"

Wilson would never forget it.

Seconds later, Dad was in the cab. The engine caught, and he rolled down his window. "You stay put. No checking on *Typhoon*, got it?"

Wilson nodded.

"You know what I love about you, Son?"

He'd never heard Dad string the words *I love you* and *son* in the same sentence. Not ever. He was too stunned to answer.

"Everything." Dad reached out the window and put his hand flat on Wilson's chest. He closed his fist around the gator tooth necklace hanging there. "You're all Miccosukee. Not half. You've got this."

"The eye . . . how long do we have?"

Dad released the necklace and glanced at the sky. "Not sure. An hour? Keep that silly helmet on."

He backed away from the house and plowed through the waters, throwing a wake behind him like a Boston Whaler.

"Dad! Get back safe!"

Dad raised one hand out the open window and tapped the brakes twice. *Bye, bye.*

"You just get back here, Dad. You hear?" But of course, he didn't. Nobody did. As far as he knew, Wilson was the only one within earshot still alive.

CHAPTER 20

Jericho Prison
Saturday, October 23, 10:20 p.m.

CLAYTON KINGMAN WASN'T WAITING for the full eye of the hurricane to be overhead. The eyelashes were good enough for him. The moment he sensed the pitch of the howling had lowered, he started the 4Runner and double-checked to be sure the doors were locked. He hadn't driven one-handed before. After the monster gator had been done with his arm, the doctors hadn't been able to save it. From the hospital, he'd gone directly to the lockup. Handling the SUV with one hand might be a challenge, but he'd do it. He could do anything. He was free.

He shifted into four-wheel drive and set his wipers on the highest speed. The instant the rain slacked enough for them to keep up, he was gone.

Clayton saw no guards. If any of them were alive, they weren't out to catch escapees, that was for sure. He balled up his bloody prison jumpsuit—complete with his inmate number—and rolled down his window. He unrolled the severed pant leg, held it up so the wind caught

77

it. The thing disappeared over the swamp. He did the same with the rest of the jumpsuit. Searchers would guess he ditched the coveralls so he wouldn't be spotted as easily—but never made it out of the swamps. If traces of blood still remained, it would look like a gator helped him out of his jumpsuit.

He pulled onto Route 27, and two men in orange jumpsuits leaped in front of his high beams. Hands up, blocking the road, signaling for him to pick them up.

This won't do.

He stopped. Rolled down his window a couple of inches. "Hop in the back. The tailgate is open." He still had to shout to be heard. "The seats are filled with enough supplies for all of us. Hurry!"

"Thanks, man!" Both men ran for the back. He watched them in his side mirror—then gunned the gas. One of them managed to get a handhold, but Clayton was already moving too fast for the moocher to hang on. Both men tumbled into the flooded ditch. "Find your own ride, fellas."

Do the unexpected. It always worked.

The storm dissolved like a bad dream. Palm fronds were strewn across the road—and debris of all kinds, but it was nothing the 4Runner couldn't handle. He mashed the accelerator.

He knew exactly what he was going to do next. If the eye was big enough and he kept his speed up, he was going to make it.

CHAPTER 21

WILSON STOOD OUTSIDE THE HOUSE, watching the road—or rather, where the road was supposed to be. Endless water—and no approaching headlights. He'd gotten all the supplies he could scrounge up, but even that wasn't much. The stars were gone—and the stillness with them. It was as if a giant storm factory had been idle, and now the break was over. Somewhere in the universe, switches were being flipped. Cosmic levers were being pulled . . . and like some giant turbine, the storm was whirring back to life.

"C'mon, Dad." He cupped his hands around his eyes. "Where are you?"

The wind multiplied its velocity. Doubling. Tripling. He had to get in the house. Had to. "Dad . . . come on!"

The demons were coming.

Shingles flew by, spinning like buzz saw blades. The wind changed the angle of the rain until it sliced sideways again—but from the other direction. It lashed at him with a stinging fierceness, making it impossible to see anything. Something flew out of the black—whacking him right in the bike helmet. The Styrofoam shell snapped in two like it'd been hit with a meat cleaver. He pulled the helmet off his head without having to unbuckle it. The wind ripped it from his hands and wedged the busted helmet into a pile of rubble.

Wilson lunged for the door. Pulled it open. Had to use all his weight to close it again.

Looking out the windows was like peering through a windshield in a car wash. And with the way the glass was flexing and throbbing? It could burst at any second—and he'd get a face full of shards.

A new coven of demons had arrived. Their claws tore at the roof as they swooped by the house. Howling. Howling.

He pressed his back against the wall, wishing his dad's arm were around him. Wilson covered his ears. Kept his head down. And pleaded with the God of the universe to stop this storm.

CHAPTER 22

THE AIRBOAT WAS A BEAUTY. A beefed-up, 500-horsepower Chevy V-8 engine. Dual props. Powerful searchlights mounted to the top of the propeller cage. Two raised captain chairs up front with the rudder stick between them. A double-wide bench seat for a second row. The thing had to be twenty feet long—with plenty of deck space to pick up survivors. The name *Welcome Sight* was painted on the rudder panels mounted behind the propeller cage. Parker sent a picture to Harley before he left the parking lot. Sent one to Wilson, too, even though they'd be down there long before phone service was restored. Somehow it made him feel like Wilson was okay.

Four texts had dropped in since he'd turned the ringer off. A couple from Harley. And two from Jelly.

He opened the first one.

Another definition. But this time the word was simply Sorry . . . with the words I really am tacked on the end.

Her second text? `Forgive . . .` followed by the words `Will you?`

He smiled. Whipped off a text.

`Thanks. And I have. Sorry I didn't tell you sooner about the trip south.`

She sent a row of smiling emojis. `I get why you didn't tell me to my face. I'm just too quick for you.`

What?

She must have guessed his reaction. Her next text explained.

`If you'd said goodbye in person, I'd have snagged your hat.`

Ha. He'd play along: hit the one thing he guessed was *really* on her mind.

`Busted. But it was my favorite hat. I couldn't let you take it. Don't worry . . . I'll be safe.`

She texted back at lightning speed.

`It's the hat I'm concerned about.`

He reread the text and smiled. *Welcome back, Jelly.*

Uncle Sammy was driving now. "You two get some shut-eye. I'm good. We're going to have our hands full when we get down there."

Parker thumbed off one group text—to Harley, Ella, and Jelly.

`Getting some rest now. Talk to you tomorrow.`

Not that he was sleepy. He was antsy to get there. To start. He wished there were something he could do right now. Something to make a difference.

He reached for his pack. Unzipped it quietly. He rummaged inside until he found his survival knife. He strapped it to his calf and snugged the nylon straps. Okay, so it wasn't going to do him any good now, but it made him feel a bit more ready to jump in.

Hang on, Wilson. Parker turned in his seat and stared at the airboat they had in tow. It truly was a welcome sight. And if the flooding was as bad as reported, it might be their only hope of finding him.

CHAPTER 23

Southbound on Route 27
Sunday, October 24, 12:30 a.m.

AFTER A WHOLE SEQUENCE OF UNEXPECTED MOVES, Clayton Kingman added one more to make his trail that much more impossible to follow. And this one was a doozy. He'd tapped *Home* on the dead warden's dashboard GPS. As it turned out, the man lived in a western suburb of Miami, not far from the Everglades Correctional Institution, where Clayton had been an inmate just days before. And the warden's house turned out to be right on Clayton's route for the second phase of his master escape plan.

He'd passed countless cars in ditches on southbound Route 27. He kept his speed up, and the timing worked out perfectly. He arrived at the warden's subdivision just as Morgan squeezed shut its eye.

The warden had lived in a gated community. The guard house sat empty—with the gate up. It'd probably been in that position since the last resident from the neighborhood had raced north. No guard would stick around in a hurricane to watch over a bunch of empty houses. Clayton would be safe here. He drove through the open gate like he owned the place. In a way, he did. He had the keys now—and it seemed to him that this was a clear case of the good old "finders keepers" principle.

The houses in this little community were big. Solid. So far, they'd handled Morgan well. RVs and boats from the neighborhood were a different matter. They were overturned, smashed into homes, and bunched in small clusters. Clayton drove on soggy lawns or across sidewalks to avoid the obstacles.

Apparently, Florida wardens raked in a decent salary. His house was *nice*, and Clayton absolutely knew he'd find the place empty. It was a safe bet that the warden's family had evacuated. Clayton turned into the driveway. Some lights still blazed inside the home—and the garage remote worked. So the warden had a generator. The guy really had thought ahead—except for that little matter of posting himself in an ancient guard tower during a Cat 5 hurricane.

Clayton pulled into the attached garage, closed the overhead door, and did a little victory dance the moment he stepped out of the 4-Runner. He had the warden's house key and stepped inside a home built like Fort Knox—and dry as the desert. For now, he was safe. But this was no time to relax. There was work to do.

The warden may have been a pig, but his home was no pigpen. Everything was neat. In its place. And full of surprises. The first was the docking station on the kitchen counter with two Axon 7 Tasers waiting . . . fully charged. Yellow, with charcoal-gray grips and accents, the things looked like something out of an epic space sci-fi movie. Why the warden had a set of Tasers at the house was a mystery. Why not just keep the charging station at his office? The guy had great taste, though. These electroshock weapons were amazingly powerful—and had the two-shot capability. Just a quick flick of the wrist between shots was enough to toggle a fresh cartridge in place. He picked one up. Found himself dying to try it on someone. And the truth was the pair of these could work perfectly with his plan. He inspected the Taser from all angles. "Looks like you'll be leaving with me."

The generator powered the refrigerator and freezer—and the man had stocked both well. While he had a frozen pizza heating in the oven, Clayton did a systematic search of the house. He needed cash—and it was here somewhere. Rich people always had a good hunk of change stashed in their home for emergencies. As a teenager, Clayton remembered his dad bragging that he'd squirreled cash away in a dozen places that no burglar would ever find. Clayton had made that a personal challenge—and in time he found every one of them. He'd left a note in each spot—so his dad would realize just how much he'd underestimated his son.

As it turned out, the warden wasn't nearly as clever as Clayton's dad. Clayton found his emergency fund before the pizza was even finished. The warden had over five thousand dollars in twenties, fifties, and hundreds. Clayton also found two Glock 19s and several boxes of 9mm hollow-point ammo. Warden Powers wasn't just prepared for an emergency; he was ready for a zombie apocalypse.

Clayton found a set of three matching duffel bags. *Cute.* He'd use all three, but for now, he stacked the cash neatly inside one of them, followed by the guns, Tasers, and docking station. He searched for more items on his list—and it was only 2 a.m.

By two thirty, he'd gathered most of what he needed. He showered and crashed in the warden's bed. He thought of how the other inmates had raced for the swamps. Rushing to their doom like a herd of pigs off a cliff.

How many were already dead? Plenty. The idiots had done it to themselves. They didn't *think*. But honestly? Clayton was grateful for every convict who took to the water. They'd keep authorities busy for days after the hurricane. Identifying bodies mostly—or remains. Many of the missing would likely be presumed dead. They'd assume Clayton was among them. But he'd been smarter than that, and now he'd never be found.

A part of him wanted to contact his dad, to show him that he could do something right. His dad would probably still find a way to put him down, though. Like when he used to use big words to prove how smart he was. "Why so *lugubrious* this morning, Clayton?" Well, Clayton wasn't so lugubrious anymore, was he?

His dad always had to get the upper hand, get the last laugh. It was an obsession. Even when he'd visited Clayton in prison, his dad had given him the complete rundown on Parker Buckman's exit from Florida. Thanks to his dad's stalker tendencies, Clayton knew where Parker and Angelica lived now: Rockport, Massachusetts. Clayton had their home addresses, knew where they both worked and went to school. He'd memorized it all. His dad's detective work was going to pay off.

He set his alarm for three hours. It would be enough. And he wanted to be up when the storm was weakening—but not over.

There was more work to do. He would continue to do the unexpected—so he could make his surprise appearance.

And that would be *truly* unexpected.

CHAPTER 24

ELLA ROLLED ONTO HER SIDE AND STRAINED to see in the dim light. She'd been drifting in and out of sleep. Mostly out, it felt like. "Jelly . . . you awake?"

"Barely."

"I keep thinking about Harley. Where do you think he went this afternoon—and why was he so secretive?"

Jelly was quiet for a moment. "Maybe he went to the doctor for some game injury."

Ella picked up her phone. They'd both agreed not to look up any more reports on the hurricane—or Jericho Prison—until morning. They'd never sleep if they did that. She flipped on the flashlight app instead and shined it on the ceiling. "He didn't act hurt. And if he was, why the big hush-hush about it?"

"Agreed."

"What if his foster dad doesn't want him anymore?" That was Ella's biggest concern. "Maybe they saw the caseworker about finding a new family."

Jelly hesitated. "That would be horrible."

But it made sense. "Can I ask you something?"

"Shoot."

It was something that needed to be asked—or said. But suddenly Ella wasn't so sure she actually wanted to do that *now*.

"Ella? C'mon. What?"

"You know how you texted Parker—and straightened things out?"

"Mmmm-hmmm."

"It felt good, didn't it? I mean, it was the right thing to do—don't you think?"

"Definitely." Jelly propped herself on one elbow. "Are you thinking you need to apologize to someone? Do it. You'll feel better."

She wasn't making this easy. "Actually, it's you."

"What do you need to say you're sorry to me for?"

Okay, she had to be way more clear. "No, I mean, I think *you* need to say something. To Harley. You made things right with Parker, but you said some things to Harley that were pretty rough."

Jelly flopped onto her back and didn't say a word at first. "I hate when I say things that hurt others. Things I regret later." Another long silence. "Poor Harley. He was just being a good friend to Parker, wasn't he?"

"Kind of the way I'm seeing it now."

"It's a little late to be texting him, but I'll take care of it tomorrow." Ella smiled.

"I got myself scared about Parker heading back to the very place that nearly killed him. And the prison evacuation didn't help. But c'mon. What are the chances of a one-armed prisoner climbing the walls and escaping—even if the prison is ancient?"

"And then finding Parker doing search and rescues."

Jelly laughed. "Exactly. I can get carried away, you know that?"

"We both have pretty good imaginations." Ella placed her hand in front of the app light and created a giant alligator head shadow on the ceiling.

"He should never be free. Never ever," Jelly whispered. "Because no matter how bad you imagine him to be, I can tell you this . . ."

Ella waited for her to finish. And when Jelly didn't, she angled the light her way. "Tell me *what?*"

Another pause. Jelly finally looked her way. Her eyes wide with whatever scene she'd been replaying in her mind. "He's worse."

CHAPTER 25

"MAKE THIS END!" Wilson shouted over the roar of the rabid winds. All of nature had gone insane. The entire world was breaking apart. "God of Parker Buckman, please make this stop!" But clearly God hadn't heard him over the amped-up madness outside.

Wilson was alone.

Dad was gone. If he had found a better place to ride out Morgan, he'd have come back for Wilson. The demons got him instead. And now they were coming for Wilson.

Wilson flicked on his flashlight. There must have been two feet of water on the floor now—and it was rising fast. Water ran down the walls from the trim around every window. The seams around the ceiling looked more like overflowing gutters.

SLAP-SLAP-SLAP-SLAP-SLAP-SLAP. The plywood sheeting on the roof. He checked the corners where the walls and ceiling met. The crack he'd seen earlier was a split now.

"God, make this stop!"

But still the demons howled. The corner of the roof rose with a sickening crack.

"Oh, God. Oh, God!"

There wasn't another living soul in southern Florida. Nobody could survive this assault. A massive chunk of the ceiling tore away, exposing the green darkness outside. The demons had found him!

Another section ripped free—sucked away into the blackness. Plaster chunks blasted him like they'd been fired from a Gatling gun. Two-by-fours snapped free across the room and sank deep into the wall beside him—hurled like spears from the hands of evil spirits. Searing pain tore through his arm.

The house was ready to blow—like an ammunition factory in a fire. If he stayed, he'd get impaled by a piece of his own home—or he'd be sucked into the sky, ripped to shreds, and scattered to the four corners of the Glades. But what chance did he have outside?

Suddenly the house shook, and the far wall imploded. The bow of a commercial fishing boat plowed through, listing horribly to starboard. The pilothouse was shattered—and empty. The boat shuddered for a moment—as if run aground. But it broke free, and the phantom vessel continued its ghostly voyage.

Here we go. Here we go. Wilson shouldered his bug-out bag. Leaped clear of the boat. Sloshed to the door, cinching tight the straps of his pack. He grabbed the doorknob. The instant the door cleared the jamb, Morgan tore it from its hinges, whirlybirding it out of sight. There was nobody—and nothing—to stop the demons now.

He took one step outside the house. Immediately the legs were swept out from under him. Wilson was down. Tumbling. Unable to see. Barely able to breathe. This was it. The way it would end. His dad was dead. And Wilson would be joining him soon.

CHAPTER 26

Suburban Miami, Florida
Sunday, October 24, 5:45 a.m.

CLAYTON WOKE FROM A DEEP SLEEP, and he'd never felt more alive. The hurricane still did battle outside, but the warden's home was like a bunker . . . holding strong. Unmovable.

A song rolled through his head—one he hadn't thought about in years. He found himself singing what few lyrics he remembered—and making up the rest.

Every breath you take, and every move you make,
It's no use to run, gonna have my fun.
I'll be stalking you.

How many times had he heard his dad singing that song to Mom before she disappeared? As Clayton got older, he realized Dad's song was a warning. In a way, he didn't blame Mom for taking off. Clayton's dad was a controlling, manipulating, and abusive pig. Sometimes a charmer—and other times a snake. But either way, he could always make Clayton's skin crawl.

At first, Clayton had expected Mom would come back for him. Absolutely believed if her love was strong enough, she'd find a way to take him away too.

She never did.

He'd grown to hate her for that. Wherever she'd disappeared to, wasn't there room for two? Even if all she'd had was a one-bedroom trailer somewhere, he'd have curled up on the couch—or in a closet. It didn't matter where Mom took him, as long as it was far from Dad.

She'd confided in Clayton about how she hated that song. But thinking back, she'd seemed more afraid than anything. After she was gone, his dad got in the habit of singing it to Clayton. Kind of a nighttime ritual. It was supposed to keep him from getting out of bed, Clayton figured. But as a kid, he honestly thought his dad had some way of seeing him—even in the dark. Even now, for an instant, he feared his dad was watching. It was time to get his mind on other things.

He made the warden's bed—careful to leave everything just as he'd found it. If anyone suspected an uninvited guest had spent the night, they'd look closer. And that could put the police on his trail.

The warden's house became his base of operations. He did a more careful search and found more things for his duffels. A set of never-used Everglades postcards sat on the warden's desk. A thought popped into his head, and he smiled. The warden must have had a pen pal somewhere with all the supplies he'd hoarded. Clayton slipped postcards, stamps, and a couple of pens into a gallon resealable bag and added it to the luggage.

The master bedroom closet held another nice surprise. Desert-tan camouflage jackets and pants. T-shirts. A pair of regulation boots that were amazingly just one size bigger than Clayton would have chosen for himself. So the warden also played army—or had in the past? Clayton rolled two sets of clothes and stuffed them in the pack—leaving a third on the bed for later.

Honestly, this was working out incredibly well. He really should send the warden a thank-you card. But the warden's ride on the for-real Tower of Terror made that pointless now—unless USPS delivered postcards to wherever the nasty warden had ended up.

From his base of operations, Clayton circled out through the neighborhood, breaking into homes for the other things he needed. It took colossal effort with the wind and rain, but he managed. He left no fingerprints anywhere, thanks to a box of Nitrile gloves he'd found at the warden's. Leftovers from the COVID-19 fiasco, no doubt.

Cash was what he really wanted—and he found thousands. Old people gained peace of mind by stashing cash. Obviously, this was largely a snowbird neighborhood. They lived up north and hadn't come down for winter yet. Being the survivors they were, they made a habit of spreading out their moolah. So even though they weren't living in the house, they had lots of money hidden there.

And for those who actually did live here and evacuated, why would they leave money behind in the house? Maybe because they thought they'd be back in twenty-four hours—and only took what they felt they'd need. After all, if another disaster followed, they'd want to have more cash on hand to tap. And what if they carried all that cash and got robbed? Heaven forbid they didn't have plenty of money still at the house.

Clayton knew older people tended to stockpile, but these people were ridiculous. And their hiding spots were incredibly predictable.

The freezer was always Clayton's first go-to spot. Hiding money in a hollowed-out loaf of bread was a front-runner in this neighborhood. His own dad had done the same stupid thing. *Dough-dough*. That's what Clayton had called it when he needed to snag a little extra pocket money.

In the six homes Clayton busted into around the warden's house, he picked up over eighteen grand in freezers alone. Cold cash. Maybe there'd been an article in some *AARP* magazine once upon a time outlining the old freezer trick. The tip the article must have missed was the need to rotate out the bread once in a while. When Clayton spotted a frozen loaf with an expiration date that was years old, he knew he'd found a bread bank.

Clayton wasn't out to get rich, but he'd need plenty of cash to make his plans work. Finding cash was so easy, he forced himself not to get greedy. He had to move on to the next phase of his plan. If he needed more cash down the line, he'd hit another retirement community. He had to congratulate himself, though. Hitting these homes now—all of them empty with the evacuation—was the easiest way to get money in a hurry, and it was a whole lot safer than robbing an armored truck. He was set.

The other thing he'd been looking for was a new vehicle. Leaving the warden's 4Runner in his garage wouldn't raise any suspicions. It wouldn't lead anyone to Clayton's trail—so searchers would keep looking for him in the swamps far north of here. Police would think the warden had wanted to keep his SUV safe from the storm, so he'd parked the 4Runner at home and caught a ride to Jericho Prison with one of the guards—now deceased.

Clayton checked the garage of every house he'd entered. He'd need a pickup or SUV to get through the flooded streets. And he'd need one with keys available—and a full tank of gas. Deep tinted windows would be nice, but hey, beggars couldn't be choosers, right?

He settled on the silver Ford F-150 with four-wheel drive and a four-door cab—found in the garage next door. It checked all the boxes on his wish list—including the tinted glass. And the sticker on the rear window was very helpful:

Don't get smart with me. I can take you with one finger—because it'll be on the trigger.

It was a no-brainer that the guy had guns hidden in the house. And it didn't take long to find them. Clayton didn't even have to bust open a gun safe to get them. Guys with bumper stickers like that wanted their guns easily accessible. Clayton tucked a pair of Sig Sauers under the second seat along with thousands of rounds of 9mm bullets from the bedroom closet shelf. He'd never shot a handgun lefty before, and now he'd have plenty of ammo to practice with. Between the Glocks from the warden's house and the Sig Sauers here, Clayton would have enough firepower to keep one loaded gun on him at all times and the other three spread out in his gear.

Clayton made one last trip to his base. Peeled off the warden's wet clothes. Dropped them in the dryer and turned it on high. He showered and changed into the camo. He made himself some sandwiches, stuffed the now-dry warden clothes into the hamper, and grabbed his duffel bags. Hurricane Morgan was on life support now, and it was time to go. With one last check to be sure everything was the way he'd found it, he slipped out of the warden's house and sprinted to the neighbor's garage.

He loaded the F-150 with the last of the supplies he'd gathered. Unscrewed the license plate and replaced it with one he'd removed from another garage on his circuit. F-150s were probably the most common truck around, so it wouldn't stand out on the road. But if by some chance the owner hurried back after the storm and reported the truck stolen, Clayton didn't want a little thing like a license number to mess him up.

Clayton raised the garage door—then stopped. Three vehicles cruised down the flooded street—including an old Chevy Econoline van. The vehicles stopped, and five guys piled out of the van carrying baseball bats. Others jumped out of the cars. They all rushed the house across the street.

Looters. Clayton smiled. They—not an escaped convict—would be blamed for everything missing. Once again, there would be no trail to follow—as long as Clayton got out fast . . . before they turned on him.

He dropped the truck into four-wheel drive and swung wide of the looters. He honked his horn and would have saluted them if he'd had a second hand.

"Good luck, fellas. You're a day late and a dollar short. I already cleaned these houses out."

Wipers on full blast, he hunkered over the wheel, straining to see. He set the GPS to Miami. But he wouldn't be stopping at the airport. And he wasn't headed for a train station or bus depot. All those were far too predictable.

What he had in mind was way smarter. He just needed his luck to hold out a little longer.

CHAPTER 27

Rockport, Massachusetts
Sunday, October 24, 7:30 a.m.

ANGELICA WOKE TO THE SOUNDS OF SURF POUNDING the Headlands. Was this some kind of ripple effect from Morgan?

The hurricane should be over by now. The worst of it, anyway. Was Parker there yet?

"Take a deep breath, Jelly." Ella sat in her bed, totally captivated by whatever she was reading on her phone. "This kind of thing doesn't happen in real life. You called this right, 100 percent."

Angelica whipped off her covers and raced to Ella's bed. A news article was open, and the headline couldn't have scared her more than if it had grabbed her by the shoulders and screamed in her face.

Jericho's Walls Come Tumbling Down

"No." Angelica scanned for the who, what, and when. She already knew the why. The prison was old. In bad shape. And Morgan had turned its head Jericho's way. "I knew it. I *knew* it."

Declaring this the largest prison break in US history, the National

Guard had been deployed to hunt down escapees. But mayhem resulting from Hurricane Morgan would severely delay all efforts.

Ella read over Angelica's shoulder. "Massive casualties expected." She stared at Angelica for a moment. "National Guard—or convicts?"

Angelica's stomach twisted and tightened. The prison break was a disaster within a disaster. And Parker was driving right into it.

"Likely some inmates got crushed when the walls went down," Ella said.

"Not Kingman." Angelica felt it deep inside her soul. "There's no way he's that easy to kill."

"You make him sound inhuman."

"He *isn't* human," Angelica said. "Kingman survived the alligator attack that cost him his arm—and the gator died. That's a fact."

"You think he'd really be out for revenge?"

Clayton would do it just to prove a point. "He hates Parker."

"But still," Ella said. "He's only got one arm. How much can he really do, right?"

Ella just didn't get it, and Angelica couldn't really blame her. "You have no idea what Kingman is capable of."

Ella nodded real slowly, like the truth was finally sinking in. "So, what do we do?"

Angelica rushed to the night table beside her bed. Grabbed her phone. "Send out a text to warn Parker." A text was already waiting from Parker—sent nearly an hour earlier. "How did I not hear this come in?"

Almost there, and phone signal expected to be zero—so this text is it for who knows how long. My dad has satellite phone—he'll update my mom. Sun almost up. Not believing what I'm seeing here.

"I *missed* him." There was no point sending him a text now. He may not get it for days. "He's on a collision course with Clayton Kingman—and has no idea he's in danger." Just like that day deep in the Glades when Kingman had tried killing him.

"Is that something you fear *could* happen?" Ella locked eyes with her. "Or something you feel *will* happen?"

Angelica shook her head. "I don't know. I fear it *because* I feel it."

"Okay." Ella was holding her cross now. "Good enough for me. We'll talk to Parker's mom. She'll be at church this morning. She can get word to Parker's dad on that satellite phone, right? Tell him to be extra careful."

"Careful isn't enough," Angelica said. "Not with Kingman on the loose. I've got to convince her to get Parker *home*—before Clayton Kingman finds him."

CHAPTER 28

Miami, Florida
Sunday, October 24, 8:55 a.m.

HURRICANE MORGAN PROVED TO BE THE best friend Clayton had ever had. Morgan broke him out of prison and provided a house to stay in overnight. Morgan handed him an empty subdivision like a giant mall to get everything on his supplies list for free. Morgan gave him this pickup. And Morgan would provide his next ride too.

The waterfront was a mess. Boats submerged at the docks, kept off the bottom only by the heavy nylon dock lines secured to the posts. Others had been swept onto shore or had ripped free from their moorings and huddled in corners of the harbor like retreating and trapped soldiers. Over and over, they slammed into each other with every wave that rolled through their ranks. Floating boards, seats, cushions, and other debris gathered there, battering the hulls incessantly.

Most of the dock boards were gone. Just rows of posts sticking out of the water, outlining where a pier had once been.

Some yachts had turtled, exposing every barnacle on their hull to the troubled sky. Tips of masts dotted the bay, like dozens of submarines had invaded the harbor—with only their periscopes rising above the water to betray their position. It was pure, joyful chaos.

Few yachts or boats of any size remained at a mooring or in a slip. And Clayton chose one of them.

A Boston Whaler 405 Conquest. A 41-footer—with a quartet of Mercury 300 HP motors mounted on the transom. Deep V-hull. High bow. Snug cabin that would be comfortable—even with passengers. The thing was beyond perfect. And remarkably, there were enough boards left on this particular pier to get his supplies on board without risk of falling into the harbor. *Thank you, Morgan!*

The spare keys didn't take long to find—and the gas tank was full. A brass nameplate secured to the dash revealed the boat's name in all-caps: *RETRIBUTION.* In that moment, he was even more convinced that fate smiled on him—and was sending him a message. Urging him on. Promising success.

Wind and rain lashed the pier, which suited Clayton just fine. The aftermath of Morgan was still aggressive enough to keep most people indoors. Which meant nobody was hanging around the harbor to question him, either. It would have taken him a dozen trips to get all the supplies to the boat, but there'd been a hand truck in the garage with the F-150. Right now, Clayton was glad he'd had the foresight to heft it into the bed of the pickup. In four quick trips, the truck was emptied, the gear stowed inside the cabin. Cases of water. Plenty of food. He was set. Fully stocked to get where he needed to go and do what he needed to do. And he'd have plenty left over besides.

Other escapees who made it out of the swamps likely reached out to family or old friends. A predictable, desperate, amateur mistake—making it easy for the police. But Clayton was smarter than that. Would his dad help him? Sure. Clayton would have to listen to some ridiculous lecture, but in the end his dad would come through. But Clayton didn't need anyone else's help—making him even more impossible to track down.

He had to get the timing right for leaving the dock. With every minute that passed, the city would come out of hiding. More people out, more potential witnesses. But the longer he waited, the more the waters might settle—and the better his chances of getting out of the harbor without hitting anything that might damage the hull.

The fact that *Retribution* rode out the storm was impressive. If the Boston Whaler engineering team had designed Jericho Prison, the towers and walls might never have come down. The cabin was dry inside. Not a drop of water. *Very* impressive.

The pier itself had worked as a shield, keeping other boats and flotsam from ramming into it. It was as if fate had stood guard, protecting the boat for him.

Clayton closed the cabin door behind him. He had a couple of things he needed to do, and it wasn't quite the right time to leave. He had a sense about these things. He felt in touch with the universe. With fate. How else could he explain all the good things that had gone his way?

The boat had a computer, and it wasn't hard finding the addresses, phone numbers, and every other bit of information he needed to make his surprise for Parker work. It was crazy how much intel he could get just by spending a bit of time online. He found one of the postcards from his pack, with the head of a nasty-looking gator staring back at him. Jaws open to show its massive, yellow teeth. "Wish You Were Here" was scrawled across the top in a bold, loose script. He pulled out a pen and wrote a brief message, grinning the whole time. He slapped a stamp on the card and slipped it inside his pocket. He chose a second card—an airboat nosed up to a patch of sawgrass, with a massive gator floating alongside. And a third card. This one featured an alligator at night, with glowing eyes. He addressed and stamped them, then jotted a cryptic message. Three cards . . . they would be more than enough. The moment he dropped the first one in a mailbox, the next phase of his plan would begin.

He pocketed the boat keys, stepped onto the dock, and rolled the hand truck off the edge into the churning water. He was tempted to leave the harbor immediately, but he had to play this smart. Leaving the stolen pickup in the parking lot would raise the wrong kind of questions. Why would a looter park the truck there? Wouldn't the authorities guess that whoever stole the truck was now driving a stolen boat? No, he had to resist the urge to leave before carefully covering his tracks.

And he had postcards to mail. He'd find a mailbox far from the harbor.

In the end, he parked the truck at a Metrorail station at least twelve blocks from the waterfront. He locked the doors, dropped the keys in a storm sewer, and flipped open a huge golf umbrella he'd found inside.

Would there be traffic cams recording him? Something that might be checked once the stolen truck was discovered? The umbrella hid his face but would certainly be easy to follow.

He ducked inside a hotel lobby. A woman stood near the entrance, clutching an umbrella much smaller than his own. She could have been fifty—and had a kind face.

"Excuse me, ma'am," he said. "I wouldn't feel right with this big umbrella while a pretty lady like yourself tried to manage with that itty-bitty thing."

He watched her eyes. In a quick scan she took in the camo pants and jacket. The missing arm. He held the umbrella out to her. "It's a strong one. It won't be turning inside out on you with the wind, either. Please . . . take it."

She made the exchange—but took his hand, too. "Thank you, son, for this." Her eyes darted to his empty sleeve. "And for what you gave for our country."

He raised her hand to his lips and gave her a light kiss. "You remind me of my mom. It's just the type of thing she'd say."

"You're an honorable young man."

It felt sooo good being seen as a hero. The camo duds were a brilliant move. "Well, freedom doesn't come free, does it?"

"Bless your heart." The woman actually teared up. "I suspect"—she looked at his sleeve again—"this could have been much worse. I'm grateful you're able to enjoy this freedom too."

Okay, he had to smile at that. "I can't tell you how good it feels to be out on the street."

"We need more young men like you!" The woman reached for her purse. "Let me pay you for this umbrella."

Clayton took a step back. "No, ma'am. I don't need money. I'm fine." Clearly she was the kind of woman who felt a whole lot more comfortable knowing she'd given more than she'd taken.

"Tell you what," he said. "There is one little thing you could do for me." He pulled two of the postcards from his pocket. "Would you drop these in a mailbox?"

"Absolutely," she said. "But I won't be back in New York until tomorrow. Will that be soon enough?"

"That's ideal. And they're still heading in the right direction." He liked the idea of two of the cards coming from an entirely different postmark from the one he'd drop in a box here. Even if she completely forgot, his card would get through.

She smiled and slid the cards into her purse. "You don't give this another thought."

He held the door for her and watched her battle her way up the block against the gusts. If anybody reviewed the traffic cam footage days from now, the umbrella would probably lead them to the airport—and a very dead end. He was being far more careful than he probably needed to be, but he was leaving nothing to chance. He hadn't left a single clue that would lead to his recapture. From the moment he had left Jericho, there had been no trail for anyone to follow. Except his jumpsuit, of course. And that would lead trackers in entirely the wrong direction. He'd thought of everything. And because he had, he was a free man—with no posse dogging his trail either.

Clayton waited inside the building another five minutes. When he did leave, it was with the woman's umbrella—and definitely some extra spring to his step. He found a mailbox right on the route. He liked the idea of the cards being spaced out a day from each other. He pulled out the remaining card—the close-up of the alligator—and dropped it in the slot. "And so . . . it begins." He stood there a moment longer, relishing the start.

The distance back to the waterfront seemed longer on foot than he'd realized. But that was good. When the abandoned car was found, nobody would guess he'd gone anywhere other than the Metrorail station. When he finally did get to the boat, he closed himself inside the pilothouse and began checking the instruments and gauges.

The boat had it all. GPS. Radar. Ship-to-shore radio. Everything he needed for a trip into some very rough seas. The motors started immediately. He took out his knife and used the serrated edge to hack and saw the dock lines rather than simply untying them. If he made the lines look like they'd frayed and finally snapped, anybody looking for the boat would be checking along the shore somewhere—or figure the hurricane had driven it away from the pier before *Retribution* went to the bottom. Clayton didn't need the lines. A boat this size would have extra lines stowed below, anyway.

Navigating out of the harbor was like going through a minefield. He took it slow, and the Whaler responded like a champ. He cleared the breakwaters and let out a whoop.

"I am Clayton Kingman—and I am king!" He was truly free now. His escape was a complete success. Every step of the way, he'd used his head. Done the unexpected. The unpredictable. And he wasn't done yet. Not nearly. The best was yet to come.

He hadn't just made one unexpected move. He'd heaped up layer upon layer of choices seemingly so illogical that his next move would be unpredictable.

The postcards were a risk but a calculated one. It couldn't be used to prove anything—but would just add to the confusion and fear. That was a good thing.

He kept to a course straight out to sea. Then he'd turn south. It was a logical choice—and he did exactly that for the sake of anyone who might be watching—however unlikely that was. If anyone did see a one-armed man leaving in the boat, they'd think he was making a run for the Bahamas. It was really tempting, too. With the money he already had, he could disappear.

But he wasn't about to start doing the expected things now. He'd turn south for a time before heading the other way. And nobody—not a soul on earth—would guess what he planned to do next.

CHAPTER 29

HARLEY SPOTTED PARKER'S MOM SITTING WITH Miss Lopez at the end of a pew. Definitely closer to the front than he normally sat with Parks. The light from the colored glass window filtered all around them, like they were sitting in a rainbow. With Parker and his dad gone, the least Harley could do was keep an eye on her. Make sure she was doing okay . . . even if that meant sitting somewhere way more visible than he liked.

He worked his way to the row, and Mrs. Buckman motioned for him to sit beside her.

She patted his leg and smiled like she was really glad he was there. "They arrived safe."

He nodded.

The church filled up. Only seats in front of them were open now. People drifted in, silencing their phones as they did. Ella and Jelly were among them. Ella flashed him a smile that was as encouraging as her text had been.

Jelly didn't even look his way. Hey, she wanted to protect her friends.

So did he. They just had different ideas of how to do that. The way Harley saw it? Sometimes protecting friends meant encouraging them to do the right thing—even if it didn't seem safe.

A restless, antsy feeling came over him. The same sense he'd get while waiting on the sideline, watching his teammates fight to keep the opposing team's offense from gaining yards. With each down, he'd get more wired for the chance to be on the field himself.

He should have gone with Parker. Somehow. Whatever Harley was trying to do now . . . this being the man of the family while Mr. Buckman was gone? It was stupid.

God . . . You made me a protector, right? But who am I kidding? I have no family to protect, and nobody is asking me to step up, either.

He checked over his shoulder. Eyeballed the back doors. Maybe he should just slip out before the service started—and not come back. He tightened and relaxed his legs. Clenched and unclenched his fists. Should he bolt?

Mrs. Buckman patted his hand. Did she sense what he was thinking now too? Did she guess how uneasy he felt being here, in church, without Parks?

"Turns out getting the airboat was a stroke of genius. Uncle Sammy hopped on the satellite phone and said there were only a few others in the area that had survived the storm."

Uncle Sammy. Like Harley wasn't just Parker's friend. Almost like he belonged to the family. *Right.* "Wilson?"

"Chokoloskee is their first priority, but it's been hard to get there." Mrs. Buckman's lips got tight for a moment, like she was trying to hold it together. "They'll call when they find him."

Harley raised his eyebrows and held up his phone.

"And then I'll call you," Mrs. Buckman said.

He smiled. "You're a mind reader."

"You remember that, Harley. That's what moms do."

Something he'd never had. Maybe that was good. He didn't know what he was missing.

CHAPTER 30

PARKER STILL COULDN'T BELIEVE WHAT HE WAS SEEING. Most of the town was under two feet of water. They'd parked on a bit of higher ground—a half block in front of Everglades High. Whether the high water was still part of the surge or the hurricane had so reshaped the area that it would always be underwater, he had no idea. But the parts of roads that were above water had heaved and split. It looked like some monster unable to escape its underground caverns had taken out its wrath on the ground overhead.

Debris everywhere. Palms. Boards. Siding. Whole sections of houses and roofs. Cars and trucks jammed up like beaver dams. Some on their side. Others with all four wheels up like dead bugs. It was almost like the town had been attacked by a giant mudslide—except it wasn't mud. The flow was made up of the shattered bits of what had once been a town.

Boats no longer floated at the docks. The piers were gone. The boats were tangled up in between cars—or bottom up in places a boat should never be.

And the smell . . . unreal. Oil and gas. Dead fish. Rotting garbage. Sewage. All that hung in the air, warmed by the sun like a putrid stew. There was a deadness to the smell. Like the town itself was an open grave.

Parker looked across the town and counted on one hand the number of homes that still had four walls intact. Half the school had been carried away. What was left had become a giant flotsam pocket. Crates. Boats. Cars. Patio furniture. Sections of piers or decks. Basketballs. Soccer balls. A kid's plastic slide. Even a couple of shipping containers huddled inside.

Electric poles were down, and wires were everywhere. Some snaked across houses like they'd been sniffing for a way inside. Others disappeared into the water. Some boats were half off lifts. Others were stacked—boats on boats.

Bark had been ripped and torn off trees like it had been chipped and flaking paint. The trees had survived the hurricane, but they'd been given a death sentence anyway.

Dad and Uncle Sammy had picked up over a dozen survivors—and hadn't made it all the way out to Chokoloskee yet in *Welcome Sight*. Every time they'd tried, some desperate person had flagged them down for a rescue. Dad and Uncle Sammy set up a base camp on high ground. Between the rescued survivors and other rangers joining them, the place was filling up.

The Coast Guard had promised help, but nobody had seen them yet. Estimates of the number of people stranded up and down the coast were staggering—and with the high water and shortage of usable boats, the Coast Guard was doing the best they could.

Just before noon, a crew of volunteers from Samaritan's Purse showed up in orange T-shirts. They unpacked massive amounts of supplies. Blankets. Water. Meals-ready-to-eat. The MRE bags contained a meal that would heat up—just by adding half a bottle of water. They brought tents and began setting them up immediately.

110

"We gas up and go out again." Dad had gotten the report about Jericho Prison from Mom. If he was truly worried, he was careful to hide it.

"They'll likely find him buried under the wall," Uncle Sammy said. "If he actually made it to the swamps, he may not have gotten off quite that easy."

Like an alligator got him? "He knows how to handle himself in the Glades, Uncle Sammy."

"So did a lot of people who became gator snacks. With all the damage from Morgan, the manhunt for prisoners has had its share of setbacks." He tapped his satellite phone. "But the word we got? Helicopter flyovers report scores of orange jumpsuits in the swamps. And nobody is moving inside them."

"The 180-mile-per-hour winds hurled rocks, branches, anything that wasn't welded down," Dad said. "It was brutal out there—and the chances of anyone surviving without some kind of shelter?"

Immediately, Parker thought of Wilson. Would Chokoloskee be any different than Everglades City? Was his house still standing? And if not . . . what would it have been like in open water with the gators? They'd gobble down a meal when it dropped on their plate.

"I can't really think about Kingman right now," Parker said. "I'm with you two—and I'm sticking close. Even if he survived somehow, he'd never get to me."

Uncle Sammy threw his arm around him. "Got that right, Parker."

The thing that *was* getting to Parker was a rising sense of urgency. "We have to get out to Chokoloskee. Wilson could be hurt."

Dad agreed. "We race out there—no stops. If someone waves us down, we'll signal that we'll be back."

Minutes later, *Welcome Sight* flew them through town on flooded streets. Dad and Uncle Sammy in the twin chairs up front, weaving to avoid floating hazards. Slowing and using Parker's gator stick to move obstacles when the way was hopelessly blocked. Parker sat in the double seat mounted behind theirs and a bit higher.

He could see fine—but the view was horrific. Everglades City had been scraped from the face of the earth. Swept with the broom of destruction. They approached the spot where the three-mile causeway led to Chokoloskee. But all he saw was angry water. The only way Parker even knew a bridge was still below the surface was from cars stopped at weird angles, water to their windshields. In some spots, sections of the road were heaved up, like a drawbridge. How many other parts would prove to be missing when the water did recede? The water table was still messed up—and the tide was coming in now. He had no idea how awful things would look when the water finally went back where it belonged.

Two bodies floated side by side, facedown. Like they were friends who stuck together, even in death. Both males, if their broad shoulders were reliable indicators. If not for the fact that they wore jeans and T-shirts, they would've looked like a couple of snorkelers on a reef tour. Could one of them be Wilson?

Dad must have had the same question. He throttled back and pulled alongside.

Uncle Sammy used Amos Moses to turn the bodies—but not before making Parker look the other way.

"Gators have been busy." Uncle Sammy rolled them back over. "Neither one is Wilson."

Parker rushed to the opposite side of the airboat. He planted his hands on the edge and tossed his Oreos. Who were those people? How horrible it must have been for them. He looked at his own arm, with the frenzy of scars that never let him forget his own encounters with gators.

Dad left both bodies where they floated—which wasn't something he looked comfortable doing. "Nothing we can do for them now." Dad planted a marker buoy. "There'll be time to pick up the bodies later."

It was true. If they pulled the bodies onto the airboat, they'd have to take them back to the base camp. But right now, they had to use every bit of daylight to find those who might still be alive. And he prayed that included Wilson.

CHAPTER 31

HARLEY SLIPPED OUT OF CHURCH IMMEDIATELY after the service ended
while Mrs. B turned to talk with Miss Lopez.

A big part of him wanted to stick around. He was pretty sure Parker's
mom would have invited him for lunch if he'd stayed. But he wasn't
really family. She'd just try to make him feel like he was. Uncle Ray's
words still messed with his head. He hated not talking to Ella afterward,
but if Jelly was half as angry with him as she'd been the day before, it was
best he stayed away. At least until she cooled down.

Harley left his bike locked in the rack at church and walked down
to Front Beach. He mounted the rocks on the south end and walked
the shoreline along Bearskin Neck, stopping now and then to watch the
lobster boats. When he reached the circle turnaround, he headed up the
street and grabbed lunch. He'd taken his time—and killed two hours.

From there, he went out to the breakwater. All the way to the end.
He sat. Settled in. This was where Parks liked to go lately when he

needed to think. But it didn't seem to do a thing for Harley. After fifteen minutes, he felt more alone than he had since his dad's funeral. He stood to head back—but saw Ella and Jelly at the start of the jetty. Ella had her watercolor duffel, so she was going to be there for a while. There was no way he wanted to see Jelly right now. He sat back down, as close to the water as he could without getting wet. There was no chance the girls would see him here.

He let his mind drift like the gulls overhead riding the breeze. The things Uncle Ray had said to him were true, weren't they?

"You're on your own, Harley Lotitto. You've got no family now. And the people you're living with don't care about you."

He wished his dad were still alive. Wished Kemosabe were still parked in the shed, waiting for Harley to get his driver's license. Wished a lot of things.

But wishes were the stuff of fairy tales, right? In real life, wishes just didn't come true. Not for guys like Harley, anyway.

CHAPTER 32

ELLA SET UP HER EASEL AND COLLAPSIBLE STOOL on the breakwater. Clipped a sheet of watercolor paper in place. She arranged her brushes, rinse water, and paints. And then she sat there staring at the blank page. Jelly walked the breakwater but not on the crown where it was smoother. She stayed close to the water, where the gaps between the granite blocks were bigger.

Painting always calmed Ella. But obviously there was only so much the paints could do.

Pez called to her from the circle at the end of Bearskin Neck. "Want company?"

Ella motioned her over.

Pez glanced at the canvas and smiled. "Stuck—or did you just paint the world's worst blizzard?"

"Totally stuck." And not just about what to paint. "Harley has been so distant. I mean, why didn't he stick around after church?"

Pez shook her head. "He's wrestling with something."

"His mystery outing after work yesterday holds the answer key."

"I'm sure that's part of it," Pez said. "Wherever he went, it was hard for him. Did Jelly smooth things over with him?"

"She was going to do it after church."

Pez sat on a granite block, staring over Rockport Harbor. "Once she does, Harley will come around. And I'm thinking he'll open up a bit too."

Ella definitely hoped so. "You understand guys so well. I wish I had that gift."

Pez laughed. "If I was that good at reading men, I wouldn't have ever gotten engaged to the man I almost married."

"But you *did* figure it out in time."

"Well," Pez rocked her hand back and forth. "Technically, he broke it off. But I think he realized I'd discovered who he really was—and feared I'd change him."

"Do you think you could have?"

Pez thought for a long moment. "Looking back? No. Only God can change a man's heart—and that's what was needed. But at the time, I convinced myself I was enough to do it—that I understood him and that he'd change for me. It just doesn't work like that."

Jelly walked up, definitely looking like she needed something to pick her spirits up.

"Well," Ella said, "if you ask me, the guy totally made the wrong choice."

Pez laughed again in that way that was as light as the breeze blowing her hair. "I will tell you this: No man deserves to be treated as good as I would have treated that man!"

"So, two questions," Jelly said. "First, what did you do with the engagement ring? Throw it at him? Sell it?"

"True story." Pez raised one hand. "I turned it into a pull for my ceiling fan chain. For months afterward, whenever I was ready to blow a gasket—just stewing about the jerk—I'd yank on that ring and cool down."

Victoria Lopez. She was one of a kind. Ella would have worked at her coffee shop for free, just to be near her.

"Question number two." Jelly paused. "Ever see yourself getting engaged again?"

Pez angled her head slightly. Looked at Jelly out of the corner of her eyes. "I'm hoping so. But God will show me when the time—and his heart—is ready."

"You mean *your* heart, right?"

"My heart *is* ready, girl. But the man will need more than a heart that beats for me. He'd better grow a heart for God."

"Sounds like you have someone in mind." Jelly said it casually enough, but she was way too easy to read.

Pez laughed. "Well, I'm a whole lot more interested in who God has in mind."

The conversation drifted to Wilson. And Parker. And the dangers they faced.

"Do you worry about them at all, Pez?"

She didn't answer right away. "Wilson . . . he's the biggest concern. He was in the middle of the worst hurricane in years. Parker?" She shook her head. "He's got his dad. And your dad, Jelly. He's in good hands."

"And the men—aren't you even a tiny bit afraid for them?"

Ella stared at Jelly. Wasn't she being a bit obvious?

"*Those* two men—guys who've hunted rogue monster gators? Nothing to worry about there, honey. Besides, those five boys—Sammy, Vaughn, Parker, Wilson, and Harley—all of them have an advantage going for them that even they aren't aware of. A secret weapon."

Both Ella and Jelly stared at her for a moment.

Pez winked. "They've got me praying for them."

Which was good. Because before this was over, Ella was absolutely convinced they were going to need it.

CHAPTER 33

Chokoloskee, Florida
Sunday, October 24, 1:45 p.m.

CHOKOLOSKEE LOOKED EVEN WORSE than Everglades City. Water everywhere—like there was no island here at all. No high ground. Battered cars, trucks, boats . . . all of them ghastly headstones in a watery graveyard. Random posts were all that remained of once-sturdy piers.

Logs, trees, whole chunks of houses. Thousands of dock boards. Refrigerators. Washers. Dryers. Trailer homes that looked to Parker how he'd imagine aluminum cans would look after a run through a blender. The entire area was an absolute maze of prop-busting potential. If they hadn't been in an airboat, they'd have definitely had to replace the propellor before this. Parker was off the seat now. He stood to one side of the bow, using Amos Moses to push debris out of their path.

Jelly's old house. Gone. If the slab was still there, it was anybody's guess. The water would have to go down more before anyone would know. Bits of neighboring houses stood like cracked and shattered tombs. Black mold was already advancing. The whole place reeked of death.

Dad cruised by their old house too. At least where it had once stood. Stubs of walls peeked above the surface, like they were checking to see if the storm was really gone. The only way they could even be sure they had the right house was the paint in what had once been Parker's room. Apparently, the new owners hadn't changed the color. Nothing about Chokoloskee felt right. Home was north now . . . a million miles from here.

Dad turned toward what would have been the shoreline and the marina. He maneuvered around dozens of boats. Some on their side—still strapped on trailers. Others upside down. But none of them still floating.

"Vaughn." Uncle Sammy pointed toward a pickup truck lying on its passenger side, with water halfway up the cab. "Stillwaters's pickup?"

Ford F-150. Charcoal gray. Right make, model, color. They steered closer and swung around the other side.

"Somebody's inside," Dad said.

Wilson's dad. Waves rolled through the missing windshield, covering the man's head momentarily. The moment the wave passed, he wiped his eyes clear. He was alive!

"My leg," Mr. Stillwaters said the instant they killed the motor. "It's caught good. Broken, I think."

Parker took the bow line and tied it to a cleat in the bed of the pickup. "Where's Wilson?"

"The house." Wilson's dad explained how they'd gotten separated. "Get him and come back for me."

As much as Parker wanted to do that, they couldn't just leave Mr. Stillwaters in the water like this.

"The tide is rising." Dad didn't have to say more. All of them knew Mr. Stillwaters would be gone long before they'd get back.

Dad and Uncle Sammy were already off the airboat, standing on the driver's side of the pickup—still above water. They opened the door, and Dad surveyed the situation.

"My right foot is the problem." Stillwaters raised his other foot. "Left is clear, though."

Dad sat on the side of the truck. He whipped off his belt and slid it under Stillwaters's arms. Dad gripped an end of the belt in each hand and pulled, raising Stillwaters above the lip of the waves. "We have to see what's holding him back."

Uncle Sammy balanced himself on the side of the pickup and reached between the man's legs and the floorboards. He pulled himself farther and farther into the cab, until his head was just above the water. "I need a knife."

Parker released the survival knife strapped to his calf and passed it to Uncle Sammy, handle first. In seconds, Uncle Sammy had the water sloshing in the cab.

"Don't saw his leg off," Dad said.

"Laces," Sammy said. "Tangled on something. I'm cutting everything I can reach."

A bigger set of waves rolled in. "Parker," Dad said. "Give me a hand."

Parker got in there the best he could and pulled. Mr. Stillwaters rose slightly.

"Keep at it," Dad said. "We're getting there."

Wilson's dad grabbed the cab roof. "Don't stop. Don't stop."

Suddenly whatever was holding Mr. Stillwaters back snapped free. With a shout of pain, the man lurched upward, and Parker lost his balance. He tumbled backward into the waters—imagining a gator rushing for him. Instantly, Parker got his footing, clawing his way onto the airboat. The three of them helped Stillwaters onto the deck. His leg was twisted at a slight angle at about the mid-shin point.

"Strap me in one of those seats," he said. "We got to find my boy."

The men got him up on his good foot and helped him hop to a seat and buckle up.

Uncle Sammy handed Parker back his knife. "Nice blade. Something tells me we'll be needing that a lot on the trip."

"Hold tight." Dad fired up the airboat and swung it around. He headed straight for Wilson's place.

How many times had Parker ridden his bike from the marina to

Wilson's house? Too many to count. But it was as if he'd never been this way before. All the familiar landmarks were gone. "There." Parker pointed the way for his dad. The smallest portion of two walls was all that remained. Waves traveled right through what was left of the house.

Mr. Stillwaters wailed. "Wilson! Wilson!" He looked at Parker's dad. Pointed at the corner of the house. "I left him right here. Told him to sit tight and wait for me."

A gator had taken up residence. Ten-footer at least. Had the thing gotten Wilson? Stashed his body under some debris? It was way more than possible.

Dad brought the airboat in close.

"Gimme that gator stick of yours," Uncle Sammy shouted.

Parker snagged Amos Moses from the deck and handed it to Uncle Sammy. The ranger grabbed the stick and jumped over the side in knee-deep water. Stomped toward the gator. "You get out of here now, or I'll shish kebab you." He jabbed at the gator. "Go on. Vamoose."

The thing showed its teeth. Hissed.

Dad tugged the Ithaca pump-action shotgun from the driver's seat holster. He held it by the pistol grip in one hand and pumped a round in the chamber with the other. He checked to make sure the safety was engaged before stepping to the front of the grass catcher. "I don't have a clear shot." Without hesitation, he jumped into the water and waded closer, shotgun trained on the gator now. "Last chance, Mr. Hungry ally-gator. If you don't, I won't."

The gator must not have liked the odds. With a violent twist, the thing turned the other way, thrashing up spray with its tail. He dropped below the waters and was gone.

"Wilson!" Mr. Stillwaters released his seatbelt and stood on his good leg. "Wilson!"

Parker stepped off the bow into the water and immediately started checking the rubble where one of the walls had collapsed and a dam of debris had collected. The water was too stirred up for a look underneath. He looked for a scrap of clothing. Anything to show where Wilson might be pinned. He picked up a bike helmet, trapped in an eddy of debris. The thing was in two pieces . . . split right down the middle. The chin strap was still clasped. Parker recognized it immediately.

"When I left him, he was wearing the fool thing!" Mr. Stillwaters said.

Dad, Uncle Sammy, and Parker searched the area hard, looking for any other sign of Wilson.

"Try there!" Stillwaters pointed at a debris island nearby.

Uncle Sammy stretched to hand the gator stick back to Parker. "Use this. And be careful. You don't know what's under there."

He was right. Some people thought gators and snakes didn't attack unless provoked. That wasn't entirely true. But right now, the hurricane had done a pretty good job of provoking everything—wildlife included.

Gradually, the three of them spread farther apart and searched while Mr. Stillwaters shouted directions from the airboat deck.

Parker poked and prodded the blunt end of the gator stick under anything floating. He swept Amos Moses left to right just below the water's surface ahead of him as he moved to the next debris dam—just in case.

"Stay closer, Parker." Dad motioned him back toward the remnants of Wilson's house. "Too dangerous."

Parker swept Amos Moses under a section of roofing. "I feel something!" It had to be Wilson. His leg—or arm—and he felt Wilson move. Clearly, there was an air pocket underneath. "He's alive!"

Dad and Uncle Sammy sloshed over in seconds. Parker dropped the gator stick and helped them pull the section of roof up on one end. A fifteen-foot Burmese python struck at Uncle Sammy. He leaped back, and the sickly-yellow and black reptile slithered by, brushing Parker's leg as he did.

"Ahhhh!" Parker grabbed Amos Moses with a death grip and sliced the waters with the dive knife bayonet.

Dad fired a couple of rounds into the water where the thing disappeared. "Everyone back on the airboat," he said. "Pronto."

Parker didn't need to be told twice. The three of them moved in a tight group, backing their way to the boat. Parker held Amos Moses at the ready. "I thought it was him."

"We all did for a moment." Dad pointed the shotgun at the dark water. "But we've got to stay on the deck and out of the water. There's no telling what we'll step into."

And it wasn't just the gators and snakes. There were beams and sections of houses. Cable. Any number of things capable of entangling them. And then there were the electric lines. Obviously all power to the area was gone, but what if?

Once aboard *Welcome Sight*, they joined Mr. Stillwaters in shouting for Wilson—but spaced with intervals between so they could listen. But there was nothing. Just wind. Waves. And a deep sense of despair.

Finally, Dad fired up the airboat and did a series of slow, concentric circles around the house. All four of them studied the water. Periodically, Dad cut the motor so they could shout and listen.

With every minute that passed, the reality closed in with a choke hold. If Wilson was alive, he'd be up on a wall or on a section of roof. He'd be perched on one of the refrigerators angling out of the water. The only thing they'd find under the debris would be his body.

"After the eye," Mr. Stillwaters pointed, "the wind was blowing this way. Let's check a wider circle."

The minutes passed, and there was still no sign of him. But they picked up two other survivors nearby—and one was in rough shape.

"We have to get him to base camp," Uncle Sammy said. "But we'll come back, okay?"

"Let me stay here," Mr. Stillwaters said. "Just find me a high spot. I'll keep calling for him."

Dad looked like he was about to cry himself. He grabbed Mr. Stillwaters in a man-hug. "We can't do that. Your leg. We'll get you patched up and get right back out here."

Stillwaters's eyes. Desperate. Haunted. But he nodded. "As fast as you can."

Even as Dad swung back into the driver's chair, Mr. Stillwaters stood on his one leg. "Wilson! Wil—son!"

He kept shouting—even after the roar of the airboat engine effectively drowned him out. The only thing Parker heard was the sound of that motor . . . and the wind.

There was no answer. Because nobody was there.

CHAPTER 34

THE SEARCH AND RESCUE BASE CAMP WAS BUZZING. Some water had receded, and more pickups were parked alongside Dad's now. Someone had salvaged a table, and a group of rangers and volunteers clustered around it. Three more airboats had nosed onto the high spot—two from Wooten's Airboat Tours and one from Captain Jack's.

Some of the survivors they'd picked up in earlier runs were still there, doing what they could to help. Or maybe they had no other place to go.

Dad eased the nose of the airboat onto the rise and cut the engine.

A couple of men with Wooten's T-shirts rushed to help Mr. Stillwaters off the boat. Coworkers of his, by the way it looked. They clapped him on the back. Slung their arms around him. Handed him a water bottle.

A map of the area had been spread on the table, and rangers had drawn a grid pattern of horizontal and vertical lines. Dad wrote his name in one of three empty boxes that covered Chokoloskee. He glanced at Parker.

"Thanks, Dad." Parker mouthed the words, but Dad got the message.

Mr. Stillwaters's Wooten buddies claimed the other two Chokoloskee boxes.

Parker learned that at least two other trucks had already left for Miami hospitals with injured survivors. The other pickups waited—and were on call to do the same. Mr. Stillwaters refused a ride. "I'm searching for Wilson while there's still daylight." Nobody told him he was being stupid, that going back out in his condition wasn't safe, or that he needed to take care of himself first. Too many of them were dads themselves.

Both Wooten's boats were being made ready to go. Stillwaters kept an eye on their progress from his chair, where a ranger was wrapping his leg. "They're almost done," he said. "Don't leave without me."

Being with the men . . . seeing them in action . . . it was like downing some kind of energy drink. Parker was itching to get back out to Chokoloskee himself—although he'd stay on the airboat this time.

A ten-by-ten canopy had been set up. It had become a collection center for fuel. Jerry cans and various gas containers were being dropped off for the airboats and makeshift ambulances.

Dad and Uncle Sammy were studying the map and talking to another ranger.

Parker hovered nearby. *Tell me what I can do.* He didn't want to interrupt, but he hated feeling useless while others worked. Then again, why did he have to ask his dad what needed to be done? All he had to do was look around.

He hustled to the fuel depot, grabbed two cans, and marched off to the airboat. It took another trip to fill the tank, but the job was done. He restocked the container under his seat with extra water bottles and granola bars and secured the thing tight to the deck.

A couple of exhausted-looking survivors stood in the bed of Dad's pickup, holding their phones up to the gray sky like they thought it might beam them out of there. Good luck with that.

When one of them shouted "Hallelujah," Parker climbed up there with them and whipped out his phone. Unbelievably, he had a signal. Just the slightest pulse, but his phone was alive.

He needed to encourage everyone back home. Especially Jelly. He started a group text.

`Found Mr. Stillwaters trapped in truck—half underwater. Rescued alive.`

He sent it off before the signal was gone—and attached pictures he'd taken of the massive destruction.

A message came back from Harley immediately. He'd started a new thread, just the two of them.

`Only Wilson's dad?`

Harley was smart enough to keep Jelly out of the conversation. How would she react if she found out Wilson was MIA?

Parker's dad whistled and motioned him over. He and Uncle Sammy trotted for the airboat. Time to go.

He still had that one little tiny bar—and didn't want to lose the chance to send a message. He whipped off a quick answer, hoping the satellite caught it before he vaulted out of the pickup truck.

`He was alone in truck. He lost Wilson after the eye.`

CHAPTER 35

THE GROUP TEXT HAD HARLEY ON HIS FEET. This was good news, and he wanted to celebrate with Ella . . . and hopefully Jelly. He'd been moping around at the end of the breakwater too long. Thinking too deep. Feeling sorry for himself way too much. He'd fired off a private text to Parks, just to clarify his last message. But with Wilson's dad found safe, it wouldn't be long before they'd pick up Wilson, too.

Harley stood, stretched, and ran along the breakwater from one massive granite block to another. Leaping over the spaces between them. Dodging left and right to miss the crags like he was avoiding defenders on the field.

Ella still sat behind her easel at the base of the jetty. Miss Lopez and Jelly stood beside her, looking at a phone. Probably reading Parker's text. Hopefully that put Jelly in a better mood.

Harley whistled and waved his phone.

All three of them looked his way. Jelly smiled like she'd gotten over being ticked at him. Finally. She motioned for him to hurry over.

Harley picked up his pace.

Parker's response to his private text dinged in, and Harley opened it on the run. The message slammed him harder than a linebacker. He hit the brakes. Slowed to a stop. Read the text again. It *had* to mean that Wilson's dad lost *touch* with him somehow, right? They got separated; that's all. If Wilson was *lost* lost . . . Parks would have said that. But until he knew more, Harley couldn't share this text with the girls. Jelly was already worried enough—and this wouldn't help.

Get your game face on, Harley. They're expecting you to celebrate with them. If you don't . . . they'll want to know why. You can do this. You're a rock. A brick. A steel vault. Jelly wouldn't get anything out of him *this* time. Neither would Ella—and she was the one to really watch out for. She was a human truth serum. A safecracker when it came to getting in his head. If she guessed Harley was hiding something, he'd be in trouble.

But he could handle Ella—and Jelly, right? Hey, all three of them could tie him to her artist stool, stick a bright light in his face, and grill him relentlessly. He'd never crack.

Okay, he'd just fire off one more text—and hopefully Parks would clear this all up. *And until he does, Harley, my man, we'll just put this information deep in the vault. You're a sphinx, Harley. Nobody will get a word out of you.*

CHAPTER 36

"OKAY," ANGELICA SAID. "This is really good news, right?" She didn't want to always be the one finding a worst-case scenario. "They already have Wilson's dad. They'll find Wilson next—and get home." Until they found Wilson, there wasn't much chance they'd be coming home early. That's what Parker's mom had said after church—even after hearing the news about Kingman.

Personal videos and pictures posted by rescuers had been showing up online—and she'd watched them all. Not just to see what was really going on down there but in hopes of catching a glimpse of Parker. A news station started a feed, and announcers repeatedly warned volunteers to use extreme caution. The aftermath of Morgan had left huge areas flooded—even after a surge would have normally subsided. Dangerous currents swirled through debris dams. And naturally, the alligators had turned aggressive. Gators were opportunistic feeders—and every volunteer was an opportunity.

"Harley stopped," Ella said.

Phone in one hand, Harley had turned his back to them like he didn't want them to see what he was doing—even though it was obvious.

"Who's he texting?" Maybe Parker had sent a second text. Angelica checked her phone. Nothing. "C'mon, Harley!" She needed to make things right with him.

Harley drove his phone into his pocket and jogged toward them. Not a speed thing this time. Like he was returning to the field with the rest of the offense, mind focused on outplaying his opponents. What was he up to?

He smiled when he got close, but it looked a little too staged.

"I have no idea how you do as good as you do in football," Ella said. "Your face is soooo easy to read. The guy on the other side of the line of scrimmage can probably tell every time you expect to get the ball."

"Line of scrimmage?" His smile looked real now. "I had no idea you even knew what that was."

"I know more than you think, Harley Davidson Lotitto. And right now, I know that *you* know something."

Oooh, Ella was good. Angelica silently urged her on.

Harley took a step back. Looked at Pez like he thought she might bail him out somehow.

"Did you get a text?" Ella stepped closer to Harley. "Is that what happened?"

Harley shrugged. "We were all on that text. They found Wilson's dad. We need to celebrate. Got some snacks stashed in that art duffel of yours?"

"You are trying so hard to change the topic, Mr. Lotitto," Ella said. "Did you get another text. From Parker?"

Harley actually looked uncomfortable. "What makes you say that?"

"Your face." Ella nodded, like she saw something there that confirmed her suspicions. "You *did* get a text from Parker. What did it say?"

"Even if I got a text, what makes you think it was Parker?"

Ella laughed. "It wasn't Jelly. Or me. Or Pez. Who else would text you? So it *was* Parker."

Harley froze. Jelly was pretty sure he was holding his breath. "We'll take that as a *yes*, Harley. So . . . are you going to tell us what he said?"

Again he looked to Pez for help. She looked apologetic but didn't make a move to get him off the hot seat. Angelica loved that woman!

"Harley . . ." Ella's voice was so quiet. "We're all friends here."

He locked eyes with her a moment before staring at the granite again. "Tell us."

"It was a message just to me . . . not to the group."

All the more reason why they needed to see it.

"Look." Ella pulled out her phone. Unlocked it. Flipped onto the text messages app. Handed it to Harley. "Open any of my messages."

He looked at her like he thought she was crazy.

"I mean it." She opened one for him. "This was between Jelly and me—during church. Jelly told me how grateful she was that you didn't blow her cover when she was hiding from Scorza. Read it."

Harley hesitated.

"We're practically family," Ella said. "I'm okay with you reading *anything* on my phone. Go on."

Harley scanned the text. His face got red immediately. He handed the phone back.

"And I really meant it," Angelica said. "I overreacted. And that wasn't fair to you. I'm sorry, Harley."

He smiled. "Looks like we've got lots to celebrate. Maybe we can—"

"Hold on, Harley," Ella said. "I showed you my phone. Now, your turn." She snapped her fingers and held her palm up. "Put it right there."

Pez laughed. "Harley . . . don't get pressured to do or say something you don't think you should."

"I agree," Ella said. "In fact, don't say a word. Just give me your phone."

Harley dug the phone out of his pocket. Made sure the screen was locked. He smiled and placed it in her hand, like he thought he was in control and the whole thing was a joke. But Ella was taking him one step at a time. Getting him to do whatever she wanted him to do. It was like Ella had some kind of power over him. Angelica was completely impressed.

"Your password, Harley." Ella held one finger poised over the keyboard like she had no doubt he'd give it to her.

And somehow the spell was broken. "You're crazy." He reached for his phone, but she pulled back.

"Let's see how well I know you, Harley." She glanced at the screen. "Only four digits for your code. Interesting. How hard can that be to crack? Just four little numbers—or is it letters?" She slid a watercolor brush from her hair. Twirled it in one hand like a drummer.

"I'll bet it's letters." She wet the brush, dipped it in a tiny pool of orange paint, and wrote *COOL* on her watercolor paper. "Or maybe something more like *DUDE*."

Harley seemed to relax. Like she was so cold he had no worries of her cracking the code.

"How about *FOOT*—or *BALL*? Short. Easy for you to remember. Even after a game when you've taken a couple of hard ones to the ol' noggin." With amazing speed, she swiped his forehead with her brush, leaving an orange line.

"I'm not giving you the passcode." He wiped the paint off his forehead and held out his hand. "My phone, please."

Ella pulled back again, hugging the phone to her chest with both hands. "You're afraid I'll get it right. You're *afraid* I know you better than you think."

"Ha!" Harley seemed to be totally enjoying this now. He held both hands out—real steady. "How scared do I look?"

Ella raised her chin slightly, her eyes alive. "Not as much as you should be."

Harley laughed. "Okay . . . I'll give you *one* chance. You miss it on the first guess, and you put the phone right here." He held his palm out to her again.

"Deal." She shook his hand, then shooed him away. "Give me space, big guy."

Angelica looked over Ella's shoulder. She was up to something—and was playing Harley perfectly.

"Let's see. Maybe it's not a word after all." Ella walked around Harley once, like he was wearing the answer. "Maybe it's some number you know you'll never forget, but you think it's really clever, too. Like 1-2-3-4." She looked at him in a teasing way. "Yes, I'll bet that's it, isn't it?" She waggled her fingers over the keyboard.

"One try," Harley said. "Make it good."

Ella moved her forefinger in a lazy circle an inch above the screen. "Or maybe the numbers are a year. A birthday. Am I getting warm?"

Harley shrugged. "Try it."

"Hmmmm," Ella stepped back from him just a bit. "A birthday . . . yes. I'm sure of it now. Not *your* birthday, though. Do me a favor and concentrate on your passcode. Real hard."

He laughed this time, but he placed a forefinger on each of his temples. "There. I'm thinking about the number. Do you have it now?"

"Naughty Harley is making fun of Ella?" She wagged her finger at him. "Shame, shame."

She held one hand in front of Harley's face like she was able to read his thoughts better that way. "Oh, I'm feeling that passcode now. I was right. Four numbers. A birthday. But not your birthday, Harley. It was the year a trusted friend of yours was born."

Harley grinned. "Parks? Try it. Put in the year."

"A *different* trusted friend," Ella said. "I was referring to when Kemosabe was born." Ella tapped in the numbers 1-9-9-9. The phone opened, and Ella handed it off to Angelica.

"Hold on." Harley rushed for Angelica, but Ella blocked his way. Harley held her by the shoulders and moved her to one side. "Jelly—no. You don't want to read that. I mean it . . . stop . . . please!"

Angelica was already into the messages—and found the exchange from Parker. She stared at the screen. Froze. "What does this mean?"

She angled the phone for Pez and Ella to read. "He *lost* Wilson after the eye?" She dropped to her knees and wailed. "So Wilson is lost . . . as in dead?"

"That's not what it says." Harley shook his head. "They got separated after the eye. That's all."

"That's *all?*" He was only seeing what he wanted to see. "Read between the lines, Harley. Look at what Parker *isn't* saying."

"I am. And Parks isn't saying Wilson is dead."

Pez stepped up beside Angelica. Slipped her arm around her and held her tight. Clearly, she understood. She knew what Parker's text really said.

Jelly stood. "If he wasn't dead, why didn't Parker text *me* the news? He couldn't bear breaking the horrible news to me. That's what I think."

"Or *maybe*"—Harley tapped his head—"Parks knows you've got a crazy imagination. Or maybe he knew your logic center can be a little understaffed or underused or something . . . and you were likely to overreact like this."

Angelica gasped. "Seriously?"

"It's happened before." Harley glanced at Ella. "When my uncle had it out for me—you read Ella's text and thought Parker and I were—"

"That was completely different, and you know it."

"What was so diff—"

"Oh, come *on.* I can't believe you're even bringing that up."

Ella lined up on Angelica's other side and took her hand. "Wilson is okay. You know how I know?"

Harley looked heavenward with an exaggerated look of relief. "Because maybe *you* know how to read a text?"

"Harley." Ella put one hand on her hip. "You're not helping."

Amazingly, Harley didn't have a comeback for her.

"If something bad had happened to Wilson," Ella said, "you'd be the first one he would've texted."

She sounded so sure—which was a lot more than Angelica felt. "You think so?"

"I *know* so." Ella looked Angelica right in the eyes. "Give me one reason he'd text Harley first."

Harley made a face like the answer was obvious. "Ah . . . because maybe we're closer than you think? I'm the brother he never had."

That one almost made Angelica laugh. "Now who's got the crazy imagination?"

Harley's face turned red. He looked like he was about to fire something back, but he caught himself. He just held out his hand for his phone. "Can I have that back now, please?"

Angelica slapped the phone into his open palm.

He pocketed it and, without a word, headed toward Bearskin Neck.

"If Wilson was truly gone," Pez said, "don't you think that amazing dad of yours would've grabbed his satellite phone and called you? He wouldn't want you hearing that from Parker or Harley—or anyone else."

"He waited hours to tell me he'd left for the Everglades," Angelica said.

"And I think he learned his lesson. Let's hold on to hope where we can." Pez said it so nicely, so carefully, that her words got through.

"Okay. I'll try not to think the worst." Not yet anyway. Not until she absolutely knew Wilson was gone.

"And right now," Pez said, "I'm more worried about your other friend."

"Parker? I know. That's just it—he'll be taking more and more chances to find Wilson."

"I was talking about *that* friend." Pez nodded toward Harley.

He was nearing the circle at the end of Bearskin Neck now. Not walking at his typical football-guy stride but not dragging his feet, either.

"Harley!" Ella cupped her hands around her mouth. "Where are you going?"

Harley raised both hands to his shoulders like he had no idea.

"Well, what are you going to do?"

He turned and walked backwards for a few steps. He held up his phone and pointed to it. "I've got to figure out a new passcode."

CHAPTER 37

CLAYTON KINGMAN HAD TURNED NORTH LATE this morning—after he'd traveled south for nearly an hour. He'd waited until he was far from shore and absolutely sure nobody followed him. But he had nothing to worry about. He hadn't even seen the harbormaster—or anyone else—when he'd left the Miami area.

The four outboards on the transom were extraordinary. They never faltered. Never missed. He'd never driven anything with nearly this much horsepower.

He felt almost giddy. Another leg of his journey, and he hadn't even been detected. He was in the clear.

"Who says dreams don't come true?" Clayton shouted into the wind. "I'm living the dream right now, baby!"

Had Gatorbait learned of the prison break? Did the thought of Clayton on the loose send a clammy chill down his spine? Of course it did.

Clayton would love to see Gatorbait right now. At this very minute. To see the fear in his eyes. Then again, Clayton would see all that—and more—soon enough.

CHAPTER 38

Everglades City, Florida
Sunday, October 24, 6:30 p.m.

THE SEARCH AND RESCUE TEAMS ALL CONVERGED on base camp within minutes after Dad arrived. Parker fueled up the airboat, hoping that would help them get an earlier start in the morning. The sun was already at the horizon. In ten minutes, it would be gone.

They'd brought back three more survivors in the last run—and all of them were going to make it. There was a rush Parker got from knowing they'd just saved someone's life. But right now, the life he really wanted to save was nowhere to be found.

They'd checked Smallwood's Store on that last run. That place had gone through how many hurricanes in its history? Parker had no idea. But it had somehow survived another one. The water was to the top of the pylons underneath, and most of the roof was gone, but the place was in better shape than Everglades High School.

Wilson's dad hobbled ashore, looking like a ghost. He checked in with Dad and with each of the other airboat captains. He had a canoe paddle tucked under one arm, using it as a makeshift crutch. It took strong urging by one of his Wooten buddies to get him into one of the pickups for a run to Miami. He needed that leg looked at, and there would be no more searching after dark.

Base camp was alive—and growing. Tents materialized and dotted the mound. Port-a-potties had been delivered. Even a trailer with showers. Another with sleeping cubicles. Parker was wiped. Part of him wanted to hit one of those showers, set up a sleeping bag in the bed of the truck, and call it a day.

But Wilson was out there.

Or was he? They'd checked every tree, every structure that rose above the waters. Smallwood's. The marina. The rangers' station. All those buildings had been searched. What was left of them, anyway. Dad and Uncle Sammy had methodically combed their box on the search grid . . . and the box was empty.

The mood at base camp was mixed. Joy and congratulations with every survivor found. But a definite sense of doom clung to the place because they hadn't found more.

Parker grabbed a granola bar and sat on the airboat passenger seat. It was the highest spot above the waters of the Glades he could find. The encounter with the python that morning still messed with his head—and the coming darkness wasn't helping. That python coiled itself around whatever remained in the courage locker Parker possessed deep inside. And the thing was squeezing. Honestly, if Parker couldn't shake it off, the locker would be crushed—along with whatever courage he had left. And if that happened, he could kiss goodbye any chance of sleeping tonight.

He stared at the scars crisscrossing his arm. Maybe he wasn't supposed to shake off the encounter with the python. He'd really be burying it, wouldn't he? When he'd lived here before, hadn't he learned something about trying to escape the things in life that kept him from sleeping at night?

"Get it out of your system, Parker." Maybe if he let his mind process the python encounter now, he wouldn't lie awake tonight . . . haunted by it.

Uncle Sammy stepped up to the airboat. "Got her all gassed up?"

Parker nodded. They were all set for tomorrow. In a physical way, anyway. But he still had a distance to go before his head was ready. For an instant, he pictured the bodies by the marker buoy.

"Up for one more run tonight?"

Parker stared at him. He was serious. "It'll be dark." Really soon. How dangerous would it be—with all the debris in the water? What if they ran into trouble?

Then again, when there was trouble, wasn't that what men did? Step up to do what needed to be done, no matter how dangerous it might be? How many times had Uncle Sammy and Dad gone into the Glades at night when they'd lived here? Hunting down the rogue gator, Dillinger. Searching for Maria.

"Your friend is missing," Uncle Sammy said. "I know how I'd feel if I was you."

Actually, Parker was too ashamed to admit he'd rather stay away from the water until the sun rose. But the thought of Wilson out there somewhere . . . alone? That was worse.

"I'll talk to your dad," Uncle Sammy said. "Be right back."

Parker absolutely knew what Dad's answer would be.

The sun had said adios minutes before they pushed off from base camp. Other rangers stood on the edge of the water. Hands in back pockets. They nodded. Saluted. Uncle Sammy and Dad had a reputation, and even now it was still growing.

"We'll make a bonfire," someone called out. "Follow it right back home."

Home was exactly where Parker would like to be right now. But no bonfire in Everglades City was going to lead him there.

Dad kept the speed up all the way to Chokoloskee, swinging wide into the bay to avoid as much debris as possible. By that time the dark had gathered what was left of the town under its black wings. Dad cut the speed to a crawl. Which was good. If they hit a big-enough chunk of wreckage, they could flip—or be thrown into the water. No thanks.

Uncle Sammy manned the searchlight. The thing could light up the entire T-wharf if he was at home. He kept it trained ahead.

Dad cut the motor within fifty yards of where Wilson's home once stood. Parker dropped his ear protection down around his neck.

"I say we whistle," Dad said, "and listen."

Uncle Sammy stepped back to the cage covering the propellor. "And keep a scan going like a lighthouse."

Dad stood at the bow. Parker wanted to tell him to stay closer to the center of the boat, but he was afraid he'd sound too much like Jelly. He unbuckled and picked up Amos Moses, taking up a position just behind the driver's seat.

The air . . . heavy. Humid. Suffocating. And that smell. Decay and death . . . there was no getting away from it. It was everywhere. Dad whistled. Uncle Sammy scanned. Parker listened—and watched.

Never—not in the entire time he'd lived down here—had Parker seen so many alligators. The reflection from their eyes when Uncle Sammy's beam hit them just right? Unlike deer or dogs or any other animal Parker had ever seen. Gator eyes give off an angry, reddish-orange glow. Like hot coals. Embers from hell. Demon eyes. And Parker could see them as far ahead of the boat as the beam reached. There had to be a hundred, easy. And all of them coming their way. Hungry gators. Sensing there was food on board and wanting a closer look at the menu.

The airboat deck was less than fifteen inches above the water. Could the alligators climb aboard? If there was a hunk of debris against the side of the boat, they'd walk up it like a ramp.

"Creepy, right?" Parker's dad flashed him a smile. "They're on the hunt."

"Gee, Dad, you're making me feel great about being out here."

Uncle Sammy laughed. "The later it gets, the worse your dad gets. Trust me."

And Uncle Sammy would know. The two of them were ranger legends for some of the gutsy night work they'd done out in the Glades.

A thump and slide against the aluminum hull somewhere behind Parker caught his attention. Bits of flotsam were constantly drifting by, but this sounded different. Rather, it *felt* different.

Another bump just like the first. Then a third. All of them at the back of the airboat. Parker unsheathed his flashlight and swept the beam to the stern.

Gators. A dozen. Maybe more. Swirling the water. Jockeying for position. Bumping the boat like they were looking for a weak spot. A way inside. "Dad. Uncle Sammy. We've got some nasty company coming from behind, too." Big gators. Smaller ones. All of them with wicked teeth. Parker pressed his back against the seat. He painted the water with his beam from port to starboard. The water was seething with gators.

Uncle Sammy whistled quietly. "Have you ever seen anything like this, Vaughn?"

By the look on Dad's face, he hadn't. He backed away off the grass-catcher bow and stood close to Parker. "It's like we're under siege." Dad eased out his phone. "I need pictures. Nobody will ever believe this."

Uncle Sammy did a slow 360, lighting up the water all the way around the boat as Dad took videos. The gators weren't intimidated by the light at all. They nosed the boat from all sides, crawling over each other like they were in a feeding frenzy. Only they hadn't gotten their chompers on the food yet.

Parker wanted to keep it that way. "Can they get in here?"

Dad didn't answer—and neither did Uncle Sammy. Parker might have read their faces, but he couldn't stop watching the spectacle of terror surrounding them at this instant. The gators *could* get in. He'd seen them get in tougher places.

Parker swung his light away from the edge of the boat—and off into the distance. His beam reached what, fifty yards? As far as he could see, more glowing eyes were headed their way. "How could Wilson ever survive something like this?" All his friend's jokes about being half

Miccosukee—how he could live in the Glades for weeks, even months? There was no way.

"Dad!" A gator already had his lower jaw on the deck near the propellor cage. He clawed the side of the boat . . . opened his jaws. Two others were working their way up the other side. Crawling over each other, effectively making a reptilian ramp. It was like a horror movie. Not that Parker had ever seen one before . . . but he couldn't imagine a scene terrifying an audience more effectively than this.

"I think we're done here, gentlemen," Dad said. "Let's pick a new spot. Try again."

Yeah . . . the sooner the better.

"Nice and easy," Uncle Sammy said. "Not a good time to slip."

The deck glistened . . . wet from the night air. Parker climbed onto his seat and buckled in tight. The thought of falling into these waters was petrifying. He gripped Amos Moses.

"Give me that gator stick, Parker." Uncle Sammy jabbed at the gators that had managed to get their heads on deck. The gators were a boarding party, and they were figuring it out. "We gotta get outta here, Vaughn."

Dad was already on it. The engine caught, and he pushed the control stick forward. It felt like they were riding over floating dock boards. The boat wouldn't hurt the gators—even though they'd been out to kill everyone on board. "You'll never see something like that again."

Parker prayed that was true.

Uncle Sammy handed off the gator stick. "Keep that close." He swung onto his seat and buckled.

Dad stopped in two other places and repeated the whistle, listen, and search beam routine. Each time the gators surrounded them. What would happen when they went to the base camp? Would the gators find them there, too? Parker was definitely sleeping in the bed of the pickup. Or the cab. And he was keeping Amos Moses with him.

"Let's assume Wilson was in the house when the roof ripped away. Where would he go?" Uncle Sammy looked right at Parker. "Think like him."

Parker had tried. Wilson would hunt for anything he could crawl up onto. Anything that would get him out of the water. But it was a Cat 5. What if the wind and the waves didn't allow him to climb onto anything? And his helmet had been split in two. What if he'd been unconscious when the house went? "What if the hurricane dragged him out to sea?"

"Entirely possible," Uncle Sammy said.

They were surrounded again. Like gladiators in the Colosseum . . . with spectators who wanted to see blood—or in this case, taste it. Gators rammed the airboat harder. Clawed at the sides with fresh aggression.

At eight thirty, Dad fired up the airboat again. "I don't like this. Maybe we should hang it up. Get some rest."

Parker should have been relieved. But the idea of Wilson being out there somewhere in this? Terrifying. Where would Wilson have gone—or tried to go—after Morgan took the house? The bigger question? Was there any possible way Wilson could still be alive?

Dad drove slowly, with Uncle Sammy lighting the path in front of them. There was no way to avoid everything in the water. Things constantly thumped against the hull. Some hard enough to make the entire airboat shudder. Alligators? Wreckage? Could be anything. But if the aluminum skin tore, they were all goners.

Dad and Uncle Sammy both looked totally focused on the water—treating each piece of wreckage like it was an iceberg—with more danger below the surface than above. They snaked their way from Chokoloskee toward Everglades City at a sloth pace. There were no standing homes. No streetlights. No lights of any kind other than what they carried on board. The searchlight lit a path in front of them. But the view to either side of the boat—and behind them—was absolute blackness. Nature had scraped away the bits of civilization that clung to the shores of southern Florida. Hurricane Morgan had turned Chokoloskee and Everglades City upside down like a bowl of mashed potatoes—and wiped the bowl clean. The Everglades had reclaimed what was theirs. And now the deep dark of the Glades pressed in on them. Pushed them out. Or was the dark surrounding them trying to keep them in?

The drone of the engine and the ear protection isolated Parker with his thoughts.

"Bonfire!" Uncle Sammy pointed at a speck of light in the distance.

Almost there! *Thank you, God.* Parker never wanted to go into the Glades again at night. He checked the time. Nine fifteen. It felt like midnight with how long it had been dark.

"Our Fish and Wildlife friends loaned us a good airboat here." Dad tapped the rudder controls. "I wouldn't put money on her riding out that storm, but she's plenty dependable in the aftermath."

Whoa, whoa, whoa. That was it! After the house went, where *would* Wilson go to ride out Morgan, if he could? Wilson had already told him, hadn't he? In his texts before Morgan hit.

He reached forward and shook his dad's shoulders. "I know where Wilson would have holed up—if he was able!"

Dad cut the engine and turned. Uncle Sammy slid off his ear protectors. Parker was right. He felt it in his gut. And he also felt a twisting dread at what he knew they'd have to do.

"We have to go back."

CHAPTER 39

ELLA SAT ON GRAMS'S TOP PORCH STEP and leaned against the handrail post. Jelly did the same on the other side. Victoria Lopez sat between them. Maybe she had the mom-instinct gene. Maybe she'd gone from being a really great employer to something more. Whatever her motivation, Pez had stayed with them ever since reading the text on Harley's phone. Like she wanted to be with the girls as they worked through what it might mean. Maybe she knew Jelly wasn't okay.

Harley had been gone for hours. Back with his foster parents—or whatever they called them. But Ella didn't like the way things had been left between them all when he'd left. He'd looked lost. And without Parker around, who did he have to unload to?

Harley had never even met Wilson. Ella was sure he cared, but she was also sure that it was more than Wilson's unknown fate that had Harley spooked. It was death itself. He'd seen too much of it. Devin Catsakis last spring. And three years before that? His dad . . . when

Harley had been in seventh grade. Was he thinking about what might happen to Parker during the search? From the news reports—and Jelly's descriptions—the area was absolutely treacherous. Had Jelly's fears about Wilson caused Harley to think about the danger Parker was in too?

Or was Harley brooding over Jelly's comment after he'd referred to Parker as his brother?

Ella had sent Harley a text every hour or so. Yeah, she was scrounging for some way to encourage him. His answers had been short. Distant.

"Wilson has always seemed bigger than life." Jelly stared down the empty street. "I've practically seen him as immortal. I think he had me convinced that nothing could take him out."

A Category 5 hurricane was not *nothing*. But still, Jelly was getting morbid. "All we truly know is that he's missing, right?"

"With all the crazy things Wilson did," Jelly said, "I was afraid he'd get Parker killed before the transfer north came in. But did I think Wilson might die? Never."

"Mmmm." Pez had a way of making sympathetic noises that were somehow comforting.

"For a while, I used to think there was an Everglades Curse." Jelly held up one hand like she was ready to testify in court. "Actually, it was Wilson who talked about it so much, I began to believe it. The Glades exacted a toll every now and then—in human blood."

Not a place Ella would ever consider visiting. "That sounds like something Grams would say."

"What would I say?" Grams padded out of the house in bare feet, a plate of cookies in hand. She pulled the wicker rocker close and sat.

Jelly explained the whole thing while Grams listened and nodded.

"Strange things happen in this world," Grams said. "Devil doings."

"Grams," Ella said. "You aren't helping Jelly."

"Neither is denying the obvious, Ella-girl." Grams nodded like she'd just revealed an ancient truth. "There are strange forces at work. The prince and power of the air roams the earth. Sometimes he rides the vapors to shore. Wears them like a cloak. Uses them for a shroud to cover his evil handiwork."

"Grams . . . Jelly isn't going to sleep tonight if you keep that up. I'm serious."

Grams set the plate of cookies on the porch deck. "Sometimes the dark prince would like nothing more than for us to get a good night's sleep. An unsuspecting soul lulled away on the sleepy-town train? Sounds like an easy target to me. 'Sleeping sentries do not good guards make.' I read that somewhere . . . and it's true."

Jelly took a cookie but didn't take a bite. She turned it over and over in her hand. "I'm not going to sleep a wink tonight anyway. Nothing you say can make it worse, Grams."

Grams settled in. "Has Ella ever told you the story of Jedidiah Masterson?"

"No, Grams. Let's not go there." Grams had told Ella that story as a kid—and it gave Ella the love of spinning a spooky story herself. Eventually she could tell the story better than Grams.

"He lived right here in Rockport, with his pretty wife, Eliza . . . until that awful, fateful night." Grams nodded at Ella. "But why don't you tell it, Ella-girl? Grandpa loved the way you did it best. Your eyes would get so big when you got to the part—"

"Grams. Not tonight."

"Okay." Grams raised her hands in surrender. "But the prince rode the vapors that night, and that's the truth."

"*Grams.*"

Jelly looked intrigued. "Actually, I'd kind of like to hear it. Maybe it will take my mind off of worrying about Wilson—and Parker."

Even Pez shrugged. "I'm a sucker for a good scary story."

"Trust me," Ella said. "Not tonight." The possibility of death was too close. Too real.

"Okay." Grams rocked back. "You win, Ella-girl. We'll do this another time. But I will say this: The prince has a way of making people crazy. Make them do things they would never do if they'd carefully thought things out. Taking perfectly sane people and causing them to do absolutely insane things."

"Sounds like Parker," Jelly said. "What is he even doing down there?"

Ella knew the answer. They all did. He'd gone to help a friend. But so far, things hadn't completely gone the way they'd hoped.

"Honestly," Jelly said. "I've tried to shed this . . . this *responsibility* I feel for Parker. Like I'm his guardian angel or something."

Pez stroked Jelly's back. "Don't you think maybe you're taking a teensy bit more on your shoulders than you should?"

"Ask Ella," Jelly said. "I've tried to let it go. I mean, like, lots of times. But if something happened to Parker, how could I forgive myself if I had deliberately stepped back when I knew he was heading for trouble? And right now . . . I feel like he's in danger."

"Are you forgetting how Parker has someone a whole lot bigger than you or me watching out for him?" Pez pointed skyward.

She seemed so confident. Or maybe she just trusted God with whatever happened—good or bad. How was she able to do that?

"If the Everglades actually took Wilson," Jelly said, "they can take anybody."

Pez drew her into a shoulder hug. "If anything took Wilson, it was the hurricane. And that's over now. Parker is with his dad. And yours. They're not going to let him out of their sight."

"You don't know what it's like down there. There've been times when I was there and everything felt fine. But other times . . . it felt so untamed . . . almost wicked," Jelly said. "But the Glades isn't even my worst fear right now. It's Clayton Kingman."

No surprise there. Jelly was still following reports of the Jericho Prison break. She'd even called Officer Greenwood. He had ways of learning things—even from as far away as Florida. He'd promised to give her a call the moment he heard of Kingman being captured—or his body identified.

"Kingman embodies everything evil about this world. And we don't dare underestimate him," Jelly said.

"He hasn't been found yet—and he still has a vendetta against Parker."

"And you think Clayton Kingman would somehow know Parker was in Everglades City?" Pez asked the question without even a hint of a parental tone.

Jelly shook her head. "No, of course not. But what if he headed there to hide? He knows the area really well."

"And while he's there," Pez said, "you think he might run into Parker, by some freak accident? Is that it?"

"Exactly." Jelly stood. Faced the three of them. "When it comes to the Glades, freak things are the norm. Airplanes crash. People vanish. And people like Kingman can make someone disappear. The Glades will eat up all the evidence."

They were quiet for a few moments. Jelly looked desperate. Harley had been right about one thing: Jelly was overreacting. Like totally, over-the-top, taking this too far. How could Ella ease her out of the sci-fi, paranormal world she'd created—and back into the real world? Or was Jelly spot-on, and Ella just didn't want to believe it?

"I hope I never meet this nefarious Kingman," Grams said. "You make him sound like the king of terrors himself."

Jelly nodded real slowly. "The Glades can be dangerous. No doubt about it. But there is something absolutely malevolent—unspeakably evil—about Clayton Kingman."

Okay, *that* gave Ella a chill.

"I know this sounds like crazy talk. Clayton Kingman can look harmless to some. He can be deceiving that way. But I know him for what he is. Deadly. Twisted. Can you imagine living someplace where it's perpetual night?"

Ella shook her head.

"That's Kingman. Perpetual night. Darkness makes its home in his heart, anyway." Jelly sat on the bottom step, like she was spent. "We have to get Parker home before the Everglades—or Kingman—claim his soul."

Ella traced the edges of her cross necklace with the tip of her finger.

They were getting themselves worked up. Scared about a possibility that was so remote—so out there—that the odds weren't even calculable. Maybe it was the dark. Or the growing sense that Wilson may be dead. But right now, Jelly's fears—as potentially exaggerated as they might be—were making more and more sense.

"If everything you say is true"—Pez took Jelly's hands in hers—"sounds like our Parker has dodged the hurricane, but he's moving into something worse. A different kind of storm."

Jelly nodded. "Something just as terrifying . . . and even more dangerous."

"Out of the storm," Pez said, "and into the maelstrom."

CHAPTER 40

HARLEY STRETCHED OUT IN THE TOP BUNK, took the socket wrench out from under his pillow, and stared at the dark ceiling. There was nobody on the bottom bunk. The Gundersons let him choose which bed to claim as his own. He'd been on the bottom of things for so long, choosing the top was a no-brainer.

He held the socket in one hand and the ratchet handle in the other. *Click-cl-cl-cl-cl-cl-cl-click. Back.*
Click-cl-cl-cl-cl-cl-cl-click. Back.

The motion felt good in his hands. Familiar. And the sound? It brought him back to the days he'd worked on Kemosabe alongside his dad.

The foster room was his to personalize however he wanted—as long as he kept it neat. And didn't tape anything on the walls. And made his bed before leaving the room. And the list went on. Still, the room was twice the size of what Uncle Ray had given him over the dive shop. That was something, right?

There was a corkboard on one wall with assorted colored tacks. A place where other foster kids likely posted their dreams . . . and were forced to pull them down again when they messed up and got moved to a new bunk in some other foster home.

Click-cl-cl-cl-cl-cl-cl-click. Back.

Click-cl-cl-cl-cl-cl-cl-click. Back.

Harley had only one thing tacked on the cork. A picture of a 1999 Harley-Davidson XL Sportster. Not his but a printout of the model he'd be saving for. He'd customize it as close as possible to the one he'd built with his dad—right down to the straight pipes and chrome. Would he name it Kemosabe—just like the one he'd had? Maybe. But then again, there'd never be a bike that could match the one he'd had.

Right now, there was another trusted friend he needed to focus on. He'd made the mistake of referring to him as his brother when he'd been with the girls. Stupid. The deeper the feelings he shared, the deeper the hurt, right?

A night-light glowed from an outlet across the room. The yellowed seven-watt bulb added a surprising amount of light to the room. Who'd occupied the bunks before him? Did some of them need a light on—something to insulate them from the dark, haunting things in their past? Harley would unplug the thing eventually. But not tonight.

Whether or not anybody else thought of him as being Parker's brother, that didn't change Harley's thought train. And if he was Parker's brother, he needed to be there for him. But what could he do? He reread the texts that had set Jelly off. Parker wasn't saying Wilson was dead, was he? Parker had been texting him—Harley—and there was no reason to be cryptic. No reason to hide the meaning of what he was really saying.

If Wilson was truly gone, Parker would need help Harley couldn't give. But Parker's God could do the impossible—like He'd done for Parker before.

He pulled out his phone. Texting Parker would make Harley feel better, even if Parker didn't have a signal. He sent them off in short bursts.

Hoping you find Wilson.

Jelly thinks he's gone. Afraid you'll follow.

She's paranoid about your Kingman buddy. I know you'll keep your eye out for him. But maybe keep both eyes out for him, okay?

Your God has taken care of you before. Praying He does again.

Praying. It wasn't just a figure of speech. Harley had to try—even though he had no idea how to do it right. What if Parks was in trouble right now? What if he was in such danger, he forgot to pray? If Harley was serious about helping his friend, he had to go to the top, right?

He took a deep breath. Listened to make sure nobody was in the hallway. Cleared his throat.

"Parker's God . . . this is Harley Davidson Lotitto. Again. My friend Parks might be in trouble—and I know he's going to need You. Sounds like the Everglades is a really nasty corner of the world right now. And that Kingman dude isn't making the place less dangerous. Just wondering if You might keep an extra eye out for Parker. Well, that's about it."

Actually, that wasn't nearly it. There was more to say, but who was he to talk to Parker's God? And for something as awesome as talking to God, wouldn't there be a clock? A time limit . . . like maybe he'd have the Almighty's ear for fifteen seconds before God would move on to more important prayers.

There was so much he wanted to say to God. And ask. Like, why did his dad have to die? And where was his mom? Did she know where Harley lived? Did she ever think of finding him? And why did he get stuck with a clod like Uncle Ray as his only living relative? Why would God allow a man like that to take the one thing that connected Harley with his dad? Would his friends really dump him eventually, like Uncle Ray had said?

He'd tell God how badly he wanted the impossible. A dad. And a brother. A mom. A family. He'd tell God how much he wanted to help Parks—which was pretty impossible from fifteen hundred miles away.

He wanted to be a good friend to Jelly—but it might take an act of God to keep them from butting heads.

And he'd talk to God about Ella. He wouldn't have to tell God who she was, either. Ella Houston had to be one of his masterpieces. He'd tell God how he wanted to be there for her, too . . . but he had no idea how. The girl was smarter than him. Funnier. Definitely more creative. Talented. Harley couldn't begin to understand her, but she could read Harley's mind. She honestly cared about others—and put it into action. Harley was good at football . . . at hitting others. But Ella could *touch* others. She was amazing—and in a whole different league from Harley.

Yeah, there was definitely more he would have liked to talk to Parker's God about, but he was sure the meter had already run out minutes ago. And Harley wasn't so sure God actually heard anything from the foster home anyway . . . even if Harley was on the top bunk.

A text dinged in—and Harley bolted upright. *That was fast.*

But it wasn't a text from heaven—or Parks. He opened the text from Ella.

Changed that phone code yet?

He smiled. Texted back.

Still working on it.

She returned the volley.

You've been working on that for hours. How will I EVER crack it this time? 😨 😨 😨

You won't.

She sent back her own two-word response.

Challenge accepted. 😊

He really did need to change that passcode. The thing was . . . he could probably leave it the same. She'd never dream he didn't actually change it. Then again, she might try it right off the bat—to get warmed up. She'd get lucky—and never let him forget it. He hated the idea of giving up that number. He'd had the year of his bike as his code since he'd gotten a phone. Maybe he'd still use it but mix it up a bit. He'd use the same year but backwards. 9-9-9-1. Actually, he liked that. It was a change but the same all at the same time. "Okay, Ella . . . one more text for you."

New passcode is locked in. Good luck cracking this one.

So . . . you're saying it may take me a full minute instead of 20 seconds?

He wanted to fire back something clever. Something that would make her laugh. After struggling for a few minutes, he gave up. He sent a text to Parker instead, hoping he'd find a spot that had a signal soon.

Find Wilson—and get back here. These girls are killing me.

CHAPTER 41

PARKER'S DAD BROUGHT THEM RIGHT BACK to the ruins of Wilson's house. He cut the motor. "Let's get our bearings." Together they mapped out the direction Morgan's winds had shifted after the eye had passed.

"So, it's possible, right?" Parker looked from Uncle Sammy to his dad. "When the house went, Wilson could have been blown toward the airboat—if it was still where he'd parked it."

Dad glanced at him and nodded. Like he was as excited as Parker was. "Okay. We'll be leaving our box on the search grid . . . but let's find *Typhoon*. I'm going to pray."

Dad kept it short, but gators were already surrounding them by the time he'd finished.

"They aren't gathering for a prayer meeting," Uncle Sammy said. "Let's vamoose."

Dad fired up the airboat and eased *Welcome Sight* away from the Stillwaters's ruins.

Boats. RVs. Cars. They swept each one with their lights as they passed—and called Wilson's name to be sure he wasn't inside, waiting for help.

Thirty minutes later, still no Wilson. No *Typhoon*. What if he hadn't made it to the airboat? Or if he had, what if *Typhoon* had been ripped apart—and Wilson with it?

Dad jockeyed *Welcome Sight* left and right—around things big enough to stop them and over things that weren't.

"Airboat—ten o'clock." Uncle Sammy pointed. The airboat was over on one side—half submerged. The bottom of the battered airboat faced them. Deck and prop cage jammed tight against a grouping of cypress trees. Alligators patrolled the hull.

"Gators," Dad said. "Good sign."

Uncle Sammy unbuckled. Stood next to Parker's seat. Dad cut the engine and let the airboat drift the last twenty feet. The grass-catcher bow tapped the bottom of the half-sunk airboat.

"Gimme a hand, Parker." Uncle Sammy rushed forward, grabbed the edge of the wrecked airboat. Together with Parker, they used it like a handrail, hand over hand, to work them to the stern, while Dad kept the searchlight where it needed to be.

That's when Parker saw the rudder. Enough of it anyway. "This is it. *Typhoon*! Wilson?"

Gators thrashed the water, like the new airboat was trespassing on their property.

"Easy, now," Dad said. "These gators are rogue now. Think about every move you make."

"Wilson! Wilson!" Parker pulled his flashlight from his belt sheath and shined it through the battered motor cage—now twisted tight like a fishing net around the engine. Both prop blades had been broken off, leaving a splintered stump behind. Beyond the cage was a tangled maze of branches and twisted metal from the seats. "Wilson!"

A thick nest of debris—including what looked like a kitchen table—had lodged between the deck and the cypress trees. A muffled groan rose.

"Wilson?" Parker still couldn't see anyone. He needed to get onto that debris field and pull some boards away. The mass looked like it was packed tight enough to stand on. Was Wilson trapped in there somewhere? "Wilson!"

Dad was beside him now—with the bigger light. "Wilson—you in there?"

"Stuck. Behind driver's seat."

Oh, God . . . Oh, God . . . Oh, God. He's alive!

Dad and Uncle Sammy repositioned *Welcome Sight* so its side was pulled up tight to the bottom of *Typhoon*. Parker fed them dock lines, and they lashed the two boats securely together.

They hoisted themselves onto the narrow gunwale of *Typhoon* and lit the section between the deck and the cypress trees with the big light. The driver's seat base was twisted, with the seat bent nearly down to the deck—like it was bowing to royalty. Palm fronds, boards, even coconuts were jammed in every available space. A branch moved, and Wilson squinted up at them. "What took you so long?"

Shouts. Cheers. Uncle Sammy and Dad hugged—then pulled Parker into the bear hug too.

Wilson raised a shaky hand. "I'd like to join you—but I'm wedged in here pretty good."

Uncle Sammy boosted himself up onto *Typhoon* and climbed over the side. He stood on what was left of the front seat supports. Parker did the same on the mangled legs of the passenger seat. Together they tugged debris free and tossed it at the alligators that were forming their own blockade around the boats.

Dad hung over the side with a light in each hand. One on Wilson and the other on the gators. "Careful, *care*ful."

"Just get me outta here." Wilson clawed at the branches pinning him in place. His hair as long as ever. Blood-matted strands of it were plastered against his face.

He was half in the water, half out. If there hadn't been as much junk dammed up in the spot, the gators would have gotten at him long before this.

"Okay—give me one hand," Uncle Sammy said. "Parker the other."

Wilson obeyed. Not two minutes later, they helped him over the edge of *Typhoon* and onto the deck of their own airboat. He wore a backpack—with the blade of his machete sticking straight up through the zipper. How that had stayed on through the hurricane was a mystery. But the way Wilson was trapped, he hadn't been able to get anything out of his pack anyway. The men took a quick inventory of Wilson's injuries. Bruises. Cuts—some of them deep and nasty looking. But no obvious broken bones. And he was shaky—but he was standing.

Wilson grabbed Parker's dad and Uncle Sammy in a hug. He turned to Parker and did the same. "I knew you'd come, Bucky. I just knew it."

Parker hugged him back in kind of a stunned silence. What if he hadn't? What if he'd stayed in Rockport like he'd wanted to?

"My dad," Wilson said. "He—"

"He's fine," Dad said. "Except for a broken ankle—or shinbone. But he's worried sick about you."

Uncle Sammy handed Wilson a bottle of water and a granola bar. Dad grabbed the first aid kit. Both men did a quick wrap of Wilson's deepest cuts. "Another granola bar—or can you wait until after we get back to base camp?"

Wilson stared at the gators surrounding them, like he knew there was no way he should have survived. "Get me out of here."

Wilson and Parker buckled in, holding Amos Moses upright between them. Dad fired up the airboat and eased away from *Typhoon*. Parker had a million questions, but right now he marveled that Wilson was alive—and thanked God for making it so.

Wilson closed his eyes. Raised his chin. Let the wind blow his bloody hair away from his face. And smiled—which made Parker smile too.

Parker leaned close and shouted over the roar of the engine. "For a guy who could survive in the Glades for a month if he had to?" Parker grinned. "You're a mess."

Wilson gave him the side-eye. "Agreed. But you never looked better."

Parker never *felt* better either.

CHAPTER 42

Miami, Florida
Monday, October 25, 1:30 a.m.

WILSON SAT ON A FOLDING CHAIR, DEEP in one of the ER hallways at Keralty Hospital. Every exam room was filled with people in a lot worse shape than he was. Even the halls were absolute traffic jams. Injured people on gurneys and chairs. Even sitting on the floor. The waiting room was a disaster.

Wilson had been lucky. He'd been treated quickly. He'd had an IV and gotten stitches in a dozen different places. And he wasn't being held overnight. Hurricane victims were still pouring in, and they needed the space too much.

Honestly, all he wanted? Sign the paperwork and get out of here. But then what? He had no home. And for the first time in his life, he didn't want to go back to the Glades. Even the thought creeped him out. But who could he talk to about it? Nobody. He'd just get over it somehow, right?

But he felt forever changed. The wind. Rain. The gators trying to get at him while he'd been trapped. He'd had enough of the Everglades— and everything that lived there. Was this what Bucky had felt after he'd been mauled?

He wished Mr. Buckman and Parker were with him right now. But the battle-ax nurse at the admissions desk hadn't let them pass. Maybe they'd found a place to sleep. Which was more than what would happen in the ER. Moans. Cries. People rushing by, desperately searching for family. As tired as Wilson was, he didn't dare try sleeping. Images of the hurricane kept replaying in his head anytime he closed his eyes.

Wilson spotted his dad before his dad saw him. Shirt torn. Bloody. On crutches, thumping down the hall, maneuvering around the obstacles. Pulling back curtains to check the exam bays. His face a mix of desperation and hope. For a moment, he stopped. Leaned on the crutches. Scanned the room.

Wilson raised his hand—slowly so as not to rip any stitches. Did his best to swallow down the lump in his throat. "Dad!"

His dad locked in on his voice. "Wilson!" He planted the crutches and swung his body to meet him. He practically threw himself into Wilson and held him so tightly that Wilson was sure some stitches would split. "I thought I lost you. I thought you were gone!" He broke into sobs. Something Wilson had only seen once . . . after his mom left. "I'm sorry I put you through this. You okay, boy? Are you hurt bad?"

Over the course of the next thirty minutes, each shared all that had happened since they'd seen each other last. Dad was different—in a good way. He wasn't distracted. Wasn't looking for his next beer. Was it too much to hope the changes would stick?

"How'd you know I was here?"

"I was waiting for my ride back to base camp," Dad said. "Parker and his dad found me."

"That makes two of us."

His dad laughed in a way Wilson hadn't heard in years. "And I'm forever grateful. You ready to get out of here?"

More than ready. "What are we going to do? The house . . . it's gone."

Dad nodded. "But Miccosukee men can never be conquered, right?"

Maybe so. But they'd come terrifyingly close.

"Buckmans are waiting to give us a ride. And then I'll find us a tent—or something. We'll figure this out. Together."

Wilson just hoped the plan didn't involve going into the Everglades anytime soon.

CHAPTER 43

ANGELICA FELT ALMOST SILLY FOR HAVING THOUGHT Wilson had died. But he certainly could have. The death toll had climbed into triple digits now. Most were escaped convicts. Prisoners had seen the swamps as their pathway to freedom. But it turned out to be a short trip down nature's death row. The articles were sketchy on how the convicts had died. But between the swamps, the hurricane, and the gators . . . nature had played judge, jury, and executioner. Bodies were being picked up left and right by troops deployed to help in the recapture efforts.

Names hadn't been released to the public, but whatever source Officer Greenwood tapped into confirmed that Clayton Kingman hadn't been picked up . . . dead or alive—unless he was part of the group that hadn't been positively ID'd.

Which was why Angelica wasn't quite ready to celebrate Wilson's escape from death's grip. As far as she was concerned, until Clayton

Kingman was back in custody, both Parker and Wilson were in danger as long as they stayed in Florida. But Angelica was working on that one.

She'd arranged a ride to school for her and Ella with Parker's mom. *That's* when Angelica would make her case—certain that Parker's mom would take it from there. Now that Wilson was found, there was no reason for Parker to stay in Florida. And with Clayton Kingman still unaccounted for . . . there was every reason for Parker to leave.

She'd been really careful in the text exchanges with Parker while he'd been at the Miami hospital last night. Angelica had a plan to keep him safe, and she was going to make things happen, without Parker knowing what she was up to.

How upset would he be if he knew what she was doing? But there was nothing for her to worry about. He was too busy playing hero to think about anything else.

Ella ducked her head in the bedroom. "Parker's mom will be here any minute. You ready?"

Oh, yeah. Angelica smiled. She had everything under control.

CHAPTER 44

PARKER CLIMBED OUT OF DAD'S PICKUP BED STIFF AND SORE. Was it due to all the time he'd spent yesterday on the airboat or to the few hours of sleep he'd caught in the F-150 bed? Probably both.

Wilson was still zonked out, and Parker wasn't about to wake him.

There was no phone signal at base camp this morning, but he scrolled through the texts he'd exchanged with Jelly from the hospital. All her earlier frustrations about him staying safe were gone. She hadn't even reminded him to be careful of gators . . . or Kingman—which was almost weird. She was all about the excitement of the moment. Parker smiled. Maybe she was changing.

Dad hustled over, satellite phone in hand. He looked like he was still flying high because of Wilson's rescue the night before. "Just talked to your mom. Worked out a game plan. You're going home."

"We're leaving?"

Dad shook his head. "Not all of us. Uncle Sammy and I are staying a little longer. We need to help with the search and rescue."

Parker pictured the floating bodies from the night before. "And recovery efforts."

"Yeah . . . that, too."

Two days ago, he had pretty much hated the idea of being here. But now? It seemed like there was still too much to do. "I can help." And how could he leave Wilson—after just finding him?

Dad shook his head. "You've done plenty. And there's school to think about."

Wilson sat up in the pickup bed, obviously following the conversation. His T-shirt was ripped and stretched at the neck. The only thing about him that didn't look completely banged up was his gator tooth necklace. The thing was as indestructible as the power Wilson believed it held. Parker really, really wished he'd found the one Wilson had given him.

"Tomorrow is Tuesday," Parker said. "There's a teacher's institute or something. So I wouldn't be missing any classes by staying another day."

"Mom worked really hard to find this flight. You'll still have a long layover in Raleigh as it is—and won't get into Boston until early tomorrow morning."

But he was pumped now after finding Wilson. And the daylight dimmed the terror of how the gators surrounded them the night before. "Okay, what's more important—making sure I don't miss a couple of measly days out of the *years* of schooling ahead or helping you and Uncle Sammy save lives?"

Wilson snickered. "Somebody's laying it on thick. Although I completely agree with Bucky."

"Nice try, boys."

"Honestly, I miss days all the time," Wilson said. "And it hasn't hurt me none."

Dad laughed. "The truth is right now supplies are still short. Food. Water. So is space for sleeping."

Okay, that made some sense. "Is Mom just worried about me in the Glades?"

"Not a bit." Dad hesitated. "But she is concerned about Clayton

Kingman." He caught Parker and Wilson up with what he'd learned. "Mom and I talked it out. You're going home on a flight out of Fort Myers. The Miami airport is a madhouse."

Parker groaned. "When?"

"We've got to leave pronto. Uncle Sammy will take the airboat and make another sweep of Chokoloskee with Wilson's dad while I'm gone."

Already Uncle Sammy was gassing up the airboat. Wilson's dad was right there with him, leaning on the crutches, handing him another tank.

"Wilson and I haven't even had a real chance to catch up—and now I'm leaving? That stinks." Parker slid his gator stick out of the pickup bed. "And what about Amos Moses? How am I going to take him on the plane?"

"After what we saw last night?" Dad reached for the thing. "We'll need him here. I'll make sure he gets home safe."

Wilson stood. "Don't you worry, Bucky. I'll put Amos Moses to work."

"Not going to happen." Dad smiled. "Because you're booked on Parker's flight."

There was this moment—a hesitation . . . like that message took a little longer getting from Parker's ears to his brain. "Seriously?" But one look at his dad's face confirmed it.

"This is going to be an adventure, Bucky!" Wilson vaulted out of the pickup bed. He winced when he landed and checked the bandages on his legs to make sure fresh blood wasn't seeping through.

"You two have had enough adventures for a while," Dad said. "Don't you think?"

"My dad," Wilson said. "He's okay with this?"

"Loved the idea," Dad said. "Your wounds need to be kept dry. A couple weeks up north to heal will do you good. He was relieved."

Parker absolutely agreed. "I can't wait to text Jelly."

"Hit the brakes, Bucky." Wilson smiled. "Tell her about *you* going home—but don't mention me. Let's surprise her. I totally want to see her face when I show up."

CHAPTER 45

CLAYTON KINGMAN STOOD AT THE HELM, guiding *Retribution* north. He stayed a good five miles offshore. Close enough to get a visual of land if he needed it. Far enough out not to be noticed.

If his dad could see him right now, wouldn't he be surprised? Proud, in his weird way. Did Dad think Clayton died in the swamps surrounding Jericho? Clayton seriously doubted that. Maybe it all went back to the stalker song. His dad may not actually be watching him, but deep down, Clayton was sure his dad would know if he was alive or dead. He might even know what he planned to do.

He'd made incredible time—thanks to the power *Retribution* packed on the transom—and the fact that Clayton could survive on hardly any sleep.

And he'd gotten clean away. He was safe—because he was careful. He had one heckuva surprise for Parker Buckman . . . Gatorbait. Parker's face would be absolutely *aghast* when he realized he'd been outsmarted. *Aghast* was the perfect word. One his dad would likely use himself.

Again he found himself humming that song his dad had sung so often. How on earth did a song like that land a Grammy back when his dad was young? Didn't anybody back then really listen to the sicko stalker lyrics before giving the prestigious award?

Then again, Dad had landed the job of principal at Everglades High . . . at least until last year. Somehow he'd gotten past the firewalls and been awarded a prestigious job. He'd been working with kids . . . but in his own way, the guy was one sick, stalking monster.

But Mom had called Dad's bluff. Clayton had to hand it to her. She must have found a time to escape when he *wasn't* watching. And if she'd done it once, she could have done it again. She could've come back for Clayton—and slipped away undetected. Why hadn't she?

And for someone who kept such control on Mom, why hadn't his dad ever searched for her? A crazy, crazy thought ran through his mind—and he pushed it away.

Spray broke over the bow and onto the window of the pilothouse.

"Keep your head in the game, Clayton." He checked the GPS. Made a course correction.

The thing was, the song was growing on him. He could make up a thousand verses. But he didn't picture his dad singing it to him—or to his mom. It was Clayton singing the song. His own version. And he was singing it to Gatorbait. He picked up a water bottle and held it up like a mic. "This one's for you, Gatorbait."

"Every breath you take, and every move you make,
I'm keeping you in sight, gonna win the fight, I'll be coming soon."

CHAPTER 46

HARLEY TOOK HIS USUAL SEAT IN THE CAFETERIA by Ella and Jelly. He pulled out his triple-decker PB&J and took a bite.

Jelly checked the time. "When Parker is on the plane—and the thing is in the air—I'll feel a whole lot better."

Actually, Jelly looked like she was flying pretty high right now. Like somehow *she'd* been responsible for Parker's sudden return—although she didn't come right out and say that. Harley figured the real credit went a whole lot higher. Harley had asked God to protect Parker. Barely more than half a day later, Wilson had been found and Parker was on his way home. Coincidence? He'd ask Parks about that some night after he got back.

"The thing that had me worried," Jelly said, "was that—"

"I might pass your table and not take a seat?"

Harley tensed the moment he heard Scorza's voice behind him.

"Worry no more." Bryce Scorza set his tray on the other side of Jelly and sat. Four slices of pizza. Three cartons of milk. A bag of chips.

Jelly looked as annoyed as Harley felt. "That seat is taken, Mr. Scorza."

"Ah, *yeah*." Scorza made a face like she'd said something incredibly obvious. "I'm sitting here."

"Uninvited," Jelly said.

Scorza laughed. "I've been wanting to show you something for a couple days now. You're a hard one to catch."

"She's impossible to catch," Ella said. "By you, anyway."

"Black Beauty. I didn't even see you." He pulled back the sleeve of his jersey and thrust his arm in front of Jelly. "Ta-da! No more cast. What do you think?"

"I liked it better before it came off," Jelly said. "In fact, I think you'd look great in a full body cast."

Scorza looked at Harley and shook his head like the whole thing was funny. "Do you believe this girl?"

Actually, Harley did.

Scorza balled up his fist and squeezed until his knuckles turned white. He tapped his forearm. "Feel this, Everglades Girl. My strength is coming back."

"I'll take your word for it." Jelly snatched a slice of pizza off his tray, took a bite, and dropped it back where she'd found it. "Your speed could use some work, though."

Scorza actually looked impressed. He picked up the same slice and took a bite himself. "You are just full of surprises, Everglades." He held out the slice of pizza. "More?"

"Nope." She took a bite of her sandwich. "Peanut butter and jelly. That's what I want."

Ella laughed in such a free, easy way. "She is soooo telling the truth."

"So, Everglades, tell the QB what has you so worried. Maybe I can help."

She stared at him for a long moment. "Highly doubtful. Let me tell you what you'd be up against." She actually started talking about

Clayton Kingman. About how he'd almost killed Parker. How he'd escaped from prison. And how she believed he would do something awful if given the chance.

Harley stared at Ella. She looked back, wide-eyed, like she was just as shocked as he was that Jelly had opened up at all to Scorza.

"There." Apparently, Jelly was finished. "I'll feel a lot better when Parker arrives tomorrow. He'll be safe up here."

Scorza squared his shoulders. "If you're worried about this one-armed dude, stick with number eight." He tapped the number on his jersey. "I'll watch your backside."

"No thanks, Mr. Scorza." Jelly took another bite of her sandwich. "And you haven't been listening. It's not me I'm worried about. It's Parker."

"With a lousy friend like Harley here"—Scorza jerked his thumb Harley's way—"I'd worry about Gatorade too."

Okay, Scorza was really beginning to annoy Harley now. But he wasn't going to get baited into confronting the jerk.

"Look, Everglades, how about we hang out a little more, until this *dangerous* convict is caught. I'm not afraid of this guy—whoever he is."

"Which clearly shows how naive you really are. You're honestly not afraid?"

Scorza smiled. Shook his head. "Not a bit."

"Well . . . you should be."

CHAPTER 47

TO WILSON, PARKER'S ROOM FELT FAMILIAR—in good and bad ways. He'd always seen the Goliath gator skull as a trophy. But it didn't feel that way now. Gators had never bothered him.

Until now.

Something had happened to him while trapped in *Typhoon*'s wreckage. The gators had found him there. The only real access point they had to him was his legs. They'd tried over and over and over again. He'd practically worn off the heels on his boots kicking the things back.

Wilson needed to get back in the Glades. And not just in an airboat. He'd need to wade in the water until he shed the "gator-shakes," as his dad called them.

When Parker's mom had picked them up at the airport early this morning, he'd answered a million questions. By the time he got to their house and climbed into bed, all he'd wanted to do was sleep in. Easier said than done.

He'd stared at Bucky's bookcase since opening his eyes at first light.

Actually, it was Goliath's smiling jaws he'd been watching. While he'd been trapped, the gators had been relentless. So powerful. He'd been sure that on one of those attacks his reaction would be too slow—and it would be over. The thought had terrorized him. Wilson grabbed the gator tooth necklace from around his neck, still eying the skull on the bookcase.

"Sometimes that skull still gives me the creeps," Parker said. "You?"

How long had Bucky been watching him? Long enough. "Nope. Miccosukee men have no fear. Not of the Glades or anything in them."

Bucky laughed like he saw right through him. "Is that why you have a death grip on your necklace?"

"The real question is where's *your* gator tooth necklace, Bucky?"

"It's here." Bucky definitely looked embarrassed. "Somewhere."

"Well, when you find it, keep it around your neck. You never know when that thing will be just what you need to get you out of a jam."

"Really?" Bucky sat up now. "It didn't exactly get you out of the airboat, did it?"

"How do you know the necklace isn't the reason I survived until you got there?" Wilson planted the tooth in his palm, closed his fist, and wrapped the lanyard around his knuckles. The tooth poked up from between his fingers nearly an inch and a half. He jabbed his fist into the air a couple of times. "This makes a pretty fearsome survival weapon in a tight spot."

"Against a gator's hide?" Bucky shook his head. "Not buying it."

"You have to aim for the eye, Bucky." Wilson took another swing. "Man or beast, sometimes a shot in the eye is your best chance to survive." He kissed the gator tooth and slipped the lanyard around his neck.

Bucky stood. "There's no way I'll sleep in today—even if there is no school. You ready to get moving? We can get a look around while we wait to surprise Jelly."

They grabbed a quick breakfast and were out of the house by seven thirty. He walked alongside Bucky down the place called Bearskin Neck. Shops, mostly. And all of them closed, except the place with the big lobster sign. The T-shirt shops interested Wilson most. He might have to break down and buy one. The one Bucky loaned him was a little tight. The sweatshirt and jeans he'd borrowed were okay.

His friend stopped at the circle turnaround marking the end of the Neck. A massive granite breakwater stretched out beyond that, disappearing into a fogbank that crept in from the Atlantic.

"I told Jelly I'd meet her on the breakwater." He pointed to a nearby spot.

They were plenty early. Which was good—just in case Jelly showed up sooner than the rendezvous time. The girl had a day off school, and she'd volunteered to work at some donut shop she texted about so often. The girl was crazy. She'd had a perfectly good day to laze around and do nothing—and she'd kissed it goodbye. The girl needed counseling.

Wilson followed Bucky over the curb and onto the granite blocks.

"Okay," Bucky said. "I'll park myself down by the water. I've got just enough time to call my grandpa before Jelly arrives."

Wilson wasn't sure if he even had a grandpa. Dad never talked about him, anyway. But Bucky and his grandpa had been texting for the last half hour. "Where am I supposed to go?"

Bucky pointed to the fogbank. "Through that. Just stay on the rocks."

"How far?" The blocks just seemed to dissolve into the fog . . . into nothingness.

"Go right down the middle until you reach water. Then stop."

"That's helpful."

Bucky laughed. "There's a signal light at the end. Wait there and listen for my whistle. She's going to *die* when you walk out of the mist."

Wilson instinctively reached for his machete—but he'd left his pack in Bucky's room. "You expect me to go out into the unknown—without a weapon? What if I fall in—and there's a shark or something?"

Bucky made the motion of removing a lanyard from around his neck and wrapping it around his fist. "You've got the ultimate weapon, right?"

"Against a great white?"

"Man or beast." Bucky shrugged. "Just aim for the eye."

Wilson grinned. Man, he'd missed hanging out with this guy!

CHAPTER 48

PARKER DIALED HIS GRANDPA EVEN AS he watched Wilson walk down the breakwater.

"Parker, my boy. So, you're on the jetty." He could hear the smile in Grandpa's voice. "If my weather app is right, there's barely a whisper of wind—from the northeast. I want you to get as close to the water as you can—on the leeward side of the breakwater."

The side out of the direct wind. The Rockport Harbor side versus the Atlantic side. This wasn't the first time Grandpa had given him strange instructions. He climbed down a few rocks until he was inches from the water. "I'm there."

"Okay, the water surface is as flat and glassy as the Old Mill Pond, right?"

"Exactly."

"Now, kneel down on the edge—and lean out as far as you can without toppling in. What do you see?"

Parker did a quick scan of the area. Right now, he was more concerned about somebody watching him. He glanced toward the end of the breakwater. Wilson was practically translucent now. Like he'd become one with the fog. Suddenly the fog absorbed him altogether.

"Parker?"

He focused on the surface of the water again. "Nothing. Just a confused-looking face staring back at me."

Grandpa chuckled. "Keep looking. What else do you see?"

Parker did his best to describe his eyes. Nose. The Wooten's cap he wore.

"You're still describing you."

"Because . . ." Parker drew the word out a bit to make the point. "That's all I see."

"So look deeper."

"Deeper into the water—or is this supposed to be some deeper look into my soul or something?"

Again, Grandpa laughed. "Both. I'm hoping the first will lead to the second. Can you see the bottom?"

"Ah . . . yeah."

"What do you see?"

Parker cleared his throat. "Humongous chunks of granite—covered with brown sea slime—all the way to the sandy bottom."

"Uh-huh. Anything else?"

"A line—leading to a lobster trap. But the thing is all bashed up—like from a storm. Keep going?"

"If there's more."

Parker checked the circle turnaround. No Jelly or Ella yet. "Okay, more rocks. A crab crawling across the sandy bottom. A sea urchin poking out from a granite block. Looks like a shoe on the bottom too. Kelpy seaweed swaying like a hula skirt."

And as flat as the water had seemed, it had an almost indistinguishable pulse, like a giant slept on the bottom, and the surface rose slightly with his chest.

"Anything else?"

"The water had seemed dead calm, but now it seems almost . . . alive."

Grandpa clapped on the other end. "Good, Parker. Good. You've just discovered another lesson of manhood."

His focus snapped back to his own reflection, holding a phone to his ear. "Uh, you might have to remind me of exactly *what* I discovered— other than lots of interesting stuff on the bottom."

"Mmmm, mmmm. You're so close. Right there," Grandpa said. "What did you see at first . . . like . . . what was the only thing you saw?"

"Me."

"Yes. Right." Grandpa sounded way too excited about Parker's reflection. "And what did you see after looking beyond that?"

"Lots of stuff." Did Grandpa want him to run down the list again?

"Put it all together, Parker. Recap what you just told me. Text me later when you get it. Your grandpa loves you, Parker. I'll let you go."

"Whoa, whoa, whoa. Not so fast, Grandpa. I was up most of the night and didn't get all that much sleep in Everglades City. I'm not firing on all eight yet, so you've got to give me some kind of hint."

Grandpa laughed. "Fair enough." He paused for a moment. "Okay . . . think about your little exercise, and complete this sentence: *There are lots of things I'll never see unless I . . .*"

Parker waited for a couple of seconds. "That's it?"

"It's enough. Work on it. The best-learned lessons are discovered . . . not taught. I love you to the alien planet and back." It was their little twist on the common *I love you to the moon and back* line. The moon was close enough to see. But a planet—with aliens? It would be so deep in space that it hadn't been discovered yet.

"I gotta go." And Grandpa disconnected . . . just like that.

There are lots of things I'll never see unless I . . . what? "Okay, Grandpa. I'll work on it." Parker glanced out to the fogbank. Wilson was still out of sight. He checked the circle. Jelly hadn't arrived, but a woman sat on the curb, scrolling through her phone. She was laser-focused on the thing. If she'd only take a look at what surrounded her, she'd discover that almost every place she turned, there was a picture. Something worth capturing. Even the fog added a creep factor that changed the whole personality of the place. The woman raised her phone, struck a pose, and took a selfie. Did she have any idea how ridiculous she looked? A million things to photograph around her—but she couldn't get past her own face.

Suddenly it hit him. He stared at the water. At his own face . . . and then the bottom beyond. "There are lots of things I'll never see unless I *look past myself.*"

It was true, wasn't it? Hadn't he been totally focused on himself before he'd gone to the Glades? He hadn't even admitted to his dad—or Harley—how much he'd dragged his feet at the thought of going to the Glades in the first place. He'd been forced to look past himself, in a way. And what would he have missed if he hadn't? Everything that really mattered.

"Parker!" Jelly's voice pulled him from his thoughts. Ella was with her—and the two of them rushed past the woman on the curb.

He stood and climbed away from the waterline.

Jelly made an exaggerated act of looking him over. "Any new scars?"

"Got enough of those when we used to live there." He held up the arm that had been gator-mauled.

Jelly snatched his hat and slapped it on her head before he could stop her.

"So you're not still steamed at me for leaving without telling you, right?"

She raised her chin and smiled. "Mad? Just because you ran off in the middle of the night to a place that nearly got you killed before? Just because you never called to say goodbye? My goodness, Parker Buckman. You've got a *wild* imagination."

Ella patted Jelly on the head. "Something's a little off with your memory, girl."

"So . . . where's this surprise you promised me?" Jelly eyed his pockets, then lifted his cap and looked inside before settling it back on her head. "Or is it an imaginary surprise?"

Parker was absolutely going to love the moment she figured it out. And the fact that she'd have to go to work at the coffee shop so soon afterward would serve her right. "You ready?"

Jelly snapped her fingers and held out her palm. "Right here. I think you *owe* me a nice surprise. You owe Ella and me both."

"Truth." Ella shrugged. "I'm the one who had to calm her down."

"You did no such thing."

"You're right," Ella said. "Nobody could get you to stop worrying."

"Pay no attention to a thing she says, Mr. Buckman. But we shall have our surprise right now, if you please." She tapped the center of her palm. "And if it's absolutely fabulous, I'll owe you a half-dozen donuts. But if it's as lackluster as I imagine, you're going to owe me."

Parker turned toward the fogbound end of the jetty and gave a sharp whistle.

"What?" Jelly gave him an incredulous look. "Do *not* tell me you rescued a stray dog while you were down there."

"Not a dog . . . but I definitely brought back a stray." He stepped to one side, looking out to the end of the breakwater, then at the girls, and then back.

Wilson's shadow appeared—but faintly. His silhouette deepened. Took on mass. He long-stepped from rock to rock, fast enough to make his hair flow.

"Oh my gosh," Jelly whispered. "Oh my *gosh*."

Ella glanced at Parker. "Is that who I think it is?"

"Wilson!" Jelly squealed and jumped in place—and then bolted right for him.

CHAPTER 49

ELLA HAD WATCHED THE REUNION PLAY OUT, smiling the entire time. Wilson was every bit the rugged swamp guy Jelly had painted him to be. Blond hair, rough-parted down the middle and hanging below his shoulders. One strand of turquoise and red beads threaded onto a tiny braid running down one side.

His face had a tough look to it—especially with the fresh stitches to his cheek and forehead. But his eyes were kind. Almost like Harley's that way. His hands were more like Parker's. Lots of faint scars.

It was his necklace that made her take a step closer. Like the one Parker used to wear when she first met him. It had to be a gator tooth.

The guy had one forearm wrapped in roll gauze, with a dark stain bleeding through. One of his calves was wrapped the same way. The guy could probably tell some horrific stories about Hurricane Morgan.

Jelly was still hugging Wilson. "You've *grown!*"

"That explains it," Wilson said. "I honestly thought you'd shrunk. I was thinking I'd have to start calling you Jelly*bean*."

"Not if you know what's good for you." Jelly stepped back and grabbed Ella's arm. "And this is my good friend Ella Houston."

Wilson gave Ella a sympathetic look. "I feel so sorry for you. I know what you have to put up with." He raised one hand like a talking puppet and made it do that yack-yack-yack thing. "She drives you nuts, right?"

Jelly slugged him in the arm.

"There's the Jelly we all know and love," Wilson said.

She peppered him with a million questions.

How long are you here?

How are you doing after the hurricane?

Do you think you'll need counseling?

How bad were you hurt?

Ella hated to be the bearer of bad news. "We're supposed to start our shift at BayView in fifteen minutes."

Jelly groaned. "I should have never asked to be scheduled. Parker— why didn't you tell me?"

"And spoil this surprise? Not a chance." Parker started them walking. "I have plenty to show him around town. And we'll meet Harley after I stop by the yacht club and talk to the boss."

The boys walked them to the doorway of BayView Brew, and Jelly made them promise to stop back later.

"So"—Parker snatched his cap back—"better than a stray dog?"

Jelly shrugged. "A puppy would have been cuter."

"Looks like I win the donuts," Parker said. "A half-dozen—on demand."

"Two for me," Wilson said. "One for Bucky."

"Uh . . . a half-dozen would be *six* donuts, Wilson. And I think Parker intends two for each of you three amigos."

Wilson shrugged. "Still comes out to two for me, math-wiz."

Parker held out his hand. "So, a half-dozen donuts—on demand?"

Jelly gave it a shake, protesting the entire time. "I have no idea why I'm doing this . . . but *fine.*"

Ella watched the two boys walk toward the waterfront. "Once Harley joins them, the guys outnumber us, Jelly. At least while Wilson is in town."

Jelly pulled open the door to BayView Brew. "It'll take more than three guys to be a match for us."

CHAPTER 50

PARKER SLOWED AS THEY PASSED TUCK'S CANDY. "We *will* visit this place. Trust me." He pointed out the harbormaster's office and showed Wilson the view from the end of the T-wharf. He found Tina Larson, co-manager of the yacht club. Mid-fifties. Hair with more silver than brown showing.

"Thanks for understanding when I missed work Saturday."

"You went to help in the hurricane effort, Parker. We all loved hearing that." She winked. "It was a slow day anyway."

He introduced Wilson, and she flashed him that smile that probably brought as many people back to the yacht club as the water did.

"I'm off school today. Anything you need?"

She shook her head. "Enjoy the day."

Parker led Wilson down the aluminum ramp to the slips. He showed him where the *Boy's Bomb* used to be tied and took him aboard Steadman's Whaler.

Wilson nodded approvingly at the 400-horsepower Mercury motor on the transom. Ran his hand along the edge of the hardtop over the console. Gripped the wheel. "So, you keep this boat cleaned up—and running— for a guy who will never come to claim it . . . a guy who tried to kill you?"

Parker shrugged.

"And you do it for no pay." Wilson tapped his skull. "Bucky, you gotta get your head examined."

"I keep it up because it's a really nice boat. And it needs to be run." It had become kind of a loaner boat as well. If a member of the club had a boat down for repairs, Steadman's Whaler made for a nice little membership perk. "And I get to drive it whenever I want—you did catch that part, right?"

"Tell me you haven't named this thing."

Parker acted like he didn't hear him. Yeah, he'd given it a name . . . which was more than Steadman did. But it wasn't Parker's boat—so he couldn't name it officially, could he?

"You named your gator stick. You've got Jimbo the knife. Eddie the machete. You name everything—and this boat is too sweet *not* to have a name. What did you name her?"

A crying kid caught his attention. Several slips down, a mom stood at the helm of a Carolina Skiff. She had one kid in her arms, another tugging at her jeans. She turned the key and got nothing. She slapped the helm. Growled in frustration. The little dude was wailing now. "Damsel in distress."

"You named the boat *what?*"

Parker pointed his chin toward the mom. "Forget the boat. *That* lady is in distress."

Parker introduced himself and explained he worked at the club. The lady eyed Wilson suspiciously. "He's my friend, a Hurricane Morgan refugee."

Refugee? Wilson mouthed the word.

"This is my brother's boat," the lady said. "He suggested I take the kids for a ride around the harbor. They didn't sleep well last night."

She didn't exactly look well rested herself. "Nothing like a boat ride to lull kids into a nap, if that's what you want."

"Not if I have to row."

Parker knew her brother. Nice enough guy but sloppy with the gear. Three inches of greenish water sloshing at the transom testified to that. Already the mom was trying to keep junior from splashing in it. Clearly, she needed a break. "Tell you what. BayView Brew Coffee and Donut Shop—do you know the place?"

The mom nodded. "Block and a half." She pointed. "That way."

"Right. Well, they've got a special today—until 8:45. I think it's called the *I Need a Break* special. Ask for Jelly, and she'll give you three donuts—free."

She gave him a skeptical look.

"Leave your keys. By the time you get back, we'll see if we can have this thing running for you. And if not?" He shrugged. "You can just sit inside the boat here at the dock and have a donut picnic. Either way, the kids will be happy."

Tina Larson walked halfway down the gangplank from the T-wharf. "Problems, Parker?"

"Just going to check her battery cables."

Tina waved and strode back up the ramp.

Apparently, that was just enough to convince the mom. She climbed out of the boat with the kids and headed for the ramp up to the T-wharf. "I'll be back in fifteen minutes."

Parker fired off a text to give Jelly a heads-up—and to cash in on three of the donuts she owed him.

"One battery cable is loose," Wilson said. "And the contacts are iffy."

Parker hustled to the club's shed and came back with a sandpaper scrap, a wrench, and a small bucket with a couple of sponges. He cleaned the contacts and reattached the cables. The skiff fired right up—and Parker let it idle.

By the time he and Wilson had bucketed and sponged up the rainwater, the mom was back. She held up a bag of donuts. "You were right!

There was a special." Both kids bounced with excitement now. Was it the donuts—or the fact that the boat was running? It didn't matter. She needed a break—and things already seemed to be turning around for her.

She snapped lifejackets on the kids and, moments later, backed the skiff out of its slip. The three of them looked like they were heading for Disney World. "How can I thank you two?"

It sounded way too sappy to say the expression on her face was all the thanks they needed. "Next time you go to BayView Brew, tell the girls working there about Parker and Wilson—two fine young men who helped you on the docks."

"And when they give you guff about the 'fine' part," Wilson said, "you just tell them they don't know what they're talking about."

The lady laughed. "Done."

Wilson stood watching the mom singing something with the kids as she swung wide around the docks. "Looks like I'm only getting one donut now. But that felt *good*. We gotta help more people like that."

Parker totally agreed. And all it took was looking beyond himself for a moment.

CHAPTER 51

ANGELICA WANTED TO LEAP FROM table to table at BayView Brew. She'd zigzag her way around the entire room, without touching the floor. And she could do it while carrying Ella. Like an astronaut bounding across the surface of the moon, right now gravity had no hold on her.

She could manage any feat of strength. Rearrange the granite blocks forming the breakwater? Not a problem. They'd be like giant marshmallows to her. Mere stage props.

Ella was in the back with Pez. Harley hadn't come in yet. And for the moment, it was just Angelica and her thoughts. She leaned her elbows on the counter and stared at the empty seating area.

Pez breezed by and waved a hand in front of her eyes. "Hey, day-dreamer."

"Sorry. It's just that I'm having one *terrific* day."

"So you've said. Mine hasn't been bad either. I just got a call from a gentleman who's planning a surprise for his niece—and he's hiring me to help. He'll pay cash, and he offered a generous bonus if I bring a couple of helpers to serve donuts and cider to a boatload of people. I told him I had just the right helpers in mind. So, tell me you're free this Saturday night. You, Ella, and I are catering our very first Halloween Sweet Sixteen party!"

"Not Harley?"

"No boys allowed. The girl is sixteen, not eighteen," Pez laughed. "Those were his exact words. I told him all about you and Ella. He took your names and said he'll have personalized party T-shirts for each of us. He thinks you'll get along marvelously with his niece. I should have asked him for her name."

"We might already know her from school. I'm in." And they wouldn't need Harley anyway. Angelica was sure she could deliver the donuts, cater the event, and drive the boat all by herself.

Angelica was feeling downright unbeatable. She'd pulled off the ultimate covert rescue. She'd gotten Parker out of danger, and even *he* didn't know she was behind it. It was Angelica who'd gotten through to his mom—who then turned around and convinced Uncle Vaughn to send Parker home. And Angelica's efforts had turned into a twofer. Not only had she saved Parker . . . she'd rescued Wilson at the same time. Why wouldn't Clayton want to kill Wilson if he got the chance?

Angelica had pretty much single-handedly reversed that threat of danger. Maybe she'd been wrong trying to repress her natural gift of protecting others—even those who didn't think they needed her protection. If a person has been given a gift, they should use it, right? Well, nobody could say that Angelica didn't have some crazy-good ability to know when others were in trouble . . . and to find a way to get them out of it. And when she used her gift, she had this sense of superhuman strength afterward. Like she could do anything she wanted to. Sure, dancing from table to table with someone in her arms sounded like something only Superman could do. But in reality, she'd just carried Parker and Wilson fifteen hundred miles to safety, hadn't she?

There was only one thing that seemed impossible right now. Just one little thing that she was finding really, really difficult to do.

Stop talking to people about it.

She wanted to tell everybody how she'd sensed the dangers and taken action. How it had all worked out perfectly. She wanted to tell Ella and Pez again—even though she already had. Right now, Angelica might talk Scorza's ear off if he walked into the shop. She'd hand him an apple fritter, sit him down, and amaze him with how she'd orchestrated everything.

But she had to be careful. If word got out about her abilities to sense danger and protect others, there'd be scientists showing up at her door. Wanting blood samples . . . looking for a logical reason behind her truly sci-fi abilities. In the end, they'd shake their heads . . . completely bumfuzzled. They'd conclude she simply had a gift that was as much a marvel as it was a mystery.

There was something about Parker that she both loved—and hated. The way he helped others—like the lady with the two kids who'd just been in. What wasn't to love about the way he'd given her half his donuts? But Parker didn't know his limitations. When he risked his own hide to help others, that was what got him in trouble . . . and he had a long history of doing just that.

Parker needed Angelica to balance him. It would be a lot easier to do that if he told her what he planned to do *before* he did it. But hey . . . he made it back safe and sound, no small thanks to his secret protector.

Angelica picked up a pair of tongs and set a cinnamon donut on a plate. She held the dish up and positioned her pinky underneath— dead center. She made microadjustments to compensate and get the balance just right. She smiled. If she could balance the plate as well as she balanced everything else, maybe she'd walk around the room this way—blindfolded.

"Girl—you gotta get your head out of the clouds." Pez stood in the entrance to the kitchen, holding a stack of clean plates. She smiled and shook her head. "You are really full of yourself this morning."

The spell had been broken. The plate wobbled, and Angelica caught it before it hit the ground. "Testing my limits, that's all."

"You crossed that line a *long* time ago," Pez said. "When I'm feeling particularly invincible, God has a way of bringing me back down to earth." She slid the plates onto the shelf under the counter. Pez patted Angelica's hand. "Remember . . . let God be God. This is an apron you're wearing. Not a cape. Be the girl God created you to be. You're not a superhero."

Angelica laughed. "Definitely not." She was just . . . *gifted*. In ways others didn't understand. "So don't worry. No more cape." There was no need for it now anyway. Angelica pretty much had everything under control.

CHAPTER 52

Atlantic Ocean
Tuesday, October 26, 10:00 a.m.

THIS WASN'T ABOUT REVENGE. It was a rematch.

The last time he'd squared off against Gatorbait, Clayton hadn't expected a confrontation. He'd had no time to think out his strategy. But now he'd had lots and lots of time to think about how he'd do things differently—if fate ever gave him a chance. And fate was handing him a royal do-over.

This time, there'd be no contest. Clayton wouldn't just control the situation; he'd own it. He'd dominate. Orchestrate the whole thing to the tune of Dad's creepy stalker song but with Clayton's endless new lyrics.

"Gonna make you shake, gonna make you quake,
Since the big jailbreak, you've been wide-awake, 'cuz I'm watching you."

Maybe after he'd had his rematch, he'd replace it with another tune. Some rousing sea shanty he could belt out over the waves as he made another flawless getaway.

Retribution proved to be all the boat he'd hoped—and more. The thing plowed through rough waters and charged ahead when the seas flattened. The four Mercs on the stern were more than equal to the task. It was as if *Retribution* had been looking for a captain who could push it to its limits. Clayton drove like he was being chased—even though he had no worries in that department.

The Jericho Prison failure had created such mayhem, such confusion, that likely they would never sort it all out. They'd be identifying bodies—or pieces of bodies—for a long time. Officials would never be sure what had happened to the one-armed convict they'd known as Kingman. They'd be left with only two possibilities: Either the gators hadn't saved any leftovers, or he'd gotten clean away. To cover their own failure, he was pretty sure they'd eventually make a statement that all prisoners were accounted for. Clayton Kingman had done it . . . and with style.

Retribution had the latest model of everything that mattered. The GPS navigation system allowed him to run safely after dark. Morgan had long since spent itself in the Gulf of Mexico. Here in the Atlantic, its effects were minimal—if any. *Retribution* absolutely gulped up the distance that separated Clayton from Gatorbait—and the rematch.

When he'd been forced to go to shore for gas, he'd changed into the camo duds before docking at a marina. Nobody questioned a vet. It just wasn't polite. The most they'd ask was about his unit—or where he'd served. Nobody asked about his arm, but he saw the way they'd glance at the empty sleeve. Deep down, they wanted to know.

Give people what they want—and you'll never be at a loss for friends. He'd heard that somewhere. And he did that—every time he stopped. He'd actually had fun concocting stories about how he'd lost his arm. His favorite?

"I was an EOD tech—sorry, that's an explosive ordnance disposal specialist. And I was good at my job. When a bomb was found, it was my duty to render it useless. My last mission . . . it was dark. Raining. We were under fire. We were ordered to fall back, but an IED was found—an improvised explosive device—that blocked our escape. The enemy was closing in—and I went to work on the thing. Unfortunately, it had a remote activator. So instead of me disarming it, it disarmed me."

That story always got gasps. It also earned him free coffee, fresh donuts, and crisp salutes. He explained that now he was just a vet who'd been given a couple of months on his uncle's boat to run the coast and find himself before adjusting to single-handed civilian life.

Maybe when this was all over and he'd given time for things to cool down, he'd do charter trips among the countless Bahama Islands. Business execs. Millionaires. Honeymooners. He'd anchor in some secluded bay at night. Maybe he'd schmooze with the guests on deck for a bit and spin the kinds of stories they'd want to hear. He smiled. It wasn't a bad plan. There would be a time for that . . . a time for everything, really. He just couldn't rush things.

His dad had been obsessed with time. As a principal, he'd loved the bell that signaled the change of periods throughout the school day. And he'd been no less time-conscious when he got home. He was all about time. *Hurry up. You're late. I don't have all day. Nickels holding up dimes.*

Clayton appreciated time too . . . but without his dad's OCD focus on it.

Time was important. Right now, Kingman was *making* good time. But time was about a whole lot more than just hours and minutes. The important thing about time was simply how you spent it. And once Clayton got to Rockport, he was going to have the time of his life.

CHAPTER 53

HARLEY LIKED WILSON. The guy fit right in. And he treated Ella with respect. The Hurricane Morgan survivor sat at the counter, sampling apple fritters, cinnamon donuts, vanilla bars, and everything else Pez slid in front of him.

"Seriously, Miss Lopez," Wilson said, "you should think about expanding. Opening a southern branch. You'd have every blue crab fisherman, airboat jockey—every local, and every tourist lining up outside your doors. And National Park rangers. Scads of them."

Miss Lopez laughed. "Hmmm. Tempting, Wilson. But I have rangers up here, too."

"She isn't going to the Glades," Jelly said. "I won't let her. Besides, from the video footage I saw, there's nothing left down there anyway."

Wilson shrugged. "See? No competition." The guy played it off, but even Harley saw a little twinge when Jelly mentioned all the destruction.

Miss Lopez pointed at the tooth necklace hanging around Wilson's neck. "I like your necklace."

Harley liked it too. It fit Wilson. Defined him. Parks used to wear its twin, once upon a time.

"But I'm not so sure I'd like a place with so many alligators," Miss Lopez said.

"Are you kidding? Once the gators get a taste of these apple fritters, they'll be lining up too."

"Okay, that's it." Jelly stepped up behind Wilson and helped him off the stool. "Any guy who romanticizes the Glades *cannot* sit at this counter."

"Oh, there's nothing romantic about them," Wilson said. "But that's what I love. Every time you leave the Glades, you know you've cheated death. Kind of a good feeling."

Harley understood that. Like surviving a football game against a big rival.

"And this guy is one of the more sane ones." Jelly said. "There are some real crazies down there. They basically choose to live in the swamp."

"The fearless type," Harley said.

Wilson grinned and clapped Harley on the back.

"Or brainless, Harley." Jelly shooed Wilson away. "Now go take a tour of town with Parker or something. We'll catch you later. You're going to scare away our customers with your wild hair and gator talk."

Parker promised they'd all meet later, and Harley walked the two of them to the door. He stood there for a moment, watching them laugh and talk with each other as they walked down Bearskin Neck.

Guys like Wilson had the ability to make friends easily. Harley? Not so much. Miss Lopez, Ella, and Jelly were still talking about him when the Amazon driver dropped a package a good fifteen minutes later.

Harley grabbed a bucket and rag and rubbed out a sticky spot on the floor. Wilson had a way of fitting in. Like he was already part of the family. And he was a great addition.

Was Harley jealous? No. He honestly didn't feel that at all. Wilson was fun. Definitely his own person. But there was nothing about him that Harley wished for himself. To live in the Glades? No. To mesmerize people with his stories of alligators and snakes and brushes with death? No, thanks. To be able to drive an airboat anytime he wanted? Nope. There was only one thing Wilson had that Harley desperately wanted. A dad.

It struck him that out of their little group—Parks, Ella, Jelly, and now Wilson—Harley was the only one with no family. It was the one way he was so different from the others. One way he just didn't fit. Sure, he had an uncle, but after that last visit, Harley couldn't call him family anymore.

He was on his own. His uncle's words replayed in his mind. How long would the others want him around? It wasn't like he was family—or had a long history with them.

"Harley," Miss Lopez motioned him over. "Got something for you."

He dropped the rag in the bucket and hustled over.

She was smiling and held out the package that had been delivered minutes earlier. "I think this is for you."

"O . . . kay."

Ella and Jelly watched. Jelly looked clueless, but clearly Ella knew exactly what was going on.

Harley took the open package and pulled out a BayView Brew Coffee and Donut Shop apron—with his name embroidered below the logo.

"You're officially part of the Brew Crew now." Miss Lopez beamed. "And the Crew has each other's back. You've already showed you can do that. You're a protector. Every family needs one—even work families."

Family.

"Whoa, whoa, whoa." Jelly waved both hands like she was trying to stop traffic. "Protector . . . isn't that a tad extreme? We're talking about Harley here, remember?"

"Says the girl who hid under a table," Ella said, "while Harley *protected* her from an obnoxious customer."

"I could've handled Scorza," Jelly said. "If anyone is a protector around here, the obvious answer is—"

"Harley." Miss Lopez ended the discussion right there.

Harley slipped the new apron over his head and tied it behind his back. He ran his thumb across the raised stitching. "Thanks, Miss Lopez. It means a lot." And not just because of his name on the apron.

The owner of BayView Brew seemed pleased.

"Look at the smile on Harley's face," Ella said. "You'd think he won a million bucks."

To be called part of a family—even in a joking way? "I kinda did."

CHAPTER 54

PARKER AND WILSON SAT AT THE KITCHEN TABLE, working on a mid-afternoon snack. Wilson's gator-tooth necklace hung outside his T-shirt—looking absolutely menacing.

Mom set glasses on the counter, and Parker gave the carton of chocolate milk a good shake. He filled the cups to the top, with the bubbly froth rising above the brim.

Mom produced a plate piled high and deep with fresh chocolate chip cookies. "Something to help heal Wilson's wounds—or take his mind off them." She stared at his bandaged arm for a moment. "Have you been changing those dressings?"

He grabbed a cookie but with a look like he'd just been caught stealing the thing.

"You stay right here."

"Busted, Amigo," Parker said. "She's going to make you get that changed morning, noon, and night."

She was back in minutes with gauze and wrap and antibiotic ointment. Parker watched the great unveiling. The edges of the wound, jagged and angry-looking. There must have been fifty stitches in his forearm alone. "Oh, Wilson," Mom said. "A few more like this, and your arm will look like Parker's."

Wilson grinned. "I'm thinking of saving up for a tattoo when it heals. Let the artist get creative—you know, where they use the scar as part of the picture."

She patted the back of his hand. "Like the head of Frankenstein's monster? Promise you'll run any tattoo ideas by me before you ink up this strong arm of yours."

He gave a half smile.

Parker grabbed a couple of cookies, gulped down half the glass of chocolate milk, and trotted off to his bedroom. He rummaged through drawers. Checked under his bed—and the guest bed. No gator-tooth necklace. He had to find the thing. It had meant something when Wilson gave it to him . . . and he kicked himself for getting sloppy.

Maybe his mom had found it and stashed it somewhere. Parker drifted back into the kitchen. Wilson's arm had been rewrapped, and now she was working on his leg.

"Why this thing didn't get totally infected is a mystery," Mom said. "So is the fact that you're alive, young man."

"I'd call it a miracle."

Mom looked him right in the eyes. "Do you really believe that? Because I do . . . with all my heart."

He reached for the gator tooth and held it. "I don't know. Maybe. When I was trapped between *Typhoon* and the cypress trees . . . and those gators were on the hunt for me? I *might* have prayed."

Okay, Parker definitely hadn't expected the conversation to go there.

"To the Almighty God of the universe?" There was no judgment in Mom's tone, but she pointed at his necklace. "Or some god of the Everglades?"

Wilson laughed. "The exact words out of my mouth?" Wilson paused like he wasn't sure he wanted to say more. "I cried out to 'Parker's God.'"

Parker stared at him. "You said *that?*"

Wilson shrugged, looking really uncomfortable now. "I was desperate." He stuffed a cookie in his mouth, like maybe if he filled it enough, he wouldn't have to say more.

"And not only did you make it," Mom said, "but Parker's God sent *Parker*—led him right to you. *Miracle* absolutely *is* the right word. You want to talk about this some more?"

His hesitation said it all. "How about another time?"

"I'm going to hold you to that." Mom shook her finger at him. "And I mean before you go back home."

Wilson laughed. "You have my word."

Over the last of the cookies and chocolate milk, details of a plan came together for the whole group to meet at the Headlands after dinner. Parker texted the invites just as Mom breezed back in.

"Has your grandpa mentioned anything about planning another trip to Rockport?"

Parker loved the idea. His visit in August had been too short. "Nope."

Mom fanned a postcard in the air. "That's what I thought. So I wonder why he's getting mail here? From Florida of all places." The postcard pictured a closeup of a nasty-looking gator.

Parker frowned and held his hands out to block the card from his line of vision. "Put that thing away, Mom. I've seen enough gators for a while." *For a lifetime.*

Wilson stared at the thing. "Me, too."

CHAPTER 55

WILSON KICKED OFF HIS SHOES BY THE FIRE and wandered closer to the water. He lived by the water. Lived *in* it sometimes. But the Atlantic was a whole different animal than the Everglades.

Still waters versus wild ones. Shallow versus deep. But both places possessed an untamed wildness. Unspeakable dangers.

From a distance, the rocky coastline looked like the boulders had been rounded and worn smooth by the surf, but the rock under his feet was plenty rough.

The water looked black, with foaming crests as white as an egret's feathers. The swells rose and mounted their attack on the shore. In a rush of sudden speed, dark water marbled by streaks of foam charged into spaces and fissures between the rocks. Like victory was assured, the water raced upward until it ran out of gas or met an unmoving boulder face.

How many times had he charged into the Glades like it was a test of manhood? And every time he'd returned as unchanged as when he'd gone in. Not in retreat but in complete control. Except this last time.

Now he saw the Glades for what they really were. Unbeatable. Hard as rock. The Glades were so much bigger than he was. Wilson wasn't conquering the Everglades every time he went in—the way he'd always seen it before. He was inconsequential. Like a water beetle resting on a gator's tail. He wasn't part of the Glades. He didn't belong. Who was he anymore?

Shake it off, Wilson. You're a Miccosukee. You conquer . . . not the other way around.

"Gorgeous, isn't it?" Jelly stepped up beside him.

"But the waves never learn." Wilson watched a swell rise. "They keep beating themselves against the shore—only to get sucked back out again. Seems pointless."

"I see persistence," Jelly said. "The shore doesn't permanently break them. They draw back. Regroup. And show they can do this all night."

"Maybe the waves are just stupid. Maybe they think they're more than they are."

"Or maybe they're relentless."

He smiled. "I like relentless." The Atlantic stormed up a rock alley and left a geyser of spray—as if to tell the world it was there—before retreating. "Relentless."

She hooked his arm in hers and dragged him from the water's edge. "Everybody is here—and they're asking where our Hurricane Morgan survivor is hiding."

Hiding. Another good word . . . and maybe the best word to describe who he really was right now.

CHAPTER 56

ELLA JOINED THE OTHERS AROUND THE FIRE made from sun-dried drift-wood. She took off her cowgirl boots and set them close to the blaze. They'd feel nice and toasty when she put them back on later. Ella and Jelly shared a boulder on one side of the fire. Harley, Parker, and Wilson each had rocks on the other side.

Anybody who said boys didn't think just didn't know how to watch them. That was Ella's theory, anyway. Maybe it was her love for art—for capturing both the seen and unseen on canvas—that taught her to notice what others didn't. She'd learned to watch faces. Body language. She paid attention to tone of voice. To the things said. And more importantly, the things not said.

And there were things both Wilson and Harley weren't saying. Sure, they laughed. Joked. Talked loud. But there was a silent cry coming from deep inside both of them. A nameless, deep pain. Different for each—but real. Ella heard it. But until she knew the source of that pain . . . she was powerless to help.

She loved what Pez had done for Harley. Okay, it was just a silly apron . . . but calling him a protector? It was perfect. How many times could Ella have put that label on him herself?

The moon twinkled off the surface of the water—even with the swells pounding in. The dancing lights formed a magical-looking path out to sea. The lights created an illusion of safety, beckoning dreamers to hop in a boat and follow the light—to nowhere. Ella had no desire to follow some make-believe path to happiness. Whether seen or unseen, she wanted what was real. And much of what she wanted was right here around the fire.

Normally, fires draw mosquitos at night. They hover over the people sitting around the flames. They look for an unprotected, vulnerable spot where they can insert their stinger and draw blood. In one unguarded moment, the damage is done. Some mosquitos carry disease. Others are just an irritant. But long after they've been swatted away, the poison they've left under the skin continues to itch. It has the power to keep you from sleeping at night. But here, this night on the Headlands, the air was too chilly for mosquitos. The night was perfect—and up to that point, bug-free. But one bug slipped through, and it was a big one.

Bryce Scorza shuffled up to the fire, wearing his football jersey over his hoodie. One hand gripped a football, and the other rode in his back pocket. "Hey."

His greeting was met by groans.

Wilson looked at him. "Hey, Abercrombie. If you're looking for the photo shoot, you've got the wrong place."

"Abercrombie?" Scorza smiled like he thought the name was a compliment. "Like the store . . . with the pictures of really cool people doing really cool things?"

"If you think sleazy is cool." Wilson laughed. "They're actors and models . . . pretending to be somebody they're not. They pretend to be cool—and pretend to do cool things. They're fakes—trying to sell you on something."

Scorza struck a pose. "Abercrombie. I actually like that. Anyway, I saw the fire. Mind if the QB joins this little huddle?"

"Yes, we kinda do mind," Jelly said.

Scorza laughed. "You kill me, Everglades."

"So leave—before I really do."

Wilson smiled. Like he'd missed being around Jelly—especially when she was standing up to an egomaniac like Scorza.

"Okay. I'll leave in a minute." Scorza sat. Not exactly in the circle but slightly outside it. Closer to the girls than the guys, for sure. "I'm just resting my feet. No law against that. Just ignore me."

"Ignore you?" Jelly gave him an incredulous look. "I wish it was that easy, Mr. Scorza."

Scorza grinned. "Ah . . . so you find Abercrombie hard to ignore. I'll take that as a compliment."

"You would. It's hard to ignore someone who turns up around every corner."

"He asked us to ignore him," Harley said. "So let's do that."

And that was it. At first it was pretty obvious how hard they worked to pretend he wasn't there. And then, incredibly, it didn't seem like an act anymore. Maybe the rhythm of the surf lulled them into a bit of complacency. Maybe it was the sparks rising from the fire. But it was as if they *did* forget he'd invaded their little community. But to Ella, he was still a mosquito. Hovering. Waiting for someone to drop their guard. Looking for a way to draw blood—or get whatever it was he'd come for.

Jelly settled back, staring at the fire. She tucked her hands inside her sweatshirt sleeves. Parker gave an update he'd gotten from his dad. There'd been a few more rescues. The water was finally going down, but the morgue in Naples was filling fast. The conversation drifted to Clayton Kingman. Incredibly, Wilson hadn't heard about the prison transfer—or the jailbreak. Which said volumes about just how much of a threat Parker had really thought Kingman might be.

Jelly was more than happy to fill Wilson in on the whole fiasco. She rattled off the stats. How many had escaped, been recaptured, found dead in the swamps. But there were still convicts unaccounted for—including Kingman.

"If he was anywhere in the Glades during Morgan," Wilson said, "he's dead."

Jelly shrugged. "You made it."

The fire showed something in Wilson's face Ella couldn't quite read. "He's not that tough."

Everyone laughed—even Scorza.

They were quiet for a few moments. The troubles of Hurricane Morgan and Clayton Kingman grew more distant. The surf thundered the shoreline twice more before anyone spoke.

"I'm betting some gator is fattening himself up on the scumbag right now." Wilson nodded like it was a fact.

There was something about the way Wilson said it—with such confidence—that it was enough to turn the mood. Maybe Ella could keep the change going—at least away from Jelly's haunting memories of Clayton Kingman. Sometimes people tried to forget whatever was scaring them by watching a scary movie—or reading a scary book. Something even more scary than whatever was making them afraid deep inside. The tactic had always worked for Ella.

"Okay," Ella said. "We have a dark night and a great fire. It's spooky story time."

Harley snickered. "Like real-life experiences . . . or ghost stories?"

"You treat ghost stories as if they *aren't* real, Mr. Lotitto. Have I ever told you the story of the Mastersons? Real people—who really lived—and still haunt their old home in Gloucester, some say."

Harley covered his ears in mock horror. "Please—not the *Masterson* story! I don't know if I can handle that."

"You're right. You can't," Jelly said. "It's a terrifying story. None of you boys could handle it."

All the guys seemed to think that was hilarious.

"Well," Ella said, "when you boys get a little older—and a *lot* braver . . . maybe I'll tell you that story."

"How about some true stories," Scorza said. "Like, what was the scariest day of your life? Mine was just this past summer . . . the day my Jeep Wrangler was stolen. I didn't even have my license—and my wheels were gone? You talk about *scary*—"

"That's not even remotely scary," Harley said. "And I'm pretty sure we agreed to ignore you."

"How about you, swamp guy?" Scorza's voice carried a challenge to it. "I know it's a national park. But it can still get scary, right? Like at night, when they lock the gates?"

"National *park?*" Wilson emphasized the word. "You make it sound so civilized, Abercrombie. Like it's nothing but nature trails and scenic views. Picture spots and picnic tables. But the Glades ain't no zoo—because there are no cages. And it ain't no park. It's more like a Jurassic Park. Filled with monsters that have survived since prehistoric times. Cold-blooded carnivores. Meat-eaters.

"People think the hundreds of square miles of national park were set apart to protect wildlife?" The firelight reflected off Wilson's eyes. Cast deep shadows across his face. "I say it was the opposite. The parks were set aside to protect people *from* the wildlife. Those areas were set aside because of the vicious wildlife there that absolutely cannot be tamed. National parks are danger zones. That's why there's so many rangers and rules. All that is to keep people from becoming the prey of the monsters that hunt there . . . especially at night."

Scorza looked pleased. "Okay, then. You ought to be able to scare up a story that will send a chill up Black Beauty's back."

Wilson looked at him across the fire for a long moment. "Lots of things about the Glades can give a guy the heebie-jeebies—even a tough football player like yourself. It's a spooky place on a good day."

Scorza snickered. "Heebie-jeebies? Is that worse than the willies?"

Wilson stared at him. He brushed the hair out of his eyes. "So, what's your preference—my scariest day in the Everglades . . . or scariest hour?"

"Let's start with the scariest hour."

Ella looked from Jelly to Parker. Neither of them seemed all that sure if Wilson was going to talk or not. The surf pounded. And again.

Wilson leaned forward and rested his elbows on his knees. "I was out on an airboat. Know what that is, Abercrombie?"

Scorza rolled his eyes. "Little boats with big fans on the back."

Wilson gave him a long look. The kind that can make someone squirm a bit. "The big fans are airplane props mounted to a large-block engine. In this case it was a Chevy 350—which is capable of creating a blast behind that airboat of over one hundred miles per hour. That's hurricane force.

"And that little boat you spoke of is much more than an aluminum hull. It's the only thing between you and certain death. It is the one thing that keeps you at the top of the food chain when you're in the Glades. Without that *little* boat . . . you'll become *part* of the food chain."

"Got it." Scorza motioned with one hand. "Get on with the story— or was that it?"

"Scorza," Parker said. "Maybe you—"

"It's okay," Wilson said. "Abercrombie wants his bedtime story. And I'll give it to him." Wilson looked out into the darkness, like he was going back in time to the very day. The very spot where something horrible had happened.

"We were far enough into the Glades to get anyone lost who didn't know how to find their way out. The sun was dropping fast. And the Glades were coming alive the way they only do at night. There are only two kinds of creatures in the Glades at night: those that hunt and those that hide.

"It was feeding time . . . and the Glades were especially hungry. Two friends rode on the airboat with me. A guy—and a girl. I'd cut the engine for a closer look at a big gator. I threw chunks of French bread until I'd lured him right there beside the airboat. An eleven-foot brute. Thick black hide . . . strong enough to withstand a point-blank shot with a 9mm—unless you place it through the eye socket, or get up under that massive jaw and shoot up through his neck and into the brain. The thing was all male, all nasty, and all about wanting an easy meal."

The fire's reflection glinted off the silver cap on the gator tooth around his neck. As he leaned forward, the tooth hung suspended from the leather tie, swinging in the breeze.

"My friend—the girl—desperately wanted a picture by the gator. Just me, her . . . and the gator, you know?" He paused. His eyes narrowed. "Now, my other friend, he wanted to leave. Had a bad feeling about it all. But we pressured him to take some shots. And against his better judgment, that's what he did. He wanted to get it over with—and get out of the Glades. So he threw himself into getting those pictures. At crazy angles. His hand out over the water. Low."

Ella knew this story. Part of it anyway. But even now, Wilson told it from his unique perspective, and he filled in blanks that Ella had wondered about. She watched Jelly. Her face . . . drawn. Haunted.

"None of us saw the other gator coming. A twelve-foot male had crept up from behind the airboat. I'd been so focused on that stupid picture—and watching out for the gator in front of me." Wilson looked out over the black Atlantic for a moment before staring back at the fire.

"I screamed out a warning—knowing even as I did, I was too late. My friend pulled back—but with one thrust of its tail, that gator lunged with incredible speed. He grabbed my friend right here." He clamped his hand over the bandage on his own forearm. "And an instant later—he was gone."

Scorza's eyes were wide. "Pulled off the airboat?"

"Right into the black waters of the Everglades."

The fire popped. Scorza jumped, then settled back in. "What happened?"

"The beast put him in a death roll. Churned the water with the most sickening sound you've ever heard. That and the girl's screams combined to make a horrifying soundtrack. *Do something, Wilson . . . do something!*"

Nobody around the fire moved. Ella hadn't even swallowed in the last minute.

"The gator had the water churned into a bloody froth before he released his grip. He must have figured my friend was dead. I sure did."

"So he *didn't* die?"

Wilson stared at the fire. "He stood. Water was maybe up to his ribs. His arm—like totally mangled. We were shouting for him to hurry—to get back to the boat so we could pull him in before the gator realized he was going to lose his prey."

Did Scorza have any idea who Wilson was talking about? Ella was pretty sure he didn't. But Harley knew. He held his head in his hands like he couldn't imagine it—or maybe he was imagining what would have happened if he'd lost his very best friend before he'd had a chance to meet him.

"I should've jumped in. I don't know why I didn't. The other gator—the one I'd been taunting—was there. So maybe that was it. But there is a raw survival thing inside all of us. Maybe I knew how slim a chance my friend really had. And if I jumped in, there would be two of us who likely wouldn't make it.

"So we shouted . . . urged him on . . . and he sloshed his way to the airboat, leaving a trail of blood behind him. We struggled to pull him in, and the girl was reaching, pulling up his legs . . . her arms up to her elbows in water. If that gator had come back, he'd have gotten her, too. But we got him on the deck. Pulled his legs away from the edge of the boat so the gator couldn't rip him away from us.

"But he was bleeding bad. Bleeding out. We made a tourniquet, and the girl did her best to hold that in place—and keep him from sliding off the deck on the ride back to the docks." Wilson stopped. Still staring at the fire like he was seeing the story in his head.

"Did he . . . die?" Scorza's question seemed to shake Wilson out of his silence.

He looked at Scorza. "He made it until we got to the dock. And then, yeah, he died."

Tears streamed down Jelly's cheeks.

"But somehow, paramedics got him going again."

"Wait . . . they saved his life?"

Wilson shrugged. "It was the girl who did that. She's the one who kept him alive until we got to shore. He died seconds after she was pulled away from him."

Scorza looked a tiny bit confused. "But he . . . came back."

Wilson nodded.

"Bet he never went back in the Everglades again, am I right?"

Wilson shook his head. "A friend went missing in the Glades. Then there was no stopping him from searching."

"Sounds like an idiot," Scorza said. "All that for a picture. Did he lose that arm?"

"No, but he never got full function back either."

Scorza's eyes narrowed. "Wait, that was Gatorade?"

"You're quick." Ella looked at him in disgust. "I really hope you're faster on the field, Mr. Scorza."

"So, Gatorade," Scorza said, "I finally got to hear the real story behind the freaky arm. Gutsy girl, too."

He looked pleased with himself for insisting that Wilson share. "Great story, swamp guy. How about another one? We've heard your scariest moment story. Now—the scariest *day*."

Ella couldn't believe Scorza. How could he just sit there and not be moved more than that?

"You don't want to hear about my scariest day," Wilson said. "You'd never sleep."

Scorza snickered. "Hey, I've seen some pretty scary guys on the field. I mean, they come at you like they want to rip your head off."

"Well, the Glades ain't no game," Wilson said. "There are no whistles to stop a play. No penalty flags. Losers don't get second chances. It's predator or prey. Life or death. And when you're trapped between an upturned airboat and cypress trees, and you know you'll never be found . . . and you can't get free . . . you learn something about fear."

Ella held her breath. What had he gone through?

"And when the gators find you . . . all you can do is keep kicking.

But they keep coming. And you know if you miss one time—if just once you aren't quick enough—you're not going to lose some yardage. You're going to lose your life." He lowered his head like he was spent.

"Hey," Harley said. "Let's give Wilson a break. Somebody else tell us a story."

Harley was at it again—living up to his protector label. Looking out for someone else. Pez should buy him ten new aprons.

"I know the scariest day of *your* life, Lotitto." Scorza's voice had just the tiniest edge to it. A razor—and he was going to cut. Or was it the mosquito coming out in him—ready to draw blood?

"You know what I think?" Ella had no idea what to say, but she sensed she had to stop Scorza.

Scorza waved her off. "The scariest day of Harley's life was when he joined the Dead Dads Club." He found the unguarded spot. Jabbed his stinger deep. "Twelve years old, and he was in a car with his—"

Harley lunged—and was on him. "You shut your stinkin' mouth—"

Jelly scurried out of the way. Wilson and Parker rushed to stop Harley.

Ella stood there—unable to move. *I should have stopped him. I should have stopped him.*

Scorza was on his back—trying to push Harley away. But Harley had pinned him good—with a forearm across Scorza's throat. "You talk about my dad one more time, and I swear I'll mount your teeth on a necklace and wear it to your funeral."

Wilson had one of Harley's arms, Parker the other. Together they pulled him off Scorza. Harley's fuse extinguished almost as fast as it'd been lit. "I'm okay. I'm okay. Sorry. That's not who I want to be. Sorry." He rolled his shoulders. Raised both hands to shoulder height.

"Honest. I'm done."

Ella stared at him for a moment. He was serious. Would she have been able to flip the switch on her anger like that if she'd been in his place?

Parker let him go. Wilson gave it a second more and did the same. Harley sat. Stared at the ground. Glanced up at Ella. Met her eyes for a second before looking down again.

His eyes . . . apologetic. Like he felt she'd think less of him. Which proved how little he knew about her. But there was pain in his eyes. Yeah . . . he was hiding something. And part of it had to do with his dad—or the fact his dad was gone.

Wilson stood over Scorza, looking absolutely fearsome. "Shoes." He snapped his fingers. "Off."

"Or *what?*"

"Or I take them." Hands on hips, Wilson had a real don't-push-me look going.

Scorza must have picked up on the vibe, because he kicked off his shoes without another word. Wilson picked them up, bounced one in his palm as if testing the weight, and heaved the thing out over the Atlantic. The surf was coming in too heavy to hear the splash—or that of the second shoe that followed.

"What did you do that for?"

Wilson glared at him. "You shoot off your mouth like a guy who's never thought about someone else's pain. Never thought about what it might be like to walk in that person's shoes. Maybe if you walk home *without* shoes—because of your big mouth—you'll think about the hurt you cause others by saying stupid things."

They'd let the bug stay by their fire, and he'd drawn blood—from one of the nicest guys Ella had ever known.

"Now get out of here, Abercrombie," Wilson said. "I'm done trying to ignore you. I want you gone for real."

Scorza stood. Backed away smiling—like he wanted everyone to think he wasn't at all intimidated. The fire's light on his face dimmed. He was twenty feet away before he spoke. "I'll just call an Uber. You know that, right?"

"Then you'll wake up tomorrow just as stupid as you did this morning," Wilson said.

Scorza waved him off. "Right." He disappeared into the shadows of the woods path leading back to the street. The way Ella saw it? It was idiots like him who gave every other guy a bad name.

Harley threw his arm around Wilson's shoulder—and another around Parker's. "Well played. Both of you. And thanks."

With the exception of guys like Scorza, boys knew more about life and friendship than most girls Ella had known throughout her life—until she'd met Jelly, anyway.

"And Harley . . . I love that idea about you making a tooth necklace." Wilson shook the lanyard around his own neck. "But not with Scorza's teeth. Someday you and I . . . the three of us . . . we'll go on a hunt for teeth in the Glades."

"Don't even think about it," Jelly said. "But I did love how you winged his shoes out there."

Wilson looked off in the direction Scorza had disappeared—as if to make sure the guy wasn't coming back. "Next time I throw his shoes in the ocean, he'll be wearing them."

That made Ella laugh right along with the rest of them.

Oh yeah. Wilson's comment proved Ella was right. Boys knew how to think, all right. It's just that they usually didn't think the same way girls did. Anybody who believed boys didn't think just didn't know how to watch them.

CHAPTER 57

PARKER DID A QUICK SWEEP UNDER HIS BED with both arms. No gator tooth necklace.

"Checking for gators?" Wilson strolled into the bedroom, grinning.

Parker flopped on his bed. "After your stories tonight? Everybody at that fire circle is checking under their bed about now. Especially Scorza."

Wilson laughed. "Abercrombie. I kinda hate that guy. And that shot at Harley? That's a page out of Kingman's playbook, right?"

Parker absolutely agreed.

"You ever wonder how all these people with daggers for tongues end up using the same tactics? I mean, it's not like there's an Abuser 101 class anywhere."

Parker thought about that for a minute. "They have the same teacher." He poked both index fingers up like horns, one on each side of his head. "The king of terrors."

The conversation drifted around to Clayton Kingman and what may have happened to him.

"Personally?" Wilson stopped like he wanted to be really careful about what he said next. "I don't think he'd make it through one night. Not with the way I saw the gators acting after the hurricane. It's like they were programmed. Every switch inside them was flipped to *kill*."

Mom ducked her head inside the room. "I talked with Dad. And you *are* going to school tomorrow."

Parker groaned. "But we have a guest. What kind of a friend would I be if I left him here while—"

"Wilson will shadow you. All day. I'll call the school office in the morning. If the principal says no, then we can revisit this."

Which was pretty much guaranteeing there was no chance to get out of it. The principal would probably love the idea that a Hurricane Morgan survivor was in the school.

She kissed each of the boys good night and turned out the light. "Sleep good. Big day tomorrow."

Taking Wilson with him to school? Yeah, that would be a pretty big day.

CHAPTER 58

THERE HAD BEEN MOMENTS AT TONIGHT'S FIRE when Harley had felt like part of a family. But there had been times around that same fire when he had realized he wasn't part of the family at all. Ella had been watching him. He'd felt it. Maybe *studying* was a better word for it. She knew he was different. Like he didn't quite fit.

And he'd proved that once again tonight, hadn't he?

The Dead Dads Club. A lifetime membership Harley had never asked for. Never wanted. Never dreamed he'd have. Harley looked at Kemosabe's key on the lanyard around his neck. Parks wore a spare. And now there was a third key in his tool cabinet. Three keys. But no motorcycle to ride—and no dad to ride with. He dropped the key back underneath his T-shirt.

He hit the bedroom light. Boosted himself up to the top bunk. He grabbed the wrench and ratcheted the thing.

Click-cl-cl-cl-cl-cl-cl-click. Back.

Click-cl-cl-cl-cl-cl-cl-click. Back.

He liked the feel of it vibrating in his hands. Tightening. Tightening. For all that tightening, why was it he still felt like he was falling apart?

He stared at the blank ceiling. Actually, the ceiling wasn't totally empty. A single glow-in-the-dark star sticker had been pressed onto the plaster right within easy reach. One of those greenish, puffy ones that dads put up for their sons instead of a night-light. But the ones who slept in this room didn't have a dad to stick it onto the ceiling.

Had some other kid in the system stuck the star there so he wouldn't feel quite so alone in the dark? Maybe. He honestly hoped it had worked a lot better for that kid than it did for Harley.

How many had a membership for the Dead Dads Club worldwide? Probably too many to count. But still, Harley was on his own, wasn't he? The thing was, there were no DDC members in Rockport High School. Not that Harley had heard, anyway. And he'd been listening.

Alone.

Different from everyone else.

Parker talked about having a father in heaven. So he had a dad *and* a Father? Maybe he was just lucky that way.

"God . . . it would be nice to be part of a real family, You know?"

He stopped.

He'd seen Parker talk with his dad late at night when Harley had bunked at their house. This talking to God thing Harley had just done an instant ago. It was a little bit like talking to a dad, wasn't it? He'd done it before, hadn't he? Had God answered his prayers? Parker had made it back from the Everglades—and he'd found Wilson . . . just like Harley had asked. Was God trying to tell him that He was there for Harley . . . and that He cared?

Click-cl-cl-cl-cl-cl-cl-click. Back.

Click-cl-cl-cl-cl-cl-cl-click. Back.

Then again, maybe Harley was fooling himself. He might as well be talking to the glow-star on the ceiling. He didn't have a dad . . . or a Father . . . and he didn't have a family.

Click-cl-cl-cl-cl-cl-cl-click. Back.
Click-cl-cl-cl-cl-cl-cl-click. Back.

He was truly, completely, and utterly alone. And there was nothing he could do about it.

CHAPTER 59

Rockport, Massachusetts
Wednesday, October 27, 11:10 a.m.

WILSON STOOD INSIDE THE ROCKPORT HIGH entranceway on the way
to lunch. He did a slow 360, checking out the murals. Bucky stopped
beside him, like he sensed Wilson needed a minute. A giant Viking ship.
A lobster boat cruising past an island with twin lighthouses. Wilson was
a long way from home, but the pictures of the sea made him feel just a
little bit closer to the familiar. Quotes and sayings were painted on the
walls. Actually, they were all over the school.

Smooth seas never make a skillful sailor. He stared at the sign.
Everything he'd known was gone. His home. His hometown. His school.
Everglades City—and every business there—now like the lost city of
Atlantis. Swallowed by the sea. He'd lost *Typhoon.* Almost lost his life.
Definitely lost his nerve. Yeah, he knew a little something about rough
seas. But it hadn't made him more skilled. Not at all. It had made him
afraid. And the very *idea* of being afraid scared the heck out of him.

As the morning had gone on, students had stared. Pointed. Kept their distance like he was as wild and untamed as the Glades themselves. Bucky had only introduced him a handful of times—but word must have spread. Now it seemed everybody knew who he was. The long hair, beaded braid, bandaged arm, and assorted cuts and scrapes on his face made for a quick positive ID. *Oh, you're the crazy guy from the Everglades who ignored the evacuation orders.* It was like they wanted to steer clear of him. Maybe they feared some of his bad luck—or judgment—might rub off on them.

Wilson sat in every one of Bucky's classes until lunch. And the teachers were cool about things. They talked to him before class, or after. But not one of them put him on the spot during class. Wilson was kind of surprised and definitely relieved.

"Parker, Wilson, you coming?" Jelly stood at the top of the stairs leading down to the cafeteria and motioned for them to join her. "Lunch period goes quick. You can look at the pretty pictures later."

She laughed and bounded down the steps. Wilson and Parker caught up before she got to the table. Harley and Ella were already there.

Bucky's mom had outdone herself making the bag lunch. A sub sandwich that would rival anything a deli might serve. An apple. Bag of sour cream and onion chips. A pint bottle of chocolate milk. A couple of chocolate chip cookies in a plastic bag. "I didn't realize how much I've missed this."

Parker shrugged. "Hasn't your dad stepped up to the plate?"

"He'd have missed the chips."

Both of them laughed, but neither explained the inside joke to the others. Wilson's dad hadn't ever packed a lunch for him—not even after Mom had gone AWOL. It had been Bucky's mom who'd picked up the slack. Parker had brought two lunches to school until he'd moved north. Wilson had been making his own lunches ever since. Today's lunch showed him just how much he needed to step up his game.

Abercrombie set his tray on the table and sat. He didn't ask permission. Didn't make an apology. He acted like he belonged there. Which kind of annoyed Wilson—because it clearly bothered Jelly.

"So, Everglades Girl. Some of the other girls are, like, all gaga about your swamp friend here. I told them that you two go way back—and how we've all been hanging out."

"Is that what you call what you were doing last night?" Jelly shook her head.

"Hey, you should be thanking me." He actually looked proud. "Because of me, you might start getting a whole lot more popular around here."

"*Ugh!* I have all the friends I need—right here around this table."

Abercrombie gave a little bow. "Well, I'm glad you're seeing me as one of your closest—"

"Don't say it, Scorza," Jelly said. "Don't you say the word, or I'll knock you so far off your stupid social ladder that you'll be climbing for months just to get to ground level."

Abercrombie laughed. "You talk tough, but underneath that big act—"

"Is the toughest, smartest, fiercest girl you've ever met," Wilson said. "She's not afraid to get her hands bloody—whether it's her blood or somebody else's. Personally, if I had a choice between facing an angry gator or an angry Angelica Malnatti? I'm going to go with the gator every time."

Abercrombie didn't seem fazed. "I don't know why you're all so afraid of this girl. Now, you take me, for example—"

"And she could take you," Bucky said. "With one hand tied behind her back . . . so be careful what you say to her."

Harley glanced under the table like he wanted to see if Abercrombie wore shoes. "Wilson was right, you know. You did wake up just as stupid today as you did yesterday."

"Speaking of our swamp friend," Abercrombie said, "when are you going home to all your reptile pals?" Like maybe Abercrombie hoped it would be soon.

"No idea. Maybe when there's a place for me to live down there."

"And that doesn't bother you—even a little bit—that you don't know when you're heading back?"

No. That didn't bother Wilson at all. The thing that was sticking in his craw right now was something completely different—and worse. He wasn't sure he wanted to go back.

CHAPTER 60

ELLA TRAILED BEHIND WILSON AND PARKER to Miss Tivoli's social studies class. Jelly and Harley had a different schedule, and the two of them really looked like they wanted to shadow right along with Wilson all afternoon.

Students scurried in right at the bell. Parker's desk sat on the aisle closest to the window. Ella watched as he pulled up a chair for Wilson just as Miss Tivoli stepped over to meet the real live Hurricane Morgan survivor. She talked with the two of them for a minute before quieting the class.

"Can anybody tell me why our state makes social studies a requirement for graduation?"

There were laughs and groans. "Because they love torturing us." It sounded like Scorza's voice, and the exaggerated laughter from the puppets sitting around him pretty well confirmed it.

"Anybody?" She waited . . . like she hadn't heard Scorza's comment.

Usually, if you hold out long enough, a teacher will fill in the blanks. Fill the void. But Miss Tivoli wasn't like that. She walked the aisles. Up one, down the next. She treated the dry erase marker in her hand like some kind of fidget device. Now tapping it against one palm. Then releasing the cap and snapping it back in place.

"Why study the forces that have shaped—and continue to shape—our world?" She did the slow pacing thing. She obviously wasn't giving up. She'd start calling on people before she'd feed anyone an answer.

Ella kept her eyes down, like most of the others. To make eye contact with her was to practically guarantee being put on the spot.

"Sal?"

Sal "Salami" Rocco slunk a little lower in his seat. "Still working on that one."

"Hmmm." She continued her hunt. "Jackie?"

"Actually, I'm with Salami. We're making this a team project." That earned her some laughs.

Miss Tivoli passed Ella's desk. "Finn. Why study things that shape our world?"

Finn Bilba had a short stack of Oreos on his desk. He usually did—and Miss Tivoli had always been cool with it. If the guy needed brain food, she wasn't about to stop him from snacking. Finn popped an Oreo in his mouth, gave it a solid crunch, and moved both halves to one cheek.

"Maybe it's the best way to know who we are . . . or why we are who we are. Maybe it gives us a crystal ball too."

"A crystal ball?"

"Yeah," Finn said. "To see who we're going to be if we keep going this way."

Miss Tivoli stopped, beaming. "Finn . . . you nailed it. Say that again—and, class . . . listen up. Finn is about to say something incredibly profound."

The class erupted, like putting the name *Finn* and the word *profound* in the same sentence was too much for them to handle. But Ella totally agreed with Miss Tivoli on this one. She jotted down the words *who we are*, *why*, and *crystal ball* on the blank notebook page on her desk.

Miss Tivoli raised her hand to quiet the class. "Finn?"

He slid a bit lower in his seat. "I'm not sure I can say that again."

She breezed over to his desk. "Eat another cookie."

Finn slid another Oreo in his mouth like he was feeding a coin into a vending machine. He shrugged like the thought still wasn't coming back.

Miss Tivoli glanced at the paper on Ella's desk, then met her eyes. "Can you tell the class what Finn said?"

Ella gave a quick look at her notes. "Finn said we need to understand what shapes our world, because that tells us who we are—and how we got here. And most importantly, it gives us a peek into the future . . . a preview as to who we'll become if we stay on this trajectory."

Miss Tivoli gave Ella a thumbs-up, and patted Finn's shoulder. "Well said, Finn."

Finn held up a cookie and twisted off the chocolate wafer top. "That was the double-stuff cream filling talking."

"Keep eating those Oreos," she said. "Obviously they inspire you."

Miss Tivoli went on for twenty minutes about how life shapes us as individuals—and sometimes as societies. "The course of our lives will change. You can wake up someday and wonder who you are—and how you got there. Social studies helps you see the things that change us—so you can fight back if you don't like where that change will take you. It's not just the national things—or the world events. Sometimes it's local—like here in our community back in 1991."

The event that was later to be known as the perfect storm. Yeah, that changed some lives—and ended others. Ella's grandpa knew a couple of them well.

"Sometimes the changes feel so personal, so unique to you, that you feel isolated. Like you're the only person in the world facing this. But you're not. People—societies all over the world—have had the same struggles." She went on to say how important it was to process . . . to talk about what is happening around us. "Make sure the changes are moving you in a good direction. If they're not? Fight . . . and surround yourselves with friends who will help you do that."

Scorza raised his hand. "Kind of like me on game day. We gotta move that ball in the right direction. And I've got an offensive line to help do that." He looked around the room and raised his eyebrows—like he'd said something truly profound too.

"Next time you want to share your wisdom," Ella said, "eat an Oreo first."

The class laughed, and Wilson gave her an approving nod.

"So, let's bring this home." Miss Tivoli raised her hand. "Someone want to share a personal story of something that happened to you or your family . . . something that had the potential to change the course of your life?"

Not a student in the room raised their hand. Finn didn't even move his hand to grab a cookie. Wilson stared out the window—like maybe he was just an unseen observer in the room.

"Okay. Raise your hand if you *don't* want to share."

Hands shot up all over the room, and Ella raised both arms. Wilson still didn't move—like he wasn't expected to respond at all because he was only an observer here. But he looked Miss Tivoli's way—as if he guessed she was looking at him.

"Wilson, you survived one of the worst hurricanes to make landfall in southern Florida. Worse than Hurricane Ian . . . and that was bad. Do you think that will change your life?"

It was too early to ask him a question like that, wasn't it? Miss Tivoli was usually so good at listening and understanding students.

"I don't want to put you on the spot," she said. "Talking about it is hard—but needed."

Wilson sat straighter. Looked at Parker. At Ella. Like he wasn't sure what he should do.

Miss Tivoli sat on the counter below the windows, not three feet from Wilson. It was like the class wasn't there. She focused solely on him.

"I grew up in the Midwest. Something happened when I was in middle school." She talked so softly, the rest of the room got dead quiet just so they didn't miss a word. She described the tornado that had ripped through her community when she was only twelve. How it had changed her town. Changed her. And not all in good ways. She had never processed it. Never had anyone who could help her with that.

And in that moment, Ella knew Miss Tivoli wasn't putting Wilson on the spot at all. She was throwing him a lifeline. Maybe she saw herself in him and wanted to give him the help she hadn't gotten. She knew he needed a nudge to talk about what had happened so he could heal.

Miss Tivoli's words had a soothing effect. Wilson visibly relaxed. His jaw. His hands. Ella glanced at the clock, not wondering when class would be over but hoping there was more time than she feared there was.

"You did what most would say is impossible. You rode out a Category 5 hurricane." She tapped her own forearm. "You picked up some souvenirs along the way, I'd guess."

She talked again about the tornado of her childhood. The sound. The terror. She described the tornado as a giant top that somebody had set loose. The thing had spun into town, destroying everything it touched.

"So, Hurricane Morgan . . . was it like my tornado in some ways?"

There it was—a direct question to Wilson. Something easy. Something to draw him out a bit. She was a master at this.

He took a deep breath. Blew it out. Wilson seemed to be searching for the right words.

Finn leaned across the aisle and handed him a couple of Oreos.

Wilson stared at the cookies in his hand. "You ever wonder why tornados aren't given names?"

Miss Tivoli angled her head slightly, like she'd never thought of that.

"They come and go so quick. They blow through a town in what, thirty seconds? There's no time for introductions. They rev themselves up and spin themselves out before they can be given a name. Hurricanes are different. Hurricane Morgan was no giant's toy. It was an enemy invasion. It destroyed every wall of resistance. It occupied our entire town. Morgan owned Chokoloskee . . . and Everglades City . . . and more. It stayed and stayed and stayed—until it searched out every spot where a soul might hide . . . and tore it apart."

Ella was holding her breath. She was pretty sure everybody in class was doing the same.

"Morgan was a demon—hungry for blood. It shredded the home of every one of my neighbors. But I couldn't help anybody—because Morgan had me pinned down too."

Ella had a feeling Wilson had never said so much at one time in his entire life. The class sat in a stunned silence.

"So, no, Miss Tivoli," Wilson said. "Hurricane Morgan wasn't like a tornado at all. It was a hundred tornadoes . . . holding hands . . . walking across town."

Miss Tivoli sat there a long moment. "Your home?"

"Gone. Everything was taken. I left with my bug-out bag. And the friend who cared enough to find me."

Now Parker was the one staring at the floor. Wilson slid a little lower in his seat. Clearly he was done.

"World events shape us," Miss Tivoli said. "Personal events shape us. Honestly looking at and *talking* about where we are—and how we got there—is important. And it may give us the chance to make changes before those events turn our world—personal or global—into a place we don't want it to become."

The bell rang, and it broke the spell Wilson and Miss Tivoli had cast in the room. Suddenly, the room was buzzing. Ella heard words like *Category 5, so brave,* and—from more than a couple of girls—*cute.* A few of the guys hung near Parker and Wilson, like they thought some hero status might rub off on them somehow. Scorza brushed by, bragging about how he'd whipped a football team called the Hurricanes when he was a kid.

Ella stared at him. "You're *still* just a kid." How could he talk about a football game after all that?

Miss Tivoli hugged Wilson and said something close to his ear. He nodded, and she let him go.

Ella fell in alongside Parker and Wilson. The three of them hurried down the hall. Not to get to the next class but to keep from being stopped. Finn caught them anyway—and held out a plastic sandwich bag of Oreos. "I'll never forget what you said. Take this, okay?"

Wilson didn't hesitate—which seemed to make Finn happy.

"Food can't really fix things. But sometimes it helps." Finn turned and headed the other way.

Parker rounded the corner, pulled up, and leaned against the wall. "Sorry, Wilson. Miss Tivoli put you on the spot."

He shook his head. "She was trying to help. I don't like talking about it. But I might need to."

"Just not aloud—in front of a class of students," Ella said. "Right?"

He smiled but was staring across the hall. "Something like that."

She followed his gaze. Another quote on the wall. *Let go of who you think you're supposed to be. Embrace who you are.* "Yeah, that's an interesting quote. What do you think of that?"

"Sounds off. Like something Abercrombie lives by." Wilson stuffed an Oreo in his mouth. "Parks?"

"Agreed. I need to think on it a bit more." Parker shot a picture of it. She imagined the two of them kicking it around late tonight. "But first reaction? I want to be more than who I am now. I want to improve. I want to be like my heroes. That's not something I plan to let go of. It's something I'm reaching for."

Ella could see that.

"I totally get that." Wilson looked at the quote for a long moment. "And how can a guy embrace himself—especially if he doesn't really know who he is anymore, right?"

CHAPTER 61

PARKER AND WILSON POLISHED OFF THE LAST of Mom's cookies.

"Your grandpa got another postcard today." Mom pointed to the stack of mail on the counter. "Actually, two more."

Parker scanned the counter to be sure there were no more cookies around. "Sounds like he's got a friend in Florida."

Wilson smiled. "*Every* senior has a friend living in Florida."

"Well, these two are postmarked from New York. But clearly they're from the same person. There's something weird about them."

"About the cards—or the sender?" Actually, to Parker it was a little weird that Grandpa got any mail at their house. But there was a first time for everything, right?

Mom placed the new cards on the table, including the one from the day before. "You tell me."

All three postcards pictured gators on the front. He turned them over. There were only initials, GB, where Grandpa's name should have been.

Otherwise, the address was fine. "GB? Seems odd not to write his full name—Gabe Buckman. I guess the mail carrier figured it out, though."

"That's just it," Mom said. "I've never heard anyone call him GB."

Parker shrugged. He really wasn't sure why Mom was making such a big deal about all this.

"That's not all." Mom looked at him like he was missing something. "Read the cards."

Parker picked one up.

Been a long time. Since you haven't come for a visit, I'll come to you.

Nothing all that weird about that one—except for the fact it hadn't been signed. The word *Breath* was written on the bottom . . . like maybe the sender used it for scratch paper. He handed it off to Wilson and grabbed another one. The handwriting was the same. Sloppy. Maybe shaky, like whoever wrote it was somewhere north of eighty years old.

Got a huge surprise for you. Can't wait to see your face.

Another word was scrawled at the bottom: *Every.* Again, no signature. No indication of who had sent it. "Must be someone Grandpa knows well—enough not to have to sign it, anyway."

"Exactly," Mom said. "To send a card but not sign it? I find that strange."

The third card wasn't much longer than the other two.

Got this song in my head. Find myself singing it at the strangest times . . . and it always makes me think of you. Maybe I'll sing it to you when I see you.

You Take was jotted along the bottom, with a single line through it, like whoever wrote it was in the middle of a thought, forgot what he wanted to say, and decided to just cross it out.

He looked at Wilson and shrugged.

"Simple," Wilson said. "Some old codger in Florida has got dementia or something . . . and he's sending cards that don't make a lot of sense."

Which would explain the random words at the bottom of the cards.

"Maybe that's it." Mom studied one of the cards. "At first I hardly gave it a second thought. GB—for Gabe Buckman. Had to be Grandpa's mail. But why send the cards here? Grandpa has never actually lived at this address. It's a mystery."

And one that probably wasn't worth the time it would take to solve it. "He must have given the address to someone. What else can it be, right?"

"That has to be it. Next time you talk to Grandpa, let him know he's getting mail." Mom smiled. "Maybe he's moving to Rockport and he hasn't told us yet."

Parker laughed. He wouldn't mind that a bit. "I'll talk to him."

Mom tossed the postcards on the counter. The pictures fanned out with the gators gaping at him. Parker restacked them and turned them upside down.

Mom gave an approving nod and then a detailed report of the situation in the search and recovery efforts. "Dinner is at six. What are you two going to do until then?"

Parker went over the plans. Meet up with Harley after football practice. Tool around the harbor in Mr. Steadman's boat. Then after dinner, another fire at the Headlands. But this time, they'd find a spot that wasn't as likely to be seen by Scorza.

On the walk to town, he phoned Grandpa to tell him about the cards. He tapped on the speakerphone so Wilson could hear.

"Well, nobody ever calls me GB. Strike one. And that bit about singing to me? Not something one of my friends would ever suggest. Strike two. And I've never given out your address—to anyone. Strike three. So, it doesn't sound like a friend of mine," Grandpa said. "Maybe the sender has the right address but the wrong people. Somebody owned the house before your parents bought it. Maybe GB was part of *that* family."

That made sense. "They can't be close friends if they didn't know the family moved."

Wilson grinned. "Or GB didn't *want* the guy to know they'd moved—or where they went. Maybe they're hiding from the guy because he's one of those totally demented guys who live on the fringe of the swamp—and sanity. Mystery solved."

"Oh, I feel much better," Parker said. "So you're saying some wacko might be coming to pay ol' GB a visit."

"But instead?" Wilson grinned. "He'll find you."

CHAPTER 62

ANGELICA STOOD ON THE ROCKY SHORE of the Headlands. East Coast sunsets differed from so many other US shorelines. California, the Gulf side of Florida . . . places like that had the postcard sunsets. Sky and clouds ablaze above the water with reds, oranges, pinks, and everything in between. The sun cooling its feet in the ocean. Those picture-perfect sunsets actually made the idea of an early evening swim look inviting. They gave an illusion of safety. Of course, if somebody fell for that, they might become a sharky snack.

That was just one more thing Angelica loved about the East Coast, and especially here in Rockport. When she gazed out over the water at the end of the day, the sun was setting *behind* her. It gave the truer picture. Land was the safe place to be. Terra firma. Solid ground. With the horizon dark, the ocean itself picked up an ominous look. There was no false sense of safety that might lure someone into taking a swim—if the water was warm enough.

Here in Rockport—in her safe place—Angelica should have felt more settled at this moment. Secure. Hey, Parker and Wilson were here. Safe. Clayton Kingman was likely hiding in Florida somewhere, too busy eluding the police to think about getting even with Parker. She should be breathing a sigh of relief. So why did it feel like sometimes she was still holding her breath? That blissful euphoria she'd felt yesterday at the coffee shop had faded with the sunlight. Her ability to jump from table to table was gone. She couldn't put her finger on it, but she had a sense that something wasn't right. Something important.

"Jelly . . . you going to join us?" Parker's voice tugged her from her silly thoughts.

There were a hundred great spots to hang out at the Headlands. And tonight, they'd found one closer to the water—and more secluded. Parker brought a kerosene camping lantern instead of building a fire. One more tactic to be sure there were no uninvited guests.

And no brawls, either.

Sweatshirts. Jeans. The glow from the lantern. The five of them found places to kick back and enjoy the cool air riding to shore on the shoulders of the dark water.

Ella slid her cowgirl boots off. "Remember the story corner idea for the coffee shop?" She set her boots in the circle, like they were one of them. "We could have Wilson there as a guest, telling Everglades stories. After the way he mesmerized everyone in class today? It would draw a crowd."

"Great idea," Harley said. "Kids screaming bloody murder—arms outstretched for their mamas. And this being Halloween week? Perfect timing."

"I was just thinking it could bring Pez even more business."

"Right," Harley said. "And maybe a lawsuit or two."

"Actually, I like Ella's idea," Wilson said. "Free donuts, and I'd get to terrorize kids? Sounds like a fun gig. And maybe, between gator stories . . . we can have *you* tell that Mastodon house story you promised us."

"*Masterson* house," Ella said. "And I'd love to tell you the story—if you think you can handle it."

"Oh, please, Ella." Wilson dropped on his knees. "Don't tell that spooky story. You'll give me the heebie-jeebies for sure."

It was good to see Wilson loosening up. There was so much more Angelica wanted to ask him about. Mostly she wanted to make sure he was really okay. But there was a balance . . . and keeping things light right now seemed like the best medicine for him. Maybe for her, too.

Wilson stared out over the black water. "You sure there's no gators out there?"

"Why?" Angelica poked him with her foot. "You miss them that much?"

"No." He laughed. "I'm just not used to a body of water I dare turn my back to. There was always something there that could kill you if you weren't careful."

But Wilson was the guy who was invisible to gators, right?

"No alligators," Parker said. "But we've got great whites. That dangerous enough for you?"

"Actually," Wilson said, "sounds like a nice change from gators."

Again . . . not at all what Angelica would expect coming out of his mouth. "You just can't get those horrific beasts out of your head, can you? No more alligator talk."

Wilson raised both hands. "Fine with me. But right now, Bucky is the one who can't get away from the gators. He can't even go to the mailbox without thinking of gators. Tell the girls about the postcards."

Parker shrugged. "Not much to say. Somebody sent postcards to my house . . . and all of them have gators on them. At first, my mom thought maybe they were for my grandpa, from a friend in Florida. But I just talked to Grandpa and he said that it doesn't sound like any friend of his."

"What do the cards say?"

Parker put on an act like he was offended. "You think I'd read other people's mail?"

"They're postcards, Mr. Buckman," Angelica said. "You're *supposed* to read them."

Wilson laughed. "Wait, run that by me again?"

"If the person writing the card wanted his message private, he would have put it in an envelope. Postcards are a way of people bragging. *Hey, look where I'm at. Don't you wish you were me?* So, what did the guy say?"

"We don't even know if it *was* a guy," Parker said. "It could be some long-lost love from high school or something like that."

She looked at Wilson. "The cards weren't signed? Now I really want to know what they wrote."

"It wasn't much," Parker said. "He—or *she*—has a surprise for someone. 'Can't wait to see you.' Stuff like that."

Something bothered Angelica about it—but she wasn't sure what. "Has your grandpa ever even lived at that address?"

Parker shook his head. "He thinks someone is sending cards to the former owner of our house. The cards sounded like they'd been out of touch for a long time. Maybe the mystery sender didn't know they'd moved."

"Grams knows everybody. She probably knew the people who used to live there," Ella said. "And if she knows where they moved, we can forward the cards to them."

"There," Harley said. "I guess that wraps up the great postcard mystery. Too bad there wasn't more to it—like something actually interesting. Maybe you could have worked it into a story time feature for the shop."

Angelica picked up one of Ella's boots and threw it at him. He caught it, tucked it under his forearm and ran a wide loop around the entire group. He circled back, dodging invisible defenders as he leaped from rock to rock. He held the boot up high like he was going to spike a football in the end zone. Instead, he set it down with an air of reverence, right next to Ella's other boot.

"You're *ridiculous*, Harley." Angelica pointed at the three boys. "All of you are. You make fun of us girls, but it's because you're missing an entire wavelength that girls possess." She swept her hand over her head. "We pick up on things that *boys* totally miss."

Wilson held up one hand. Sat upright. "Shhhhh. Listen."

Angelica looked at him—and listened—but didn't hear anything other than the sound of the ocean testing the rocks. "What are we—?"

"Shhhh." Wilson half stood. "A voice." He motioned for Parker to douse the lantern and stared off in the direction of the trees.

Angelica strained to hear, but there was nothing. She glanced at Ella. Clearly she didn't hear anything either.

Wilson crouched down. "Somebody's calling. Listen."

"I hear it," Harley whispered.

Parker nodded like he did too. Angelica still couldn't hear a thing.

Wilson cupped his hand over his mouth. "Everglades Girl." He obviously did his best to imitate some kind of warbly, haunting voice. "Ever . . . glades . . . Girl . . . where are you?"

That was it. She looked at Ella. "Hit him with your boot. And make sure it's on your foot."

The three boys were laughing hysterically now.

"Sometimes us boys pick up on things you girls miss too," Wilson said.

"The only thing we're missing"—Angelica pointed at Ella and back at herself—"is the Y chromosome that you boys have. And the *Y* stands for *why* are boys so stupid?"

It was hard not to laugh along with them. There was no way she was going to get them to talk seriously about the postcards tonight—or anything else. Maybe the guys needed the break. They all did. But there was still something about the postcards that bothered her.

"Do me a favor, would you, Parker? Bring the postcards tomorrow to lunch."

"Why?" Harley tried to hold a straight face—but he wasn't that good at acting. "You want to read somebody else's private mail now too?"

Again, the laughter—and that was okay. Angelica looked out at the dark waters. She probably *was* overreacting. Seeing shadows where they weren't. But viewing the postcards herself was probably the only way to shed whatever it was about them that bothered her. "Tease me all you want. Knock yourself out. Just bring the postcards."

CHAPTER 63

PARKER SAT AT THE USUAL CAFETERIA TABLE. Harley and Wilson dropped onto seats on either side of him. Ella and Jelly looked to be in a deep discussion as they came out of the hot lunch line. They stopped—and seemed in no hurry to get to the table.

"Mind if I join you?" Finn stood behind one of the empty seats. He held up four bags of snack-size Oreos. "I brought dessert." The guy was a sophomore just like them—but looked two years younger. He had an honest face—and an easy, hair-trigger smile. It took almost nothing to get him grinning—which he was doing at the moment.

Wilson motioned for him to sit—and Finn tossed each of them a bag of Oreos after he did.

Out of nowhere, Bryce Scorza scooted onto one of the other empty seats, tray in hand.

"Nobody invited you, Scorza," Harley said. "That seat was reserved."

"Relax. There's still room for the girls." Scorza stretched to look toward the hot lunch line. "Where are they, anyway?"

Harley glared at him. "Probably looking for a different table, now that you're here."

"I'm a dessert *first* kind of guy." Finn wrestled to tear open the bag of Oreos.

"Let me see that." Wilson whipped off his necklace and put the tooth in his palm. He closed his fist so that the point of the tooth stuck up between his fingers.

Finn handed him the bag, and Wilson jabbed it—punching a nice hole in the bag.

"That necklace is like a multitool." Finn poked his finger in the hole and ripped the bag open easily.

"More of a multi-*weapon*," Wilson said. "I could stop a great white with this." He feigned a jab again. "Pow, right in the eye." He handed the necklace to Finn.

Finn popped an Oreo in his mouth and inspected the tooth. "Did you do the extraction?"

Wilson told about the alligator he'd hunted and killed—and how he'd taken all the teeth. He'd only used two of them to make necklaces . . . one for himself—and the other for Parker.

His necklace and Wilson's—both teeth from the same gator? That was one bit of information Parker hadn't known.

Wilson explained his belief that the necklace brought him luck—or protection. Maybe both.

Finn held it up, measured the tooth with his fingers, and thumbed the point of it. "Not as sharp as I'd have guessed."

"But there's massive power in those jaws," Wilson said. "With enough pressure to hold their prey . . . so they can shred the skin while snapping bone and—"

"Dude." Scorza stared at him. "Abercrombie is trying to eat lunch here."

Wilson ignored him and stayed focused on Finn. "Trust me. The teeth don't have to look sharp to do a world of damage." He pointed at Parker's arm. "Exhibit A."

Finn's eyes were about the size of Oreos now. He looked at the necklace in his open palm with total respect.

Scorza snatched the necklace from Finn. "You should make me one of those sometime. I'll pay you."

"No can do," Wilson said. "It's only for the closest friends. Guys who've set themselves apart in an act of friendship—or a feat of courage."

Which just about made Parker want to crawl into a hole. Why had he treated the gift so casually?

Scorza hooked the leather strap around his finger and gave it a twirl. "You really think this has some kind of supernatural power?"

"When I was trapped—with no hope—I wore that necklace," Wilson said. "I wanted to be rescued so bad—and it happened. Parks and his dad—and Jelly's dad—found me. So you tell *me* if the thing has special powers."

Parker laughed. "We have a difference of opinion on that. Finding you was a miracle . . . and it was Almighty God who saved your hide."

"So"—Scorza closed his hand around the gator tooth—"this can bring me what I really wish for?" He squeezed his eyes shut and pressed his fist against his forehead, like he was putting the thing to the test.

Jelly and Ella took the last empty seats while Scorza was totally absorbed in his little exercise. He opened his eyes—and stared at Jelly with a stunned look on his face. "Whoa. That was *fast*." He opened his hand and stared at the necklace. "I definitely got to get me one of these!"

Finn snapped up the necklace from Scorza so quickly, the QB didn't have time to react. Finn wiped it with his napkin and handed it back to Wilson. "Sorry about that."

Wilson nodded in an approving way and slipped the necklace over his head. "Fast hands."

Finn shrugged. "I'm a drummer."

"Okay," Jelly said. "The postcards. Tell me you brought them."

Parker fished them out of his pack and slid them across the table. Jelly examined the pictures for a few moments before flipping them over and studying the backs. Scorza leaned closer, probably trying to figure out why the cards seemed so important to Jelly.

Parker finished his lunch, and like Wilson and Harley, washed it all down with a carton of chocolate milk.

"GB isn't the initials of one of the people who used to own your house," Ella said. "I checked with Grams."

Jelly seemed to be thinking that one through. "Two postmarked from New York. One from Miami. And all of them"—she gave them a closer look—"mailed after riding out maybe the worst hurricane of their lifetime—yet they don't mention Morgan at all? Am I the only one who thinks that's weird?"

"What's weird is your obsession with it," Wilson said. "Or is this one of those things somebody with a Y chromosome can't understand?"

"That's exactly it." The bell rang—and Jelly growled. "That wasn't nearly enough time—I gotta think on this more."

"Take them." Parker stacked the postcards and handed them to her. "Knock yourself out. Just give them back when you're done—although I'm not sure what I'm supposed to do with them anyway. We have no idea who they were really intended for."

She nodded. "We're going to solve this mystery."

The way Parker saw it? The postcards were a dead end. But until she figured that out for herself, there'd be no changing her mind.

CHAPTER 64

CLAYTON KINGMAN LOVED THIS BOAT. He wished he could find a way to keep it. But that would mean changing a very-well-thought-out plan. Eventually, he could pick up another boat—but he'd swipe the name from this one. *Retribution.* It had become part of him now. Maybe someday he'd write his own memoir. He already had the title: *In the Wake of Retribution.* It had a powerful ring to it . . . just like the name Clayton Kingman.

He'd write it—and tuck it away somewhere, of course. But someday, he'd release it. And people all over the world would marvel at his ingenuity. How he'd used his head every step of the way. He'd eluded all the Florida National Guard and the US Marshals searching for him, outsmarting every one of them. Even now he was someplace nobody would think of looking.

Do the unexpected. And he definitely had. But the best was yet to come.

He'd managed to get news about the Jericho Prison break. The body count was high. And the number of unidentified bodies was still impressive. Officials were quoted as saying "on good authority" that likely not one of the prisoners had made it out of the swamp. Chalk it up to great instincts—or fate—but Clayton had made the right choices every step of the way.

Even now, he was nearing his goal—and it was only Thursday. Tonight, he'd find a safe harbor where he could drop anchor . . . and his guard a bit. Tomorrow he'd pass Boston—and by tomorrow night, he'd reach his destination. Then he'd start prep for Gatorbait's surprise Saturday night. Halloween Eve. That would add a nice creep factor to the whole thing, wouldn't it?

Would his dad be grieving as he watched the body count rise from the Jericho Prison escape? Clayton thought about that for a long time. He concluded that his dad wouldn't believe Clayton was dead—no matter what the reports said. Until he saw a body, he'd know his son was alive—and as free as he was. He was likely the only one on earth who would guess Clayton had gotten clean away—and where he was headed. And when the news came out about a ranger's kid disappearing in Rockport, Massachusetts, his dad would connect the dots. He'd know his son was more alive than he'd ever been before.

The more he thought about it, the more he was sure Dad should be in prison—for crimes committed when Clayton was a boy. Dad had covered his tracks—and his dark side—well. And Clayton would build a new life too.

But first . . . the surprise. The rematch. And afterward, he'd disappear in the wake of *Retribution*. It was a good feeling. So good, he couldn't help but sing.

I'll be watching you . . .

CHAPTER 65

HARLEY HAD NEVER BEEN IN THE Gundersons' two-car garage before, but somehow it felt familiar. Maybe it was the satisfying smell of gas and oil. A rolling chest of tools stood at one end. Not quite as big as Harley's but close. He slid open a drawer. Pulled out a ratchet wrench and snapped a socket in place. He worked the action in his hands as he explored the rest of the garage. The wrench wasn't quite as nice as his own, but he still liked the feel of it.

A tarp covered a car in the second bay. He lifted a corner of the canvas and carefully pulled it back to the windshield. An AMC Javelin . . . maybe 1971? The hood and fender were perfectly sprayed in dull gray primer. Not the car Harley would choose to restore, but Mr. Gunderson was doing a nice job.

Maybe this would be a way to connect with his foster dad. Harley was good with the tools. Maybe Harley could help. If Mr. G had read Harley's background sheet, he would've known Harley helped restore Kemosabe with his dad. Funny Mr. G hadn't told him about the Javelin.

The service door to the garage opened. Gunderson strode in. "Saw the light. What are you doing out here?" Okay, Mr. G did not look happy.

"I, uh—"

"The garage is off limits," his eyes flitted to the wrench in Harley's hands. "Only two people are allowed in here. My son—who is away at school—and me."

Of course. Another reminder that Harley *lived* with the family—but wasn't part of it.

Gunderson brushed past him and went to the exposed section of the Javelin. He bent over it, inspecting the hood in the light. What, did he think Harley was stupid enough to touch the thing?

Harley set the wrench back in the drawer and slid it shut without a sound. He couldn't get out of the garage fast enough. Mr. G was still searching for a scratch that wasn't there.

Without a word, Harley slipped out and closed the door behind him.

Harley went straight to his room and hit the lights. He kicked back on the top bunk and stared at the single star, barely glowing on the ceiling. He pulled out his own socket wrench and turned it over in his hands. He felt the smooth chrome of the socket attachment. The handle with its perfect grip. He held the socket in one hand and cranked the handle with the other to feel the ratchet action vibrate in his palm. It actually did seem a tiny bit smoother than Mr. G's wrench.

Would Gunderson give him a strike for being in the garage? Probably not—unless he stepped in there again.

How had Harley's life gotten so messed up? He lived in a house . . . but it wasn't a home. Not like what he'd experienced when he'd stayed with Parks. Even football was messed up. He'd never wished for a season to be over—until this year. They weren't playing like a single unit, and they were at the bottom of the league. This Friday would be the last game of the season, and they were going to get creamed. Some blamed it on the fact that Scorza hadn't played. There was probably some truth to that. He had a good arm—before he'd gotten the thing snapped by *Deep Trouble*, anyway. But the problem wasn't so much that Scorza couldn't play. It was that he couldn't give the team some space to find their way. He came to every practice. He sat on the bench for the games. He critiqued every play. Swore at guys who messed up.

Harley cranked the socket wrench a couple more times. A good team captain should encourage the other players, right? That was pretty important when it came to building unity—at least the way Harley saw things. But Scorza had a different style. Even before the broken arm had taken him out of active play, he'd badgered and insulted any player who made him "look bad." A missed catch. A sack. A play that failed to get a first down. None were the fault of the QB. It was always someone else's mistake. Scorza stayed on top by putting others down. The more a player kissed up to Scorza, the less he rode him.

Last year, when Harley had been a freshman, the team had become almost like family to him. They had been brothers. But not this year. He wore the Vikings jersey, but he wasn't part of the family anymore.

Scorza had systematically undermined Harley. Said things that weren't completely true. Convinced other players that Harley had horns under his helmet. It was like his foster life had followed him to school. He was a foster Viking now too.

He slowly ratcheted the wrench in his hands. *Click-cl-cl-cl-cl-cl-cl-click. Back.* The only place he still seemed to belong was with Parker and the others. But for how long? Every family Harley had been part of had crumbled. Uncle Ray's predictions played in his mind. Would he stay close with Parker and Ella and Jelly—and now even Wilson? It was the only group Harley fit in with at all . . . and now Scorza was trying to horn his way in. Would he divide them somehow? Would Scorza try to mess up Harley's friendship with Parker and Ella and Jelly if he could? Oh, yeah.

Click-cl-cl-cl-cl-cl-cl-click. Back. If Scorza could figure out a way to insert himself into *that* family, Harley would be an orphan for good.

CHAPTER 66

ANGELICA SHUFFLED INTO THE KITCHEN and sat at the table. Ella followed right behind her. She'd invited Pez, but she hadn't been able to make it. Did she somehow see right through Angelica? Did she know that this was more about finding an excuse to be around her—and put in a pitch for her dad? Grams brought each of them a slice of her Blueberry Ghost Pie and pulled up a chair herself.

Angelica gave them the short version of her conversation with her dad. Most of the water had receded . . . but it made things look worse, not better. He'd sent pictures—and it was beyond anything she could have imagined. He'd avoided her question about finding bodies. People who'd been determined to ride out the storm—but got a ride in the coroner's van instead. Wilson could have been one of them. He probably would have been if Angelica had kept Parker from going down there.

For just a second, she wondered about her whole "protector" mentality. How many other times had she made things worse by trying to control the situation? How many more times would she make a mess if she didn't learn? But hey, she got the boys back, right? That was something.

Grams fanned out the postcards on the table. "I've been looking at these. I sense an evil about them—and it has nothing to do with the dreadful creatures on the front."

Okay, that got Angelica's attention. Grams was superstitious—everybody knew that—but sometimes it was just her keen insight leading her, wasn't it?

Grams turned them over. One at a time. Slowly. "There is something here. Something dark. Secret. Something we're not seeing—but I believe we need to."

Grams, Ella, and Angelica pulled their chairs in close and hovered over the cards.

"GB." Angelica pointed to the initials on each card. "We're certain this isn't for Gabriel Buckman. And this isn't the former owner of the house, for sure?"

Ella shook her head. "The previous owners of the Buckman home were Leo and Faye Marvin, right Grams?"

"Mmmm-hmmm."

Angelica wished Parker's mom were with them at this moment. She would have prayed, enlisting the help of Almighty God to sort out the puzzle. "Do dates matter? If so, this one came first." Angelica moved the card mailed from Miami to the number one position. "The other two are postmarked a day later." She slid the other two cards in a position below the first to make a triangle on the table.

Grams read the three cards right in a row—except for the random words that were crossed out or didn't make sense at the bottom.

Been a long time. Since you haven't come for a visit, I'll come to you.
Got a huge surprise for you. Can't wait to see your face.

Got this song in my head. Find myself singing it at the strangest times . . . and it always makes me think of you. Maybe I'll sing it to you when I see you.

"Okay . . . every one of these three cards refers to seeing *someone* in person, so whoever wrote this is coming for a visit," Angelica said. "Can we all agree on that?"

Grams nodded. Ella jotted the assumption on a pad of paper.

"And here's something," Ella said. "Whoever wrote these didn't sign their name. How did they forget that *every* time?"

"They didn't," Grams said. "Let's assume they kept their identity a secret—on *purpose*."

Ella scribbled that on the pad.

Grams tapped the new assumption. "Now think, girls. Why not put their name—or return address, for that matter?"

Ella stared at the pad and took a bite of her pie. "They don't want their identity known because it's like they said on the card—they want to surprise the person. If he knew *who* was bringing the surprise, maybe our mystery person thinks he'll guess *what* the surprise is too."

"So." Grams thought for a moment more. "They didn't give their identity because it might *spoil* the surprise. And the sender of the card wants to enjoy the look of surprise."

That made sense. And the deep dark mystery of the postcards wasn't looking so dark anymore. Angelica took a giant forkful of the pie. Grams had certainly not lost her touch.

"What about the song bit," Ella said. "It's got to be a love song, right?"

Angelica nodded. "Seems like some old flame is trying to reconnect with someone who doesn't even live at Parker's house."

"Well, when she finds her long lost love doesn't live there, the real surprise will be on her." Ella stood and put her empty plate in the sink. "And with no return address, there's no way to contact her."

Angelica licked her fork, collected the empty plate from Grams, and set them all in the sink.

Grams studied the postcards again and shook her head. "The feeling was so strong. But I'm not sensing it now."

Her sense of foreboding could come and go. Just like the fog.

Angelica collected the cards. Tapped them into a neat stack. "Well, sorry, whoever you are. You're going to miss whoever you'd hoped to surprise."

Grams gave a tired sigh. "I just hope it's not *us* who are missing something."

CHAPTER 67

PARKER HAD SEARCHED HIS ROOM AGAIN while Wilson hit the shower. Still no gator tooth necklace. Why had he stopped wearing it? Jelly had once said it was his mind subconsciously trying to help him forget the traumatic memories from the Everglades. But if that was true, why did he leave the alligator skull on his bookcase and his gator stick propped in the corner?

The real reason he'd stopped wearing it was because he'd drifted apart from Wilson. Sure, they shot texts to each other pretty regularly, but it wasn't the same as being with him. And now that they'd spent these days together, Parker wanted that necklace again. It had taken some work, but their connection was back. And he'd do better at keeping it that way when Wilson went home. If part of being a man involved caring for others, certainly Parker should expect it would take some effort on his part.

Mom poked her head inside the room. "When you're ready for Mom's help, you let me know."

Parker motioned her into the room and flopped back on the bed. "It's gone. It could be anywhere."

"You still looking for that gator tooth?" Wilson stepped in from the hall. He passed it off like it was no big deal. But it definitely had been important to Wilson when he'd given it to Parker.

"It's in this room," Mom said. "And I could find it in five minutes—unless you're so pigheaded about finding it yourself."

Wilson laughed. "Ooooh, Mom scores a point."

"*Five* minutes?"

Mom smiled—which she'd been doing a lot these last few days with Wilson here. She had a bigger family—and seemed to thrive with it. "That's three hundred seconds, if that's easier for you to keep track."

"Mrs. B scores again!" Clearly Wilson was loving this.

Maybe Parker should call her bluff. "Why do you think the necklace is still in this room? I've searched."

"Searched?" Mom gave him a look like that was the most ridiculous thing she'd heard. "You've skimmed. You've scanned. You have *not* searched. And it's in this room because you were never careless with it. You wore it. You hung it on the bedpost."

"I'm afraid it ended up in the garbage," Parker said. The trash basket was near the bedpost.

"Not possible."

Parker gave Wilson a can-you-believe-this? look. "Okay, Mom . . . what makes you so sure?"

"When's the last time you emptied the garbage from that basket?"

Wilson laughed. "Mrs. B is on a roll."

"*I* take out your garbage," Mom said. "You let things pile up until the basket overflows. And I'd have seen a necklace when I dumped the garbage for sure." She smiled and scanned the room. "It's here. Trust me."

"Okay, Mom. Let's see what you got," Parker said. "Five minutes."

"Challenge accepted." Mom stood there for a second, taking in the room—like she was deep in thought.

Wilson sat back on the guest bed and leaned against the wall. "This

I want to see. A real mom in action. I'll handle the timer." He flipped to the stopwatch app. "And the time starts . . . now."

Mom flipped on the room light and stood staring at the bed—with Parker on it.

"Time is flying, Mom."

She held up her hand. "Shhh."

Parker was loving this. "You think the necklace is going to *call* to you or something?"

"Wilson, it looks like your friend is getting nervous that I'm better at this than he is." She marched to Parker's bed. "Off."

Parker moved to the guest bed and sat next to Wilson like it was a set of bleachers.

Mom pulled off the covers. Sheets. Shook each one carefully. She slid the mattress off the box spring and let it drop in the middle of the room. She inspected the box spring for a moment, then eased it off the frame. The space under the bed was pretty well filled. Baseball bat. Machete. Another survival knife. Shoeboxes taped shut with stuff inside that hadn't been opened since the move up. "You checked through all this?"

"I moved some stuff. Yeah." But from the edges. He didn't take the whole thing apart.

"Wilson," Mom said. "Would you be so kind as to pile all this junk up in front of the bookcase?"

Parker's friend sprang into action. He quickly propped the mattress and box spring out of the way. The moment he had the floor under the bed cleared, Mom motioned for him to help move the frame and headboard away from the wall. Even from here, Parker could see the baseboard on the far side of the bed. As much as he wanted the necklace, he definitely didn't want her finding it *that* easily. "Well, it looks like some moms are all promises and no deliveries."

Mom laughed and scooted behind the headboard. She stopped and smiled. "Stop the clock."

What? "No way."

She reached behind the headboard and held up a leather lace, with an alligator tooth hanging from the end. She wiggled her finger a bit . . . putting the tooth in motion, like a pendulum. "Time, Wilson?"

Wilson whooped. "Three minutes and change. And how long have *you* been looking for this, Parker?"

"Where was it?" Parker was on his feet, straining to see behind the headboard.

She pointed at a tiny nail sticking out of the back of the headboard, or maybe it was a staple. "The leather was hooked right there."

Wilson squeezed in to check it out himself. "You are an absolute wonder, Mrs. Buckman."

"When you can't figure something out, always go back to what you know. Stay there until you get your answer." She turned to Parker. "You were searching all over the room—because you didn't find it on your headboard post—or on the floor under your bed, right?"

"I'd searched." And Parker had. "It wasn't there—so I moved on."

"You were on the right trail . . . but you let one bad assumption keep you from finding it. You didn't think you'd missed anything, but you needed to stick with it until you'd turned everything upside down." Mom seemed really, really happy with herself.

He reached for the necklace, but she pulled it back and pointed to her cheek. "Right here, Buster."

Parker gave her a quick kiss on the cheek—and a hug that wasn't quite as quick. "I still don't believe it. Thanks, Mom!" He slipped the gator tooth over his neck. There was something that felt right about it being there—along with the key from Kemosabe. Maybe it was the weight of it. Or the way his friendship with Wilson had regained some mass in the last few days.

"A definite improvement, Bucky."

"I'm not taking it off, either."

"I'm glad you're happy." Mom breezed back into the hallway. "Good night, boys. Have fun cleaning up the room."

They put the bed together and tucked all the other junk underneath.

Wilson raised the window before flopping back on his bed. He talked about his dad . . . and how he'd seemed changed since the hurricane. In good ways.

They talked about the changes ahead for Wilson. And the huge questions—when he'd go back down to be with his dad and where they'd live when he did.

Over the course of the next hour, they pretty well solved the problems of the world—except Jelly and Ella. Those two were mysteries beyond figuring out.

"I think Jelly is kind of a control freak," Wilson said. "She's got to beat that one—or she'll drive herself crazy."

"Us, too."

Wilson laughed. "Like the way she obsessed over that prison escape. You really think we were in any danger of Kingman showing up while we were down there?"

"Zero chance," Parker said. And he meant it. But it was just one more example of how Jelly could get all worked up about things she couldn't control. It boiled down to not trusting God, didn't it?

"How about the postcards?" Wilson snickered. "She's obsessed with the most insane things—don't you think?"

Parker wasn't going to argue. The postcards were meaningless. "She won't rest until she finds some dark plot behind them."

Their laughter settled into a quiet listening of the swells pounding the Headlands.

"So how was it," Wilson said, finally. "Going back to the Everglades? Do the gators still creep you out, or are you totally over that?"

The room was too dark to see Wilson's face, but even in the tone, Parker picked up a seriousness. Maybe that was the wrong word. But the question didn't feel random. More rehearsed than off the top of his head.

"It was okay. I mean, I still hate gators—which makes me super cautious around them." Parker thought about it for a moment. "I don't think that's a bad thing."

The waves continued their suicide march to the Headlands.

"So, you were fine. The fear, or whatever, just kind of went away, right?"

Why was Wilson asking him this now? And was it really about Parker at all?

"There's still some fear . . . but the good kind. The kind that keeps you sharp, not the kind that paralyzes."

"Yeah, that's good." Wilson rolled like he was trying to get comfortable. "I'm sure after what happened to people in Everglades City or Chokoloskee, some will feel . . . different. Not me, of course. Miccosukee are sort of like brothers to alligators. They don't see us like they see other people."

Right. Parker wanted to ask him more. But then again, what was to ask? He'd been trapped, fighting off gators with his feet for how many hours? "Getting traumatized by gators would make *anybody* extra cautious . . . Miccosukee or not. I'm Exhibit A."

"But you changed. I mean, you said you got over it."

Parker wanted to get this right. "Mostly. But I had help. I couldn't do it alone."

"Your dad?"

"And Uncle Sammy. And God." *Especially* God. "I even had some really solid phone sessions with Dale . . . a psychologist friend of my dad's."

Wilson didn't say anything. After a couple of minutes, Parker was pretty sure Wilson had drifted off. Parker rolled to one side . . . face close to the window. Even here, he could feel the Atlantic breeze.

"Thanks, Parker. That's all I needed to know."

For now. There was a lot more to talk through—eventually. But he'd wait until Wilson was ready. Parker slipped his hand around the gator tooth at the end of the lanyard. Oh, yeah. Wilson was still fighting those gators, wasn't he? And Parker had to find a way to help.

CHAPTER 68

Friday, October 29, 7:15 a.m.

ANGELICA TAPPED OFF HER ALARM AND dropped back on her pillow. She thought through the whole postcard thing again. It was probably nothing. She tended to go overboard seeing danger—when there really wasn't any at all.

Daylight greeted Ella and Angelica with a rousing "Good morning." The sun definitely softened the shadows in Angelica's head too. And for the first time since she'd heard about the prison transfer—and Jericho's walls falling—she felt like somehow that was behind her. The massive escape had happened nearly a week earlier. Angelica sensed they were in the clear now. Clayton Kingman was probably dead. What was left of him was in some gator's belly over a thousand miles away. Good riddance.

She didn't have that familiar dread like there was something she needed to get under control—because everything actually *was* under control. It was Friday, and it was promising to be a good one.

She'd barely rolled out of bed when she got the text from Pez.

Sorry I couldn't make the meeting last night. I was soooo
hoping to be there.

Me too, Pez. Maybe it was the way she reminded her of Parker's mom.
She sure seemed to have a rock-solid relationship with Jesus like her. She
was strong like Mrs. Buckman too . . . but in her own way. Maybe it was
her sassiness that Angelica liked best. She was no pushover—but never
pushy. She'd mastered that balance. Add the coffee shop to all that, and
it seemed Pez had really found her place in life. Angelica just wished
that place might someday include her even more—or rather, her dad.
But Pez did say she was praying for him, right? That was something.
Another text zinged in.

Let me make it up to you. Stop by the shop after school.
We'll look at those postcards—and you and Ella can help me
clean up!!! ☺☺☺!!!

The three smiling emojis made Angelica laugh. She pecked out a
quick reply.

I'm in. I think we have our postcard mystery solved, but
I'll bring them.

The big draw for Angelica? She'd have a great time hanging out with
Pez . . . and maybe she could slip in another good word about her dad
without being too obvious.

Angelica, Ella, Wilson, and Parker would all go to the football game
afterward and watch the Rockport Vikings end their season by getting
killed. There would be no postgame Valhalla party for them. No cele-
brations at all. Poor Harley. Tonight would be an agonizing end to a
crushing season. But other than that one *minor* detail, this truly was
shaping up to be a great day! And nothing—or nobody—was going to
change that.

CHAPTER 69

Gloucester, Massachusetts
Friday, October 29, 7:30 a.m.

HARLEY FINISHED BREAKFAST EARLY AND retreated to his room for a few minutes before heading to school. He reached under his pillow and grabbed his socket wrench.

Click-cl-cl-cl-cl-cl-cl-click. Back.

Click-cl-cl-cl-cl-cl-cl-click. Back.

They were going to get pounded tonight. Would he even get any playing time? Probably not. The upperclassmen would be on the field until they dropped. The coach would give them this last chance to redeem themselves—or to live with the worst football record Rockport High had seen in a decade. For most of the seniors, it would be the last time they'd play football in anything but a pickup game. A family Thanksgiving Day Turkey Bowl.

While Harley rode the bench, Scorza would pace the sidelines like he was a coach—instead of the out-of-commission QB that he was. He'd shout orders and insults and be his obnoxious self. He'd purposely stand in front of Harley to block his view of the game. All part of Scorza's way of showing he had control. Or that he had serious mental issues.

Click-cl-cl-cl-cl-cl-cl-click. Back. Two bunkbeds in the room. Three empty mattresses. Harley should have been happy to have a room all to himself, right? He could have been forced to room with a total moron. But would that be so bad? At least he wouldn't feel so alone. He'd slept alone in a room when he'd lived with Uncle Ray above the dive shop, but that was different. That room was barely big enough to fit his bed. With this room at the Gundersons', it always looked like someone was missing. Like everybody in the world had moved on—and Harley had been left behind. How many others had struck out in Mr. Gunderson's little foster baseball game? If Harley wasn't careful, his bunk would be empty soon too. He couldn't let that happen.

Harley pulled the sheet and covers tight and tucked the hanging edges neatly under his mattress. He gave the room a quick scan to be sure everything else was in its place. If Gunderson did an inspection while Harley was in school, he wanted the man to find nothing that could be seen as a strike. And depending on Mr. G's mood . . . it wouldn't take much.

Click-cl-cl-cl-cl-cl-cl-click. Back. He checked the corkboard. Two strikes. Mr. Gunderson kept the score—and he was the ump, too. He called 'em the way he saw 'em. Not sending an answer for over an hour after Mr. G texted, asking where Harley was? Strike one. Arguing with Mr. G about that being a bad call? Strike two.

The door swung open—and Mr. Gunderson strode in. Immediately his eyes locked onto the socket wrench. "I thought I told you the garage was off bounds?"

Harley held up the wrench. "This is mine, Mr. Gunderson. I actually have my own set of tools—at my friend's house."

Mr. Gunderson held out his hand. "Let me see that."

Harley placed it in Mr. G's palm. "Sir, you can check your tools—"

"And if I find this is mine—you've picked up your third strike."

Harley stared at him. "I-I can prove it's mine. We could go to Parker's house and see the empty spot for that wrench—and the one-inch socket."

"All I care about is that there's no empty spot in *my* tool drawer."

Harley wanted his wrench back. It belonged to *him*. His shed. His motorcycle. He was so stinking tired of people taking things that belonged to him.

Mr. Gunderson slapped the wrench into his own open palm. "If I find this is truly yours, you'll get it back."

It truly *was* his. And he *would* get it back. "I could go to the garage with you. Help you find yours."

Gunderson laughed. "If it's there, I'll find it. You better get hustling. Game day today." For a split second, his eyes flitted to the corkboard. "You don't want to be late."

He really didn't care about a tardy. But he definitely couldn't afford a strike. Harley eyed the board. "So, end of the month is in two days. Does the ball game start all over again?" He could make it two days without a strike. He had to.

"You mean, do I *hand* you a fresh slate at the start of the month?"

He had a way of making it sound like Harley was asking for the moon. His stomach sunk. "Yes, sir."

"It doesn't work that way, Harley."

And Harley had no idea how this was going to work any other way, either.

CHAPTER 70

WILSON WALKED THE HEADLANDS AIMLESSLY for a bit before finding a spot to park himself. The rock made a natural chair. Close enough to the water to feel its power—but far enough back not to take a direct hit from a wave. Spray was another thing altogether, but he didn't mind getting misted a bit.

Bucky's mom had packed him a lunch, and he pawed through it to find the cookies before setting the personal cooler down beside him.

He didn't mind shadowing Bucky at school. It was the shadows in his head that were the problem right now. Mrs. B had given him the green light to skip school today. Maybe she knew there were some things he had to learn that couldn't be taught from a textbook—or in a classroom.

Wilson had been made for the water. Practically lived on the water. Felt part of it. But the things living *underwater* haunted him now.

There was no way he should have survived Hurricane Morgan. No way he should have lived after the airboat pinned him with his legs in the water. The gators had been in some kind of feeding frenzy. Relentless.

When Wilson was a kid, his dad had taught him about the Everglades Curse. How the place was alive—and how the Glades saw man as trespassing every time they fished or hunted or flew over without paying something back. The Everglades kept score—and exacted a heavy penalty when the numbers reached some mysterious level. A trespassing toll, paid in human blood. Sometimes the Glades took its victims one by one. Other times, by the dozens. That was the real reason for airplane crashes in the Glades. The explanation for all the deaths caused by Morgan, too.

Once upon a time, he'd thought Bucky had been marked as a toll. Selected, in some supernatural way. Bucky had nearly lost his life in the Glades—over and over. But somehow, Bucky escaped. Was the same price now being demanded of Wilson? Had he been selected as a toll? Would the Everglades Curse hang over him—until its bloodthirst was satisfied? Would he only be safe if he stayed out of the Everglades, or was there a way he could escape the curse like Bucky did?

Everything looked different to Wilson right now. Even here, fifteen hundred miles away, he looked over the water and wondered if a great white was out there. Patrolling the coastline like there was a bounty on Wilson's head—and the shark intended to succeed where the alligators failed.

Maybe the curse wasn't limited to the Glades. Maybe it included the entire Atlantic, too. Like the universe itself had selected him and marked him for death. It wasn't the waters themselves that would get him. It was the carnivores lurking there. If he was truly selected, maybe it wasn't random. Maybe it was because Wilson had hunted and killed his fair share of gators. And now they were hunting him. The alligators had tried their worst to get him after the hurricane . . . but thanks to Parker, he'd escaped. But had he truly gotten away from the curse?

Seagulls wheeled and cawed overhead. They dove at him—or at the cookie in his hand—veering away at the last second. "You want this?" Wilson held up the plastic bag of chocolate chip cookies. "Too bad."

More gulls circled. Screeching. Calling to each other. Were they all here for food—or were they broadcasting his location? Like they were in league with nature itself. They'd found the cursed one . . . and they were telling every other creature in the wild kingdom exactly where he was.

"Shake it off, Wilson." He held up a cookie so the gulls could see it, then stuffed it in his mouth. "I'm not afraid of you."

But he was afraid of *something*. And the fact that he was afraid at all really, really bothered him. Back when Bucky had lived in Chokoloskee, his friend had insisted there was no Everglades Curse. And Wilson wanted to believe he was right. But he had to face the fact that he was marked somehow . . . and except for taking a shower, he needed to stay out of the water until he figured this out.

CHAPTER 71

ANGELICA CUPPED HER HANDS ON EITHER SIDE of her face and peered through the window at BayView Brew Coffee and Donut Shop.

Ella set her bookbag on the sidewalk. "See her?"

The place looked completely swept up and wiped down. "Looks empty." Maybe Pez forgot she'd invited Angelica to stop by. A twinge of disappointment skipped through her.

"Maybe she's in the kitchen." Ella pulled out her cross necklace and used it to tap on the window.

Within seconds, Pez stepped into view, waving and laughing. She opened the door. "Wouldn't you know it. I go into the back for two seconds and that's when you show up."

Pez led the way to a table with a window looking over the water. "Let's see these postcards."

Angelica shrugged off her pack. "I may have overreacted a bit." She pulled out the paper outlining the conclusions they'd come to—and how the postcards didn't seem quite so mysterious as she'd imagined.

"That's a good thing," Pez said. "Right?" She wiped her hands on the towel apron around her waist. "Mind if I see them—just for fun?"

Angelica set the stack on the table. What she really wanted to do right now was see if her dad and Pez had been talking. "So . . . heard any more from southern Florida?"

Pez put her hands over the postcards. "Ladies, do you mind if I pray?"

Angelica shouldn't have been surprised, but she kind of was. Praying over postcards? That seemed just a tiny bit extreme.

Without waiting for an answer, Pez bowed her head. "God, great revealer of secrets, we pray that You will lead us now. We need to interpret these postcards correctly, if they are important. And if they're not, we need to know that, too. You say if we ask for wisdom—and come to You for direction, trusting You for both—You will deliver. I pray You'll be pleased to reveal answers to us now."

She sighed. Smiled. And she spread all three cards out on the table—photo side up. "Nasty-looking beasts, aren't they." Not really a question.

Ella locked eyes with Angelica for a moment. Like she knew exactly how Angelica wanted to steer the conversation. "I wonder if the men have seen any unusually big gators down there during the search efforts? Like maybe Hurricane Morgan dredged them out of some lair that had been unknown for generations."

Okay, Ella was laying it on a little thick. But in a way, Angelica could see it happening.

Pez studied the front of each card and then flipped each one over, arranging them in a triangle on the table. She rotated the order of the postcards slightly, forming a new triangle. She leaned in. After studying them for a quiet minute, she went back to Angelica's list. "You're making some big assumptions about these postcards."

"Big assumptions or logical conclusions?" Angelica quickly recapped their line of reasoning. "You see anything that seems like a stretch?"

Pez gave a combination shrug and nod. "First, you're assuming GB has nothing to do with the Buckman family—Grandpa or otherwise—yet each one is addressed correctly to their house."

Okay . . . that actually made sense. "But we ruled out every possible explanation."

Pez took out a pad and pen. "Just because we can't explain GB doesn't mean the cards are all addressed wrong." She wrote GB in bold letters. "And another thing: You assume this is a woman—and that she was in love with GB—whoever that is."

Ella pointed out the line about the writer smiling every time they think of GB. "And then there's the love song bit."

"Just because the person smiles doesn't mean it's a good smile. And it just says a song comes to mind . . . you're assuming it's a love song."

In two minutes, Pez had dismantled everything they'd concluded after spending an hour kicking ideas around the night before.

"Couldn't we draw some different conclusions—about everything you've assumed so far?"

Pez got back to work on her list.

GB—could be written to anyone—but because of the right address, can't totally rule the Buckmans out

Cards not sent by an old flame

Could be a male sender, not female

Smile may not be friendly

Song may not be a love song . . . not a good song

"And if *these* assumptions above are true"—Pez studied the cards for another moment—"then the visit is not a good thing at all." She added a line to her list:

The surprise is a bad thing

Angelica didn't like the look of the list now. "How do we find out which are the right assumptions?"

Pez studied the postcards. "Three ways."

Ella and Angelica exchanged a glance. Pez changed the order of the cards again.

"Three ways," Ella said. "And the first would be . . ."

"Well, you'd have to find out exactly who GB is—which may be impossible to do beyond a shadow of a doubt," Pez said. "Second . . . figure out the song. If it is a nice love song, maybe your assumptions are legit."

Angelica waited, but Pez was back at the cards again. How were they supposed to figure out what the song was? "I feel like this is another dead end."

Pez pointed at the words that made no sense. "What are these random words along the bottom of each of the cards?"

"Mistakes," Ella said.

"On every card?" Pez jotted down the words on her pad.

They were losing focus here. "What's the third way to find out which way to interpret these cards?" Hopefully Pez would suggest something that was a bit more doable.

"Wait until the person shows up at the Buckmans' door." Pez shrugged. "We'll find out pretty quick if the surprise is good or bad. But if it's bad . . ."

She didn't have to finish the sentence. It would be too late to do anything about it.

"What if the words *aren't* random?" Pez tapped the words she'd written on the tablet. "*Breath you take every. You take every breath.*" She looked up. "That's a sentence—if we got the order right."

But what did it mean?

"The postmark," Ella said. "That will give you the right order."

Pez's eyes got wide. "Brilliant." She slid the earlier postmark to the top of the triangle. The other two had exactly the same date. "Okay . . . so *Every* is our first word. *Every you take breath.*"

Angelica swapped the order of the last two postcards. "Or *Every breath you take*." It still didn't make a whole lot of sense. "It's not a complete thought. Every breath you take . . . *what?*"

Pez sat back. "Hold on a sec." She stared out the window for a moment. "Is that it?"

Angelica glanced at Ella. She looked just as clueless as Angelica was. "Is that *what?*"

"Wait . . ." Pez whipped her phone out. She opened YouTube.

"Pez," Ella said. "What is it?"

She typed something into the app. "It's not a sentence. That's a song title . . . definitely popular back before my day. But I've heard it before."

"'Every Breath You Take' . . . a good song," Ella whispered, "or a bad song?"

Pez moaned. Flipped the phone around to show them the screen. It definitely was the title of a song by some group called The Police. "Good—in that it ranked high on the charts. It was popular. But in my opinion? It's creepy. It's a stalker song."

She hit the *play* arrow . . . and the three of them sat back and took the song in. The opening riff definitely sounded familiar. Angelica didn't catch all the words, but she got enough. The chorus echoed eerily in the empty coffee shop. Two lines stood out—and stuck.

Every step you take
I'll be watching you

"Sheesh," Ella said the moment the song ended. "The name of the group was The Police? That sounds like one cop we've met. Remember Officer Rankin?"

Pez went back to the list she'd made and circled the new assumptions that the song wasn't good—and the writer wasn't an old flame. "I think we can agree on these, right?"

"Which means"—Ella pointed to *Smile may not be friendly* and *The surprise is a bad thing*—"we should assume these are true too."

Pez nodded slowly.

"No!" Angelica stood so fast that her chair tipped and clattered to the floor. "No—no—no!" Instantly her eyes flooded with tears—hoping against all logic that she was wrong. But she wasn't. "I've got it. But I don't *want* to have it. I want to be wrong. Why can't I just be dead wrong for once?"

"Jelly?" Pez took her hands, her eyes searching.

"It's a bad surprise. A vicious, horrible, evil surprise!" Angelica wanted to scream. "I know who GB is."

Pez pulled her close. Rocked her. "Okay . . . talk to us. GB. What does it stand for?"

"Gatorbait," Angelica wailed. "That's what Clayton Kingman called Parker. These were sent *after* the hurricane. It all fits now. He's alive, Pez—and he's coming for Parker."

CHAPTER 72

"WHAT?" Parker sat at the helm of Steadman's boat and reread Jelly's text.

Wilson stretched to read over Parker's shoulder. "What's up with her *now?*"

"She just sent out a huge group text. My mom. Dad. Grams. Ella. Harley. She put her dad on the thread too." Parker steered around the yacht club and headed for the slip.

"I can't wait to hear this," Wilson said. He motioned for Parker to read it aloud.

Parker dropped the shifter into neutral. "Emergency family meeting. New development. Meet at BayView Brew in fifteen minutes. This could be life or death. Sorry, Harley—I was going to be at the game. Honest."

"Life or *death?*" Wilson shrugged. "Drama queen."

It was the last game—and Harley could use the support. Parker shot back a quick text.

How about after the game?

Jelly was back.

That may be too late. Please get here, fast. Ella and Pez are with me—and in total agreement.

"Even Pez is in on this?" Parker couldn't be at both places at once. He thought for a moment. "I hate missing the game."

Wilson snickered. "I haven't seen Jelly this worked up in a while. I'd hate to miss *that*."

"You should have seen her when the hurricane was headed your way." Parker pulled into the slip and the two of them secured the lines. They really didn't have a choice, did they? He whipped off a reply.

Wilson and I will be there. This better be really, really good.

She was back . . . like she'd been waiting for his reply.

No—not good at all. Really, REALLY BAD.

CHAPTER 73

HARLEY BROKE OUT INTO AN INSTANT SWEAT—and it had nothing to do with the fact he was standing in the suffocating locker room, fully suited up for the game.

Helmet in one hand, phone in the other, he read Jelly's texts again—and ran through his options. Miss the game or miss the meeting. It was that simple.

He wasn't needed for the game. Harley probably wouldn't play a single minute anyway.

But if he didn't go to the field . . . what then?

He stared at the screen. Jelly called it a *family* meeting.

And he was included in the text. Harley. The guy from the Dead Dads Club. The guy living in a foster home. The guy who had been disowned by the only living relative he had. *That* was the Harley who'd been called to a *family* meeting.

The coach was jotting something on his clipboard. Scorza was at his shoulder, wearing his game jersey, acting like part of the coaching staff.

"Parker's God," he whispered, "guide me to the right choice . . . and give me the strength to do what I need to do—either way."

Harley took a deep breath and hustled across the locker room. "Coach." He held up his phone. "Family emergency. I gotta go."

The coach looked up at Harley like he'd been torn from someplace he really didn't want to leave. "You gotta *what?*"

He gripped his helmet by the face mask. "Go. Family emergency."

Scorza stepped in. "He doesn't *have* a family. His dad—"

Harley swung the helmet backhanded at the QB's face, catching Scorza across the chops. He went down in a heap, swearing. Players hooted and hollered. They left their lockers and formed a circle—like they'd been waiting all season for a showdown between the two of them.

Harley was shaking. "Don't you talk about my dad, Scorza. Or you'd better be wearing a helmet along with that jersey."

A few claps from the guys—but definitely a weak show of support.

The coach bent over Scorza. "Follow my finger." He swept his pointer finger high above his right shoulder and then his left. Scorza tracked perfectly. He angled the QB's head one way and then the other. "Nose doesn't look broke. Ice it—and walk it off. You'll live."

The family meeting would start soon. "I have to go. Please, coach."

The coach eyed him and glanced around the room. The fact that so many guys were within earshot could be really good—or bad. It pressured the coach—either to make an example of Harley or show what an understanding coach he could really be. If it had been Scorza asking for a pass, Harley was pretty sure he'd already have it. But Harley wasn't the team captain.

"Last game of the season," Coach said. "And a tough one. You really want to leave the rest of the team covering for you?"

Not good. Not good. What if Jelly was exaggerating? She did that sometimes, right? "Family. Emergency."

"Like what *kind* of emergency. Exactly."

Harley shook his head. "That's just it. I don't know."

"Your foster family has some kind of crisis; is that it?"

Oh, man. *Here we go.* He shook his head. "Not foster family. Just . . . family."

The coach shot him a confused look.

"Close friends. We're . . . *like* family." But he wasn't *really* family. He knew it at that moment more than ever.

Coach looked at him for a long moment like he was making a decision. Weighing everything out. Not just this moment but all the moments to come when there'd be other family emergencies for any number of players. "*This* is your family." He looped his index finger in a circle. "Right here. In this locker room."

But they weren't. They *weren't.* They were a hopelessly splintered team. He had enemies in the room—and not just Scorza.

"Family comes first, Mr. Lotitto." Coach took a deep breath and gave a loud sigh. "I've said that a time or two. You need to take care of your family."

Wait, he was letting him leave? Relief. "Thank you, Coach. I'll make it up to you somehow."

Coach shook his head. "You misunderstand me. *This* family needs you. Right now. Right here."

Harley took a step back as the coach's meaning sunk in. "It's an *emergency.*"

"We got an emergency too," Coach said. "It's called having a home game on the line. And I want full support—even if that means you're only cheering from the bench—for the entire game."

Scorza was back on his feet. Blood draining from his nose. Fire crackling from his eyes. "You can't cut a game and be part of the team."

Coach shrugged. "I gotta agree with the team captain here. You walk out the locker room door now—and you're off the team. For as long as I'm the coach here."

There was no mistaking his meaning. Unless the coach left the school, Harley would never play high school ball again. JV. Varsity. Not another game. Harley's stomach knotted tight. He was trapped, wasn't he? He didn't have a choice.

"Now break it up, fellas," the coach said. "And get focused. We got a big game tonight. And we got some *family* honor to defend."

CHAPTER 74

IT HAD BEEN ONE BUSY DAY, BUT CLAYTON KINGMAN wasn't complaining. He felt good. Invincible. How could so many things be going so right? He'd arrived at Gloucester long before sundown. He'd changed into his camo gear just before turning into the harbor. He'd headed right for the canal, and he'd picked up a salute from the guy in the bridge house. He'd docked at the Cape Anne Marina and paid cash for gas.

He needed a skiff—something he could tow behind *Retribution*. Something that could handle rough seas outside the harbor. There were plenty to pick from at the marina. In the end, he chose a twelve-foot inflatable Catalina with a twenty-horse Mercury outboard motor clamped to the transom. Small enough not to attract attention. Big enough to do what had to be done. The Catalina had two bench seats and a wood floor. It could definitely hold plenty of weight. It was all he needed. And the grey and white color wouldn't be easy to spot, either.

There was enough stagnant water in the bottom of it to assure Clayton the boat didn't see much action. It was a pretty safe bet the owner wasn't going to need it this Halloween weekend. The motor fired right up. He had a full tank of gas and a spare container on board. An anchor was stowed up front, with plenty of line. He was good. A makeshift flagpole holder had been attached to the transom. A scuba tank rack had been secured at the stern as well. Clayton smiled. Tucked behind the set of oars was a six-foot pole with a red and white diver's flag wrapped around it. *Perfect.*

The party store delivery van arrived right on time. Everything he'd ordered was there. Plates. Cups. Plastic utensils. Helium balloons. Purple and orange twinkle lights—and strings of the bigger clear glass bulb lights too. Clayton found that money definitely could buy just about anything—if you offered enough. For the extra promised cash, the delivery guy from the party store was willing to provide even things the party store didn't carry. He brought Clayton the two phones he'd requested—and had even loaded the mix of songs on one of them . . . just like Clayton had asked.

Clayton had thrown in an extra hundred bucks to get the driver's help stringing the lights. Taking that kind of money from a one-armed vet almost seemed to shame the driver, but in the end, he pocketed the cash.

The guy was big—but agile. He looked like he could handle himself in all kinds of situations way beyond doing deliveries. It turned out Clayton had pegged him right. He learned the driver did late-night work as a bouncer at a local bar. Delivering for the party store was apparently just one of many ways he earned extra cash. He was resourceful. Clayton liked that.

The driver went all out with the lights, too. Did a whole lot better job than Clayton could have done single-handed. *Retribution* looked magnificent, proving once again that Clayton did the unexpected. Anybody else would have hidden a stolen boat. Clayton decorated it—and lit it up.

The costume the man had picked up for him was the best. Clayton actually tried it on while the guy worked. It would accomplish exactly what he needed it to. "Clayton, my man," he whispered, "you're a genius." He changed back into his camo gear, practically shaking with excitement. This was happening. Absolutely. Positively. Happening.

The moment the driver finished with the lights, Clayton fired up the motors and flashed him one more crisp, hundred-dollar bill. "I need to surprise someone. Would this help you keep our secret?"

The driver laughed. "Your secret is safe with me. My number is already in both phones," the driver said. "Vinny Torino. If you ever need *any*thing, night or day, I'm your man."

Clayton believed him. The man could be an asset, depending on how Clayton's plans played out. "I may take you up on that, Vinny. See you."

"I see nothing." Vinny pocketed the money and pushed *Retribution* from the slip. "Have a nice party."

Clayton nodded. "The best ever." At exactly 5:45 p.m., Clayton left the marina, taking the channel to Gloucester Harbor with the skiff trailing obediently behind *Retribution*. The bridge operator saluted again as Clayton passed. Even as he pulled away from shore, he plugged the phone into the boat's dash. The music blasted through who knew how many speakers hidden around the boat. Party songs, most of them.

He didn't especially like leaving Gloucester Harbor after dark, but *Retribution* was outfitted with state-of-the-art navigation. He'd watch the screen, and he'd be okay. And reaching Rockport would be the perfect end to a pretty darn perfect day.

Clayton guided *Retribution* far out from the harbor before turning north. So far, he'd been really careful not to leave any kind of trail to be followed. He wasn't going to get sloppy now. As far as he knew, Clayton Kingman, escaped convict, was presumed dead. Soon enough, the truth would come out. He'd do what he'd come to do, and then slip away without a trace.

The familiar opening notes of "Every Breath You Take" blasted over the waves as Clayton headed north. He sang along—at the top of his lungs. The day had been perfect. He'd be anchored in Sandy Bay, just off the town of Rockport, in an hour, easy.

"Ready or not, Parker Buckman, here I come. And do I have a surprise for you."

CHAPTER 75

PARKER FILED INTO THE COFFEE SHOP right behind his mom and Grams. Wilson followed, and Pez locked the door. She gave him a sad smile. *Sheesh . . . what was this all about?* Jelly sat at a table back by the rear windows, with Ella beside her.

Honestly, he kind of resented the meeting. Things had just been getting back to normal. Yeah, Dad and Uncle Sammy were still down in the Everglades. But it was about cleanup and recovery now. They were safe—and were going to stay that way. Things with Wilson were good. Even the fears about Kingman escaping seemed so . . . remote. Parker had a good feeling about it all. A confidence, really. Everything was going to be okay, and he didn't need Jelly putting some gloom-and-doom damper on that. And on top of all that, he was missing the game—which was important to Harley.

Parker was definitely trying to look beyond himself, but it was kind of hard when he felt he needed to be in two places at the same time. "Emergency. Life and death. What's going on?"

That's when he saw the postcards on the table.

Wilson groaned. "I thought we were *done* with those."

A rough circle was forming. Parker and Wilson hiked themselves up on tables along the fringe. It would make it easier to slip out and get back to the game if this meeting was as lame as it was beginning to look.

Pez motioned them closer. "Let's all sit where we can't be seen from the front windows."

"I'm good," Parker said. But he wasn't. They'd already analyzed the postcards to death, hadn't they? They were all ditching the football game to be here—for nothing.

A sharp knock at the door made both Mom and Grams shriek. Harley was on the other side of the glass—in his uniform. He propped his bike against the window.

Parker couldn't believe it. "*What?*"

Ella was on her feet—rushing to the door before anyone else had moved. She let him in and locked the door behind him.

"Sorry I'm late." Harley was breathing hard. "What did I miss?"

"Uh . . . the *game?*" Parker stared at him. Except for the helmet, he was wearing all the gear. "What are you *doing* here? You're supposed to be—"

"Jelly's text. Emergency. Life and death, right?" Harley shrugged. "It said we all needed to be here . . . for our family." He drew a circle in the air that seemed to loop around all of them.

Parker still couldn't get his head wrapped around this. "But the team . . . the game . . ."

"That's all it is. A game," Harley said. "But this is *family* . . . and where I felt maybe I belonged, or something." Now he didn't look so sure—of anything.

Ella hooked his elbow and pulled him toward the rest of the group. "We *are* a family, and you *are* a big part of it, Harley Davidson Lotitto. I for one am totally impressed with what you've just done."

Ditching a game . . . the last of the season? "The coach let you go?"

Harley locked eyes with Parker for an instant, but it was long enough for him to know.

"So the coach *didn't* give you a hall pass on this?" Parker wasn't so sure Ella even realized what this might mean for Harley.

"You haven't missed a thing," Pez said. "Now that Harley is here, we can officially start."

Harley boosted himself up on a table by Parker and Wilson.

"First"—Pez held up one card—"GB." She locked eyes with Parker. "Gatorbait."

It was like Parker had just taken a punch to the gut. He couldn't speak. He wasn't even sure he was breathing.

Pez explained the completely different way she'd interpreted the postcards—and she played the song. "So, to sum it all up, we think Clayton Kingman escaped the prison, survived the storm, and is headed up here to settle a score with Parker."

Instantly, the room went up for grabs. And deep inside, Parker lost his grip on every bit of confidence he'd had. If Pez and Jelly and Ella were right . . . Kingman's escape wasn't behind Parker.

His mom was there, hugging him tight. He squeezed her right back. "It's going to be okay, Mom."

Why did he even say that? Was it a knee-jerk reaction? Was it about wanting to keep Mom from being afraid? Or was he in denial . . . trying to convince himself things would be okay?

But that's not at all what his heart told him. Because deep down, he knew that everything definitely . . . positively . . . *wasn't* going to be okay.

CHAPTER 76

HARLEY WAITED UNTIL SOME OF THE initial commotion passed. Questions were flying around the room, but no real answers were coming in for a landing.

He gave a sharp whistle, and there was the slightest pause in the chaos as they looked his way. "If this is really that Clayton Kingman guy, why are we only worried about Parker? Wouldn't Jelly be a target too?"

"I can answer that." Jelly explained how she'd never gotten on Kingman's bad side like Parker had. She'd never ratted him out, either. In fact, she'd kept Kingman's dirty little secret until the very end. "As creepy as it sounds, I think he actually liked me," Jelly said. "He had a pet name for me and everything."

Okay, Harley wasn't going to let that slip past. "What did he call you?"

She shook her head. "Not important. The point is . . . he likes me. I never made myself his enemy like Parker did."

"Hold your horses, Jelly." Wilson smiled. "I know what he called you. And I, for one, hate keeping secrets from my brother here." He slung his arm around Harley. "Kingman called her *Angel*."

Jelly glared at him. "We all know the man was crazy."

"Crazy 'bout *you*, anyway," Wilson said.

The room erupted in laughter and teasing. The way Harley always thought it would be in a big family. And the little sidetrack about Jelly's nickname seemed to take the edge off the tension that'd been building.

"Maybe Clayton has no intention of coming up here—and the postcards are his idea of a sick joke," Mrs. Buckman said. "But we have to treat the threat as absolutely real." For an instant, Mrs. Buckman's eyes met Harley's. Was she counting on him to help bodyguard Parker or something? He gave her a slight nod.

"I just don't think he'd do it," Parks said. "*If* he survived Jericho's walls coming down—and *if* he got out of the swamps alive—it would be insane to come up here."

"He *is* insane." Jelly used her whole body to emphasize the words.

"But why send not one but three postcards to announce it?" Parks shook his head.

"What better way to create some fear?" Mrs. Buckman sighed. "Look, there are things we know about Clayton Kingman. He doesn't think like we do. And that's how he almost got away with what he did to Jelly's sister, right?"

Harley had heard part of the story. And even from what little he knew, Mrs. Buckman was spot-on.

She held up the postcards. Fanned them out. "If this is *him*, he's cheated death how many times? He wasn't crushed by the walls—or hurled to his death by Morgan. He's survived the swamps—and eluded the authorities. Almost every other inmate was taken down by one of those. When others struck out into the wilds to get away"—she tapped the postmark on one of the cards—"apparently, he went to the city and sent out some mail. Who would have guessed any of that?"

Parker stared at his feet. Harley didn't know if his mom's words had finally gotten through or if he just didn't want to argue a losing battle.

"Something wicked this way comes," Grams said.

It sounded like a quote, but Harley couldn't be sure. Her words definitely added a creepy vibe to the whole meeting.

"We have to be smart," Mrs. Buckman said. "We have to take some steps as if we truly believe he *is* coming up here."

That made sense. Ella. Grams. Miss Lopez. Even Wilson nodded on that one.

Over the next hour and fifteen minutes, they hammered out a plan. Decisions were made. A path forward was mapped. Phone calls were placed.

And Harley was in awe.

Even though they weren't all related by blood, *this* was how a family functioned. Sometimes the voices got loud, but that wasn't the same thing as yelling. There was passion, sure . . . but all of it was based on a kind of mutual respect. It wasn't like they always agreed, but they didn't let differing opinions stop all forward motion, either. Some ideas got yardage. Others didn't. But they kept making the first downs . . . and marched up the field.

Jelly erased the *Specials of the Day* chalkboard and brought the thing to the table. She kept a list of the confirmed action steps, and Harley snapped a picture. There were things he could help with there. He just had to figure out the right places to fit in.

Call the police. And they had already done that. Officer Greenwood promised to look into the possibility that Kingman had eluded the net cast for him in Florida. He promised to heighten the alert at bus stations, airports, and train stations in the greater Boston area . . . over a thousand miles beyond the current search perimeter in Florida. And he'd worked other cases with Uber and Lyft before, and he already knew a way to get Kingman's picture out to all their drivers in the area.

Don't let Parker out of our sight. Harley could help with that. He was pretty sure Wilson was on that one too.

Get out of the Buckman house. The postcards proved Kingman had Parker's address. How had he gotten that? The internet? So they had to make sure nobody was there if Kingman showed up. Harley saw himself helping with that one too. His room had three empty bunks. There was more than enough room for Parker and Wilson. He sent a quick text to Mr. Gunderson to get permission.

Dads fly home. Okay . . . this was the one that knocked Harley off his feet. Parker's mom had slipped out of the room and talked to them. And both men were coming back on the earliest flight Mrs. Buckman could book. They'd go back down and help in the effort after everyone was sure Clayton was gone—or had been captured. This was how real dads operated. They dropped everything when family was in trouble. There was something so strong about that. Reinforcements were coming. Something inside Harley wanted that. Ached for it.

Girls stay with Grams. Ella. Jelly. Even Mrs. Buckman. Nobody was taking any chances until the men came home. There'd be no easy breadcrumbs for Kingman to follow if he did come to town. If Kingman went to Parker's house, he'd find it empty. If he decided to press Jelly into telling where Parker was hiding out, he'd run into an empty house there, too . . . with no clue as to where they really were.

Never go anywhere alone. Ella. Jelly. Mrs. Buckman. All of them agreed not to go anywhere alone. Harley thought that was a little over the top. None of *them* were targets. Were they doing that so they could convince Parker and Wilson to do the same? Harley suspected that was what it was really about. And when Mrs. B came right out and said it, his suspicions were confirmed.

Wilson wanted weapons on the action list. He'd had to check his backpack as luggage on the flight here so he could bring his machete, survival knife, and whatever else he'd stowed in his pack that would make TSA freak. Along with what Parker had in his room, there was more than enough gear to make sure everyone had one or two surprises on them. Unfortunately, the idea met a wall of resistance from the ladies in the group.

"So you expect me to walk into Rockport High School next week with a machete sticking out of my pack?" Jelly added just enough sarcasm to make Wilson's idea look stupid.

"We need an edge," Wilson said. "And a machete has a nice sharp one."

He was fighting a losing battle, but he exchanged looks with Harley and Parker. Without a word, Harley knew they were all in agreement. *They* would be armed. Always. Except when they were in school.

They were still stuck on where to have Wilson and Parks sleep. Harley checked his phone, but Mr. Gunderson hadn't sent a message back yet. But it had to work. Otherwise, how could Harley really help protect them?

"I got extra mattresses in my bedroom," he said. "A whole extra bunkbed. Kingman can spend all day trying to track you down in Rockport. You'll be in Gloucester."

The idea of them staying in a different town definitely made Jelly and Ella happy.

"You sure that will be okay with your foster dad?"

Harley held up his phone. "Well, he hasn't said *no* yet." And the very fact that the Gundersons took in foster kids said something, right? Deep down, it couldn't only be about the money. Didn't that say they wanted to help protect kids who were at risk in some way? Well, Parks was at risk. Gunderson would go along with this. He just had to.

"Holed up at Harley's?" Parks shook his head. "No offense, but it feels like we're being quarantined. Or being sent to jail."

"And you'll go *directly* to jail," Ella said. "Do not pass Go. Do not collect $200."

Pez gave her leg a pat. "Love that Monopoly reference, girl."

Harley kind of did too.

"We can all do this for tonight." Mrs. Buckman smiled. "Vaughn and Sammy will be home by three o'clock tomorrow afternoon. We can talk about adjustments then."

And just like that, something changed. The ball had been snapped.

The play was in motion. The clock was running—and it wasn't going to stop until even the slightest threat of Kingman showing up was gone.

Mrs. Buckman prayed after that. Nothing fakey or flowery. It felt like she really was talking to God. Like she was standing before His throne . . . and somehow, she'd brought Harley with her.

"You have paid my ransom. You have become my reward. Now, Father . . . now, oh my Jesus . . . I need my rescuer."

An antsy restlessness gripped Harley. Like maybe he shouldn't be here. Like maybe a guy in the DDC wasn't quite qualified. He wished he had the wrench in his hands. He needed to do something. He settled for easing the lanyard out from under his T-shirt and holding Kemosabe's ignition key in his fist.

Grams prayed along with Parker's mom. "Yes, Lord. Sweet Jesus. Mmmm-hmmm. Just like that, Lord, just like that."

Harley tried to keep his eyes closed. But there was something about what was going on around him that he needed to see. He opened his eyes—but not wide. Just slits. Miss Lopez had her hands raised high. Silent tears ran down her cheeks. *Just how bad can this Kingman guy be?*

"Now, Almighty God . . . protect our boys," Mrs. Buckman prayed. "Our men. Deliver us from evil."

Ella clutched her cross necklace with both hands. Her eyes opened—and she looked directly at Harley. He held her gaze for an instant before bowing his head.

"You have delivered our Wilson—and Parker, Sammy, and Vaughn—from the dangers of the hurricane . . . and its aftermath. But in my heart, I sense we're moving into a second danger now."

For an instant, it was like someone slipped an ice cube down Harley's jersey—and held it against the small of his back. The chills radiated to his fingertips. He peeked again. Mrs. Buckman's lips were tight—like she was fighting back breaking into sobs or something.

She took a shaky breath and continued, "Oh, God . . . we're moving into something darker. Deadlier. Something infinitely more sinister. Something personal and targeted against our family. Grams was right when she said *something wicked this way comes*. He is coming. . . . I believe that. And his twisted mind is bent on some unspeakable evil. We've set up a plan—but we know ultimately only You can protect our men . . . Vaughn and Sammy. Only You can keep this threat from harming our young men . . . Wilson, Parker, and Harley."

She said *his* name? Prayed it. Actually spoke his name to God . . . like Harley was really a part of the family?

"Father"—Mrs. Buckman's voice was down to a whisper now—"watch over them as we are thrust into this second storm."

Second storm. That's exactly what this was. Only they were all in it now . . . not just Wilson. Harley rubbed down the goosebumps on his arms.

"And we pray all this in the powerful name of Jesus. Amen."

And that was it—the prayer was over. But to Harley? It felt like something was just beginning.

There was a strange awkwardness when he opened his eyes. He felt closer to everyone in the room somehow, and yet he still felt like he was on the sidelines. Harley looked at the list Jelly had chalked on the board. "This is a good plan. We'll keep one step ahead of this Kingman guy."

Jelly shook her head—with the saddest expression he'd ever seen on her. "We can't stay a step ahead. Not really. He's sick." She tapped her head. "We don't understand how he thinks. All we can do is pray he doesn't find Parker." It looked like she was ready to lose it herself.

"And if Kingman does find Parks?" Harley probably shouldn't have even asked the question.

Jelly's eyes were closed. "Then all we can do . . . is pray that we can stop Clayton in time."

CHAPTER 77

ANGELICA KICKED BACK ON THE EXTRA BED IN ELLA'S ROOM. She walked her bare feet up and down the wall above the headboard, every step perfectly placed on the footsteps painted there days earlier.

If only there were a sure path—a way to know that every step she took in real life would be right. Safe.

Mrs. Buckman had already grabbed some essentials from her house and had moved in with Grams. Pez had joined them—and was actually sleeping over. "More sets of eyes and ears—until the men get back anyway." That was all she'd said by way of explanation. She was amazing.

Even now, Angelica could hear snippets from the three of them in some deep conversation downstairs. Part of her wanted to be there. To hear what they were talking about . . . or who. But even more than that, she needed to be here . . . with Ella.

Parker had loaded a backpack and disappeared with Wilson and Harley—off to the Gunderson foster home, if they kept with the plan.

"We did it," Ella said. "We made our case. And they listened."

"You really think the guys are all in?"

Ella didn't answer for a moment. "Harley is. I saw it in his eyes."

"Yeah, well, I kind of picked up on that when he showed up in full uniform."

They both laughed for a moment. Angelica repositioned her feet on the wall. "And Wilson?"

"I don't know him like you do . . . but I think he's actually *hoping* something happens." El rolled onto her side to face her. "Do you really think he'll carry a machete around when he's not in school?"

"Oh, yeah. He'll have it. And I think you've got him pegged just right. What about Parker?"

Ella didn't say anything for what seemed like a minute. "He's harder to read. Sometimes I think he just doesn't see it—or doesn't want to believe it. Because if he does . . . it makes the danger that much more real."

That sounded about right too. The conversation drifted to Clayton Kingman. The sleazy way he'd called her Angel so many times. The uneasy feeling she'd always gotten when he had. Ella doused the room light. She didn't say why, but she didn't need to explain. She was probably feeling the same thing Angelica was. The more they talked about Kingman, the more she felt exposed—or vulnerable. Like he could see her if he really wanted. *I'll be watching you.* But here in the darkness, she could hide. They both could.

"Airports. Bus depots. Train stations. Uber. Lyft. All are going to be on high alert," Ella said. "But you're worried he'll still get through somehow, right?"

It made no sense, but yeah, she was. "He's got *one* arm. His picture has been *everywhere*. There's no way a normal person should get through." Even now, Officer Greenwood was probably patrolling the neighborhood. "But there's nothing normal about Clayton Kingman. He's a Houdini or something. The postcards proved he'd made it to New York—and those were mailed days ago."

Angelica checked her phone. She'd hoped the boys would be at Harley's foster home by now, but what were the chances of that happening? They'd have to have been pedaling hard, all the way. She had to let it go. For at least a minute.

"Calling that meeting was brilliant." Ella's comment pulled Angelica from her thoughts. Maybe it had been a good move, but that didn't make up for all the dumb ones Angelica had already made.

"When am I ever going to learn?" Angelica could barely make out her painted footprints in the darkened room. "I think I can be the protector . . . but I always seem to make the wrong call."

"Such as?"

"I wanted to keep Parker from going back down to the Glades. But I was wrong. If he *hadn't* gone . . . would Wilson have been found in time?"

Ella stayed quiet. She was good that way. Some friends would be quick to convince Angelica that she was being too hard on herself. Ella seemed to know when to let Angelica just vent her heart.

"And once Parker was down there . . . I pushed and pushed to convince his mom to get him back after they found Wilson. Parker was what, within a hundred miles of the prison break? All I could think about was the danger he could be in.

"But Kingman would've had no idea Parker was so close. He was making his way north somehow—distancing himself from Parker with every mile he traveled. Parker was actually safer down in the Glades than he is up here. I've basically delivered Parker to the place Kingman expects to find him." And that was no exaggeration. "Angelica Malnatti, the great protector of her friends. Yeah, there's an escaped convict on the loose . . . bent on killing him. And I've put Parker on a collision course with the psycho. Again. Some protector."

The two of them were silent for a bit. There was something about the dark room that helped her see herself more clearly than if she'd been looking in a mirror on a bright day.

"I'm telling you, El, here's the honest to goodness truth: Whenever I try to scheme and connive to protect Parker . . . I always make things worse."

CHAPTER 78

PARKER DIDN'T LIKE THE ATTENTION. It was like he was a celebrity or something—but in a bad way. Wilson and Harley were his bodyguards. He just wanted to be regular Parker. But thanks to Jelly, that was impossible now.

After the emergency meeting, they'd sidetracked to the school on their way to Harley's foster home. A custodian let them in so Harley could change back into his street clothes. And the word was out. He'd been officially cut from the team. A dishonorable discharge, for sure.

And all because he felt Parker needed protecting. Mom. Dad. Uncle Sammy. Jelly. And now Harley and Wilson. Everybody changing plans—and focused on protecting him . . . like he was a little kid playing too close to the street.

He'd wanted to go to the Headlands—just the three of them. But Harley wouldn't have any of it. It seemed the ball game with Mr. Gunderson was too close to call, and he didn't want to risk anything that might earn him another strike. Parker was pretty sure that Harley wanted to get Parker out of sight, too, just in case Kingman showed. They'd made a quick stop at the Dollar Store on the way to Harley's foster home. Harley went in by himself while they watched his bike. He came back with a bag. He didn't tell them what he'd bought—and they didn't ask. They followed Harley as they rode the last few blocks.

Harley circled around to the back side of the house, just outside his bedroom window. "You guys wait out here. I have to talk to Mr. G."

Parker set down his pack with all his overnight stuff—including the weapons. "Wait. I thought you said you'd texted him about all this?"

"I did. But he hasn't answered me yet."

Wilson snickered. "Uh-oh. Do we have a Plan B?"

There was no place else. "Grams's guest house?" But as soon as Parker suggested it, he knew it was a bad idea. There was definitely a renter coming in late tonight.

"I'll talk to Mr. G in person. I'm sure he'll give us one night to see how it goes," Harley said. "Stay right here—and keep your voices down, okay? We'll be in. I guarantee it."

Wilson laughed again. "I'm betting we'll be camping somewhere tonight. We may get to the Headlands yet, Bucky."

"Shhhh. Give me five minutes. We got this."

He sounded absolutely sure of himself. But even in the dim light, that's not what his eyes said.

CHAPTER 79

WILSON LOOKED AT THE DARK BEDROOM WINDOWS of Harley's room again. "Think he forgot us?"

Bucky laughed.

"It's been a lot longer than five minutes." But there were plenty of places they could sleep if this didn't work, right? "We should have grabbed some blankets from your house."

The light snapped on in Harley's bedroom, and a moment later he raised the window. "We're good."

Wilson gave Parker the side-eye, then looked at Harley. "You want us to cli—"

"Shhhh!" Harley motioned with both hands. "Keep it down. Mr. Gunderson isn't wild about the idea."

"Should we find another place?"

Harley shook his head. "If you do, I'll be stuck here . . . and we agreed to stay together, right?"

Parker looked like he was ready to back out of the whole thing. "Yeah, but . . ."

"Come on," Wilson said. "Gimme a boost."

Parker hesitated for just a moment, then knit his hands together to make a stirrup. Wilson stepped into it, and Parker hefted him a little higher. For just an instant, Wilson pictured that moment when Parker and his dad had rescued him from the airboat. They reached for him . . . pulled him free. Even now, Wilson climbed through the window like the gators were still nipping at his feet.

The moment he was inside, he offered a hand to Parker. Seconds later, the three of them stood in the saddest room Wilson had ever seen. Two bunk beds. Four mattresses. Gray walls—with nothing hanging on them except a corkboard with a small picture of a motorcycle. There was no bookcase. Besides the motorcycle picture, there was nothing personal in the room to make it Harley's. The rescue workers' tents in Everglades City had more of a homey feeling than Harley's room did.

"Nice place," Wilson said. "A *tad* depressing, though, don't you think?"

The three of them did their best to muffle their laughter. Parker stepped closer to the corkboard. "What's with the two strikes?"

Harley shrugged. "Three-strike rule."

"And then what . . . you're grounded or something?"

"Or something." Harley pointed to a top bunk. "I've got this spot. Sleep wherever you want."

Had he deliberately dodged Parker's question? "You've got a full count here, Harley."

"Yeah, and I'm lucky it's only two strikes. Mr. Gunderson came to the game tonight. Found out I ditched it. I have no idea how I talked him out of a strike for that one. He was *not* happy, though."

Wilson eyed him. "So . . . if you get a third strike . . . exactly *what* happens?"

Harley winced. "The top bunk will be empty again."

Sheesh. And Wilson thought *his* dad was tough. The Gunderson guy was an idiot. "Did you tell him you're trying to help a friend? Want me to talk to the guy?"

"No." Harley grinned. "I want you to stay really quiet, okay?"

Parker had that suspicious look on his face. "He did say it was okay for us to stay, though, right?"

"Look, I'm kind of on probation here." Harley glanced over his shoulder at the bedroom door. "I'm thinking if we're quiet—and we don't cause him to lose any sleep—maybe he'll warm up to the idea. Just grab a mattress."

Wilson still wasn't sure if that Gunderson dude had agreed to allow them to stay or not. Parker sat on the edge of the bottom bunk. He pulled his phone charger from his pack and plugged it in.

"We're together—and Kingman has no way of knowing where we are. We're safe. That's all that matters." Harley looked like he was about to climb into bed, but he stopped dead. He picked up a socket wrench that was lying on his pillow. "Huh."

Wilson snickered and climbed to the other top bunk. "You sleep with a ratchet wrench? Talk about a total gearhead."

Harley smiled and ratcheted the tool a few times, then dropped it in his pack in the corner. He kicked off his shoes and boosted himself up to the top bunk, still carrying the bag from the Dollar Store. He pulled out a sheet of glow-in-the-dark stars, picked one off, and stuck it to the ceiling next to one that clearly had been there for a long time. He added another, and another, until the group of stars covered the space of a large pizza. He pulled out a pen and made smiley faces on the stars.

"You have got some strange sleeping habits, Harley." Wilson leaned on one elbow. "What are you doing now?"

Harley leaned back and surveyed his tiny galaxy. "Giving that little star a family."

"What are you," Wilson said, "six?"

"I wish." Harley said it real quiet. Like he was just thinking out loud.

"So," Parker said, "what *is* the story with the stars?"

Harley dropped back onto his pillow. "Just making sure the next guy doesn't feel like he's all alone."

CHAPTER 80

PARKER WOKE WITH A START.

"What in *tarnation* is going on here?!" To say Mr. Gunderson shouted wouldn't do it justice. *Bellowed* was a better word. "Didn't I say *no* friends in this room? I got a wife and daughter living under this roof."

What was that supposed to mean? Should Parker leave? Probably—but at the moment, he couldn't move.

"I took you in—a kid with *no* family—to let you live in my home with a safe, *normal* family." Gunderson's face was incredibly red. "And *this* is how you thank me?" He strode deeper into the room. Pointed at Wilson's pack. "Is that a *machete* sticking out of his backpack? You brought in some gangbangers—and let them bring weapons in my house? What else does he have in there—an AK-47?"

Harley leaped off the top bunk to the ground. "A *real* family helps each other, right? And I needed help—but you brushed me off."

"You went against my direct orders."

"I just wanted to prove they'd be no trouble. Then you'd let them st—"

"*No* trouble?" Gunderson shook his head in mock confusion. "They're nothing *but* trouble. They got you kicked off the football team last night. And now they earned you another big fat strike."

Harley looked like he'd been hit by the pitch. "They're good guys; they're—"

"Out of here," Gunderson roared. "And so are you. Strike three." He gestured with his thumb. "You're out."

Parker swung his feet over the bed and pulled on his shoes. He wanted nothing more than to get out of the place. He wished he'd slept in Steadman's boat. Anywhere would have been better than this. But Harley needed this place.

Harley looked desperate. Like he was beginning to realize that without a foster home locally, the state could move him anywhere. "I'm sorry, Mr. Gunderson. Look—"

"No. *You* look." Gunderson stormed to the scoreboard and grabbed a number three from an envelope tacked in the corner. He tore the number two off the wall and slapped the three in its place. "You swung. You missed. You chose your friends over family—and you're out."

"They're all I've got." Harley still didn't look like he understood the obvious . . . that this conversation was over. "They're more than friends. They're—"

"Trespassing." Mr. Gunderson pointed at Wilson and then at Parker. "You're both trespassing. And you've got about thirty seconds to vamoose before I call 911—and tell them I've got armed trespassers in the house."

Wilson vaulted off the mattress above him and landed on his feet.

"I'm calling your social worker, Mr. Lotitto. You just spent your last night in the Gunderson home."

This was no home. Not like anything Parker had ever experienced.

"You two." Gunderson pointed at Wilson and Parker. "Be out of here before I get back." He stormed out of the room.

Parker stuffed his charger in his pack. "Man, Harley . . . I am so sorry." This was his fault, right? Harley was just trying to be a good friend. "I can't believe he's kicking you out."

Harley's face . . . so red. "Yeah. I'm part of the family. Then suddenly I'm not. Same old story." He jammed the few things he owned into his pack.

Wilson watched the door like he expected Gunderson to come back with a baseball bat. "We gotta get out of here. Now."

Harley nodded. "But not out the front door." He motioned toward the window. "Trespassers aren't allowed through the house. Now that he bounced me, I guess I'm a trespasser too."

Wilson had the window open—and threw his pack outside. A second later, he followed.

Harley gave the room a last look—like he wanted to be sure he didn't leave anything behind. He stared at the cluster of stars on the ceiling. "Tell the next kid good luck from me."

Parker tossed his pack outside. "Harley . . . what are you going to do now?" It was a stupid question. How would Harley know? He was a ward of the state—and they'd decide.

"Get out of this rat hole." Harley offered Parker a boost. "After you."

Parker climbed through and jumped onto the back lawn. Harley was halfway through the window himself when Gunderson's voice boomed from somewhere behind him.

"The social worker is going to want to talk to you, Son."

Harley didn't look back. "She's got my number." He dropped to the ground.

"Yeah." Gunderson leaned out the window. "Looks like I got your number too."

CHAPTER 81

ELLA WORKED THE COUNTER ALONGSIDE JELLY at the coffee shop. Harley's apron hung from the peg at the entrance to the kitchen. He should have been wearing it an hour ago. Where was he?

The counter wasn't just a place for customers to sit on stools and enjoy their coffee and donuts. It formed a natural separation between them and the workers. But even the counter couldn't keep Scorza from invading the little workspace they had behind it. He leaned forward, constantly yacking as Ella and Jelly served donuts and coffee to real customers.

Scorza's nose was taped and red—like maybe he'd played in last night's game . . . without his helmet. "It was incredible. I mean, the guy just ran out of the locker room. Last game of the season—and he threw it all away. Boom. Just like that."

Would he never shut up? "You're not telling us anything we don't know."

"Coach was hotter than you-know-what. Harley is *so* done with football—and not just this year. You know Coach will never let him play again, right?"

Okay . . . Ella didn't know *that*. And by the look on Jelly's face, she hadn't figured that either.

"Coach warned him he'd never play ball again. But Harley left anyway. The dumbest thing I ever saw."

Oh, Harley.

"We're not in trouble," Jelly said. "Do we look like we're in trouble?"

Scorza took a bite of his sprinkled donut. "Somebody's in trouble. That's why Harley ditched the team. So, who is it?"

The bell on the front door chimed, and Mr. Gunderson stalked in. Wide at the shoulders. Wider at the waist. Like a guy who used to play high school ball—and still ate like he was burning off thousands of calories at practice every day. There was nothing warm and fuzzy about Harley's foster dad. He stood at the counter. "Harley Lotitto. Where is he?"

Poor Harley. What had he done to get Mr. Gunderson so riled up?

"Harley's not in yet." Pez stepped out of the back room. "How can I make your day a little brighter?"

Ella loved the way Pez greeted customers.

Gunderson slapped a phone charging cord onto the counter along with a folded piece of paper. "Give these to Harley. I don't want to see his face again."

What? Ella stared at him.

Pez opened the paper. It was a picture of a motorcycle. A 1999 Harley-Davidson XL Sportster.

Oh, Harley!

Gunderson went on a tirade. Harley had told him about Parker being hunted by an escaped convict—and needing a safe place to crash at night. "I told him no—but he did it anyway. Can't have a boy like that around my family. Who knows where the state will put him now."

Ella stood there—in a stunned silence. But inside, she was scream-ing. *No. No. No.*

"Oh, dear." Pez smiled apologetically. "So, Harley risked everything to protect someone he really cared about? Someone in danger? Seems to me Harley is just the kind of young man you *do* want staying at your house."

"You don't get it," Gunderson said. "I have a family to protect."

"But as a foster dad, wasn't the state paying you to make Harley part of your family?" Pez asked the question in an innocent enough way, but Ella saw right through her. "It seemed to me that Harley needed protecting—and he went to you for help."

Gunderson's eyes narrowed, like he wasn't sure if Pez was that naive or just really shrewd. "I don't get paid enough to risk my *real* family."

Pez grabbed a pair of tongs and slipped an apple fritter into a bag. She held it out to Mr. Gunderson. "For your trouble. I'll see to it that Harley gets the charger."

Gunderson hesitated, like he was looking for the catch.

Pez shook the bag slightly. "You've had a tough morning. I guarantee this will make it a tiny bit better."

He took the bag this time. Mumbled a weak thanks, then strode out the door.

"Pez." Ella tried to keep her voice steady. She didn't want to burst out into tears . . . not with Scorza watching. "What does this mean? What will happen to H—"

Pez touched Ella's lips with her finger. "Not here, sweetie."

Scorza's eyes were wide—and alive. Like he'd just thrown a touch-down pass.

"You were way nicer to Gunderson than I would have been," Jelly said. "If it were me—"

"Return good for evil," Pez said, "whenever you can."

"So, *Gatorade* may be a hunted man?" Scorza shook his head, smiling in wonder. "And Harley's stupid need to be the hero—to play personal bodyguard—got him booted off the team *and* kicked out of his foster home?"

Ella wanted to kick Scorza right out of the coffee shop. "Looks like there's no end to what some guys will do to help their friends."

"Sounds like Harley needs an apple fritter—because he's definitely *not* having a good day." Scorza grinned and scanned the room. "Where is he anyway? Or wait . . . did he get fired, too? Oh, that would be rich . . . a perfect hat trick—in a loser sort of way."

Pez patted Scorza's arm. "Don't you worry. That young man has a job here as long as he wants it." She marched off to the back room with Ella drafting behind her.

It was too much. Too much. Ella's eyes burned with hot tears. "Pez," she said the moment they got out of earshot of the counter. She grabbed Harley's apron from the peg and held it up. "Where is he? Do you know?"

She nodded. "He called. Told me everything. He's out in the boat with Parker and Wilson right now. I figured we could handle things here. Give him some time."

What if Harley's social worker couldn't find him a home in the area. "This is really bad, isn't it."

Pez smiled apologetically. "It's not good."

Jelly stormed into the back room, grabbing fistfuls of her own hair. "Scorza is driving me berserk! He says I should think about my own safety and distance myself from Parker. Do you believe that guy?"

Pez motioned for her to lower her voice.

"Scorza *reminded* me that Parker almost got him killed this summer at the Salvages. Scorza claims he only got run over by the boat because he was helping *Parker*—and he stayed too close. He doesn't want that happening to me."

Pez put a finger on Jelly's lips. "Whisper, honey."

"He rewrites history. He's a self-serving, egotistical pig and—"

Ella stepped in and helped cover her mouth. "He's a jerk. We know that." He was no more than a bug. An irritation. The fact that Harley would be reassigned to a different home—anywhere in Massachusetts? That was the real problem.

Jelly seemed calmer.

Ella hoped it was contagious, because there was nothing calm going on inside her. "Deep breath, Jelly." She lifted her hand from Jelly's mouth and hesitated, then lowered it altogether.

"I'll whisper," Jelly said. "Scorza says I need to look out for myself— or let *him* do it." She scrunched her face up in an agonizing expression. "Ew, right? His exact words? 'Why don't you hang with me for a while, Everglades Girl?'"

Ella peeked around the corner. Scorza was still at the counter, scrolling through his phone. "What did you tell him?"

"I told him there was a better chance of me *hanging* him than hanging *out* with him." She turned to Pez. "What do we do about Harley? We have to *do* something."

Pez seemed to be thinking about that for a moment. "I'll tell you what I'm going to do. The next right thing. And then the next right thing after that. I'm going to pray that God guides my steps—and works something out."

"But what about Harley? They *can't* take him away. We need him. And what about Parker and Wilson? They're in danger." Jelly asked the questions burning in Ella's heart. "This is even worse than the hurricane."

It was the maelstrom Pez had talked about when they'd heard about Kingman's escape. It was the sound of approaching thunder. An ominous wind shift. It was thickening clouds. Darkening skies. It was what Parker's mom had mentioned in her prayer—the start of the second storm.

"You're right." Pez reached out to hold Jelly's hand—and Ella's. "Some very scary things have happened—and I fear more are coming. But right now, we're going to give the boys some space. And we're going to take care of our customers all day. And after we close, we're going to clean the place up and cater that Halloween sweet sixteen birthday party tonight."

Ella groaned inside. She'd forgotten about that. Not that she didn't want to help—it was just that the timing was so bad now. How would any of this help Harley—or Parker and Wilson?

"Harley was here for us last night . . . for the meeting we called," Jelly said. "And he gave up football to do it—something he loved."

Ella pictured him—the way he'd shown up with his uniform and pads and everything. "And now he lost his home because he wanted to protect Parker—and Wilson? Don't you ever wonder *where* God is, Pez?"

She smiled. "You think God has missed anything that's happened in the last twenty-four hours?"

Ella was pretty sure God saw everything. Would He *do* anything about it, though? That was the question. "But what if Mr. Gunderson won't take Harley back?"

"One step at a time, Ella."

Not an assuring "everything is going to be okay" kind of answer. More of a "yeah, this is bad, but let's deal with it later" kind of thing. To Ella, it sounded like even Pez believed there would be no changing Gunderson's mind. Harley would be sent to a new foster home.

And the worst thing? This time it could be really far away.

CHAPTER 82

THE HARBOR BY NEARBY GRANITE PIER PROVIDED Clayton Kingman with exactly what he'd need tonight. A new boat.

He motored the inflatable skiff along the fringes of the harbor until he found one that bobbed at a mooring far from shore. The name *Escape Room* was painted across the transom. Definitely a pleasure craft—but with all the telltale signs that it didn't get out much. What were the chances that the owner would drive up from Boston, or wherever he lived, and take it for a ride on a raw Halloween weekend? Slim enough for Clayton to risk it.

Escape Room was easily a 28-footer with a snug little cabin. An inboard motor. It was a safe bet that it had considerably less muscle than *Retribution*. But it would still have plenty to get him to Rhode Island or even Maine if he decided to take it that far. It looked like the owner couldn't decide if he wanted the boat for cruising or fishing, and he'd settled on a compromise of both.

Once aboard, Clayton took a long look at the shoreline to be sure he had no audience. Satisfied, he jimmied the cabin door lock and stepped inside. It was compact, for sure, but he'd have all the room he really needed for himself—and a passenger. Clayton gave the cabin a quick search until he found the spare key for *Escape Room*. Every boater kept at least one hidden on board—and finding this one proved to be no challenge whatsoever. Once he had the key, Clayton checked the gas, started the motors, and unloaded the supplies from the inflatable.

He'd thought ahead on what he'd need—even for this stage of the plan. From the get-go, he'd divided his essentials into three duffel bags. Each had the same contents. A change of clothes, a Glock 19 or a Sig Sauer, a couple of boxes of 9-mm, and enough cash to disappear for a long, long time. He stowed one duffel in *Escape Room*'s cabin. The other two were still on *Retribution*. If all went well, one more of those duffels would end up in *Escape Room* tonight. The other would stay aboard *Retribution* to complete his ruse.

The cabin windows were old school. Just streamlined, narrow things that were all about bringing light into the cabin but didn't provide much of a view. Exactly what he'd hoped for. And it made covering them with duct tape quick and easy.

He did one careful sweep of the cabin to make sure there was nothing sharp or dangerous. Nothing someone could use to cut their bonds—or attack him.

Finally, he unloaded the chum buckets Vinny Torino had supplied. The four of those would do the job—and then some. And Vinny had included a couple of five-pound bags of Bloodstream Shark Chum—his personal chum of choice. The product claimed that the chum slick it created was the equivalent of a hundred pounds of fresh, bloody chum—and would last for up to eight hours. The most impressive feature? Bloodstream boasted that it could effectively draw sharks from up to 47 miles away.

Okay, that was way more chum than he needed, but sometimes

that kind of overkill was effective at creating debilitating fear. That was exactly what Clayton wanted.

Satisfied with his preparations, Clayton pocketed the ignition key for *Escape Room*, made sure the boat looked exactly the way he'd found it, and stepped back into the inflatable for the short run back to *Retribution*. By the time he pulled up alongside the bigger boat, he was slick with spray that chilled him to the bone. He'd accomplished his mission, though, and that was all that mattered.

He'd anchored the mother ship in Sandy Bay, a couple hundred yards from shore. *Retribution* nosed into the wind. The bow rose and fell in rhythm with the waves. It was almost like the boat itself was chanting, "Let's go, let's go, let's go . . ." just as eager as Clayton was to put the next phase of his plan in motion.

But it would come soon enough.

He tied the inflatable's bow line to a cleat mounted on *Retribution*'s gunwale for now. The time to move the little boat would come later. For now, everything was in place. He sat in the captain's chair and swiveled it to face Front Beach, directly off his stern. Behind it was Beach Street, and beyond that a cemetery climbed a fairly steep rise. The idea of anchoring so close to a graveyard intrigued him. If everything continued to go as well as it had so far, there'd be at least one fresh grave in Rockport before this was over. Maybe more.

CHAPTER 83

THE RIDE WAS NEARLY OVER, but Wilson wished Bucky would keep driving his nameless boat all day. The Boston Whaler had to be ten feet longer than the old *Boy's Bomb*, had ten times the horsepower on the transom, and handled the light chop a whole lot better too. Bucky drove them north all the way to Pigeon Cove, then turned back and followed the coast past the Granite Pier, Back Beach, and now Front Beach.

"You ready yet to tell me what you named this thing?"

Bucky ran his hand over the console like he was admiring the wax job. "Steadman's boat."

"Liar. That's what you *call* it. What's its name?"

Even Harley looked interested in hearing it.

"If it's ever really mine, I'll tell you."

"So you *do* have a name for it." Wilson had been right. "I know you, Parker Buckman. And I'm not buying your line that the boat is too good to just sit at the dock without somebody giving it a little attention. I know why you wipe it down and keep it running and check and recheck the dock lines a million times when we get to the pier."

"Yeah?"

"You're in love with the boat, man." Wilson grinned. "You look at this boat the way I look at *Typhoon*. Or at least the way I did before the hurricane. You're going to tell me that name."

"Wouldn't that be nice?" Bucky swung wide around a huge Boston Whaler anchored in Sandy Bay. The thing had to be forty feet long. The name *Retribution* was painted on the side near the stern. Four Mercury outboards on the transom. Unbelievable power. A gray and white inflatable bobbed behind it, tugging at the line as if the little dinghy thought it might drag *Retribution* to shore.

"Why don't we stay out on the water, Bucky?" There was no risk of Kingman sneaking up on them. They'd see anybody approaching them by water for miles.

"We've kept Harley from work long enough—and Dad's flight will be landing soon. Mom wants us riding to the airport with her."

"Whew," Wilson said. "I feel a whole lot better knowing your mom is there to protect us."

Harley snickered.

The Everglades—with its gators—seemed a million miles away. Wilson liked that fact, although he'd never admit that to the others.

In a way, each one of them was facing their own demons. Harley was just as homeless as Wilson right now. And Bucky—the target of a psycho?

"You really think the whole postcard thing is legit?"

Parker cut way back on the throttle. "Not like Jelly does."

"You believe the postcards are from Kingman," Harley said, "but they're only a scare tactic—not a real threat?"

"Exactly." Parker shrugged. "I can't see him risking recapture just to get even with me."

Maybe it was the daylight. Or the sense of safety out here on the water. But that was exactly what Wilson was beginning to think. "I got a feeling your dad—and Jelly's—bought a plane ticket for nothing."

Parker agreed, but Harley still looked like he was riding the fence.

"So what do we do, Bucky? It's like we're stuck in some witness protection program. We've got to have chaperones and bodyguards wherever we go. It's so over-the-top, don't you think?"

Parker slid the gearshift into neutral and turned to face him. "Definitely. But if we go along with it, the whole thing will blow over fast."

"So, for now," Harley said, "no pushback?"

"Not unless we want Jelly to strap tracking devices on us."

"She hasn't changed much," Wilson said. "Anybody have an idea where we'll be sleeping tonight?"

Parker shifted the boat back into gear. "My dad said he'd work on that. The bigger question is what you're going to do, Harley. Did the social worker call?"

"No idea." Harley shrugged. "I turned my phone off after talking to Miss Lopez."

Wilson laughed—and didn't blame him a bit. "Get ready for a blitz of messages when you turn it back on."

Nobody spoke as they pulled back into Rockport Harbor. They drove through Outer Harbor. Past the Tuna Wharf. Motif Number 1. T-wharf.

"Let's just go along with what they tell us to do," Harley said. "Jelly will calm down. Everybody will."

"Unless . . . Jelly is right." Wilson did his best to talk in an ominous tone. "And there really *is* something to all this." He stood—one arm tucked behind his back, the other outstretched like Frankenstein's monster. He stepped toward Bucky . . . reaching for him. "And even now, Clayton Kingman is close. His twisted, demented mind fixed on one thing . . . on one person." Wilson grabbed Bucky's T-shirt at the collar, shaking and stretching it like a madman.

Bucky, Harley, and Wilson laughed hard enough for any one of them to dislodge their Adam's apple.

Bucky pulled into the slip, and Wilson and Harley jumped to the dock to secure the lines.

"Okay." Bucky cut the motor. "We got just enough time to walk with Harley to BayView Brew. Then the two of us will meet my mom for the airport run."

Wilson did his best to put on a mock face of terror. "We gotta walk all the way from the coffee shop—to your house? Just the two of us? Without your mama?"

"No worries," Bucky said. "Maybe we'll ask Jelly if she'll escort us home."

CHAPTER 84

CLAYTON KINGMAN EASED BACK ON *RETRIBUTION*'S THROTTLE. The team of Mercury outboards idled restlessly, like they wanted to show Clayton what they could *really* do.

"I feel the same way, boys." He was itching—no, *craving*—to throttle ahead to the grand event tonight. But this little detail was the lynchpin to the ultimate ending for his little rematch. Without it, his door to freedom would never stay open long enough to truly get away.

He checked the distant shoreline. He was far enough south of Rockport, and a good five miles off Straitsmouth Island. He pulled the Catalina inflatable alongside *Retribution* and climbed in. He stowed one of the last two duffel bags under the rear bench seat. He added flashlights, an extra sweatshirt, and a rain jacket to the gear already inside. He could have left the bag in *Retribution* until tonight, but the transfer would need to be done quick. Every minute would count. And if for some reason he had to change plans at the last minute and couldn't get back to *Escape Room*, the duffel would have everything he needed to disappear.

Clayton dropped an anchor off the inflatable's bow and watched the line play out and disappear into the green-black depths. He unfurled the diver's flag and set the pole securely in its holder. Climbing back aboard *Retribution*, he untied the inflatable from the cleat—and tossed the bow line into the dinghy. Mission accomplished. Clayton hustled to *Retribution*'s console and dropped a pin to mark the exact location. He gave the inflatable a salute, then throttled forward.

The Catalina bobbed in *Retribution*'s wake, setting the diver's flag into a frantic waving motion. The universal red and white diver's flag would keep any curious boaters away. Anybody passing the Catalina would give it a wide berth. They'd think somebody was scuba diving without a topside spotter. Some might call it reckless, but it was done all the time.

"Sit tight, buddy. I'll be back." Clayton Kingman smiled. "And I won't be alone."

CHAPTER 85

DID DAD HAVE AS MANY DOUBTS AS Parker did about the Kingman threat being real? If he did, he hid all signs of it. Ever since they'd picked Uncle Sammy and him up at Logan International Airport in Boston, he'd been in "dad mode." Or maybe it was National Park ranger mode. But clearly, two of the three most important men in Parker's life weren't taking any chances.

Miss Lopez had a third-story attic bedroom above the coffee shop. She'd called Dad and offered it as a crash pad for the boys. Dad had jumped on the idea. Based on the postcards, Kingman knew exactly where Parker lived. But there was no connection to Pez's place. It was the perfect hideaway.

Dad stopped at the Walmart in Danvers on the ride back from the airport. He bought three sleeping bags, pillows, toothbrushes, and a tube of toothpaste. The plan was that he'd drop the boys off at BayView Brew before heading home. If, by some remote chance, Kingman had made it all the way to Rockport—and was watching the Buckman house? There was no sense stopping there for gear—and leading him right to where the boys would be hiding out.

After dropping off the boys, Dad would drop Mom off at Grams's place for the night. Jelly and Ella would join them after they'd finished helping Pez cater the Halloween sweet sixteen party they'd committed to. After that, everybody was to stay put.

Dad and Uncle Sammy would be posted all night at Parker's home. If Kingman showed up, they'd be ready. Even Officer Greenwood promised he'd patrol the neighborhood—keeping a tight watch over Parker's place and Jelly's.

Dad took 127 into Rockport. "Everybody good with the plan?"

Wilson shrugged. "Bring it on, Mr. B. It would kind of be a letdown if he doesn't show up after this."

"I'm with you, Wilson," Uncle Sammy said. "Nothing would make me happier than to find that animal slinking around Rockport. We gotta finish this."

Wilson laughed. "Finish *him*, you mean."

Uncle Sammy gave Wilson a quick wink. "He's like a gator gone rogue. You have to deal with that kind."

Like Uncle Sammy and Dad had dealt with the gator they'd named Dillinger? But just the thought of what Uncle Sammy was saying was terrifying in its own way. Or was the thing that really scared him something more personal? Closer to home. Like the fact that deep down inside, Parker agreed that someone had to *finish* Kingman.

"Parker, you keep your phone on—and make sure your charge is good." Dad looked at him in the rearview mirror. "Mom and I will do the same. And we'll be praying, too." That was a given. Something Parker needed to put more effort into himself.

Mom took a deep breath and let it out. She turned and smiled back at Parker and Wilson as they pulled up to BayView. "You boys be careful, you hear?" She reached for Parker's hand. Squeezed it hard like she didn't want to let go. Didn't want to say goodbye. "I mean it." Desperation haunted Mom's eyes. A flash of fear. The kind you get when you strap on a tank and plunge into a dark quarry. Or step off the back of a dive boat miles offshore—and you know a great white could be waiting.

"We'll be okay, Mom." Even as he said it, an uneasiness settled over him.

She unbuckled and turned in the seat. "You, Wilson, and Harley—you'll all be watching out for each other. That makes me feel a little bit better. We'll all follow the plan, right? Everything's set."

But for the first time all day, Parker wasn't so sure things were set at all.

CHAPTER 86

CLAYTON KINGMAN DROPPED ANCHOR in Sandy Bay, directly north of Bearskin Neck—just about where he'd been anchored before. He eased *Retribution* into reverse and tested to be sure the anchor held. There was something incredibly satisfying about anchoring a boat so that it wouldn't drift. The secret was using plenty of line. Too many weekend boaters had no clue. They thought the key was using a heavier anchor, but that wasn't it at all. Clayton could secure a ten-thousand-pound boat with a twenty-pound anchor. Easy. You just had to know how much line to use.

Retribution's anchor gripped the bottom of Sandy Bay tight. Satisfied, Clayton ducked into the cabin and changed into the costume purchased for him by the party store guy who'd proved he was a lot more than a delivery driver. Clayton told him to find a good one, and Vinny Torino hadn't disappointed. This one looked like it could have been used on a movie set.

He checked himself in the mirror. Wig. Pirate captain's hat. Massively full beard—separated into a series of braids, each tied off with ribbon. There wasn't much of Clayton's face showing. "Aye, you be lookin' more like Blackbeard than the bloke himself." With the eyepatch in place, even Clayton's dad wouldn't recognize him.

The pirate topcoat fit nicely. Wide leather belts crisscrossed his chest with imitation pirate pistols sticking out conspicuously. A sword swung at his side. Plastic—but not exactly looking like a kid's toy, either. Wide-legged pirate pants—and boots rising up to his knees. "You be lookin' fine as full sails and following seas, says I."

The missing arm might have been an issue if Clayton hadn't thought ahead. Vinny Torino had promised him a really good fake arm. The kind sold at the Halloween stores that pop up every Fall. Torino even brought a sling made from black cloth. With the fake arm tucked neatly inside, it just looked like Clayton put a lot of effort into the costume for his niece's party. Anybody could tell the arm was fake . . . but nobody would guess he didn't have a real arm tucked inside the jacket. Nobody would suspect he was the one-armed convict who'd successfully escaped, survived a hurricane, and eluded the massive manhunt that had turned Florida inside-out looking for him.

The way Clayton saw things, fate smiled on a guy who could land on his feet like he did. That sense of being immortal was unexplainable but so, so real.

Hadn't Blackbeard continued to fight—even after taking more than one bullet? Even the costume was the right choice for the occasion. Clayton would draw on his own immortality and on the legendary sense of invincibility the costume added.

Blackbeard would shock his opponents with his bizarre tactics. Even *they* believed he was unbeatable—and as soon as that thought was in their head, Blackbeard became exactly that.

Blackbeard was known to carry multiple weapons, and Clayton would live up to the reputation. He tucked a fully loaded Glock 19 into the back of his waistband. The hip pockets on his topcoat were deep.

He slipped a completely charged Axon Taser 7 into each pocket. He was set. So completely set.

Clayton took the sweet sixteen helium balloons from the cabin and tied all six of them in place—from the rails on the bow to the corners of the stern. He flipped on the twinkle lights Vinny Torino had been kind enough to string around *Retribution*'s cabin, pilothouse, and open deck area. The boat looked absolutely fabulous.

And so did Clayton.

If there was a way to conjure up Blackbeard's persona—his mojo—Clayton would do it. Blackbeard created unprecedented levels of terror in the hearts of everyone he encountered. And tonight . . . Blackbeard would sail again.

CHAPTER 87

TWO FLOORS ABOVE BAYVIEW BREW, Parker looked at the room that would be his home until Clayton was captured—or ruled out as a threat. Pez called it the Crow's Nest, and the name fit. With the front window looking over Main Street, and the back with a full view of Sandy Bay, the attic room was like a lookout tower, giving nearly a 360-degree view. The sharply angled roof made the room look like a giant pup tent.

The attic apartment was empty but big enough for a twin bed, a small desk, a comfy chair, and probably a dresser or bookcase. A 40-inch flat-screen sat on a low stand in one corner. There was even a compact bathroom with a shower. Pez had a back-burner plan to rent the room out, but right now the coffee shop kept her busy enough—and it seemed she wasn't all that concerned about extra income.

"What a setup." Harley stood at the window looking out over Sandy Bay. "And with a view. This is perfect."

Wilson tossed his sleeping bag in the corner and unzipped his backpack. He started lining up his weapons on the wood plank floor. Machete. Survival knife. A second machete. "I wish they'd just let us stay at your house, Bucky."

"You really want a rematch with Kingman?"

"Don't you?" Wilson gave a half laugh. "Neither of us totally believes he's within a thousand miles of here."

It didn't really matter what Parker thought. Nobody was taking any chances.

Harley picked up one of the machetes and slid it from its sheath. "You've got an arsenal here."

"And if Kingman *does* show up?" Wilson raised his eyebrows in a knowing look. "We'll need it."

Parker had a similar weapons cache in his backpack. He strapped Jimbo, his survival knife, on his calf. Slung his own machete across his back. "Arm yourself, Harley."

Harley didn't commit at first, but he kept going back to a second survival knife Parker pulled from his pack. Harley slid the sheath onto his belt so it rode on his hip. Harley practiced drawing the knife. "It's got a nice feel, right?"

It absolutely did.

By five thirty, Jelly and Ella had arrived to help Pez. The two of them took the stairs up to the Crow's Nest to check it out.

"Take a good look now, Ella," Jelly said. "This is the neatest this room will look until these three bozos move out."

"*Armed* bozos," El said. "What's with all the GI Joe gear, boys?"

If she had to ask the question, there was no way she'd understand Parker's answer. "Some guys don't feel they're fully dressed—or ready for their day—if they aren't properly equipped."

"That's it?" Ella stared at him a moment. "That's all you got?"

Time for Parker to try a different tack. "Do you have ChapStick in your purse, El?"

She gave him a look like he'd just asked the weirdest question. "Uh . . . yeah."

326

"Why?"

"Because . . . it's essential. I may need it."

Parker took a bow. "Thank you. You've just explained why we carry blades."

"Lip moisturizer and machetes have nothing in common," Jelly said.

"Except," Parker said, "they both bring nice big smiles to the people who carry them."

Jelly gave him an exasperated look, but she was smiling. "Touché."

Wilson raised his machete. "We're ready—just in case Kingman does the impossible and actually makes his way up here."

Jelly stiffened immediately. "The *impossible?* Are you implying that you don't think he could be here?"

"Let's just say"—Wilson smiled—"the chances are slim."

Jelly went on about how he needed to take the threat seriously, and if he didn't, he might take chances that could put them all in danger.

"I was in that hurricane," Wilson said. "And so was Kingman. Nobody could survive Morgan without picking up serious injuries. Without help, I can't see him getting up here."

Jelly wasn't one to let it go. "If he had just a quarter of the Miccosukee blood in him that you have, he'd have made it. Am I right?"

Wilson grinned. "When you put it *that* way . . . how can I argue? But how would he actually get up here, with Florida under lockdown?"

"Forget it, Wilson," Harley said. "You can't win this debate with simple common sense and logic."

Jelly gave them her high-chin, single-nod thing. "Well said, Mr. Lotitto. Maybe we'll pick up this conversation after we do our little donut delivery."

Wilson groaned. "Can't wait."

"There's our rich client." Ella stood at the window overlooking the bay. "That's got to be him, right?" She stepped aside so as not to block the view.

Even from here, Parker could read the giant *16* on a couple of the birthday balloons. Faint orange and purple lights had been strung along the entire length of the boat. Brighter, white twinkle lights gave the boat an inviting look. What a great spot for a party. "He's got a lucky niece."

A fogbank had materialized on the horizon since Parker had last looked out over the bay. With the darkening sky, the fog itself seemed even more dense than usual.

"The vapors are thick tonight," El whispered. "Grams wouldn't like that."

It didn't sound like El was too wild about it either.

The birthday girl's ride with the quad of Mercury engines had pulled anchor and was trolling along the breakwater toward Rockport Harbor now.

Harley turned on the big screen. Synced it with his phone. Pulled up YouTube. He played a couple of football recaps but, incredibly, was tuned enough to Ella and Jelly to see they just weren't into it. He scrolled to a whole series of stories about Hurricane Morgan. "Pick one, El."

The four of them watched the collections of footage from survivors who'd captured incredible storm shots. The sound of the wind . . . like nothing Parker had ever heard. Ungodly. Unearthly. Unreal.

Wilson sat on the floor. Back against the wall. Maybe it was the light from the screen. Maybe it was what was showing on the screen itself. But the color in Wilson's face seemed to drain. His hands disappeared under the hair at the sides of his head. Was he holding his ears?

"Harley." Parker nodded his head toward Wilson the moment Harley looked his way.

Harley's eyes got wide, and he scrolled to a new clip immediately. This one had been taken on one of the Miami beaches. The waves . . . incredible. How anybody out in the open could have survived was beyond Parker.

El's phone dinged, and she swiped open a text. "What did I tell you? Grams just asked if I've seen the sea smoke . . . how it's building out there." She stepped back to the window. "It does look thicker somehow. More than I've seen it in a really long time."

There was something about her tone. The word *foreboding* came to Parker's mind—which was weird. It wasn't a word he'd use in any conversation.

"She'll still let you do the donut run with us, right?" Jelly sounded concerned.

El sent off a return text. "I guess so. I mean, she didn't exactly say I couldn't. But the way she ended the text tells me she's plenty worried."

All eyes turned her way. Jelly stretched to see Ella's phone. "You're not going to leave us hanging, are you?"

"She said . . ." Ella stared at her screen. "Stay away from the vapors, Ella-girl. I have a bad feeling. Are you armed?"

Wilson snapped to attention. "Look—see? Even your Grams knows how important it is to carry a weapon." He rummaged in his backpack. "I got a couple of great jackknives. Want to borrow one?"

Ella gave a weak smile. "She was talking about a different kind of weapon, Wilson. Something even more effective than a knife. And I was way ahead of her. I've already got it."

Wilson looked at her in kind of a stunned awe. "Okay, I think I really love your Grams now. What is she talking about? Mace? Taser? Or are we talking seriously hardcore? Are you carrying a gun in that cowgirl boot of yours?"

"Think even *more* powerful." El locked eyes with Wilson . . . and held up the silver cross hanging around her neck.

CHAPTER 88

CLAYTON KINGMAN PULLED UP TO the floating platform just off the east end of the T-wharf. He was early, but he didn't want to be caught rushing. That led to mistakes. People short on time tended to take shortcuts—which could prove disastrous.

He kept *Retribution* idling and stepped onto the floating dock, boat lines in hand. He tied off to the heavy cleats on the platform and eyed the ramp to the top of the granite block wharf. Part of him wanted to walk up and see if Victoria Lopez was there . . . with her helpers. He'd wave her over . . . and get this party started.

Every time he stepped ashore, he risked someone recognizing him from news reports. The wig and beard were saviors. Fate had planned the timing of the hurricane to hit when it did . . . and for his journey to end on Halloween weekend. The costume, with so many layers, did more than mask his missing arm—and who he really was. It hid the hammering of his heart—which almost definitely would betray him if he was wearing only a T-shirt.

He'd lined everything up in advance with Victoria Lopez. She'd have the cash when the donuts were delivered. She'd loved his idea of having personalized T-shirts. He'd only asked for first names—or nicknames—whichever she'd prefer. She'd given him three. Pez. El. Jelly. He'd nearly whooped out loud in all his excitement. Angel would be there. Naturally, when the girls made the delivery, they wouldn't find the personalized T-shirts onboard that he'd promised, but there'd definitely be a surprise waiting for them.

He climbed back over the gunwale and up to the helm. He'd wait from that vantage point. Putting more distance between him and Angel would help reduce any chance of recognition.

"Hey there." A guy stood at the top of the ramp. Friendly-looking face. Fleece jacket with a harbormaster emblem on a patch stitched to the chest pocket. Solid build—but not just gym muscle. He gave off a vibe of strength that didn't come from doing reps but by doing life. By being active. A guy who didn't back down from hard work. Not the kind of guy Clayton could take lightly.

"Aye, matey." Staying in character was the smart move. Clayton fully believed that. "Well, aren't I the one what should be keelhauled? Docking without yer permission. My apologies, sir. After I picks up me cargo, I'll be off quicker than a musket ball, says I."

"Eric. Harbormaster."

Clayton bowed at the waist. "Pleased to make your acquaintance, Admiral."

"Looks like you've got quite a party planned." Eric walked down the ramp toward the floating platform.

"Truer words was never spoken." So what did the harbormaster want? The donuts would be here in minutes. This guy could mess things up.

Eric walked the platform alongside the boat. "Where are you out of?"

Clayton had already seen the harbormaster glance at the registration numbers on the bow. To try lying to the guy now would be a mistake.

"Florida." Give as little info as he could get away with—and change the topic. That was the ticket. "Little party for my niece. I'll pick up the caterers, then wait out in the harbor until my niece gets here. I'm a bit early for her." He winked. "You'll pardon me, Admiral, if I get back in me character. Doing me best to make this a reg'lar *fair winds and following seas* event, if you understand my meaning."

"*Nice* boat you have here."

And Clayton was a little young to have something so nice? Is that what the guy was driving at? "That it is. It be me brother's boat, Admiral. He be bringing me niece presently. Aye, and I think they'll love the way we've outfitted her for the festivities. What says you?"

"And you drove it up—all the way from Florida—for a party *here?*"

The harbormaster walked along the edge of the floating platform again, his hand gliding along the top of the gunwale this time.

Decision time. To admit driving it up from Florida would send a red flag right up the main mast. Why would the owner have someone drive it that far? If the guy lived in Florida, why not do the party there? "Florida be the home port, to be sure," Clayton said. "And will be again, soon enough. But Gloucester be me brother's Port Royal for the season. He has a slip at the Cape Ann Marina, he does." It sounded reasonable.

Eric nodded. "Got it. So you only drove it up from Gloucester."

"Aye."

"Wonder why he didn't arrange for the birthday cruise in Gloucester?"

He was fishing. One of those "ask an innocent-sounding question" kind of guys. And as strong as the harbormaster looked, Clayton was beginning to think the guy was even smarter. And not just book-smart. There was a street-smartness about him. He'd toy with the man a bit longer. But the timer was ticking.

"Charting a course in familiar waters be no way to surprise the young lass. Besides, me niece has a love for the donuts from BayView Brew, she does. So here I be." Clayton swept his hand out toward the Outer Harbor. "And disagree ye can't . . . a better view for a birthday cruise nary can be found."

Tick-tock. Tick-tock. He needed to lose this guy. If the harbormaster kept going with the questions, Clayton couldn't be blamed for what happened next.

The harbormaster glanced at the registration numbers again. "Where exactly does your brother dock this in Florida?"

Okay . . . Clayton had to take control. Something had made the harbormaster suspicious—whether or not the man on the platform could put his finger on it. Would he keep probing until he figured it out?

"A fair question, says I. But that would be one for me brother to answer when he gets here." This was it. How the harbormaster responded would tell Clayton what he needed to know—or rather what he needed to do.

Eric checked his watch. "Maybe I'll hang around a bit. I'd like to meet your brother."

"Aye. And you'll like him, says I." He stood from the pilot seat. "And while you be waiting, maybe you can solve a riddle that be following me wake. Just off Straitsmouth Island, I picked up a bit of flotsam. Just a wee thing, but it be looking like it be part of a seaplane, says I. I'd love to hear the harbormaster's mind on the matter." Make the story just out there enough to hook that curious nature of the guy.

"A seaplane?" Eric stood there for a moment. "Sure. Happy to."

"It be on the table." Clayton motioned toward the open cabin door. "Climb aboard and feast your eyes, mate."

Eric the harbormaster swung over the gunwale in one smooth move. He ducked into the cabin, and Clayton followed two steps behind him. He drew the Axon 7 Taser, held it up, and waited.

"Where'd you say the thing was?" The harbormaster turned—his eyes growing wide as he spotted the Taser.

The harbormaster lunged—but Clayton had him. The Taser was impressively effective—even through the guy's fleece jacket. The poor harbormaster dropped face-first like he'd been hit by lightning. Clayton kicked the guy's shaking feet together, lassoed his ankles with an oversize nylon zip tie, and ratcheted it tight. He did the same with the wrists.

He slapped a length of duct tape over his mouth—which was tricky with one hand—especially with the way the guy was drooling.

Move, Clayton. He dragged Curious George to the door sealing off the head. Stuffing him inside took some real work, but in the end, Clayton managed. "Now, Admiral. How you play your cards next will determine what happens to you. Capisce? You control your destiny."

Even now the harbormaster strained against the ties, which only made them dig deeper into his skin.

"Control your anger, Admiral. Your heart tells you this is your moment, doesn't it? A turning point. Do what you're told, and fate lets you live. So I'm telling you to stay quiet. That's all you have to do. But if you insult fate by thinking you can change it? Fate will gobble you up whole. You know what I say is true."

The guy growled. It was the best he could do with all the duct tape.

Clayton shrugged. "You're smarter than that, Admiral. I'm warning you. Don't spit in fate's face and expect not to pay a price. You stay quiet—and in the end, you'll be found alive. You'll be a hero and can go on saving boaters or seals—or whatever you like to do. That's a promise."

There was an absolute rush Clayton got by besting another man like this. And though he'd rather have women for hostages, a man would do. There was a fifty-fifty chance he'd need hostages for his plan—depending on how things played out. The world would know who Clayton was—and *where* he was—soon enough. Hostages would likely be needed to help him disappear again. "Do you know who I am?"

The harbormaster glanced at Clayton's wig and beard like he was trying to figure that out. He gave a three-syllable grunt.

"Blackbeard's ghost?" Clayton grinned. "Is that what you said?" This guy was funny. Clayton added two more lengths of duct tape. Something told him the admiral wasn't going to cooperate with fate, but was determined to create his own.

"Well, I'm worse than Blackbeard, Admiral." Clayton showed him the Glock 19. "And I be packing a whole lot more firepower."

CHAPTER 89

HARLEY STARED OUT THE WINDOW OF THE CROW'S NEST. It wasn't the view of Sandy Bay that had Harley in awe. It was what he'd seen in the last twenty-four hours. Parker's dad. Jelly's dad. It was what men did when there was a threat to the family—no matter how remote that threat might be.

They'd dropped everything to be close. Made sure the family was safe. Then they left to deal with the threat. And in that moment Harley knew he wanted more than just to be part of this family. He wanted to fight for it.

He wished his dad could be here. But if he were alive, he wouldn't be here in the room with Harley, would he? No . . . he'd be with Mr. Buckman—and Mr. Malnatti. He'd be buds with Officer Greenwood. Men who knew something about family . . . and manhood.

Images of the destruction in Florida rolled on the flat-screen.

Jelly rubbed down goosebumps on her arms. "Clayton Kingman. He's here."

Okay . . . that pulled all eyes from the big screen—onto her.

"Don't ask me how I know," she said. "But I know."

"How did he get here?" Harley wasn't questioning her spooky sense of intuition—or whatever it was girls had. Maybe he was just looking for direction . . . a clue as to where the threat was coming from . . . so he could be ready.

"Well, he didn't take a plane," Wilson said. "I think we can all agree he'd never get through TSA without an ID. And a train? With other passengers walking by him every time they wanted to use the can? And them thinking, *Where did I see that face? Hmmm. A one-armed man. Didn't I hear something on the news about him?*" He shook his head. "Bus? Same thing."

Jelly's face was getting way too red.

"If he'd boosted a car and blown a roadblock or something, they'd have had a cop chopper flying over him . . . taking him down." Wilson shrugged.

"I'm sorry I mentioned it." Jelly looked like she was ready to leave.

Suddenly Wilson bolted from where he was sitting. "Wait a sec. Hold on. Actually, there *is* a way." He stood there, looking at the floor, like he was putting something together in his head.

Jelly gave him the side-eye. "Is this another Wilson joke?"

"Plane. Car. Bus. Train. None of those worked for me . . . which was the big hole in the *Kingman is here* theory. But there is one way that *could* work." Wilson lowered his voice. "Something we've all overlooked. And not just us. The police, too." He actually looked scared. "How could we be so stupid?"

Ella definitely looked like she was dying to know. Jelly looked a little suspicious, but the anger was gone.

"Wilson," Parker said. "Are you going to tell us?"

"Not until the girls step away from the windows. He could be looking for Parker right now."

Ella and Jelly stepped closer.

Wilson nodded. Licked dry lips. "Okay." Took a couple of deep breaths. "This all makes sense now. You both know Kingman does the unexpected, right, Jelly?"

She nodded. She seemed to be totally reeled in now.

"Okay. Here's how Kingman got out of Florida . . . and nobody would've seen this coming." Wilson looked from face to face. Either he was getting pretty great at acting, or he was dead serious. "Skateboard."

Jelly sucked in her breath like she'd just been betrayed. She hauled off and slugged Wilson in the arm. Ella targeted his other arm. Wilson tucked and rolled, laughing his head off.

"What?" Wilson looked from Ella to Jelly. "You think he used roller skates?"

Jelly slugged him again. "Make fun all you want. But stay inside—and *you* stay away from the window, Buster."

"Girls." Miss Lopez's cheery voice echoed up the stairs. "Time to load up. We've got a sweet sixteen party to cater."

Wilson was still on the floor—flat on his back. Jelly placed one foot on his chest. "We'll finish with you when we get back."

The girls hustled for the stairs.

Harley followed. "Need some help loading?" Kingman wasn't looking for him, after all.

Miss Lopez looked up from the bottom of the stairway. "Sit tight." She pointed to the room behind him. "And keep those two in the Crow's Nest."

Harley sat halfway down the stairs as the girls loaded Miss Lopez's SUV. Was there anything to Jelly's intuitions? He had no idea. But he definitely liked how the men took the threat seriously. It was time he stopped messing around and followed their lead.

"God in heaven . . . I want a family . . . to be worthy of one," he whispered. "And if that means fighting for them"—he flexed his fingers: open, shut; open, shut—"teach me to fight well."

CHAPTER 90

ANGELICA WAS THE FIRST ONE OUT OF THE CAR after Pez slid the gearshift into Park. She stood there, box of donuts in hand, staring at the boat. As great as it had looked from the Crow's Nest, the thing looked that much more magnificent at the end of the T-wharf. All four motors on the transom rumbled at an idle, with a stream of water shooting out the side of each.

A large banner was taped along the side of the boat:

Halloween Sweet Sixteen! Thar be a birthday girl aboard!!

The pirate captain seemed busy at the console with something. Whoever the birthday girl was, Jelly hoped she appreciated how lucky she was. The guy had gone all out with his Halloween costume—and the decorations. The strings of purple and orange lights gave the boat a deliciously creepy Halloween feel. The white lights seemed brighter against the distant, dark wall of fog. It was always hard to tell just how far from shore the fog sat. But from here, the breakwater was perfectly clear. If she had to guess, she'd say the fogbank met the ocean somewhere just east of the Salvages. So maybe four miles out—at most?

There was no wind, and the water had become an eerie, almost dead calm. It wouldn't take much to get the fog moving to shore, but for now, it gathered strength and waited. For a moment, her mind flitted to something Grams had said once. About demons . . . and the devil himself being the prince and power of the air. Did he have the power to order the fog to advance—or was that ability reserved for only God?

"Looking for me?" Scorza's cocky voice.

Angelica groaned loud enough for him to hear.

"And you brought me donuts? We're going to get along just great, Everglades."

If he expected her to look at him with even a hint of amusement, he was going to be disappointed. "Dream on, delusional one. I'm here to work, not babysit. Now excuse me; we have an order to deliver."

Pez handed Ella a box of donuts—and took one herself. "One box at a time, ladies—and let's be sure we're holding the handrail when you take that ramp."

Angelica got it. The catering job was important—and could lead to more business. It was definitely smarter to make a second trip for the rest of the donuts. She certainly wasn't going to ask Scorza to help.

She fell in step behind Pez and Ella. Scorza tagged along beside her. "So, you're ditching Parker and Harley and that savage from the Everglades. You're finally wising up and coming to the dark side." He splayed his hand on his chest. "Am I right?"

His question didn't even merit an answer. Angelica shot him an annoyed look. "I'm working. Please leave."

"Okay. I'll wait up here for you." Scorza pulled out his phone at the top of the ramp while the three of them carried their precious cargo like they were gifts of gold, frankincense, and myrrh.

"Ahoy, me hearties." Blackbeard waved from his perch at the captain's chair. "Ye be right on time, which be more than I can say about the birthday lass." He motioned toward Scorza. "That bilge-sucking scalawag with you?"

"He most certainly is *not* with us," Angelica said.

Blackbeard nodded like he'd caught her drift. Obviously, he was a little quicker than Scorza in that department.

"Aye, and *thar* be the treasure chests." He motioned them to bring the donut boxes onto the boat. "Welcome aboard, me ladies, says I."

Pez led the way, beaming, and Ella followed. The captain's costume was good. Lots of attention to detail. Obviously, it had cost him some serious doubloons, but looking at the boat, that didn't really surprise her.

She felt Blackbeard's eyes on her even as she handed off the donuts to Pez and swung a leg over the side. Angelica looked up . . . and the pirate captain smiled. At least she thought he did. It was hard to tell with that full beard and mustache thing going on.

Pez scanned the deck, as if looking for a safe place to set the boxes.

"Aye, and stow that precious cargo in the cabin, ladies, if you please." Blackbeard pointed toward the cabin door.

Pez paused . . . long enough for Angelica's antenna to go up. Some guy dressed up as a notorious pirate instructed them to go to his cabin—and they were obeying? But he was a client. And this was a sweet sixteen party. There were three of them—and Scorza was still there at the top of the ramp, although he was absorbed with the screen on his phone now.

"Aye, the door be locked, is that it?" Blackbeard was on his feet. "Let ol' Blackbeard give it the heave-ho. The loot I owe you be on the table—along with a handsome bonus. The T-shirts be in the box on the floor."

He moved with more speed than Angelica would have expected. He opened the door, then took a step back and to the side, waving them in with a bow. "Me ladies."

Angelica's arms tingled, and even with her sweatshirt on she felt the hair rising as she followed the other two inside. Something was wrong. Something was—

The cabin door shut behind them. Angelica turned. Blackbeard held what looked like a yellow toy gun between his teeth, and another one in his hand. He pulled the trigger, rocked the gun to one side, and shot again.

Not a toy—a Taser!

Pez—then Ella—dropped hard. Both rigid and shaking on the cabin floor.

Blackbeard tossed the spent Taser on the bed—and instantly had the other one in his hand.

"*Hello,* Angel."

God. No. Shock. Fear. Not a flight-or-fight sensation at all. She couldn't move . . . even before he squeezed the trigger.

CHAPTER 91

ELLA WIGGLED HER FINGERS. Her toes. For the longest moment, she'd thought the Taser had paralyzed her forever. She hadn't noticed the floor vibrating from the motors when she'd climbed aboard, but now she felt everything.

Her wrists were snugged tight behind her. Ankles, too. Her mouth—sealed closed with tape or something. Pez was just coming out of it to one side of her. Blackbeard stooped over Jelly, zip-tying her wrists—then pulling it tight with his teeth.

"Three wenches. Aye, the fishing be good in Rockport, says I." Blackbeard stood, giving each of them a once-over as if to make sure the ties were sufficiently cutting off all circulation to their hands and feet. The three of them were on the floor, partially tangled with each other.

"I'm Clayton Kingman, in case you haven't guessed." All pirate jargon was gone. There was something absolutely terrifying about his voice.

Like he got some kind of twisted joy from revealing his identity—and what that would mean to them. "Welcome aboard the *Retribution*."

Ella's stomach tightened and did a series of backflips. This couldn't be happening.

"I have your mobile phones, and I'll toss them into the briny deep before we leave the harbor. There's no cavalry coming—and no way you can call for help." He let that tidbit sink in for a moment. "I'm here for a reason—which doesn't include killing you. *But don't push me.* Angel here knows what I'm capable of."

Ella felt her friend shudder.

"You want to stay alive? Do exactly what I tell you. And right now, I'm telling each of you to keep your traps shut."

How could she do anything else? Her mouth was sealed tighter than his grip on the gun in his hand. A real gun this time. The Taser was gone.

"I'll explain everything you're *dying* to know in a few minutes. But we're going to leave the dock first. I don't want any more visitors."

He scooted out the cabin door and locked it behind him. Ella could just barely make out what he said.

"Yo, landlubber."

Was he talking to Scorza?

"Twenty dollars if you untie me frigate and give me a good heave-ho from the pier. And fifty dollars if you're here to help dock me when I get back in an hour."

She couldn't make out what Scorza said, but Ella was pretty sure he agreed. The idiot. *Idiot!*

"Much obliged, mate!" Blackbeard—Kingman shouted above the noise of the motors.

The boat pulled away and turned hard to port. Ella's legs were over Pez. She wriggled to untangle herself. Pez's eyes were wide. Blood seeped down from above her hairline from whatever she'd hit when she went down. The instant Ella rolled off Pez, the owner of BayView Brew worked herself to a sitting position. She pressed her cheek against the edge of the mattress and rubbed hard. One corner of the duct tape lifted. Pez worked harder.

Ella and Jelly scooted to the mattress and did the same.

Retribution's nose rose slightly as the boat picked up speed.

With a pained squeal, Pez succeeded in ripping off the duct tape. "Father, help us!"

Prayer was good. Right now, Ella would love a whole church full of people praying against the evil at the helm of *Retribution*.

"Ella—honey—put your face in my hands." Pez spread her palms as wide as she could with the nylon tie around her wrists. She wiggled her fingers. "Hurry."

Ella obeyed. She felt Pez groping for a corner of the duct tape—and picking at it with her nail when she found it.

"Got it. Pull back, Ella. Hard."

Ella jerked away from Pez—and half the duct tape pulled free. She dropped her head in Pez's hands again.

"Okay, baby. Now."

This time Ella flipped her head to one side as she threw herself back—and the duct tape tore free.

"Now do that for Jelly," Pez said. "We need something sharp to cut through these ties."

Seconds later, Jelly's duct tape was gone. Ella wished she'd taken Wilson up on one of those jackknives . . . but Kingman would have found it when he snatched their mobile phones.

"We've got to get out of here," Jelly gasped. "He's insane."

Ella frantically scanned the cabin for something—anything—sharp. "Teeth?"

"Try it." Pez turned and raised her wrists slightly.

Ella gnawed at the thick nylon, trying to make a groove and keep her teeth in it. The tone of the motors lowered. The nose dipped. And *Retribution* came to a rocking stop.

"No." Jelly's eyes were so very wide. "He's coming."

Moments later, the cabin door swung open. Kingman was half

Blackbeard, half escaped convict now. The eyepatch was gone. The hat and wig too—along with the beard. The pirate jacket and pants were still in place.

"You've been busy, I see." He circled his own lips with his finger. "And you didn't scream. Good girls." He checked out the cabin window. "We're in the Outer Harbor . . . ready to go out the channel and on to the little adventure I have planned for us. I could go one of a couple ways, so I'll be looking for your opinions. But first I need some introductions. Angel I know. And Miss Lopez, a pleasure to meet you in person. And who are you again?" He looked directly at Ella.

Was he for real? "I'm . . . Ella Houston."

"I've always wanted to visit Houston." Kingman smiled. "And I guess now I have."

The guy was sick.

"Now let me fill in a few blanks for you." Kingman told of his escape, his stay in the warden's home, and how he'd made his way north. He stopped at points, it seemed, just to revel in the shock he must have seen on their faces.

"I told them you were unpredictable," Jelly said.

"Yes! I absolutely am! See, Angel? You know me so well. I think you understand me better than your sister did. And I must say, you've grown up a lot in the year since I've seen you." An oily smile slid across his face.

All the things Jelly had told Ella about Kingman somehow hadn't captured half of the monster he was.

He told of the postcards—and how it was all a ruse to make it look like Parker was his target. "But it was you, Angel. From the very start. I told Parker I had a big surprise for him. And this is it. I came . . . for *you.*"

Tears ran down Jelly's face. Pez tried to get close, like she wanted to hold her, but of course she couldn't. "Why? I actually *helped* you."

"And here you are, helping me again."

She shook her head. "I don't understand."

"I wanted a *rematch* . . . not revenge," Kingman said. "I get you?

I hurt Gatorbait—real bad. I hurt the whole Buckman clan—and your dear old man, too. I take one person—and I have it all. Just by getting you . . . I've already won the rematch. It's like taking Maria all over again. Even better, I'd say."

Jelly squeezed her eyes shut tight. Shook her head. "No-no-no."

"Maria was mine—and then Gatorbait set out to find her. And by sheer, dumb luck . . . he did," Kingman said. "But now *you're* mine. It's a redo, see? All I have to do to stay on top is keep Parker from bringing you back alive."

Ella did not like the way he said the word *alive*. She had to think. How could they turn this around? "We'll be missed. Parker will come after us."

"Exactly what I'm hoping," Kingman said. "And why I'm stalling here in the harbor a bit. If I see him come out after us . . . I'll take a chance in getting a twofer. If not . . . well . . . I'm totally satisfied walking away with you, Angel." He reached over and petted her hair. "Spoils of war."

"I hate you!" Jelly said. "Hate you!"

"We'll see. Ever heard of Stockholm syndrome? Abducted girls actually grow to love the one who provides for them." Kingman leaned in close. "That will be you and me."

"Never!"

"Please," Pez said, "Mr. Kingman . . . have mercy. You've given everyone a good scare. You've shown the world you can do what most would find impossible. Escape prison. Survive a hurricane. Elude authorities. You've *already* won. So drop us off—and disappear. You can still escape."

"I *know* I can escape—and have my Angel, too. We'll disappear. Do you have any idea how many islands there are in the Bahamas?"

Had he just tipped them off as to where he would take her?

"What happens to Pez," Jelly said, "and Ella?"

"That's where I need your help," Kingman said. "If everyone cooperates, there's no need to hurt anyone. So what happens to them is really up to you."

How did he think he could get away? The boys had seen the boat anchored in Sandy Bay. They'd call the police once they realized the girls were gone. The Coast Guard would come after them. But then again, Kingman had made it pretty clear, hadn't he? All he had to do to win was keep Jelly—or keep her from being taken from him alive.

"Listen," Pez said. "I'm a follower of Jesus . . . who happens to be God's Son. You don't want me praying against you right now. You do not want my heavenly Father steamed at you. Turn around—and drop us at the T-wharf. Do it now."

She spoke with authority. Like maybe she felt giving him a direct order might sway him. Or was her faith in God that strong?

Kingman looked at her in amazement. "Do it . . . *now?* And what if I do . . . you'll put in a good word for me with the man upstairs?"

"That's not going to happen . . . but I'll let you keep the donuts. That's the best I can do."

Kingman threw his head back and roared. "I like you, lady. I really do. If I ever get bored with Angel, maybe I'll come back for you, how's that?"

"Have you no fear of God?"

Kingman smiled. "Not even a tiny bit."

"The harbormaster probably already figured out where the boat is from," Jelly said. "He's probably having the harbor sealed off as we speak."

Kingman put on a mock face of terror. "Really?" He stepped over and around them until he got to a small door in the cabin. He swung it open. "*This* harbormaster?"

Eric glared back at him.

"Oh, God," Ella whispered. "Oh, God. Oh, God. Oh, God. Help us!"

Kingman spun to face her. "Pray your heart out, girlie. You'll be the first to go." He stepped over them to the cabin door. "Time for me to go topside, ladies and gentleman. I'll give young Gatorbait another few minutes. If he's a no-show"—he winked at Jelly—"it's just you and me, Angel. And I'm really good with that."

CHAPTER 92

PARKER PACED THE LENGTH OF THE CROW'S NEST. "Jelly's going to pick up where she left off when she gets back, Wilson."

"I'd be totally shocked if she didn't," he said. "But you got to admit, Kingman coming this way is a longshot. A total *moon*shot. Yeah, he sent postcards like he had some kind of no-fail method to get up here. But it doesn't exist."

"One hundred percent," Parker said.

"I still say he was just trying to get everyone running scared." Wilson put on a mock terrified face. "Hiding out—like we're doing now."

Harley didn't seem to know what to think. "So where is he—or where's he going if not here?"

"Mexico. South America," Wilson said. "I'd put money on either one of those."

"That doesn't add up either," Harley said. "If he found a way to travel south, he could find a way to travel north. I still say we have to be careful."

348

Parker's phone rang, and his dad's picture flashed on the screen. Right on time. Parker picked up. "Yes, we're in the Crow's Nest—and no, we haven't seen or heard anything suspicious. How are things at the house?"

As it turned out, Dad had taken a walk to the waterfront with Uncle Sammy. Officer Greenwood had well-hidden men staking out both houses. If Kingman was watching and saw Dad and Uncle Sammy leave, maybe he'd make a move to see if Parker was inside. "It's pretty much a shot in the dark," Dad said. "But worth a try. We're dropping in at the harbormaster's office before heading back," Dad said. "I'll call you every thirty minutes."

Dad was definitely sticking to the "stay in contact" part of the plan.

The images on the Crow's Nest flat-screen showed the Miami waterfront again. Wilson turned the volume up just enough to hear the announcer talking about the damage to the harbors. Few boat owners got their boats to more northern ports before Morgan arrived. Most left the boats to ride out the hurricane. Which was a mistake.

Pictures of boats stranded on roads, parking lots, and buried halfway inside houses scrolled across the screen. The newscaster explained that hundreds of boats had been sunk or were missing. It would take months to figure it all out—if they ever did.

Suddenly Parker's gut twisted. "Hold on . . . that's it! Kingman took a boat from a harbor in Miami." He grabbed the remote and cut the power. "Guys—I know I'm right. A *boat*. That's a surefire way for him to get up here—without being spotted."

"A boat would be unexpected," Harley said. "Which is his MO, right?"

"Totally." Parker could picture it now. "Somehow, he travelled *into* the hurricane after his escape. Into the city. And with all the confusion right after Morgan, he could pick any boat that was still floating without anyone questioning him."

Even Wilson's eyes were wide. "He knows how to handle a boat, that's for sure. And all he had to do is get something big enough to be seaworthy. Boats like that have all the fancy navigation tech stuff. He'd have no problem getting here."

"And everybody would think the missing boat got lost in the storm," Parker said. "Nobody would be looking for it *here*."

Parker whipped out his phone and dialed his dad, put him on speakerphone, and bounced the idea off him. Dad must have had his on speaker, too, because Uncle Sammy and even Maggie interrupted with input.

"The postcard said Kingman had a surprise for you," Harley said. "Think that was it . . . that he took a boat?"

Parker thought about it for a moment and shook his head. "The surprise is more than him getting here or taking a boat. He's bringing something—or he'll do something totally unexpected to surprise me when he gets here."

Wilson slipped on his backpack. "Machete at the ready."

"We've got to tell the girls when they get back." Parker stepped to window overlooking Sandy Bay.

"We usually touch base with out-of-town boats that visit our harbor," Maggie said. "Eric is checking one right now. Actually, I'm surprised he's not back. But moving forward, we'll be watching extra careful."

Parker stared at the screen for a moment. "Whoa, whoa, whoa. Out-of-town boat? Dad . . . Jelly, Pez, Ella . . . they're delivering to a boat right *now*. The guy ordered donuts for a *surprise* party. What if it's Kingman—and this is his big surprise!" Parker was right. He knew it somehow. "He's not after me—he wants *Jelly!*"

"God help us!" Dad disconnected.

Parker bolted for the stairs, Harley and Wilson right behind him. "While we've been hiding away, Jelly—all of them—are walking into a trap!"

CHAPTER 93

PARKER SPRINTED ALONGSIDE HARLEY and Wilson straight up the middle of the T-wharf. The party Whaler with the strings of lights and balloons was far out in the Outer Harbor, crawling toward the channel.

Harley pointed to the ramp at the very end of the T-wharf. "The girls must be down on the floating platform."

With the tide as low as it was, Parker couldn't even see the float. But that had to be the answer. The girls would be there, splitting a great tip or something.

Harley reached the granite-block edge of the wharf first. "Empty!" He bounced on the balls of his feet like he was overjuiced with adrenaline—and had no idea how to put it to good use.

Music pulsed over the still water, like the party had started on the big boat—but without the people. Parker strained to see from this distance, but except for someone standing at the helm, the entire deck looked deserted. Okay, so the girls weren't on board. *Thank you, God!* So where were they?

Alert 1, the harbormaster's patrol boat, raced around the corner of the yacht club. Maggie was at the wheel, flanked by Dad and Uncle Sammy.

"Parker!" Dad motioned as they passed. He pointed at the party boat. Did Jelly and the others go aboard? Is that what he was saying—or did he want Parker to follow?

Scorza stepped out from between a couple of parked cars. "Too late, gents. Blackbeard hired *me* to be the dock boy."

"The girls—have you seen them?"

Scorza gave him a funny look. "They went on that big party boat leaving the harbor." He pointed. "*Retribution*. Driven by a guy dressed like Blackbeard."

Parker ran both hands through his hair. "They were *delivering* donuts—and serving them to guests. I don't see anyone on board—why are they leaving without the guests?"

Scorza shrugged. "Blackbeard told them to put the donuts in his cabin. They must've decided to go for a boat ride before the guests got here."

"And that didn't make you suspicious?"

"Hey, I didn't see anything weird." Scorza looked at Parker like he was the crazy one. "Next thing I know, Blackbeard is asking me to cut him loose. I'm going to help him dock when he gets back too."

If Blackbeard was who Parker feared he was, he had no intention of coming back.

"Parks!" Harley pointed at a Honda CRV in a parking slot—with the hatchback window still open. "Isn't that Miss Lopez's?"

The three of them ran—leaving Scorza behind. It was hers, for sure. And two boxes of donuts were still neatly stacked inside.

Retribution swung into the channel now. *Alert 1* was closing in. The music was still blaring . . . and the familiar intro to "Every Breath You Take" echoed across the harbor.

"It's Kingman!" Parker sprinted for the boat slip. "Steadman's boat. We've got to go after them."

The boys piled into Steadman's Whaler. Wilson had the boat untied and the lines in the boat by the time Parker had it started. He backed out of the slip and sliced through South Basin and then the Outer Harbor at full throttle.

As soon as they cleared the channel and were in open water, they spotted both boats. The party boat cut a wake heading for deep water—and the fog bank. *Alert 1* was close, lights flashing. The party boat wasn't stopping, but it couldn't possibly be using all the horses on the transom either. The big boat seemed to go just fast enough to lure both pursuers farther from shore—and reinforcements. As fast and light as Steadman's boat was, he wasn't sure he could keep up if it turned into a real chase. One by one, the sweet sixteen balloons snapped free and wriggled to freedom. The banner peeled off the side of the boat and disappeared.

Parker stood at the helm, staying at full throttle until he'd caught up to the harbormasters' boat. Where was Eric?

"*Retribution.*" Harley pointed at the boat with all the lights. "Is that your Kingman guy?"

A man in pirate costume was at the helm. He turned and smiled—as if he'd been waiting for them to catch up. Even from this distance Parker could tell. "It's him!"

Kingman saluted—and throttled forward as if daring them to give chase . . . which is exactly what Parker did.

CHAPTER 94

Atlantic Ocean, off the coast of Rockport, Massachusetts
Saturday, October 30, 6:18 p.m.

TWO BOATS TRAILING *RETRIBUTION*? Clayton didn't like the odds. But that didn't mean the tagalongs could wreck any of his plans. Not at all. This only dictated which fork in the road he'd take. Each fork had an upside. If there'd only been one boat, with Gatorbait alone, he'd have his showdown with the park ranger's son. But there was the harbormasters' boat to consider. And Gatorbait had a posse with him. The choice was easy. No showdown.

When he'd planned it all out, he'd known the chance of getting Gatorbait alone would be remote, anyway. And there was an upside to having so many on his stern right now. He'd have the fun of using the hostages. Honestly, both forks provided their own kind of rush . . . and both led to exactly the same place—with Angel as his prize.

The harbormaster maneuvered closer to *Retribution*'s stern on the starboard side. There were enough lumens on that thing to put on a light show. It seemed almost comical. Did she really think flashing lights would force him to surrender . . . after all he'd been through to get here? Hardly. Gatorbait's dad was there—and Angel's? Fate genuinely smiled on Clayton. Both dads would have a front-row seat to a horror show. And neither of the rangers would be able to stop him.

Gatorbait kept to a course off *Retribution*'s port side. He had a couple of others with him. Likely high school friends who pictured themselves being heroes. "Not today, fellas." Clayton could lose Gatorbait whenever he wanted to. He'd peel him off like a dirty shirt. But first he'd toy with him. With all of them. Let them get close . . . which would only make the agony of their defeat worse.

Even now, the harbormaster had likely called in the coordinates. The Coast Guard would join the hunt. More boats were of no real concern. The Coast Guard chopper was a different matter. But the fog—and soon darkness of night—would take care of that problem. Clayton could stay and play for a few minutes more, but after that he'd get serious. He'd let them think they had him cornered or trapped or confused or some such nonsense. Then he'd whisk them off his tail.

He cut the wheel hard to port—and gave *Retribution* a whole lot more throttle. The boat responded like it had been waiting for this. Gatorbait swerved to avoid him and throttled back so completely that water washed over his transom.

Clayton swung in a wide arc, then cut back toward Gatorbait. "The hunted becomes the hunter," he shouted.

Gatorbait made a run for it, but Clayton pulled alongside—and let *Retribution* drift toward the smaller boat. Clayton had to keep his focus on what he was doing, but he could imagine Gatorbait scrambling at the wheel to get out of *Retribution*'s way.

He opened up to full throttle. Pulled ahead. Cut in front of the Boston Whaler. He chanced a look over his shoulder and grinned. Gatorbait was working the wheel with all he had to keep the boat from filling or flipping. His two compadres were hunkered down, hanging on for dear life. Gatorbait slowed way up—likely to regroup or gather his nerve.

The harbormaster was a different story. She hung with him but kept enough distance to give herself plenty of reaction time. Clayton did a couple more circles, churning up the water like some monster leviathan from the depths. But she was good. There was no shaking her.

Gatorbait pulled it together and joined the mayhem again. Clayton had to hand it to him. He was better at handling a boat than Clayton had figured.

Clayton had seen the hate and fear on the faces of the rangers—and Gatorbait, too. It was incredibly gratifying. They would live with the agony of defeat. Of being close to rescuing Angel but unable to do it. All Clayton had to do now? Keep them from ever getting her back. Easy Peasy.

"Playtime is over, gang." It was time to shake these tails for good. They'd be expecting him to try outrunning them. He wasn't even sure he could shake loose the harbormaster. And he didn't need to. He wanted to see both the rangers—and Gatorbait's face—one more time . . . when he put the next phase of his plan in motion. Would Gatorbait look absolutely *aghast?* Clayton would put money on that.

He shouted to the boats behind him—even though they wouldn't be able to make out a word of it. "Even in your wildest dreams, I'm betting you'll never guess what's coming next!"

CHAPTER 95

RETRIBUTION'S WAKE WIDENED AS THE BOAT SLOWED. Blackbeard stood at the helm. He didn't look over his shoulder in some kind of panic or desperation. Made no indication that he intended to surrender. The boat continued to decelerate, like Kingman was approaching an invisible pier. What was he up to?

Parker matched Kingman's speed and held back about thirty yards off *Retribution*'s port side stern. Maggie did the same off the starboard. The fogbank was close now. If Kingman hadn't stopped when he did, he'd already be in the thick of it.

Dad motioned to Parker to keep his distance from *Retribution*. Parker waved back.

The churning behind the quad of *Retribution*'s motors settled. The eerie strains of the stalker song crept across the waves. Kingman turned to face them and leaned back against the helm, arm across his chest like he'd invited them to a meeting. He looked at them for a few long moments.

"Think he's giving up?" Harley took a wide stance near the bow. "I'm soaked."

All of them were wet—and freezing in the late-October air. Kingman looked dry. Happy. And there was no way Kingman was surrendering.

"Throwing in the towel now would be unexpected," Harley said. "Right?"

"*Unlikely* is a better word." Parker watched Kingman work his way to the cabin. "Unexpected is a whole different thing."

Kingman disappeared inside the cabin.

"Parker," Dad shouted. "Keep distance!" He held up his hand like a gun and pointed at *Retribution*.

Good point. Kingman might be planning a regular shootout. Parker had Jimbo on his calf and Eddie on his back . . . but that was it for weapons. Wilson seemed to be doing a personal weapon inventory himself. He dropped the backpack and slung the machete over his head and one arm so the thing rode perfectly on his back as well. He clutched the gator tooth necklace hanging at his chest, caught Parker's eye, and pointed to him.

"Got it." Parker thumped his chest. Felt the giant tooth under his T-shirt. But he'd need a whole lot more than that if Kingman pulled out a gun.

"We hang back at a safe distance," Dad shouted. "We'll just keep a visual on them until the Coast Guard catches up."

Retribution might outrun Steadman's boat, but he'd never shake *Alert 1*. Not with Maggie driving—and her infrared vision capability. Parker flashed his dad an okay sign.

"If he goes into the fog—head back." Dad pointed toward shore. "Too dangerous."

Kingman appeared in the cabin door, holding a fistful of Pez's collar. Her hands were secured behind her back. And by the way she walked— so unsteady—her ankles had probably been tied until moments ago.

"Miss Lopez!" Harley was on his feet.

Kingman pulled out a gun and motioned her to the top of a small staircase leading up to the gunwale.

"Hold on, Kingman!" Uncle Sammy shouted. "Nobody needs to get hurt."

"And they won't—if you back off. Like, turn around and head back to Rockport Harbor. Now."

Maggie didn't budge. Parker followed her lead.

Kingman grinned like they'd done exactly as he'd hoped. He jammed the barrel against Pez's thigh—and pulled the trigger. With a shriek, she dropped into the sea.

"No!" Uncle Sammy was the only one who could talk. Parker couldn't even breathe.

Maggie sprang into action and charged forward with *Alert 1* even as Kingman scurried back up to the console. *Retribution* stormed ahead.

Parker raced ahead—his eyes fixed on where he'd seen Pez go down.

Pez partially broke the surface but not enough to get a breath. With her hands tied—and only one working leg? She slipped under *Retribution*'s wake, then surfaced again.

Maggie pulled alongside Pez—and both Dad and Uncle Sammy rolled her into the boat. Parker circled them once. Pez was moving. Talking.

"She's alive!" Harley leaned over the side like he'd been ready to dive in after her.

Kingman hadn't driven more than a hundred yards—but he was stopping again. He dragged Ella from the cabin.

"Parks!" Harley pointed. "Parks—get there!"

Harley's voice moved Parker from shock to action. He slammed the throttle forward, blitzing past *Alert 1* and on toward *Retribution*.

Ella fought against Kingman, but it was over before it started. He said something—or did something—and she stood dead still.

Harley stood at the bow—one hand on the gunwale, the other wrapped tight around the bow line. "*No!*"

Kingman prodded her up the steps until she balanced on the gunwale. Another shot, and Ella dropped hard—like someone had swept her feet out from under her. She landed on the edge—upper body inside the boat, legs hanging over the water. She screamed and thrashed in agony. Kingman tucked the gun in his waistband. Took out a knife and released her wrists. Immediately he shouldered her over the side.

"Surface, El. Surface!" Parker shouted over the sound of the wind and motors.

Kingman took off again. *Retribution*'s quad of motors churned up the water where Ella had disappeared. Her hand broke the surface—then her face. Eyes wide in panic. Parker came in hard and fast. Even as Parker throttled back and threw the gearshift in reverse, Harley dove in after her.

Harley held her head above water, scissor-kicking hard. Wilson and Parker reached over the side and pulled Ella aboard. Total dead weight—which was only made worse with the soaked jeans and sweatshirt.

"We got you, El; we got you."

They left her on the deck, and Parker and Wilson struggled together to pull Harley on board.

Blood spread from Ella's leg in a wide arc on the nonslip deck.

Alert 1 roared up and pulled alongside. Uncle Sammy was on his knees, keeping pressure on Pez's leg.

Maggie swung over the side and into Steadman's boat as Dad held the boats together. "She's losing too much blood."

Another shot. Parker caught a glimpse of Harbormaster Eric dropping headlong into the dark waters of the Atlantic—fifty yards away.

"Get a visual, Vaughn," Maggie shouted. "Don't lose him."

"He's insane," Harley whispered. "Psychotic."

"Hands. Here." Maggie took Harley's hands and pushed them on Ella's thigh. "Pressure—or she'll die."

Harley obeyed immediately. Maggie vaulted back onto *Alert 1*—and roared off for the next victim. Steadman's boat rocked in the backwash.

Dad stood beside Maggie, his arm outstretched, pointed to a spot in the water where Eric was. Or maybe it was where he'd seen Eric last, because there was nothing there. No splashing. No hand waving. Just black water that looked way too still.

Retribution built up speed. Leveled off. The white foam crest of the wake was like a giant arrow, pointing to the boat that was getting farther away by the second. The boat where Jelly was still a hostage. What if Kingman stopped now . . . and did the same to her? They were too far away. Parker would never get there in time.

God, what do I do?

To chase *Retribution* into the fog was out of the question. He'd never catch the boat anyway. And if he were flying at full speed, would Harley even be able to maintain the pressure on Ella's leg like she needed? The party lights grew dimmer. Even now, the boat was barely visible. *Retribution* lost density and mass as it entered the fogbank, as if the boat itself was becoming part of the sea smoke. *Retribution* banked hard to the south . . . and the party lights dissolved into nothingness. Only the haunting melody of *Every Breath You Take* gave any evidence that the boat still existed. And then . . . even the music was gone.

The vapors were real. Alive somehow. They'd made the 41-foot *Retribution* vanish . . . and they'd just swallowed Jelly Malnatti whole.

CHAPTER 96

ANGELICA COULDN'T STOP SHAKING. She'd heard the shots. The splashes. And now that Clayton had her back on deck, she could see the blood on the gunwale and down the inside wall of the boat. Clayton had run at full speed for how long before stopping this time? And there was nobody following them. They were alone. "I'm going to be sick."

He'd snipped the nylon tie holding her ankles together, and she rushed to the side. Leaned over—and lost everything.

"Avast, thar be a retching wench aboard me frigate." Kingman stood watching. He still had on his Blackbeard garb, except for the wig and beard.

How he could function—let alone joke—at a time like this was beyond shocking.

"You killed"—she could barely say the words—"my friends."

"If I did, the boats would still be following. They'd have rolled the bodies aboard, strapped them down, and be in hot pursuit right now."

He held a hand out toward the dense fog as if to prove they were completely alone. "I couldn't have that."

So the only reason he *hadn't* killed them was because it would've made it harder for him to escape? "Why not just push them over the side? By the time they got picked up, you would've been gone."

"Risky move, Angel. Your daddy was on one of those boats. You think he'd run back to the harbor with the swimmers—just to make sure they got a warm blankie?" He shook his head. "Not him. They'd have piled all your wet friends in Gatorbait's boat and sent *them* back. The harbormaster boat would still be right here with us."

Suddenly Kingman cocked his head slightly. He rushed to the back of the boat. Peered out over the motors. "Hear that?"

Was he insane? Of course he was. "I don't hear a thing."

Kingman smiled. "Precisely. Three people shot? That'll keep everyone busy in both boats—and they absolutely would've raced back to shore . . . to the hospital. If anybody dies, it's on their heads. Not mine. Honestly, unless I nicked their femoral artery—or the boats didn't get to them before they went down—they should be okay."

She leaned over the side again with the dry heaves. She turned to face him. "They'll get you. And then what? You could have been free."

That seemed to amuse Kingman. "I deliberately headed south—while I could still see their boats. One of them would have noticed that change of direction. They'll find the boat . . . but not us."

What did that mean?

Kingman eased the throttle forward. Studied the screen on the console. Strained to peer through the fog.

"What are we looking for?"

"We?" Kingman looked pleased. "We're already a team, you and I."

She wanted to tell him how they were never—and would never be—a team. She wanted to scream to his face that she would take him down. But for now, she had to be smart. Had to use her head.

"There." Kingman pointed. An inflatable boat materialized out of nowhere. A diver's flag hung limp—as if in mourning, like whoever had been diving had been under far too long to be coming back.

He pulled alongside, dropped the motors into neutral, and grabbed the dinghy's bow line with a gaff hook. He secured it to a gunwale cleat. For a few minutes, it seemed like he hardly knew she was there. He scrawled out a note and taped it to *Retribution*'s wheel. He dropped the bow anchor, then promptly cut the line.

"Your hand." He motioned for her to turn around. "I need to draw a bit of blood."

Angelica backed away.

He held the knife in his hand and stepped closer. "I need to make sure I keep my prize."

She pressed herself against the side of the boat so hard that he wouldn't be able to get at her hands. He'd need two hands himself.

"I'm not going to *stab* you, Angel. Just a slice." Clayton leaned in against her. She felt a deep burning in her shoulder—like a papercut, only a hundred times worse.

"Hand. Shoulder. Makes no difference. I need some blood."

"What are you now, a vampire?"

Clayton laughed. He ripped off her sleeve and squeezed the slice so the blood trickled down her arm . . . her hand . . . her fingertips. "Now walk with me." He grabbed her wrist and half led, half dragged her up the steps and around the pilothouse to the bow—where the anchor had been stowed. He shook drips of blood from her fingertips as he did. A Hansel and Gretel path went from the deck behind the cabin—all the way to the front. But the trail was in blood, not breadcrumbs.

"Again." He walked her to the main deck and back. "Dig your heels in this time. Fight me a bit."

She was only too happy to obey. She leaned back. Tugged. Kicked. But even with only one arm, he toted her along like she was a roll-aboard bag until he had her up on the bow deck again.

"Okay," Clayton said. "You did good." He pointed at the blood. It didn't look like he'd simply staged a blood trail. There were drips, smudges, and smears. To anyone investigating, it would appear that she'd fought him every step of the way.

Clayton stood on the bow deck, surrounded by low, stainless steel railings. "Now I need you to listen carefully. I'm going to give you a chance. Fight me, Angel. Like your life depends on it. Push me overboard, and you win. The keys are still in the ignition."

Was he serious? "My hands are tied. I don't stand a—"

Clayton swept her legs out from under her. She dropped hard on the bow deck—flat on her back. "Fight."

She spun around—still on her back—and kicked.

The blow landed on his shin. His leg buckled—and he hit the deck hard.

Angelica kicked again and again. Each time she connected, her whole body slid on the deck that grew increasingly slick with her own blood. She jabbed him hard in the face with her heel—hoping some of his blood would spill on the deck too.

"Perfect. You're doing so good, Angel. Fight hard!"

She kicked him again—and he fell backward. His head smacked the deck. Blood fled from both nostrils, like even his own blood was trying to escape him.

Angelica rolled to one side and managed to get up on her knees. She sprang to her feet while Kingman lay on the bow deck—blocking her way of escape. But where would she go? She had to get him off the boat—or find his gun.

Kingman rolled on his side to face her and smiled—like he knew what she was thinking. She saw movement—but too late. He caught her with a perfect leg sweep. Her sliced shoulder thudded onto the thick fiberglass deck. *Get up, Angelica. Get up or die!*

He was on his feet before she could move, and then just as quickly disappeared. He returned holding a fire extinguisher and flashing a bloody grin.

She scooted away from him until she hit the pilot house. She tried to stand, pressing herself against a window. For a moment, she tangled herself in a string of lights that had looped over her head. She ripped them away. "Back off!"

Kingman raised the fire extinguisher and heaved it toward her. "Look alive!"

She ducked and heard a window shatter behind her.

Kingman stepped forward and kicked Angelica's feet from under her. He towered over her, looking around the boat. "Nicely done, Angel. Look at this bloody mess. Forensics will have a field day. Looks like a real knock-down, drag-out fight."

Angelica inched away, worming away from Kingman until she felt the bow rail stop her. "What do you *want* from me?"

He glanced around the boat again. "Just one more thing." He placed one foot on her—and gave a shove.

Angelica tried twisting away from him, searching for a handhold on the deck. Kingman turned his back to her and dropped to his knees. Supporting himself with his one arm, he mule-kicked her. The bow dug into her back—and seemed to give way slightly. She clawed at the edge of the bow, desperate for anything she could use to steady herself. He drew back his leg and hammered her again. A sharp snap came from the rail behind her.

"Clayton—stop—you're going to kill m—"

He kicked again. The section of bow rail broke free and Angelica slid off the bow into the icy waters of the Atlantic.

CHAPTER 97

HARLEY STOOD AT THE END OF THE T-WHARF next to Parks and Wilson. His friends looked as helpless as he felt. Rockport and Gloucester paramedics busily worked over Ella, Miss Lopez, and Eric the harbormaster.

Jelly's dad stalked along the edge of the granite blocks with a haunted look on his face. He looked like a bridge jumper, psyching himself to take the leap. When they weren't watching, the fog had followed them in. The breakwater was no longer visible. Only the beacon light at the end gave proof that the jetty was even there. The light flashed on and off, muted by the mist . . . like a weak pulse.

Mr. Buckman hustled over to the three boys. "They're going to be okay. All three of them. I'm not so sure that would have been the case if you boys hadn't followed us out."

"But Jelly," Parker's voice cracked. "Dad—"

He pulled his son into a hug. "I know, I know. Maggie dropped a pin where the boat was last seen. And she saw him turn south. The Coast Guard is out there combing the area right now."

"But the fog."

"They've got radar and infrared—just like *Alert 1*, I'm sure. He won't get far."

Was Mr. Buckman that sure—or was he hiding his fears for the sake of his son . . . for all of them? He was like Harley's dad that way. And Harley wished his own dad were here, holding him in a bear hug too.

"Now . . . you three stick together." Mr. Buckman pulled Wilson and Harley into the circle. "Be smart. Mom and Grams are on their way to the hospital right now. They'll keep me updated—and I'll update you."

Harley didn't need to ask where he was going. He'd made sure the wounded were safe. But his job wasn't done.

"We can't just wait for word," Parker said. "What can *we* do, Dad?"

Mr. Buckman hesitated. "You three have done plenty already. I know what you're feeling—but I don't have an answer."

"We could follow in Steadman's Whaler. We've got plenty of gas."

Mr. Buckman shook his head. "With this fog? I wouldn't want you out of sight of the shoreline. We'll be totally focused on spotting Kingman—and watching out for you would only make that harder. We've got to move fast, Son. With the infrared on *Alert 1*, we'll be flying."

Parker nodded like he'd known it was a bad idea from the start.

"You pray, Parker. Harley, Wilson . . . I think you've both seen the power of the God I serve . . . the God who loves you. And, Parker, you remember the Scripture you've memorized . . . you'll find strength there."

Fear ballooned inside Harley's gut. Was Parker's dad reminding him what to do while he was gone . . . or what to do if he didn't come back?

"Be on your guard," Mr. Buckman said. "Stand firm in the faith. Be men of courage." He looked at Parker and waited—like he expected his son could finish the quote.

"Be strong," Parker said. "Do everything in love."

Mr. Buckman nodded. "That's it. Now, I know you feel helpless. If there's something more for you to do, I'm going to trust that God shows you—and makes it clear. But you'd better be praying—and following His lead. No Lone Ranger stuff."

He slung his arm around Parker's neck. Pulled him close. "I love you. I'm proud of you."

He grabbed Wilson by the sides of his face and kissed the top of his head. Did the same to Harley. "I love you boys too."

Harley hugged him back. Just a quick one but harder than he'd hugged anybody—other than his own dad. And in that instant . . . Harley belonged. He was part of the family—and the DDC label couldn't change that fact. But Mr. Buckman was leaving. Going to chase a psycho. Harley couldn't lose Mr. Buckman, too.

The paramedics wheeled Ella's gurney toward one of the vans. Harley waved—and she locked eyes with him. Even from where he stood, Harley saw the fear. Not for herself anymore, he was pretty sure. She was afraid for Jelly. They all were.

Mr. Malnatti seemed to snap out of his thoughts, and he hustled over to Miss Lopez's gurney. She took his hand. Raised her head and said something to him. He nodded with a dangerous look of determination on his face. He broke free and hustled back to the edge of the T-wharf, staring out over the Outer Harbor like *Retribution* might materialize at any moment.

"You pray now, Parker," Mr. Buckman said. "Wilson. Harley . . . you, too."

Harley had no idea how to do that, but he would absolutely try.

Maggie's jacket was still wrapped around Eric. In her white harbor-master shirt, seemingly oblivious to the chill, she'd used her own paramedic skills right alongside the others. His bloody pant leg had been cut away—and lay in a heap on the ground. Eric was fully conscious, looking like he wanted to hobble off the gurney and climb back aboard *Alert 1*.

Harley stood alongside the men, watching. Sensing something was about to happen.

Maggie seemed to be assuring Eric of something. She peeled off her surgical gloves and wrung the pant leg, forming a pool of blood in her palm. She dipped two fingers into Eric's blood and painted a V on her shirtsleeve. A double chevron—like she'd become part of a blood battalion. She wiped the rest on her pants, grabbed her jacket, and hustled back toward Harley and the men.

"No turning back this time—and we're out for blood." She looked spitting mad. "Let's go get Jelly."

CHAPTER 98

ANGELICA SCISSOR-KICKED HER WAY BACK to the surface of the freezing water. Gasped for air. She kept a frantic flutter kick going to keep her head above water for a few more breaths before giving her legs a rest and sinking down again. If she got a charley horse, she'd drop like the anchor Clayton cut loose. *Retribution* drifted alongside her with all motors off. Like it was silently watching her struggle. She couldn't feel her hands . . . or feet.

She kicked her way back to the surface. Her movements were slower now. Sloppy. Like her blood had thickened. With her hands bound like they were? Terrifyingly claustrophobic. She fought back the panic, knowing if she failed . . . if she *did* panic, she'd surely die.

The sound of a small outboard motor raised her hopes for an instant. An inflatable dinghy rounded the bow—with Clayton straddling the back bench seat. He steered with the handle sticking out from the small motor on the transom.

"Need a lift?"

She'd take a ride with the devil himself at this moment. Kingman wasn't much better.

He coasted up alongside and grabbed the back of her sweatshirt. He pulled—and the thing seemed to stretch more than raise her out of the water. "Kick, Angel."

She *was* kicking, but her feet were too numb to be much help. "Cut the ties on my wrists."

"Let's not." He hooked his arm under hers and dragged her aboard.

He wore camo pants now. Black hoodie. So he'd taken the time to *change* after he'd kicked her off the bow? "What if I'd drowned?"

"Too much fight in my Angel to give up that easy."

"I was *bleeding*. What if a great white had come?"

Clayton shrugged. "I would've grabbed my camera. But I think you're missing the point. I just saved your life, Angel. You know I did."

After he'd cut her and kicked her into the water. She sensed he was waiting for something. She knew it—and every bit of emotion inside her wanted to deny him the satisfaction. But she had to be smarter than that. There were no more rescuers trailing their wake. She was on her own—and she had to survive. "Thank you." She stared at the bottom of the little boat. There was no way she would have gotten the words out of her mouth if she'd looked him in the eyes.

"You're welcome." He pulled a blanket out from under one of the bench seats. He spread it over her. Tucked in the sides. "See there? We're going to get along okay, you and I."

If there had been anything left in her stomach, she'd have deposited it on his shoes.

He zoomed once around *Retribution*, as if making sure he hadn't forgotten anything. "Party lights on. Key in the ignition. Extra phone on the console. Duffel with cash and a gun left behind. Murder-suicide note taped to the wheel."

"A *note*?"

Clayton looked pretty stinking proud of himself. "Basically, it says

I sent you to Davy Jones's locker. With the anchor line cut, and all the blood, they'll get the picture. They'll think I didn't want to get captured, strapped on an extra anchor, and took a swim myself."

"There's still time for that, Clayton. I could help you if you want."

He laughed. "I'm not desperate enough for suicide. But *they* don't know that. They wouldn't guess I had a second phone and other duffel bags with lots more cash. And plenty of other supplies. It'll look like we're both gone."

He'd truly thought of everything. Every little morbid, twisted thing.

"One more little detail." He pulled alongside *Retribution* and cut the motor. He grabbed the bow line and climbed back aboard the bigger boat.

She struggled against the nylon ties welding her wrists together. If she could free her hands, she could steer the dinghy into the fog. Lose him.

The massive speakers on *Retribution* came to life. "Every Breath You Take."

Of course.

He was back in the inflatable in seconds. "I set the song to just loop. Creepy, right?"

"Incredibly creepy." And not just the song.

Clayton bobbed his head to the pulse of the music and held the end of the bow line like a microphone. "'Baby can't you see . . . you belong to me . . .'" He grinned at her—like he was pleased she'd been watching.

Clayton started the outboard motor, pulled out his phone, and opened a compass app. How had he been so sure he'd even get a signal out here? But knowing Clayton, he'd probably checked that in advance. In seconds, the lights from *Retribution* grew softer. Weaker. And then they were gone altogether. Only the faint song betrayed that the boat was out there . . . somewhere. She was alone. A sense of hopelessness weighed on her . . . as real as her soaked sweatshirt.

"They would have found us if I'd tried to outrun the Coast Guard. Nobody will guess I had this little beauty out here . . . anchored and waiting. There were plenty of witnesses who saw us go out—without any kind of lifeboat in tow. The Coast Guard will find *Retribution* soon enough—and signs of a struggle. Clever, right?"

What, was he looking for a compliment? "Brilliant." And the thing that galled her most? It really was.

"After they find the empty boat, they'll be calling in the scuba recovery team to search for our bodies."

If nobody guessed she was alive, no one would be looking for her anyplace other than on the ocean floor. She couldn't depend on a rescue. She had to find a way to escape.

Clayton seemed more relaxed by the minute—even though they were practically running blind. No flashlight giving them a pathway of light ahead of them. The little outboard couldn't possibly be super fast, but with the limited visibility it seemed like they were on a hydrofoil.

He held up the screen so she could see. "They saw us heading south. And that's where they'll find *Retribution*. But *we're* not going south."

Of course they weren't. He was sticking to his MO: Do the unexpected. "You sure you can trust that app?" The dark. The fog. There was no way he could see a thing. "We could be heading to England, for all you know."

He laughed like she'd made the most stupid comment in the world. "Still cold?"

Not as cold as his heart.

"We won't be out here long. Then I'll get you warmed up. I'm pretty chilled myself."

The only way she wanted to see him warmed up was on a spit over glowing coals. "What happens if they find us—out here like this?"

"We're low to the water. I'm pretty sure their radar won't pick us up—even if they came way up north here."

"But if they did."

He looked at her like he couldn't understand why she'd have to ask the question. "I win. No matter what. And winning means your daddy or Gatorbait or his ranger daddy never rescues you. They don't get to take you home. No matter *what*." He slowed the motor, then lifted his sweatshirt. The faint glow from the phone was enough to show a pair of handguns tucked in his belt.

A chill swept through her—and it wasn't from the wet clothes or night air. *Angelica Malnatti. Self-proclaimed protector of the naive and impulsive.* What a joke. She'd really thought she could protect Parker. Like it was her calling or something. If she ever got out of this, she would change. She had to. She'd been so busy keeping others "safe" that she'd dropped her own guard. Protect others? What a crock. She couldn't even protect herself.

CHAPTER 99

PARKER SAT AT THE END OF THE T-WHARF with his feet hanging over the granite-block edge. The water ten feet below him was black and still. Harley sat with one foot hiked up, hugging his leg and resting his chin on his knee. His eyes looked dead, like he was in a daze. Wilson paced, machete in hand.

Parker had prayed. He'd tried, anyway. It was more of a looping prayer. *God, keep her safe. Bring Jelly home safe.*

All of them jumped when Parker's phone rang. "It's Dad." He answered immediately and put it on speaker.

"Do you have her?"

There was a pause on the other end. Too long. *Too. Long.* For good news anyway.

"We found the boat adrift . . . and empty. Nobody on board."

A ghost ship. It was that moment when every rescue scenario crumbles. When worst fears collide with reality . . . because they're on the very same path.

Dad relayed the facts. The blood. Missing anchor. Smashed window. Broken bow rail. The eerie music. The note. A duffel on board with cash and a gun. And the emergency inflatable lifeboat still onboard, secure in its pod. Dad was in that man-mode that allowed him to convey terrible information without crumbling himself. *Be men of courage.*

Parker's mind still looped in a prayer. *Oh, God. Oh, God. Help me.* The lights on Motif Number 1 blurred.

"By the looks of things, she put up one valiant fight."

And she'd fought Kingman alone. Parker hadn't been there to help her.

"Uncle Sammy . . . is he okay?" Why did he even ask that stupid question? Maria was off at school. She'd grown up. Jelly was still Uncle Sammy's little girl. Of course Uncle Sammy wasn't all right. "Forget I asked."

Wilson swung his machete, attacking one of the telephone-pole-sized posts spaced along the granite wall. He chopped away at it. If it helped—even a little—Parker was going to pull Jimbo out of its sheath and hack one of the posts down to a toothpick.

Harley covered his head with his hands. He rocked there on the edge of the granite blocks.

Parker stood. He had to do something. Hit something. "What if Kingman switched boats somehow? What if he staged everything on board beforehand?"

"Officer Greenwood said the same thing." Dad hesitated. "*Retribution* was heading south. A Coast Guard team is running a dragnet up from Boston as we speak. They'll stop every boat they see."

"What if he turns off his running lights? What if they don't see him?"

"They've got radar, Parker."

Parker tried to push the image of the empty and bloody phantom yacht out of his mind. "Do you think he met up with another boat—like he had it all arranged?"

"An accomplice?"

The idea was ridiculously far-fetched. How would Kingman have done that? The prison escape wasn't something planned months in advance. So how did he find someone willing to risk their neck for him—with so little notice? "Maybe his dad?"

"Greenwood says he's been under surveillance since the prison break, just in case Clayton came looking for help."

There had to be another explanation. "What if he flagged some random boat over—like he was in distress? He knew he had to ditch *Retribution*—that the Coast Guard would catch him if he didn't."

"And," Dad said, "when the boat came close to help, he shanghaied the thing?"

"Yeah. Something like that."

Harley looked up—like the idea made sense to him, too. Wilson was sitting on the post now. Listening. The machete dangled from the leather wrist thong.

"Parker," Dad said, "that absolutely could've happened."

"But what do *you* think?" If Dad really thought it was a possibility—Parker might dare set his hopes on it.

"It's a long shot," Dad said. "Kingman had everything too planned out to take a chance that he'd run across another boat in the fog—who'd offer to pull alongside and help."

Okay, that made way too much sense. And if Kingman did catch a ride with another boater, why leave his duffel with the money and gun behind?

"So, either it is what it appears to be," Dad said, "or there's something we're missing—and we need to figure it out."

Something they were missing. It wasn't much, but it was a sliver of hope. "We'll think on that."

"You do that. In the meantime, we're towing *Retribution* back instead of driving it, so as not to compromise the crime scene," Dad said.

Crime scene.

"It'll probably be an hour. Officer Greenwood and his team will meet us at the T-wharf." Another pause. "Parker . . . there's a lot of blood. I don't think you want to see this."

The lump in his throat burned as it swelled. He couldn't answer. Couldn't say a word.

"I'll let you decide, Son. Either way, I'm with you."

Something he never doubted. But right now, the one he really wanted with him . . . was gone.

CHAPTER 100

The harbor at Granite Pier, Rockport, Massachusetts
Saturday, October 30, 9:30 p.m.

UNUSUALLY CALM SEAS. That was the only reason the little twenty-horse motor had gotten them back to shore as quickly as it had. Angelica knew exactly where they were within moments of seeing land. Clayton scooted into the harbor by the massive old Granite Pier. He'd headed north for so long before cutting west toward the coast, she'd been sure he was lost. He was either really good at navigating in the fog or incredibly lucky.

She was so cold. Angelica promised herself that if she ever got to a shower, she'd stay in it until the hot water ran out. She hurt everywhere she still had feeling—and the rest of her was numb. Worse yet, so was her mind. She had to think, but the tired, the cold, and the fear kept easing her mind into neutral.

The harbor was socked in good with fog. Clayton probably loved that. He dropped his speed and steered past buoys with boats tied to them like sleeping dogs on leashes. He cut the motor completely and coasted to the side of an inboard cabin cruiser—with the name *Escape Room*.

She stared at the name—then at Clayton. "For real? Is that why you picked this boat—for the name?"

He motioned for her to keep her voice down. "That was just fate's way of steering me in the right direction."

Angelica had to find a way to escape. And when the opportunity came—no matter how slim—she'd have to take it. No hesitation.

Clayton tied the inflatable to a cleat on the big boat's gunwale and motioned for her to climb aboard. She just stared at him for a moment. With her hands tied, exactly how was she supposed to do that?

Clayton hiked one leg on the edge of the inflatable. "Step on my thigh."

She'd rather kick it. But she obeyed, and seconds later she dropped onto the deck of the boat. Instantly Clayton climbed aboard *Escape Room* himself. He ushered her into the cabin below—and shut the door behind them.

The cabin—so dark. Panic welled up inside her.

"Now I need you to listen good, Angel. Your whole future rides on how you play your hand over these next few hours."

"I can't even move my hands."

He laughed quietly. "Well said."

Suddenly light shone inside the cabin. He swept his phone around the tiny space. The windows were covered with duct tape—so there was no way anyone would see their light. A duffel sat on one of the bunks, zipper half open. Dry clothes. And was that the handle of a gun?

Clayton must have followed her gaze. He grabbed the duffel and winged the zipper shut. He dropped onto one bed and motioned for her to sit on the other. "We're at another crossroads—and I have two plans to choose from. Plan one? We keep moving. We pick up a car or truck right here and drive north by land—like right now. I leave you in our little hideout just long enough to find ourselves a ride. Plan two? We hunker down in *Escape Room* for the night. Sometime before sunrise, we'll fire this baby up and head north to New Hampshire. Go up to Hampton Beach. Find a car there and keep going north. Way up into Maine. And maybe we ditch the car for another boat and cross the border."

Like stealing cars and boats was as easy as calling an Uber. Yet the guy had made it this far, right?

"What do you think, Angel? Option one or two? Do we hit the road . . . or ride out the night here?"

"So, one if by land and two if by sea?"

Clayton grinned. "Paul Revere . . . nicely done, Angel. So, one or two?"

She had to think. "Cops will be everywhere. What about a plan three—where you turn yourself in? They'll even give you a warm, dry jumpsuit to wear. Doesn't that sound nice?"

"Sassy. I love that." He laughed quietly. "We are going to do *so* well together."

That urge to puke was coming back.

"Seriously. One or two?" He looked at her like he was really expecting her opinion.

Was this some kind of test? There was only one thing she hated more than the idea of riding out the night with him in this boat. And that was leaving for points unknown with him. Every hour she stayed close to Rockport increased her chances of being found, right?

"We lay low," Angelica said. "Isn't that what the bad guy does after pulling off the big crime?"

"It is indeed." He smiled. "But I'm not a bad guy—and I always lean toward the unpredictable."

Her heart sank.

"They would have found *Retribution* long before this. It only takes one on the search team to refuse to believe the obvious. And if they're still out looking for us, they'd be searching an hour south of here. Maybe more. But if they widen the search zone through the night?" He looked at the shut cabin door. "I think you're right, Angel. We should keep moving."

"That's not what—"

"I know what you said. But you actually helped me see things more clearly."

She groaned inside.

"But I think we'll let fate decide," he said. "I'll see about procuring us a vehicle with a full tank of gas. If I do, we move. If not, we lay low until morning."

He snipped the nylon tie that had turned her hands to blocks of wood. She massaged her wrists while Clayton rummaged in the duffel. He handed her a pair of pants and a sweatshirt. "Use the head to change into dry clothes. And don't get excited. I already disabled the lock."

He shined his light on the jeans label. Like he wanted her to read it. *Exactly her size.* Okay, if there was any possible way he could've creeped her out more than she already was, he'd just done it.

She changed as fast as her numb limbs allowed. He nodded approvingly when she came out. Like he was pleased she hadn't screamed for help—or tried clawing her way through the hull to freedom.

He showed her the handguns again. "I still have these. Anybody tries to stop us tonight—and we'll shoot to kill."

Weird how sometimes he talked to her like a prisoner—and other times like a partner. "One of those for me?"

He pulled one of them from his waistband. "Not the gun." He dropped the clip halfway—just long enough for her to see it was fully loaded—then snapped it back in place. "But you can have as many of the bullets as it takes to stop you if it comes to that."

His eyes . . . dead serious. This was no con he was pulling. She knew that in her heart. "I want to live."

He nodded. "Just so we're clear. That's what I want too. But I want one thing even more than you staying alive." He waited, like he wasn't going to go on until she asked.

"And that is?"

"To win this little rematch. If something happens and we can't get away—or I don't think I can get away with you . . ." He shrugged. Like the answer was obvious.

"Then I'm dead."

"It's the only way I win." He smiled apologetically. "I knew you'd understand. Now here's the thing. Since *you* want to live—and *I* want you to live—let's work together. We do that, and we'll make it. It's a sure thing."

The only sure thing? Clayton was absolutely psychotic. As crazy and unstable as a rabid dog. And if she got the chance to put him down—she absolutely must.

"I can give you a good life. You'll be happy. Down the line, we'll get married—and maybe we can come for a visit. Who knows?"

She was going to throw up again if he kept going.

"Now, here's what we're going to do." Over the next few minutes, Clayton outlined his next steps. She'd be bound again. Mouth covered too. He'd take the inflatable to shore after locking her inside the cabin. There were plenty of trucks parked in the lot at the heel of the harbor. He'd find the right one, load some essentials, and come back for her.

"I want to trust you, Angel. And that will come in time. But I need to show you something." He opened the cabin door. Pointed to a row of containers on the deck. "Know what that is?"

She had no idea.

"Chum." He let the word sink in for a moment. "I'm going to soup the waters around the boat *real* good before I leave. You'll be tied, for sure, but in case you think you can throw yourself over the side and somehow make it to shore? Think again. A great white would be one hellacious way to go . . . don't you think?" His voice grew lower. More ominous with every word. "And they're here. You can thank the growing seal population for that. Between the blood and you thrashing around? We'll bring in a good one."

CHAPTER 101

PARKER SAT SLUMP-SHOULDERED ON THE edge of the T-wharf, staring out at the channel into the open sea. His eyes were messing with him. Sometimes he was sure he saw *Retribution* ghosting through the fog. Did he want to be here when they arrived? To see her blood on the deck?

No. Definitely not. But he couldn't seem to leave, either. It was like when he was a kid in the car with his parents. There'd been a horrible accident—and rescue vehicles were still on the scene. Police routed the line of cars past the site.

"Don't look, Son," Dad had said.

But of course, he did. He didn't see a body. Not exactly. But they had made a makeshift morgue out of the two-lane. Someone had covered a victim with a tarp. Even though Parker couldn't see his face, the tarp hadn't covered the guy's hand. Palm up. Lifeless. He wore a watch with the face on the underside of his wrist. The man's hand rested across the yellow no-passing stripes. Like even in death, he was pushing his luck.

As much as Parker didn't want to see the crime scene, he knew he would when the boat arrived.

Harley cleared his throat. "Your dad said we should, uh, you know. Pray. Right?"

Which meant it was going to be up to Parker. But he felt prayed-out. Like when someone has cried and cried and cried. And at some point, the pain is still there, but the tears don't work anymore. "I got nothing."

Harley looked at him for a long moment, then squeezed his eyes shut. "God, this is Harley Davidson Lotitto. You don't really know me. I get that. But You do know Parker. And he's got something to say. But it's hard to find the words, You know? But he's gonna try. Maybe You could sort of fill in the blanks if he leaves something important out, okay? Ah . . . again, this is Harley Davidson Lotitto . . . over and out."

The prayer almost shamed Parker. Harley was desperate enough to try—and the truth? Parker was too. He bowed his head. "God . . . I know I should be praying, like, constantly. But I'm not that strong. I'm scared spitless. Help me. Help us. Help Jelly. Do what only You can do. And if we're missing something? Show us the way." His voice cracked, and that was it. The lump in his throat wasn't going to allow another word out.

"Over and out," Harley whispered. He looked at Parker. "What now?"

Parker shook his head. "This isn't exactly a science. We wait. We go back over everything—and trust Him to show us if we missed something important."

That seemed to make sense to Harley. He led off, reviewing everything they knew so far. From the postcards to the ghost ship being towed back to the harbor at this very moment.

"The whole 'rendezvous with a partner in crime' idea may be too far out there," Harley said. "And the chance that he'd flag another boat down and pull off a takeover is just as crazy. Kingman does the unexpected— but that doesn't mean he takes stupid chances."

None of them disagreed.

"Okay, your dad said the emergency lifeboat was still on board. But what if Kingman had a second lifeboat?" Harley wasn't suggesting anything Parker hadn't already thought of. "They could have left in that, right? Made a run for shore?"

"We all saw Retribution leave the harbor," Parker said. "There was no dinghy or lifeboat behind it."

None of them spoke for a long minute.

"Actually," Wilson said, "it *did* have an inflatable earlier. Gray and white. Tied off the stern."

Parker actually turned to face him. "Wait . . . *what?*"

"On the way back from Pigeon Cove this morning. We drove right by *Retribution*, and there was an inflatable tender behind it."

Parker played back the scene. He'd been wowed by the Boston Whaler and hardly noticed anything else . . . but there *had been* a boat behind it. "With an outboard motor on it. So, was that just someone delivering supplies . . . or was it Kingman's?"

"I didn't see anyone on deck," Harley said. "And why would a delivery person even go on board? What if Kingman towed the boat out to deep water earlier. Anchored it, and—"

"Staged the fight," Parker said, "so he could make his getaway. He had to know the Coast Guard would intercept *Retribution*—probably long before he'd reach Boston."

"So," Harley said, "he *didn't* commit suicide. He pulled a disappearing act. Created an illusion—and we all bought it."

Okay, maybe Parker was overly generous at connecting the dots—but this was making real sense. Kingman hadn't look one bit suicidal when they'd seen him. He looked confident. In control. "How big was the motor on the tender?"

Wilson shrugged. "*That* I didn't notice. Which means it was puny. Fifteen. Twenty-horse max. I would've noticed anything bigger."

"He has the tender anchored." Parker was on his feet now, pacing the very edge of the granite blocks. "Uses the hostages to slow us down and keep us from seeing what he's *really* up to. He had Jelly in the inflatable before setting *Retribution* adrift." He looked at Wilson and Harley. There was hope—and fire in their eyes. "So, where did he go?"

"Not far in *that* boat," Wilson said. "We check the shoreline. Look for the boat. Maybe it will give a clue as to where he's really taking her."

Right. *Right.* "We all saw him angle south. Did he make a mistake letting us see that—or was he making sure he kept us looking the wrong way?"

Harley stared out over the Outer Harbor. "He does the unexpected, right?"

"So we search north." Parker peered into the fog. Pulled out his phone and called his dad. Put it on speaker. He gave him the thirty-second recap. "How long before you're back? We gotta search the north coast."

It would be another forty minutes, anyway. That could be too long. The trail—if there was one—could be cold by then. "Dad . . . please . . . we can't wait that long."

His dad hesitated like he knew what Parker was going to ask. "Steadman's boat?"

"We'll stay close enough to see shore lights—but we'll stay off the rocks. I know the waters, Dad, you know I do." He had to say yes. Every minute counted. To say no would only increase the odds she'd never be found.

"Pigeon Cove," Dad said. "No farther."

It was far enough. How far could Kingman go in a dinghy—especially from where he would've started? Harley started for the boat at a fast jog. Wilson alongside him. Parker on the other side. He held out the phone so they could still hear.

"You three check it out. You keep in contact." There was a tension in Dad's voice. "And if you see that boat . . . you stake the thing out and wait for me and Uncle Sammy—and Maggie. Got it?"

Yeah. He got it.

"Get going, guys." Uncle Sammy's voice. "God help us. You find our girl. And God help Kingman when I get there."

CHAPTER 102

ANGELICA KNEW SHE SHOULD KEEP SEARCHING the cabin for anything that might help her break her nylon bonds and bust out of *Escape Room*. But the cabin was dark—and she'd crab-walked her way across every inch that she could reach. Kingman wasn't that sloppy.

He'd chummed the water good—actually taking her on deck to see the job before he locked her back in the cabin and drove the inflatable to shore. How long had it been since his motor had faded from earshot? Ten minutes? He wouldn't risk leaving her alone much longer. Now that he had his Angel, his prize, he wouldn't let her out of his sight for long, chum or no chum.

She'd seen the psychotic side of Clayton long before her sister had. Maria had believed that under all the ego and anger, Clayton was just a good boy who needed a girl like her to fix him.

In that moment, in the darkness of the cabin, Angelica saw her situation as vividly as she'd seen anything in her life. Clayton was scary-smart.

He'd outsmarted everyone who'd been hunting for him since Jericho's walls fell. In her heart, she knew—with absolute certainty—if Clayton took her away tonight, somehow he'd make her vanish. She'd never be found by her dad or Parker—or anyone else. She'd be an unsolved mystery. And Angelica was convinced, to the very core of her soul, that if Clayton took her away tonight . . . eventually he'd kill her. But it would be on his terms. In his cruel way. Waves of chills flashed through her body.

So that left her with one option. Only one. She had to fight. No more going along with him, hoping his guard would drop and she'd get away. No more making this easy for him. He intended to take her away tonight. She saw that caged-animal look in his eyes. So she would fight him every inch of the way—and do everything she could to escape or slow him down. If he was going to kill her, she'd make him do it now.

With her mouth duct-taped, she couldn't even scream for help—if anyone was actually out on this godforsaken Halloween Eve night. Time to fix that. She dropped to her knees and lowered her face until she felt the edge of the bunk. She pressed her cheek hard against the bare mattress and turned her head—just like Pez had done. Over and over, she rubbed at the very corner where the tape ended. The mattress felt more like a fine sandpaper as her cheeks grew raw. But the corner lifted—and she absolutely attacked the mattress until she'd peeled off the entire length of tape.

She tried to steady her breathing and listened. The motor. Faint. But it was him. *God help me. God help me.* How could she signal anyone?

The idea was stupid. Desperate. She stood, hopped to the port side bunk and threw herself onto it—hard enough to slam into the side of the boat bordering the bed . . . the hull itself. She got up and threw herself against the hull along the starboard bunk this time. Did the boat move? Rock, just a bit? It did, didn't it?

"Make waves, boat. Make waves. And somebody—please—see them!"

She struggled to her feet. Threw herself against the boat's hull again.

Repeated the same motion on the other side. Her shoulder was bleeding again. Tears wept from her eyes. She'd been so stupid. If nothing else, throwing herself from one side of the boat to the other was a great way to beat herself up for getting into this spot. She deserved that.

Angelica pictured Clayton in the darkness—as if *he* were the hull of the boat itself. She threw herself against the side of the boat with savage fury. "I will fight. I won't let you take me."

She hit the opposite bulkhead again, a cry of pain escaping her lips as she did. Make waves, *Escape Room*. Make waves.

And maybe—somehow—someone would notice. She dragged herself off the bed and launched herself at the other side.

Make waves. Start a ripple effect. And maybe she'd make a wave big enough to disrupt Clayton Kingman's plans too.

CHAPTER 103

HARLEY STOOD ALONGSIDE PARKER AT THE WHEEL. Wilson knelt in the bow, like he was ready to spring into action. All of them straining to see through the fog. Wilson and Parks likely driven by the same fear and desperation—and the tiniest sliver of hope—that Harley felt.

At the entrance to the harbor at Granite Pier, Parks eased all the way back on the throttle. He cut the motors, and Mr. Steadman's boat settled in the still waters.

He'd done this how many times since they'd left the slip at the T-wharf? Stop. Cut the motor. Listen. Struggle to see through the fog. Move on. Repeat.

At least a couple dozen boats sat anchored in the harbor, maybe more. It was impossible to know with the fog. But every boat in sight sat as still as the tombstones in the Old Parish Burial Ground off Front Beach.

Wilson held one hand up and pointed to his ear with the other.

Harley held his breath. Strained to hear.

Wilson pointed into the fog—and Harley caught the slightest sound of an outboard motor. Wilson motioned Parks forward.

Parker started the engine and crept ahead, keeping the speed down and the sound low. The fog didn't exactly part as they moved forward. More like it became part of them. Absorbing into Harley's sweatshirt. Jeans. And lungs—with every breath he took.

Wilson drew a finger across his throat. Parker cut the motor again.

They coasted silently ahead and came to rest in the shadow of a sailboat just as the silhouette of an old cabin cruiser came into view. Not nearly as big as *Retribution*. Inboard. Ripples radiated away from the hull in all directions. Like the motor was on—but clearly it wasn't. Weird.

And out of the fog an inflatable dinghy materialized out of nothingness. A man hunkered low on the seat, steering directly to the cabin cruiser. He killed the tiny outboard motor and coasted to the side of the boat. And when he stood, it was obvious . . . he only had one arm.

Harley, Wilson, Parks . . . all of them dropped low. Was Harley shaking? Parker's God had answered a prayer thrown up to Him as desperate as any Hail Mary pass Harley had ever seen.

Wilson looked back, a wicked smile on his face—and something almost devilish blazing in his eyes.

So not only did Kingman have a dinghy, but he had a second boat? Brilliant. He tied the inflatable to the back of the boat and climbed aboard himself. Where was Jelly?

Parker eased his body to the deck. He lay flat. Dimmed the screen on his phone and made a call—to his dad no doubt. Harley crouched down next to him.

"We got him, Dad," Parks whispered into his cupped hand. "Granite Pier. Southeast corner of the harbor. Cabin cruiser. No sign of Jelly—but she could be inside. I can't tell if he's coming or going."

She had to be there. *Parker's God . . . make her be there. Please. She's my friend. My family. God . . . please.*

Parks nodded. "Ten minutes, max. I got it. We'll try to wait. Honest. But we can't let him leave the harbor, right?" He pocketed the phone but stayed low.

Wilson crept back to join them. "Got a plan?"

"They're anchoring *Retribution* and racing over. Dad will call the police. Maggie will radio the Coast Guard." Parker peered into the fog toward the cruiser. "In the meantime, we get closer. See if we can spot Jelly, right?" He pointed to a lobster boat moored between them and the cruiser. The name *Something Fishy* was barely visible. "We'll pull alongside the lobster boat."

Harley nodded. The thought of just waiting at the mouth of the harbor was torture. Kingman disappeared inside the cabin—but no lights came on.

Wilson pulled a paddle from the rack mounted to the inside wall of Steadman's boat. He grabbed a second one and handed it to Harley. Each knelt on opposite sides of the boat and silently dipped their paddles into the black water of the harbor.

They pulled up alongside the lobster boat. The big fishing boat effectively hid Steadman's boat completely. The boys could stand now, with just their heads poking above the bow of *Something Fishy*.

Kingman was back on deck. He dropped a duffel into the tender, rushed back to the cabin, and disappeared inside.

"We need to know if Jelly is in there," Parker said. "But if we go any closer, he'll spot us for sure." What would stop Kingman from shooting her—or escaping again before Dad arrived?

Wilson peeled off his sweatshirt. Kicked off his shoes.

"Hey, man," Harley said. "What are you doing?"

"I'll swim over to the mooring line. Shimmy up. If Jelly is in there . . . and she's in trouble . . . there's no way we're waiting for backup. We all know that."

Parker nodded. "The water is cold. Can you handle it?"

Wilson snickered.

"What about sharks?" Harley hated to bring it up, but swimming in the ocean . . . at night? And in an area where fisherman likely dumped fish blood and guts? "I mean, there are great whites in the area, right?"

"Miccosukee Indians are invisible to sharks—*especially* great whites."

"You're only half Miccosukee," Parker said.

Wilson grinned. "A half-invisible swimmer. That'll freak the shark out." He slipped the strap of the machete's sheath over his head and slung the weapon across his back.

Harley looked at the distance to the boat. A whole lot farther than he'd want to swim if there was a great white within a mile of them. "The machete won't do any good against the shark, Wilson."

He reached back and tapped the handle. "I'm not wasting this on a shark. The machete is for Kingman." Wilson raised his gator tooth necklace to his lips. "This is for the shark." He feigned a jab. "Right in the eye, right? Wish me luck."

Wilson slipped over the side, his eyes getting wide as the chill hit his body. He struck out in a silent breaststroke through fog that clung to the surface. Parker's lips moved in silent prayer. Harley bowed his head too but kept his eyes on Wilson. When Parker finished, he pulled his own gator tooth necklace out from under his T-shirt and held it for a moment—like he was somehow urging his Miccosukee friend on.

Wilson reached the mooring line running up to a heavy eyebolt on the bow of the cruiser. He raised his machete to signal them—and slid it back in its sheath.

Suddenly the cabin door burst open. Kingman appeared, half-dragging someone behind him.

Jelly!

She squirmed. Screamed. Kingman let go. She thudded to the deck, and he hauled off and kicked her. Not a half-cocked thing. This was kickoff force, like he was aiming to send a football into the end zone.

She screamed in pain. "I'm not going! Not going!"

Parks's hands clenched and unclenched. "We can't just sit here." He shot a desperate look toward the mouth of the harbor.

Jelly balled up the best she probably could with her hands and feet bound the way they were.

"You like being dead weight?" Kingman sounded like a man losing it. "I can make that permanent."

Parks stood. Started the boat. Slammed the throttle forward. "That's it."

"Go-go-go!" Harley grabbed the console to keep from doing a backwards flip.

"Kingman!" Parker roared toward the cruiser.

Kingman stared—a stunned-stupid expression on his face.

Parker threw Steadman's boat into reverse and gave it the gas—engines screaming. Still, he hit the side of the cruiser near the stern with a glancing blow.

Kingman lost his footing for a moment, regained it, and pulled a gun from his waistband. He squeezed off two wild shots—flames rocketing from the muzzle.

Harley and Parker instinctively ducked, and when they looked up, Kingman had his arm around Jelly's neck. The bend of his arm was at her Adam's apple . . . the pistol still in his hand.

"Back off, Gatorbait. Hear me? I'll do it. You know I will."

For a moment—nobody moved. The boats had drifted ten feet apart. If Parker tried to pull close so they could rush Kingman somehow? They'd both be dead before they boarded the cruiser. Likely Jelly would be next.

"Give us Jelly," Parker said. "And we back away."

Kingman shook his head. "Not going to happen. How about you back away, and I won't shoot her?"

Parker didn't move. "She never hurt you. Let her go. I'm the one you want."

There was a moment. Like that instant before the ball is snapped—when players are staring into the helmet of the opponent . . . each intending to take the other apart.

"How about you come aboard with me—and we take a boat ride

together? The moment you climb aboard. I'll let Angel leave with your bodyguard there."

Jelly squirmed furiously. "Don't do it—it's a tra—"

Kingman cinched his arm tight. Whispered something in Jelly's ear.

"Stop! I'll do it." Parker glanced at Harley. Desperation in his eyes. "I have to."

Parker was right. He had no choice. But Jelly was absolutely right too. This was a trap.

CHAPTER 104

PARKER EASED FORWARD, closing the gap between the two boats. From this angle, he caught the boat's name for the first time. *Escape Room.* Incredible. "God . . . rescue us somehow. Help Jelly escape for real."

Harley stood shoulder to shoulder with him. "And help me fight."

Kingman had kicked the fight right out of Jelly. He steered her onto the gunwale—and forced her to sit on the very edge. Jelly's legs hung over the water—with her ankles securely zip-tied. Arms still bound behind her. If he pushed her over the side—she wouldn't have a chance.

"Take care of Jelly," Parker said. "No matter what."

"I got her, Parks."

"Weapons on the deck," Kingman ordered. "Sweatshirts. Off."

What, did he think Parker was carrying a gun, too? He took the machete off from around his neck and dropped it. Peeled off the hoodie. Tossed it to the side. Unclipped the survival knife strapped to his calf. Let it drop. He held his hands up and did a 360. "Satisfied?" He pulled off his gator-tooth necklace and shook it in front of him. "Or do you want this, too?"

"Keep your jewelry, tough guy. Just get your tail aboard. Nice and easy."

Parker placed the tooth in his palm and closed his fist around it. Wrapped the lanyard around his knuckles. His gimpy arm . . . and it had never felt weaker than at this moment. He tapped the side of *Escape Room* with his bow.

Harley held his arms above his head and stepped to the bow. "I'll hold the boats together for the exchange—okay?"

"Do it," Kingman said. "But if I so much as see you twitch, Angel goes in the water—which I massively chummed, by the way."

Harley scanned the surface. "Chummed?"

"The stuff is guaranteed to draw sharks from over forty miles away, so don't get stupid on me."

Harley pulled the boats together, still eying the water.

"Now Jelly comes aboard." Parker tried to sound confident. Like he wasn't totally at Kingman's mercy—even though he was.

"Not happening," Kingman said. "I want you on this deck—like right here—before I let Angel go."

"Don't do it, Parker!" Jelly's eyes . . . pleading—and filled with fear.

Kingman wasn't going to let her go. Parker was sure of that. But getting close to Kingman might give him the chance to stop him. Parker stepped from Steadman's boat to *Escape Room*.

"Okay," Parker said. "I'm here. Jelly goes in the other boat."

Kingman shrugged. "It doesn't work that way, Gatorbait. I have the gun. I make the rules." He motioned to Harley. "Shove off, and toss me your keys, scurvy dog."

Harley hesitated—until Kingman aimed the gun at Parker. Harley pushed Steadman's boat back, pulled the keys from the ignition, and tossed them. They dropped onto the deck near Kingman's feet.

"Good boy, scurvy dog."

Kingman didn't show a trace of fear. He had the gun, and he had

Jelly. He'd take Parker out. Maybe Harley, too. And he'd disappear with Jelly. Parker had to stall him. "*Please.* Let her go."

"*Poor* Gatorbait. I kicked your butt at every turn." Kingman's face . . . pure arrogance. "This was the mother of all rematches, and it ends with you begging for her life? You'll be begging for yours soon. You're pathetic. And you know something? Except for showing up here, every move you've made has been sooo predictable."

Parker had to make him feel there was no escape. "If you go back to prison as a convicted murderer—you'll be a lifer . . . on death row." He chanced a step closer. "You don't want that."

Kingman made an exaggerated show of scanning the harbor. "And exactly who is taking me back to prison? Scurvy dog?"

Harley raised his hand. "Hey, I'd be happy to volunteer."

"It's over, Kingman," Parker said. "I made a call before you spotted us. Help is coming. Let her go—before they come—and maybe it goes better for you."

Kingman looked at Parker like he'd just heard the most ridiculous thing. "I win the rematch. Angel comes with me—or she joins the angels."

Sirens wailed from somewhere on shore nearby. *Thank you, God. Thank you, G—*

Kingman stared toward the parking lot—the faint pulsing of red and blue lights reflecting off his face. "What will they do, swim out here?" He still had his chokehold on Jelly. "Aye, me Angel. Looks like I be needing to travel fast—and light. Can't be having a wench slow me down, says I."

Kingman dropping back into that pirate-speak thing again? He was really losing it now. Parker inched closer.

"Time for you to walk the plank, Angel-wench, so's I can deal with Gatorbait proper-like. But we can't be having that bilge-sucking scurvy dog jumping aboard to help Gatorbait, now can we?" He nodded toward Harley. "We gots to keep him busy, says I. How you be at swimming, scurvy dog?"

Harley wiggled the fingers on both hands. "A mite better than you."

Kingman laughed. "Well said, scurvy dog." He unhooked his arm from around Jelly's neck. "Now fetch, scurvy dog." He pressed the gun to Jelly's thigh—and pulled the trigger. The force of it jolted her off the side of the boat—screaming. Harley dove in after her.

Parker rushed Kingman—but Clayton stepped back and squeezed off a round into the water. "Stop—or I keep shooting." He fired again.

Parker froze—just within reach of Kingman. "Don't shoot them—please." Or was it already too late?

"It be easy to finish them off, says I." Kingman's eyes were wild. "And I've got a mind to do it." He kept the gun pointed at the surface of the water.

Harley surfaced, with his arm around Jelly. She coughed. Sputtered. She was alive.

"Watch out for shark," Kingman said, his aim still on Harley and Jelly.

The sound of a boat roaring in hot came from the harbor entrance. *Alert 1* materialized out of the fog.

Kingman swore.

"Just put the gun down, Kingman," Parker said. "It's over."

Kingman turned the gun on Parker. Stepped closer. "For you."

God . . . help me. Parker forced the point of the gator tooth up like a spike between his middle and ring fingers. Closed his fist.

"Clayton," Jelly's desperate cry rose from the water. "Nooooo!"

Kingman smiled.

And Parker knew he was going to do it. *Alert 1* came clearly into view. He clenched his fist tighter. *God, strengthen this gimpy arm—one more time.*

"Actually," Kingman said, "this is great! They're too late to stop me, but I get an audience to see me win the rematch. All three of you will be gone—right before their eyes."

Wilson's head poked up from the bow on the other side of the cabin—just out of Kingman's line of vision. He shimmied silently along the gunwale.

Kingman glared at Parker. "You're first." He pressed the barrel hard against Parker's ribs. "See ya, Gatorbait."

"Kingman!" Wilson leaped right at them—machete raised.

Kingman swung the gun toward Wilson—and Parker struck at Kingman's shocked face. The gator-tooth hit soft tissue—and sank deep.

"Aaahhhh!" The gun dropped from Kingman's hand. He cupped his hand over one eye, blood streaming from between his fingers. "Aaahhh-ahh-aaahhh!" He staggered backward until he hit the side of the boat.

Wilson met him there, ramming into him with full-blooded Miccosukee force. Arm flailing, Kingman flipped backward—heels over head—and splashed into the bay.

The dual motors powering *Alert 1* screamed as Maggie reversed hard. Uncle Sammy was on his knees at the low gunwale collar instantly, reaching for Jelly. Harley swam her to the side of the boat. Uncle Sammy—together with Dad—pulled her aboard.

Parker leaned over the gunwale. "Is she okay?"

Maggie cut the motor and rushed to check Jelly's wound. "We got you, honey. It was in and out. Nowhere near your femoral artery."

Uncle Sammy cradled Jelly. Rocked her. "My girl, my girl."

Dad stood, Jelly's blood on his hands. He smiled—and in that moment, every shadow of fear and every doubt were gone. Jelly really was okay.

Harley grinned, treading water in the triangle formed between *Alert 1*, *Escape Room*, and Steadman's boat. He swam for the empty Boston Whaler.

Wilson stood on the gunwale with the machete over his head. "Where's Kingman?" He searched the surface of the water as if he expected the guy to climb aboard and pick up where he'd left off. "There!" He pointed the machete at him.

"Stop him, Daddy!" Jelly cried. "He can't get away."

Maggie locked eyes with Uncle Sammy. "Jelly's fine—just hold on to her tight, okay?"

Dad knelt back down next to Uncle Sammy and Jelly. "We got her . . . do it."

Maggie fired up *Alert 1* and gunned the motors. She banked hard around the bow of *Escape Room*. Uncle Sammy held Jelly, one hand pressed on the bullet wound.

Kingman was on the surface, kicking hard and clawing for shore. Maggie maneuvered *Alert 1* to block his escape. Kingman changed his tack—heading for *Something Fishy*.

Maggie spun the wheel and cut him off again. "I can do this all night. Can you?"

Harley struggled to climb into Steadman's boat, but with the wet clothes, he was getting nowhere. He held on to the bow line and seemed way more interested in watching what was happening with Kingman than getting into the boat anyway.

"Harley!" Parker motioned him over to *Escape Room*. "Get over here. We'll give you a hand."

Harley dropped the bow line and struck out for Parker and Wilson.

Police cars were parked at crazy angles on the granite pier and in the parking area along shore. Their searchlights lit up the harbor. A paramedic truck roared in.

Kingman ducked underwater. What, did he think he could lose them somehow?

"Enough of this," Maggie said.

The instant Kingman surfaced, Maggie pointed behind him. "Shark! Get out of the water!" She threw a life ring. Kingman shot a desperate look behind him, then did a combination frog kick and doggy paddle straight for the lifesaving float.

Harley splashed his way toward Wilson and Parker with sloppy, numb-armed strokes.

Parker leaned far over the gunwale and slapped the side of the boat—cheering him on—and hoping the noise scared the shark away. "C'mon, Harley!"

Wilson joined him. "Dig, dig, dig! *You're* not invisible to great whites, remember?"

A moment later, Wilson and Parker hoisted Harley aboard *Escape Room*.

Kingman grabbed the life ring. "Pull me in!" He swore. "Where's the shark?"

Maggie flipped a switch on the winch and reeled him to the side of the boat. Together with Parker's dad, they dragged him half over the gunwale. Maggie whipped out nylon ties. She cinched his wrist to his belt. Dad lassoed Kingman's ankles with another tie and pulled so tight that Kingman howled.

"Well, pull me all the way in!" Blood streamed from Kingman's closed eye. "The shark!"

Maggie grabbed a line and lashed him to the cleats on the gunwale. "No shark. Just bamboozling you a little to hurry things along. And after what you did to my partner, I really don't want you on my deck."

She hit the horn—and motioned to the police on shore. "Got a live one for you!" She motored toward the waiting policemen—with Kingman strapped to the side like a giant dock bumper.

For a moment, Parker, Wilson, and Harley just stood there on the deck of *Escape Room*, watching. "We made it," Harley whispered. "We all did."

The three friends stared at each other for a long moment . . . as if the reality of that statement needed time to sink in.

Parker held out the bloody gator tooth necklace . . . the lanyard still wrapped around his knuckles.

Wilson grabbed Parker's wrist and held it up high. "Is this the ultimate weapon or *what?* Gator teeth can still draw blood—even after the gator is dead."

The three of them laughed in that hysterical way that only happens when adrenaline and raw fear collide with relief—and sheer joy.

Parker unwrapped the lanyard and slung it back around his neck. His gator tooth necklace wouldn't be coming off anytime soon.

Maggie maneuvered *Alert 1* perfectly, delivering Kingman to Officer

Greenwood. In the beams of the searchlights, Parker could make out Officer Greenwood and another policeman dragging Kingman off the collar of the harbormasters' boat. Paramedics were already at Jelly's side.

"Dad!" Parker cupped his hands around his mouth. "Jelly's really okay . . . right?"

Dad turned their way and flashed them the divers' okay sign.

All three boys whooped and cheered. Harley did a victory dance with both hands high over his head—like they'd just scored the winning touchdown. Wilson stabbed deep into the fog overhead with his machete.

"It's over." Parker grabbed Wilson's neck—and Harley's . . . pulling them both close. The three of them had been in battle together and had come out the other side. "Us three. We're more than friends. We're family. Brothers."

Parker held his gator tooth necklace out in the middle of the three of them.

"Brothers." Harley clamped his hand over Parker's. "I like the sound of that."

"Make that *blood* brothers." Wilson added his hand to theirs and squeezed. "Forever."

EPILOGUE

"WE SHOULD LEAVE IN TEN." Parker set his timer and sat beside Wilson on the granite rocks at the end of Bearskin Neck. They'd be meeting Harley, Jelly, and Ella at the coffee shop soon, but there were still a few more minutes to kill. Parker looked out over Sandy Bay, where just seven days ago *Retribution* had been anchored. The week following Jelly's rescue had been filled with so many good things.

Jelly, Ella, and Pez became local celebrities. The coffee shop closed for a couple of days. But when they opened—and all three of them were on shift? People came in just to see them working together on crutches. And it seemed every other customer couldn't resist cracking lame jokes.

"Hey, give me an extra *shot* of espresso in that one, will ya? Make it a 9mm."

"I feel dead today. Got anything with really high-caliber caffeine?"

"Can anybody get a job here, or do all your female workers have to take a bullet?"

Some customers even came in on crutches themselves. Not that they had any real injury, but it became kind of a thing. There were times when half the customers in the shop had crutches. Pez even added two new flavors to the daily specials board.

Crutch Coffee—guaranteed to keep you on your feet
Bulletproof Brew—enough caffeine to make you unstoppable

And the tips jar? The thing had to be emptied twice a shift.

Maybe employees didn't have to take a bullet to get a job at BayView Brew, but it sure brought more customers into the shop. If the traffic kept up, Pez said she'd have to hire more help. Her exact words? "Who'd have guessed a shot to the leg could be such a shot in the arm."

The bullet Eric took lodged in his femur—which meant emergency surgery. His full recovery would likely take longer than the girls', but already he'd been getting around pretty good on the crutches. He got cheers whenever he hobbled into the coffee shop.

Maggie had been respected plenty before the incident, but now? She was well on her way to becoming a Rockport legend. Sometime in the last couple of days, vinyl chevron stripes had been added to each side of the pilothouse on *Alert 1*. The thick, blood-red markings added a fierceness to the harbormasters' boat.

Dad had worked things out with Harley's social worker, allowing him to stay with them through November, anyway. When Mom had learned he'd never had a real Thanksgiving—as in a whole family sitting around the table—she'd started planning . . . and inviting guests. Jelly. Uncle Sammy. Grams. Ella. Pez. All of them would be there. And Grandpa wouldn't miss it either.

To lock in the brotherhood, Wilson awarded Harley his gator-tooth necklace, promising to bag a gator and make a new one for himself. Harley matched that by giving Wilson a leather lanyard with the last spare key from Kemosabe. All three of them would wear two necklaces now—one with the gator tooth and one with the motorcycle key. Symbols of a bond that wouldn't be broken.

Wilson, Harley, and Parker all packed into one bedroom—even though the Buckman guest room sat empty. The late-night talks had absolutely been among the best moments of the last week. Some people say nothing good happens after midnight, but Parker found that wasn't completely true. It often wasn't until after twelve that the joking stopped and the talks got serious.

Parker talked about his desire to be the kind of man he saw in his grandpa, his dad, and Uncle Sammy . . . and how he was working on that. He'd admitted how unsure he'd been about going to Florida at first. How to his total surprise, God had used that trip to answer some of Parker's deepest prayers. God had taught him that looking past himself and being there for friends in need—new and old—was part of being the kind of man he wanted to be.

Parker shared how *he'd* been helped so much—just by helping a friend. If he hadn't gone to help find Wilson—and Wilson hadn't come back with them . . . what would have happened to Parker? If Wilson hadn't distracted Kingman on the boat exactly when he had . . . Parker would never have had the chance to take that wild swing. And if Wilson hadn't been in Rockport, Parker wouldn't have been wearing the gator tooth necklace. With all his other weapons gone, how would Parker have stopped Kingman without it? The necklace proved to be the one weapon Kingman hadn't seen as a threat. But the gator tooth—along with prayer—was all that was needed to take the guy down.

Wilson admitted that Hurricane Morgan had done more than leave him with scars. He fought a growing sense of fear of going back to the Glades—something he'd never felt before . . . and he wasn't sure exactly what to do about it.

Harley opened up about his loneliness—his sense of not having any kind of real family connection. He told about the visit with his uncle in prison—and how it had messed with his head.

They talked about Jelly and Ella—a lot. Their quirks. Their fierce loyalty as friends. Lots of good things that they'd never talk about in the daylight—or tell the girls face-to-face.

But maybe Parker's favorite part of their "midnight confessions," as they came to be known, was how the talks usually gravitated to spiritual things.

Grandpa had gotten the complete rundown from Parker—the blow-by-blow of how everything had come down in that second storm. Grandpa wanted every detail—and Parker hadn't left a single one out. He'd even told Grandpa about the late-night talks since Kingman's capture. Two days later, a letter came in the mail—with instructions from Grandpa not to open it until the three boys were together, after midnight.

> *Parker, Harley, and Wilson,*
>
> *Seems to me you three have had a great display of God's power and justice and love. Real men are quick to give credit—and thanks—to their Rescuer. And real men look beyond themselves—and find a bigger, better world when they help others in need . . . as each of you did. Know that this man is awfully proud of the men you three are becoming.*
>
> *Much love and respect,*
> *Grandpa*

Harley read and reread the note. He even took a picture of it. Harley asked a lot about Jesus and "Parker's God," the way he'd referred to Him at first. In the end, Parker offered him an introduction . . . and Harley made it personal. Harley got a Father, got a brother, and became a member of a whole new family in that instant.

Yeah . . . the late-night, open-window, moonlit-room talks were pretty hard to beat. Especially with the sound of the waves thundering against the Headlands.

Parker's timer went off, bringing him back to the present . . . there on the rocks of Bearskin Neck. "Time to roll."

Wilson stood and stretched. "Jelly is going to freak. She may try to hide it, but it'll come out." He smiled. "I can't wait."

Parker and Wilson walked side by side down Bearskin Neck and up Main. Parker used the gator tooth to tap the window at BayView Brew. The plan was to meet at four o'clock, just after closing and cleanup.

Harley opened the door, still wearing his BayView Brew apron. Mom, Dad, Uncle Sammy, and Pez sat around a table near the front, laughing hysterically about something. They'd been getting together a lot lately. Parker waved as he passed and moved to the back of the dining area. Together with Harley and Wilson, Parker pulled up chairs around a booth with a killer view of Sandy Bay.

Jelly and Ella swung over on their crutches.

"Oh, no you don't," Jelly said. "We're going to the Headlands, like we always do."

But not since the shootings. "Kind of a long way with the crutches, don't you think?"

"I'm *always* thinking." Jelly nodded toward Ella. "We both are. Which is more than I can say about some boys I know."

Wilson snickered. "Here we go."

"Seriously," Jelly said. "We've been so looking forward to this and . . ."

She didn't have to finish. With Wilson leaving tomorrow, it was the last time they'd be together for who knew how long. The Headlands was a great choice. "I can ask my dad to drop us in the truck."

"You will do no such thing, Parker Buckman." Jelly looked past him at the group around the table. "Things are going wonderfully with those four—and I don't want you breaking the spell."

"Spell?" Harley circled his ear with his finger. "How *enchanting*."

Jelly stuck out her tongue. "You obviously don't understand."

"The point is," El said, "we're perfectly capable of getting there on our own two legs . . . and crutches."

The girls grabbed sweatshirts—and handed the boys a couple of blankets and a lantern. Clearly, they'd planned ahead. A half hour later, they'd settled in on the weathered rocks of the Headlands, close to the water. Jelly and Ella each had a blanket around them. The lantern was in the middle of the circle.

The ocean was nearly as calm as the night they'd chased *Retribution*. The water still rose with rhythmic swells that gurgled and gasped from a thousand cracks and crevices between the rocks.

"Harley told us about your dad's big plan," Jelly said.

Parker waited, definitely expecting her to give twenty reasons why she thought it was a bad idea. She held her tongue. *Interesting*. "Yeah, we're leaving tomorrow after church." Still no reaction from Jelly.

"So, Jelly, your dad is driving his pickup to take me down to Everglades City," Wilson said. "Parker's dad will ride along too. And Harley. And *Parker*." He paused, like he was waiting for the big push-back. "All five of us guys."

"Towing the trailer home, right?" Jelly didn't show a sign of her usual worry. What was with her? "Amazing what the church did—along with Eric and Maggie."

Beyond amazing. The congregation had taken an offering and pulled in enough to buy a twenty-five-foot trailer home. Used—but in terrific shape—and ready to tow. Eric and Maggie had come up with the idea—and convinced the owner to sell it at a ridiculously low price. Wilson's name was on the title. It would be a place for Wilson and his dad to stay until their insurance claim paid out and they rebuilt. There was even enough money left over to keep them in groceries for months.

"I hear you boys will be doing some cleanup work in Chokoloskee before you come back," Jelly said.

They'd be down there a week. Rockport High School had gotten all behind them on the project. There'd be no homework for Harley or Parker, either. Miss Tivoli had spearheaded the whole thing. They'd have to stream live reports each day—which would be easy. Miss T wanted the other students to *feel* what was happening down there. The only things Harley and Parker had to do when they got back was make an oral report—with lots of pictures.

"I'm kind of jealous," Jelly said. "It really is a great thing you're doing."

Parker exchanged glances with Wilson and Harley. Jelly's I'm-totally-okay-with-this act actually seemed sincere. After her rescue, she'd claimed she was going to work on being less OCD when it came to being protective. But in their midnight confessions, Wilson, Harley—none of them believed it would happen.

"Yeah, but we'll be in the *Glades*, Jelly," Wilson said. "You know . . . where the gators are?"

She didn't comment.

"And we won't be cleaning up the *whole* time. Bucky and Harley want me to get back on the horse. Know how they're going to help me do that?"

"Nope." Jelly waved him off. "And I don't need to."

"The three of us." Wilson motioned toward Harley and Parker. "We're going down Gator Hook Trail. Together. And after the hurricane, that water will be chest-deep. Easy. And it was Bucky's idea, if you can believe that. Doesn't that make you just hopping mad at Bucky?"

The Everglades were Wilson's home. He'd have to get over his fears. And even though Parker didn't like the idea of Gator Hook Trail one bit, he'd suggested it anyway. It was a way he could help Wilson—and that's what friends did, right?

Jelly smiled. "I'm sure you'll have a wonderful time. And it will give you an excuse to pull out all your 'guy gear.' Knives and machetes and gator sticks and carnivore-tooth necklaces—and whatever else you think you'll need."

"No pushback?" Parker studied her face. "I'm impressed, Jelly."

She raised her chin slightly and smiled. "You should be. You and Harley will come back with all kinds of wild and exaggerated stories, I'm sure. Ella and I look forward to hearing them."

"Which reminds me," Harley said. "We never got that story about the Masterson place that you promised, El."

"Hmmm. Well, that's the kind of story you can't just tell from anyplace other than right in front of the house. At night. And the later, the better."

Harley looked from Wilson to Parker. "We could go now."

Ella laughed like the idea was ridiculous. "We talked about doing exactly that. But it's not quite dark enough. And Jelly and I really don't think you boys can handle it."

"It's way too much for you," Jelly said.

Wilson laughed. "You're a piece of work, Jelly. And you're rubbing off on this one." He nodded toward Ella.

Both girls seemed to take that as a huge compliment.

"She's *totally* rubbing off—and that isn't a good thing," Harley said. "A couple months ago, Jelly lost her phone in the harbor. Now she lost another phone—in the same harbor. Ella, too."

"Ooohh . . . that is so unfair," Jelly said. "After that crack, you don't even deserve hearing a good story."

"How about this?" El gave a very parental smile. "We'll see how you boys do down in the Glades. If you can handle being around the gators *without* having nightmares, I might risk telling you the story of the Masterson place. How's that?"

Harley laughed. "I'll hold you to it."

"And if you two can sleep without leaving all the lights on after that," Ella said, "I might risk telling Wilson the story on his next visit."

"I *will* be coming back," Wilson said. "You know that, right?"

"And it better not take a hurricane to get you here next time," Jelly said.

Wilson raised one hand. "I promise."

Ella asked for Harley's phone—determined to prove she could crack his passcode again. She stepped away from the group, facing the water. Within seconds, it looked like she was typing madly on the keyboard—but Harley wasn't buying it. "She's bluffing. Trust me . . . she won't crack it this time."

When she joined the group two minutes later, she handed Harley his phone.

The screen was locked—just like it had been when he'd handed it to her. "Don't know me as well as you thought, eh?"

But El's smile was way too big for someone who *hadn't* cracked the code. "You'll see."

"Okay—what does that mean?" Harley looked to Parker—as if he had a clue.

"You're about to find out." El pulled out her own phone and pecked out a text.

Harley's phone dinged, and he stared at the screen. *"What?"*

Jelly was already laughing. She stretched to see. "Who's it from, Harley?"

"Miss Smarter-than-Harley."

Ella gave a single nod. "Glad we both agree on that, Mr. Lotitto."

"You got into *my* contacts—and edited your profile?"

"Not just mine."

Harley groaned. "You gotta be kidding me!"

Movement from outside their circle caught Parker's eyes. Scorza stepped out of the shadows. Football jersey. Hands in back pockets.

"Abercrombie!" Wilson grinned. "Here to wish me a safe trip back?"

Scorza ignored him. "Coach reversed his decision to kick you off the team, Lotitto."

"Football season is over." Harley showed zero emotion. "I'm done."

There was something final about Harley's tone. Was he talking about more than this year?

"Coach asked me to deliver the message. He felt bad about the whole thing."

"More like he *looked* bad," El said. "To teachers *and* students."

Word of Harley's sacrifice for his friends had swept through the entire school. He had Miss Tivoli to thank for that. She was likely the one behind the movement to get his jersey back too.

"Thanks for being the messenger boy," Jelly said. "See you in school Monday."

Scorza shrugged. "I thought I'd stick around. You know, in case that psycho Blackbeard guy has any friends in the area."

"His only friend was the bozo who helped him with his dock lines," Jelly said. "But I can handle him."

Scorza grinned like he thought Jelly was just teasing.

"Look," Jelly said. "This is kind of a family get-together tonight, okay?"

Harley glanced at Parker and smiled. He mouthed the word *family*.

"What if Blackbeard escapes again while these *boys* are off wrestling gators?" Scorza stepped into the circle. "You need me."

"Yeah, we need you to *leave*." Jelly raised her crutch and poked him in the gut. "We girls can handle ourselves. Adios, Scorza."

He laughed and raised his hands, backing away. "Okay, okay. I'm going. But I'll see you and Black Beauty at our lunch table Monday." With that, he turned and disappeared into the darkness.

Jelly and Ella both groaned.

"Maybe we can stow away in your dad's truck," Ella said. "I'd rather be in the Glades with alligators than spend a lunch period with Scorza."

The group grew quiet. Scorza had opened the door to the topic that all of them had so carefully avoided.

Clayton Kingman.

"He'd worked so hard to chum the water. Too bad a shark *didn't* get him," Wilson said. "But I wouldn't wish that on the poor shark. Kingman is bad blood. Not even a great white could survive a bellyful of him."

The laughter felt good.

"Okay," Ella said. "Do any of you think Kingman might ever escape again? One to ten—ten being he'll never, ever get out."

"After all he did?" Harley shook his head. "Ten. He'll be in maximum security."

"Ten," Wilson said. "Unfortunately."

Ella stared at him. "Care to explain that?"

"The first time he messed with us, he lost his arm," Wilson said. "Now he lost his eye—I promise you that little peeper is *gone*. It was like seeing a big ol' grape get burst by a—"

"Stop!" Jelly covered her ears. "I don't want to hear the gory details."

Wilson grinned. "What'll Kingman lose next time—his leg? That'd be rich. Between the eye patch and the peg leg, he won't need a pirate costume." He stood, squinted one eye closed, and took a couple of limping steps. "I'd kind of like to see that."

Okay, it might not have been the most Christian thing to do, but even Parker couldn't help laughing.

"Parker?" Jelly looked at him like she really wanted his opinion. "One to ten."

"Ten. But even if he gets parole after twenty years, he won't bother us."

Jelly gave him a skeptical look. "Give me one good reason why he wouldn't."

"Kingman has seen God's ability to rescue in the face of impossible odds—twice."

Jelly's shoulders relaxed. "I like that answer." She pointed at Parker's hat. "Might as well give me that now. You know I'll snag it before you leave tomorrow."

Parker took it off, looked at it . . . and slapped it right back in place. "Sorry, this one is my favorite."

"You'll get it back—after you *get* back." Jelly snapped her fingers, and held out her hand, palm up. "Right here."

Actually, for how well she'd handled the news of him going to the Glades? Parker ceremoniously placed his Wooten's Airboat Tours hat in her hand.

"That's more like it." Jelly looked way too pleased with herself. She snugged up the Velcro tab, then adjusted it just right on her head—like it was finally where it belonged.

"Come on, Jelly." Wilson smiled. "With all the dangers in the Glades . . . you're not even a *tiny* bit worried about Bucky?"

"Nope. You're all big boys."

"Circle this day on the calendar, Brothers," Wilson said. "Jelly *finally* admits we can take care of ourselves."

Jelly shook her head. "Not at all. In fact, you three are pros at getting yourselves into trouble. But God is even better at getting you out of it. You boys just have a good time, okay?"

Wow . . . Jelly *was* making progress.

"We're going to bag a gator," Wilson said. "A big one."

Jelly smiled. "Send photos."

"Okay. You've lost your mind, Jelly. I give up." Wilson raised both hands in surrender. "But seriously, I'm making me a gator-tooth necklace so the three of us"—he motioned toward Parker and Harley—"are connected, you know? I could make one for you girls, too. I'll send it back up with Bucky and Harley."

Ella raised her Navajo cross. "If I'm wearing a necklace, it will be *real* jewelry. And a carnivore's incisor doesn't qualify. No, thanks. If you want to send us something, just stick with texts."

"We'll do better than that," Parker said. "We'll send you postcards."

Jelly struggled to her feet. She stuck a crutch under one arm and pointed the other one directly at Parker. "You will do no such thing."

Ella stood beside her, like they were inseparable. "Don't you boys dare."

Parker was already picking out postcards in his head. Every one of them would picture a gator. Harley and Wilson both snickered like they were thinking the same thing.

"If you do?" Jelly gave him a friendly—but fiery-eyed—glare. "You will *not* get your favorite hat back. *Ever.* Understood?"

Parker nodded and smiled. "Completely."

He needed a new hat anyway.

NOTE FROM THE AUTHOR

EVERY BOOK GROWS ITS OWN WRITING CHALLENGES, and *The Second Storm* may have presented some of the biggest hurdles ever. Parker. Jelly. Ella. Harley. Wilson. Where would their story go this time? What would be their personal struggles in this story? What would they learn—if anything? How might that help you, the reader, gain beneficial perspective or wisdom? How would this book personally nudge you, the reader, to aim higher in some very real way?

God . . . I love writing this story. Thank You! While working on this story, I prayed that sentence more times than I could count. Having fun while writing is important . . . and if done right, the story is that much better because of it.

If you liked the story, tell your friends. Post reviews on Amazon and Goodreads. And send me a note. Each of these is incredibly important to me.

How can I convey all the ways God answered prayer specifically while working on this book? I can't possibly do it. I kept a journal, and there's a lot written there. But I'll say this much: Below are some of the Scripture verses I clung to while I was writing this book. My God proved faithful every step of the way. And He will be faithfully by your side on your life's journey too.

Thanks for reading, my friend!

Writing by God's grace, for God's glory, and for my good—and yours!

Tim Shoemaker

Then they cried out to the LORD in their trouble,
 and he brought them out of their distress.
He stilled the storm to a whisper;
 the waves of the sea were hushed.
They were glad when it grew calm,
 and he guided them to their desired haven.
Let them give thanks to the LORD for his unfailing love
 and his wonderful deeds for mankind.

PSALM 107:28-31

Look to the LORD and his strength;
 seek his face always.

PSALM 105:4

Many, LORD my God,
 are the wonders you have done,
 the things you planned for us.
None can compare with you;
 were I to speak and tell of your deeds,
 they would be too many to declare.

PSALM 40:5

For this God is our God for ever and ever;
 he will be our guide even to THE END.

PSALM 48:14

SPECIAL THANKS

Jim Olsen: For joining me on so many Florida dives . . . all of which helped make this High Water book series more real. And for sharing his experiences and photos of Hurricane Ian when it pummeled Pine Island.

Bill Luttrell: For sharing his powerful story of hunkering down with his family through the Category 5 Hurricane Dorian in the Bahamas. For answering my questions . . . helping me understand . . . even through his tears.

Scott Story and Rosemarie Lesch: Rockport Harbormasters, for answering my texts and emails loaded with questions. For sharing their experiences, which helped me make the story that much more powerful. For telling me all about *Alert 1*. I definitely want a ride the next time I'm there!

To Dave and Cyndi Darsch: For loaning me your pier again in July when I needed a spot to write for a few hours. It was soooo good to be back. I grieved to learn that Hurricane Ian swept that writing spot away. But not even a Cat 4 hurricane could undo all the ways the many visits to your dock added to the High Water series as a whole.

To Scott and Denyea Swartz: For providing me a place in the shade to set up my standing desk along the ocean this past July.

Dunkin: When I needed to go somewhere to write, you provided a great spot. Tina, Sarah, Arbita—and the rest . . . so often I'd hear you laughing on the other side of the counter. That made for a great atmosphere. And you kept giving me more coffee—thank you! And I'd like to think all the donut holes you gave me actually helped me catch holes in my stories.

Carlos, Iris, and the crew at Culver's: Thanks for a clean booth and a friendly atmosphere when I stopped in to write. I've grown to love those chocolate malts.

Matt and the crew at Blackwood BBQ: Just the smell of the place when I come in to work gets me off to good start. Everyone there is always friendly . . . and I always get a lot done.

Nancy Rue: Mentor, friend, and one person who really understood when I shared the challenges this book would present. Again, your "I know you . . . and you can do this" confidence makes a difference.

Larry Weeden and Danny Huerta: For continued support of this series. God only knows the long-term impact the series will make.

Vance Fry: For your trust in me as a writer—and for your balanced approach to editing. I know this book has become stronger because of your insights.

Cheryl: The woman who read this before anyone else . . . and gave me extremely essential feedback. I love you, Babe! And, as always, thanks for your encouragement and support all the way!

To my Lord and God: We did it . . . together. You planted the story somewhere deep inside. Grew it. And the characters . . . You brought them to life. I love the story. And I'm amazed at the hurdles You carried me over to write *The Second Storm*. Thanks for the countless times You gave me the words, the ideas, the boost, and the direction I needed. Thanks for the productive hours . . . when You supplied my needs. Your Word always says it best: "Look to the LORD and his strength; seek his face always" (Psalm 105:4).

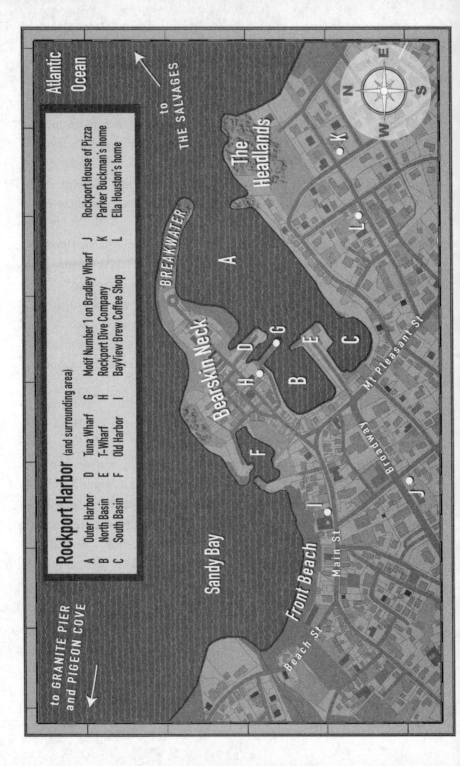

Atlantic Ocean

to THE SALVAGES

to GRANITE PIER and PIGEON COVE

Rockport Harbor (and surrounding area)

A Outer Harbor
B North Basin
C South Basin
D Tuna Wharf
E T-Wharf
F Old Harbor
G Motif Number 1 on Bradley Wharf
H Rockport Dive Company
I BayView Brew Coffee Shop
J Rockport House of Pizza
K Parker Buckman's home
L Ella Houston's home

BREAKWATER

Bearskin Neck

The Headlands

Sandy Bay

Front Beach

Beach St

Main St

Mt Pleasant St

Broadway